Chasing Summer

HELEN LACEY
CHRISTINE RIMMER
ABIGAIL GORDON

WITHDRAWN

MILLS & BOON

First Published in Great Britain 2017
By Mills & Boon, an imprint of HarperCollins*Publishers*
1 London Bridge Street, London, SE1 9GF

CHASING SUMMER © 2017 Harlequin Books S. A.

Date With Destiny, *Marooned With The Maverick* and *A Summer Wedding At Willowmere* were first published in Great Britain by Harlequin (UK) Limited.

Date With Destiny © 2013 Helen Lacey
Marooned With The Maverick © 2013 Harlequin Books S.A.
A Summer Wedding At Willowmere © 2009 Abigail Gordon

Special thanks and acknowledgment to Christine Rimmer for her contribution to the *Montana Mavericks: Rust Creek Cowboys* continuity.

ISBN: 978-0-263-92977-5

05-0817

Printed and bound in Spain
by CPI, Barcelona

DATE WITH DESTINY

BY
HELEN LACEY

Helen Lacey grew up reading *Black Beauty, Anne of Green Gables* and *Little House on the Prairie*. These childhood classics inspired her to write her first book when she was seven years old, a story about a girl and her horse. She continued to write, with the dream of one day being a published author, and writing for Mills & Boon Cherish is the realization of that dream. She loves creating stories about strong heroes with a soft heart and heroines who get their happily-ever-after. For more about Helen, visit her website, www.helenlacey.com.

For Gareth
1966–2009
Forever in my heart

Chapter One

Grace Preston stared down at her bare feet peeking out from the hem of her long dress. Her sister's beach wedding had been romantic and casual—exactly what the bride and groom wanted. But it had left her without shoes and feeling more than a little exposed.

Grace didn't bother to pull up her dress as she walked toward the water's edge. To hell with it—she'd never wear the halter style blue-green chiffon concoction again anyway. The water was cold and she ignored the wet sand clinging to her heels. The moon hung low in the sky, casting a great sliver of light across the ocean. The sound of cresting waves was faintly hypnotic and she relaxed a bit, taking a long swallow from the champagne flute in her hand. Once the glass was empty she quickly refilled it from the bottle she held in the other.

It wasn't like she intended to get drunk. That wasn't her

style. She simply needed to be alone. Away from the cloistering effects of wedding guests and the party.

She's been home for five days and already felt as though
it was time to leave.

But I won't.

She had a month. Four weeks to recharge and pull herself together. Not that *she* really believed she needed it. But
her boss did. Her therapist did. She had her instructions—
go home…go home and spend time with her family. Go
home and forget the car crash that had killed a colleague
and changed her life.

So, I'm here.

She took another sip, finishing her drink. One glass down.
Maybe getting drunk would give her some relief from the
heavy band of pressure pressing at her temples.

Relief now, perhaps. But regret in morning.

Grace Preston didn't do hangovers. She did fourteen-hour
days and skipped lunches and four-inch heels. Vacations were
usually a long weekend in her apartment with a laptop and
one eye on the stock market.

And Crystal Point, the small beachside Australian town
where she'd been born and raised, was a long way from her
office, her apartment, her Jimmy Choos and her life in New
York.

She took a few steps and cautiously dipped her toes into
the ocean. The sound of music and laughter and clinking
crockery faded as she headed farther from the huge tent and
the celebration of Evie and Scott's wedding. The stars above
seemed particularly bright, like they were mocking her, like
they knew all her secrets.

Like they knew she wasn't quite whole and there was a
tiny window of emptiness aimed directly in the center of her
chest. Maybe it was the happiness radiating from her sister
that had Grace thinking things she wouldn't normally think.

With a new husband and a baby on the way, Evie had never looked happier.

While Grace had never been more alone in her life.

The fact her boss knew as much was the reason she was back. She was home to recharge and be with the people who loved her. Not that she was about to admit that to anyone anytime soon. Her family thought she was simply home for the wedding and an extended vacation.

She kicked at the tide with her toes and gasped as cold water splashed up her calf, but then ventured in a little more. When she took a swallow of champagne the bubbles zinged up her nose and down her throat. A couple more glasses, she thought, and she might be on her way to sweet oblivion.

The idea made her laugh and she heard the sound echo and then ripple and somehow quietly disappear into the night as she took another step into the water.

Across from the river mouth, where the waterway met the sea, was Jay's Island. It had been part of the mainland once, but years of sand trenching to allow sugar cane ferries to pass had created a gulf between the two banks. Now it was home to nesting herons and sea turtles. When she was young she'd swum the distance, not put off by the fast current that dragged many swimmers along. But she hadn't done that in a long time.

Despite what some people believed, Grace didn't hate Crystal Point. She just had little in common with the small beachside community that boasted a population of barely eight hundred residents. Not after so many years anyway. Time had a way of creating distance and building walls. Grace simply didn't fit in. She never had.

"Don't think I'm gonna jump in and save you if you fall in and get pulled down by the riptide, *Princess*," she heard a deep and infuriatingly familiar voice say from behind her.

"I have no intention of ruining a perfectly good suit because you can't hold your liquor."

Grace swiveled in shock at the sudden intrusion and almost toppled over. Clenching her toes into the sand for balance, she moved up the bank to where Cameron Jakowski stood about ten feet away.

She scowled and fought a guilty look at the glass and bottle clutched between her fingers. She absolutely would not rise to his *Princess* jibe.

"What do you want, *Hot Tub?*"

She saw his smile in the moonlight, knew instinctively that his velvet brown eyes would light up, ready for battle with her. They had always called one another names—always worked out new ways to needle each other. *Hot Tub, Princess*—silly names meant to antagonize.

"Just making sure you don't drown."

Grace shrugged her bare shoulders. "I didn't realize you cared."

He came closer. "It's a wedding. I doubt Evie and Scott would want their celebration ruined by your carelessness."

Grace's temper simmered. "I'm not acting the least bit careless," she said through clenched teeth. "And I'm perfectly sober."

He looked at the bottle. "Prove it," he challenged. "Walk a straight line."

Grace bit back a scowl. "I'll do no such thing. You're not on duty now."

He chuckled and Grace forced herself to *not* think about how sexy it sounded. Okay—so he had a great smile and a handsome face and filled out his police officer's uniform as faultlessly as he did the suit he wore. She'd have to be comatose not to notice.

"So, why are you hiding out here anyway?"

Grace moved up the sand. "Who says I'm hiding?"

Cameron hooked a thumb over one shoulder. "The party's that way."

She shrugged. "Maybe I'm not in the mood for a party."

"Nothing's that simple with you."

Grace bristled. "Leave me alone. I don't want to argue with you."

Cameron stepped closer. "Now I know there's definitely something wrong with you. What's eating you tonight?"

"Nothing," she lied. "I'm my usual happy self."

"And now you're lying your shoes off."

Grace tugged at the hem off her dress and exposed her feet. "I'm not wearing shoes," she announced, holding herself upright despite a sudden surge of wooziness.

Of course, he knew that. He was a groomsman and she'd been partnered with him most of the afternoon. He'd already smirked when he'd spotted her bare feet and purple-painted toenails as she'd taken his arm to walk toward the altar.

Because Grace Preston didn't bare anything in public.

And Cameron knew that.

She glared at him some more. "I don't know why the men got to keep their shoes on. Anyway, I'll probably step on a stonefish and that will be the end of me."

Cameron laughed. "So much drama over a pair of missing shoes. Come on, I'll walk you back."

Grace shook her head. "No, thanks—I'll stay here. I've had about all the marital bliss I can stand for one evening."

He was close now and Grace could see the curious expression on his face. "Are you jealous Evie's married?"

Was she? It seemed like everyone was getting married lately and getting their happily-ever-after. First her brother, Noah, had married Callie Jones and now, less than eight months later, Evie was tying the knot with Scott, Callie's younger brother. But no, she wasn't the marrying type.

"Certainly not," she replied quickly and took another sip of

her champagne. "I'm very happy for my sister. I just meant..."
She stopped. There was no way she would explain anything
to Cameron Jakowski. "Nothing. Leave me alone."

He moved toward her again, only this time she didn't step
back. Toe-to-toe, he stood close to eight inches taller than her
and without shoes it was impossible for Grace to stare him
down without tilting her head up.

"And what if you go back into the water and get swept
away by the current?" he inquired. "I don't want that on my
conscience. I'm staying."

Grace shrugged. "Suit yourself," she said as she moved
up the bank some more and headed toward a small cluster of
rocks. She sat on the largest one and refilled her glass. "Want
a shot?" she asked, holding out the bottle.

Cameron followed her steps and took the bottle. "I reckon
you've had about enough of that." He dropped it onto the sand.

Grace watched the champagne seep away. "You're ruining my evening."

"Your evening looked well and truly ruined before you
wandered off down here."

She frowned. "Are you spying on me?"

Cameron laughed. "Hardly—but you did bail on our dance."

"I didn't want to dance," she told him flatly. "With you or
anyone else," she added.

Being partnered with Cameron for the entire celebration
had been more than she could stand. Not only because she
wasn't in any mood to combat his sarcasm or insults, but because the happy smiles and animated chatter of the wedding
party had felt like a cloistering blanket around her shoulders. Since the accident she'd become less adept at handling
crowds. Less inclined to make pointless conversation.

"You know, it wouldn't hurt you to open up a bit."

Grace almost choked on her champagne. Was he reading
her mind? "To you? You're joking, right?"

He shrugged. "Why not?"

"Because you're *you*." She shook her head. "And you and I are like...oil and water."

He stepped closer and thrust his hands in his pockets. "It's a double-edged sword," he said quietly.

Grace stared into her glass. "I have no idea what that's supposed to mean."

"Sure you do," he flipped back. "Admit it, *Princess*— fighting with me gets you all worked up."

Grace wasn't admitting anything. "You're imagining things. Not everything's about you. And stop calling me *Princess*."

"Stop calling me *Hot Tub*."

Gridlock.

As usual.

He didn't move. He stood in front of her, smiling, making Grace so mad she was tempted to toss her remaining drink in his direction. For sixteen years they'd been stuck in this groove—hurling insults, sticking it to one another at every opportunity.

But a lifetime ago it had been different. He was her brother's best friend and because of that relationship she'd known him since she was five years old. She'd liked him back then. He hadn't teased her for her bookish ways as her brother did. By the time she was preparing to leave for boarding school liking him had turned into a crush. But she didn't dare admit it or imagine he felt the same way. She left for school and took her silly dreams with her. Nothing had prepared her for the night of her sixteenth birthday when he'd unexpectedly kissed her for the first time. When school was over she'd returned to Crystal Point to take a break before she headed off to college and in those few months they'd dated one another. Cameron Jakowski had been her first real boyfriend. Her first kiss. The one man she'd never quite been able to forget.

"What's really going on with you, Grace?"

Her back straightened, shoving her into the present. "Spare me your fake concern."

He stepped closer. "It's not fake."

Grace didn't believe him. "Like you care?"

He laughed. "C'mon, Grace—lighten up. You're not in your swanky office now. There's no one to impress by pretending you've got it all together."

Grace stilled. His words hit a raw nerve. Because she'd heard the same ones from the therapist her boss had *insisted* she visit. But Cameron didn't know that. No one knew. The terrible accident and the month afterward where she'd returned to work and pretended none of it had happened, or the way she'd spectacularly unraveled in front of a client. She needed to lie through her teeth—for her own sake. "I always have it together—you know that."

"Do I? I know that you've been hanging around down here for the past hour. I know that you've barely cracked a smile all afternoon, at your own sister's wedding. I know that you're unhappy even if you don't have the courage to admit it."

Grace glared at him, hating she felt so transparent in front of Cameron, hating he could see through her. "And I know that if I admit to anything you'll just use it against me. No, thanks." She got to her feet and stumbled.

He grasped her arm quickly. "Steady," he said as he held her.

Grace tried to pull away but he held her firm. Something uncurled low in her belly, warming her blood. A familiar sensation she experienced whenever he was close. It unnerved her and she fought the feeling. "Let me go."

"You'll fall over."

"So, I'll fall." She was suddenly powerless as one strong arm came around her waist.

"I'd catch you," he said quietly.

Grace frowned. "Let me go…please."

But she wasn't afraid. She'd never feared Cameron. Despite their differences, she'd always trusted him. Grace felt the nearness of him and fought the sudden warmth spreading across her skin. That he could do this to her—make her boil with fury one moment and burn with awareness the next—only added to her resentment and determination to keep as far away from him as possible. He was the only man she'd ever known who'd been able to do that to her. The only man she'd ever thought could see through her, know her and work her out.

"Don't…"

"I'm not doing anything."

"You are. You do. You always do. I just want…" She stopped, stalled and felt herself get dragged into meeting his eyes. She was flustered, uneasy. "I can't…"

"What is it?" he asked softly. "What's going on in that beautiful head of yours?"

Grace's resistance crumbled. The champagne she'd had suddenly freed up her tongue. "I just… I don't belong here," she admitted and pulled herself from his grasp as she stepped backward. "I don't belong anywhere."

Cameron's hands burned from the feel of Grace's skin and he clenched his fists at his sides. The pain in her voice knocked through him, settling behind his ribs in a way that made him think about every feeling he'd had for her—and buried.

"What do you mean?"

She turned away, clutching her arms around herself. "Nothing," she said quietly.

Cameron pushed the heels of his shoes up from sinking in the sand and pressed on. "What do you mean you don't belong?"

Grace twirled around and her long dress billowed around her knees. "Why do you care?"

Why indeed? He shouldn't. Grace was nothing but trouble. A workaholic ice princess who had little time for anyone. *Me included.* He'd found that out the hard way. Beautiful beyond words, smart and independent—and about as warm as an Arctic winter. The perfect antidote for all his fantasies. Wanting her was about as sensible as wanting acid rain.

He shrugged. "Friendly concern."

Her beautiful face looked almost luminescent in the moonlight as she shot him a death stare. "Don't be nice to me," she said quietly, looking suspicious. "We're not friends and I just—"

"We were more than friends," he said and took hold of her hand despite his best intentions to not touch her. "Once."

She stared at their linked hands and this time, she didn't pull away. Cameron's fingertips tingled. He knew that would happen if he touched Grace...expected it...didn't like it one bit but chalked it up to chemistry and tried not to let it mess with his mind. Over the years there had been the odd touch between them, the chance gesture of hands brushing...and every time it was the same. The same vibration rattled inside him, over his skin, through his blood. He knew it wasn't like that for her, of course. Grace was supercool and controlled, with perfectly straight dark hair, immaculate clothes and haunting green eyes—like a mannequin on display. A mere touch wouldn't jangle Grace. But he remembered what it was like to touch her, to kiss her, to hold her in his arms. Those memories were burned into his soul.

As expected, she pulled away. "A lifetime ago."

Her dismissal cut deep. She'd left him without looking

back all those years ago and as much as he wanted to deny it, that rejection still stung. He smiled because he knew it would infuriate her. "So, explain what you meant about not belonging anywhere?"

"No. It was nothing." She shrugged lightly. "And now, if you don't mind, I need to get back to the party."

He didn't believe her for a second. So he pushed. Because he could. Because he wanted to know what was going on inside her beautiful head. "So, has this got anything to do with that suit you've shacked up with?"

Her lips came together. "Erik," she said after a moment. "We broke up a year ago. And we were never *shacked up*. We both kept our own apartments."

She crossed her arms. The movement pushed her breasts upward and Cameron did his best to ignore the swell of cleavage rising up and down with each breath she took. He'd never met the other man, since Grace had kept him under wraps in New York. But Cameron had heard about him from her brother. He was stupidly pleased the suit wasn't in the picture anymore. "You didn't answer the question."

"Because it's a moot point." Grace scowled, but somehow managed to still look beautiful. "And I really don't want to talk to you about my…love life."

Cameron bristled. Did he even think Grace capable of love? "So you loved him?"

"No," she replied swiftly. "I meant…I meant I have no intention of talking to you about him. Now, would you ignore everything I've said and leave me alone?"

Cameron wanted to laugh. "Ignore you? Yeah, right."

Her gaze sharpened. "Ignoring me isn't usually a problem for you. Except of course when you're making fun or insulting me."

"It goes both ways, Grace."

She moved her feet and seemed to come a little closer.

"I guess it does." She dropped her arms. "It only happens with you."

"Do you ever wonder why?"

She raised one perfectly arched brow. "Why would I bother?"

"It might explain one of the great mysteries of the world."

She laughed humorlessly. He could sense her thinking of some kind of cutting retort and wasn't disappointed. "I don't want to rain on your monumental ego, but I really don't have the time to waste wondering about things like that."

"So you never think about it?"

She stilled. "About what?"

"You and me?"

"We were over a long time ago. It was a silly teenage summer romance. I hardly remember."

Her response pushed his buttons. Because he didn't quite believe her. The tension between them had never waned. Every time she returned to Crystal Point, every time they spoke, every time he caught her stare from across a room, the awareness between them was still there. He straightened his shoulders. Down deep, in that place he'd shut off because it stirred up a whole lot of hurt, Cameron remembered what it felt like to want her so much it haunted his dreams. "Maybe you need a reminder."

She faced him with an indignant glare. "And what exactly do you propose?"

"Propose?" He smiled. "Is that what you're after, *Princess*—a proposal? Couldn't you get the suit to the altar?"

Her green eyes flashed. "I have no desire or plans in that regard. I'd think you'd know that better than anyone."

He did. He wasn't likely to forget. They'd started dating when she'd finished high school. She'd come home from boarding school that final time and he'd waited two weeks before asking her out. Three months into their relationship she'd bailed. She wanted a career and a different life...a life that didn't include a small-town police officer. A life that didn't include him or marriage or the possibility of children in the future. She'd made her intentions abundantly clear. Grace Preston wanted a career. And that's *all* she wanted. She'd left Crystal Point for New York without looking back.

Except for now. This Grace was someone new. Someone who didn't seem like she had her usual ice running through her veins. Grace never did vulnerable. And Cameron wanted to know more.

"The corporate life is still giving you everything you need, is it?" he asked, referring to her highly successful job as a finance broker.

"Of course."

"So your little outburst earlier, what was that about?"

Her brows came up. "Are we back on that subject again? It was nothing. Forget it."

"And let you off the hook?" He rocked on his heels. "No chance."

"Haven't you got anything better to do with that mouth of yours than run off with it at me about my life?"

He did. Absolutely. And her words were like a red cape to a bull.

"Did you have something in mind?"

"No, I don't," she said with a caustic smile. "And don't get any ideas."

He laughed at her prickles. Only Grace could make him do that. *Only ever Grace.* "I could kiss you," he teased. "That would shut me up."

She stepped back. "Don't even think about it."

It really was all the challenge he needed and Cameron moved closer. "Grace, you know me better than that."

Her green eyes were alight with fire and defiance. "You're right, I do know you. I know you've got a reputation for nailing anything in a skirt. The last thing I want to be is a notch on your bedpost, Jakowski...so back off."

"You shouldn't believe everything you hear." Cameron placed his hands on her shoulders. She didn't resist. Didn't move. "Kiss me, Grace?"

She shook her head slightly. "No."

The air shifted, creating a swift, uncommonly hot vacuum which somehow seemed to draw them closer. Their bodies brushed and it spiked his blood. He shouldn't want this... shouldn't do this. But everything about Grace Preston took him to another level of awareness. It was almost primitive in its intensity and it made him forget all his good intentions to stay as far away from her as possible.

"Then I'll kiss you."

"I won't kiss you back," she whispered, but he felt her slide a little closer.

Cameron's libido did a wild leap as he moved his arms around her, bringing them together. "Sure you will."

"I won't," she said boldly. "I hate you, remember?"

"You'll get over it," he said smoothly and moved one hand to her nape. For twenty years he'd wanted her like no other woman. For sixteen years he'd been angry at her for breaking his heart.

Grace stared up at him, her green eyes shining and wide in her face.

She looked more beautiful than he'd ever seen her. More desirable. More everything. Without thinking...with nothing but feeling and the need to suddenly possess her, Cameron claimed her lips with his own.

Chapter Two

I will not make out with Cameron Jakowski.

Too late. Grace allowed his mouth to slant over hers and her breath left her sharply.

Maybe just for a moment...

Because he still knew how to kiss. And she hadn't been kissed by Cameron in such a long time....

Her resistance faded and she opened her mouth, inviting him inside. Blood rushed low down in her belly, spiking her temperature upward like a roller coaster moving way too fast. Grace floated along and was quickly caught up in the deep-rooted pleasure which unexpectedly tingled across her skin. The kiss deepened and Grace felt his tongue roll gently around hers. It was so incredibly arousing she couldn't prevent a low moan from escaping deep in her throat.

I should stop this...right now. But she didn't. She just let herself float on a sigh and kissed him back. Her arms moved upward and she curled her fingers into his shoulders. The movement brought their bodies together and Grace melted against him. *Strong and safe*. The words spun around in her head and rocked her to the core. Because she knew she'd only ever felt that way with Cameron. Not with Erik. Not with any man she'd ever been with.

His arms came around her and one hand settled on her hip. And still he kissed her. Grace clung to him as heat charged between them. His touch became firmer and he bunched a handful of her dress in his fist. The tempo between them altered slightly, and the hot surge of desire fanned to life.

He said something against her mouth—her name—something…she wasn't sure. But it fueled the growing need she had to feel his touch. She lifted her leg and wrapped it against him. Her dress rose up and she shuddered when his hand made contact with the soft skin behind her knee. It felt so good to be with him like this, even though some faraway voice told her it was madness. Every part of her came alive when he touched her and she arched her back with a hazy, wanting compliance.

"Grace," he said, leaving her mouth for a moment. He trailed a line of kisses across her cheek and toward the sensitive spot below her ear. "I think it would be a good idea if we stopped…."

Grace turned her head so their lips met again. She didn't want to stop. She only wanted to feel. "No," she whispered into his mouth. "Don't stop."

"You'll hate me tomorrow," he said softly against her craving lips.

"I hate you now…"

She felt his smile against her mouth.

He's right, we have to stop…

Only Cameron's touch was mesmerizing and his kiss had her longing for more. His fingertips burned across her skin in an erotic trail, moving higher, and the blood in her veins

boiled over in a powerful surge of narcotic pleasure. She felt
his hand on the top of her thigh and she pushed closer. He
was obviously as hotly aroused as she was and the notion
drove Grace beyond rational thought, beyond reason. His
palm curved around her bottom and he drew her hard against
his body. Need uncurled low down, liquefying her bones. She
groaned as his mouth sought hers again and kissed him back
with a hunger that startled her, entwining her tongue with
his. She was dazed, on fire, out of control. Grace's knees almost gave way when his fingers traced the edge of her lace
panties. *I shouldn't want this. I shouldn't feel this turned on.*
But she was so aroused, so completely oblivious to anything
other the sudden and unexpected need to be taken to places
she suspected he'd effortlessly be able to take her.

But reality intruded and brought her back to earth with a
resounding, wrenching thud.

The music resonating from the wedding reception area
came to an abrupt halt and the silence was suddenly deafening. "Oh, my God," Grace moaned as she jerked her mouth
from his. "My speech!"

Cameron released her. "What?"

Grace staggered back and shoved her dress down her
thighs with shaking hands. "I have to give a speech. I'm the
maid of honor. I have to get back."

He looked annoyingly calm. "Okay, we'll go back."

"No," Grace said on a rush of breath. "I'm not walking
back up there with you. I look like…" She pushed a hand into
her hair and was relieved to discover that the up style was still
in its right position. But her blood raced, her breath was shallow and she was certain her mouth looked as though it had
been well and truly plundered. "I must look like I've been—"

"You have been," he agreed quietly, seeming completely
cool and relaxed. "Don't stress, *Princess.* You look fine—as
picture-perfect as always."

Grace crossed her arms and glanced toward the reception area. The big white tent stood out like a beacon in the moonlight. She heard someone speaking into a microphone and quickly recognized her father's steady voice. "I need to get back. And don't follow me."

He didn't respond immediately. He just looked at her. Looked *through* her was more the point. Humiliation burned across her skin like an out-of-control brush fire.

This was not supposed to happen. I didn't come home for this. Nothing will stop me from getting my life and career back on track.

He grabbed the bottle and glass from the sand. "Let's go," he said quietly.

Grace considered some kind of cold retort, but failed to find one.

Cameron Jakowski had his hand up my dress.

"All right," she said with a deliberate tilt of her chin and tried not to think about how good his hand had felt. "We won't ever mention this again."

"Sure we will."

Grace lifted her hem fractionally and took a few steps up the sand. "We won't," she said defiantly. "*I* won't. I intend to forget this ever happened."

"Good luck with that."

Grace stomped along the sand, headed for the boat ramp and walked back toward the reception. As she'd suspected, her father's proud speech was in full swing and Grace circumnavigated the huge tent and slipped through an opening behind the wedding table as discreetly as she could.

But Evie's hawkeyed radar caught a glimpse of her immediately and Grace did her best to squash a fresh wave of embarrassment from heating her cheeks. Evie raised both her brows inquiringly and Grace managed a barely decipherable shake of her head. It didn't help that Cameron chose that moment to make his entrance through the same opening.

Busted...

The look on her sister's face was unmistakable. She knew Evie would demand answers at some point. That was Evie's way. Grace steeled herself with a deep breath and took her conspicuously empty seat at the table. Cameron did the same a few seats away and she used every inch of effort to not look at him. Instead, she concentrated her attention on her father's heartfelt speech.

When it was her turn to say a few words, Grace stood and took the microphone from her father and softly kissed his cheek. All the guests clearly waited for her to speak. And she meant to. Only she made a fatal mistake and glanced at Cameron. And damn him—he smiled, winked and made her forget every word she'd planned to say in honor of the bride and groom.

Nothing came out, only a squeak, a kind of strangled sound that a distressed cat might make.

And it was pain-in-her-neck, thorn-in-her-side Cameron Jakowski's fault.

Supercool Grace Preston was at a loss for words. Any other time Cameron might have been happy about that. But tonight...not so much. He could still taste her lovely mouth; still feel the silky texture of her skin against his hands.

One minute they were talking, the next they were kissing like a couple of horny teenagers. Cameron couldn't remember the last time he'd felt like that. The last time he'd *done* that.

And he certainly hadn't expected to do it with Miss Icy Britches.

He'd mostly kept his hands to himself when they were dating. They'd made out plenty of times—but never quite like what had happened on the beach. She'd wanted to wait to make love and he'd respected her wishes, although he'd imagined a future together—a wedding, a wedding *night*. Until Grace had informed him of her big plans for a career and a future that didn't include Crystal Point or the small-town police officer who wanted to marry her one day.

But right now, she didn't look like the Grace he'd come to resent. It was easier that way, easier not thinking about her perfectly beautiful face and body. And yet his skin felt tight watching her, waiting for her to speak. She was off balance, askew, and he knew it wasn't the champagne doing damage.

It churned something inside him, thinking he was responsible for the kind of hazy, almost lost look on her face as she stared into the microphone. He smiled again, different this time, without mockery, with only the intent to calm her obviously fractured nerves. She met his gaze and they remained like that for a moment, linked by some invisible thread that had nothing to do with the searing kisses they'd shared, or the years of thinly veiled antagonism that had come to define their relationship. He saw her relax, watched as her jaw loosened and then she began to speak.

"Tonight is a celebration," she said and then swallowed hard, as though the words were difficult to say. "Of love. Of trust. Of the commitment between two people."

She went on to talk about the bride and groom, speaking clearly and concisely as she wished the newlyweds a long and happy life. Cameron wondered if she meant it. He'd never heard her speak about love before. When she was done she returned to her seat and didn't spare him another look.

Dessert was served after that and Cameron pushed the sugary sweet around on his plate. The dancing started again and the woman beside him dug him in the ribs with her elbow, but he was in no mood for that either. He declined her invitation and managed a smile when she scooted off her chair.

Mary-Jayne Preston was a pretty brunette with amazing green eyes—and she was Grace's younger sister.

Grace...

She didn't like him. He didn't like her. But he'd wanted her and loved her most of his adult life. He thought he was over it. Thought he had it under control.

Jackass...

"Why do you look like you want to be somewhere else?"

Cameron turned his head. Noah Preston. His best friend. And Grace's older brother. "You know me and weddings," he replied casually.

The other man ducked into the empty chair beside him. "Are you tempted to take the walk yourself?" Noah asked.

He shrugged to disguise the truth. Because he did want to get married. He wanted a wife and kids and the whole deal. Cameron longed for a family of his own. He was thirty-six years old and had dated a succession of women, none he saw for more than a few months. And none who invaded his deepest dreams like Grace Preston.

He'd built a house designed for a family and lived in it alone. Dated women he knew weren't going to figure permanently in his life. For a long time he'd avoided thinking about marriage and family. Once Grace left Crystal Point he'd pushed his focus into his career as a police officer and tried to forget about her. And their ongoing resentment for one another had fueled that focus. But now he wanted more. More than an empty house when he came home after a long shift at work, more than an empty bed. Or one filled occasionally with someone he barely knew.

He wanted what his parents had. He wanted what his best friend had.

"It's not as bad as you think," Noah said easily. "Actually, it's the smartest move I ever made. You just need to find the right woman."

Noah had married Callie Jones eight months earlier and the stunning, blue-eyed, California horse-riding instructor had transformed his friend's life. His four children had a new mother and Noah had the love of a woman he adored. And with Callie's brother, Scott, now married to Evie, it seemed like everyone around him was getting their happily-ever-after.

Just not me.

It made him think of green eyes. *Grace's eyes.* Noah would have a fit if he knew what he was thinking. Or what he'd been doing with her down by the beach.

"I never said it was bad."

Noah laughed. "I'm sure there's some sweet, easygoing girl out there who—"

"I don't want easygoing," he said swiftly. "Or sweet."

Grace again. Because Grace wasn't either of those things. She was smart and independent and reserved and coolly argumentative and...

And she's the only woman I've ever wanted.

Noah laughed again. "Can't say I blame you. I love my wife's spirit." There was a gleam in his friend's eyes. "Makes life more interesting."

"I'll bet," Cameron said agreeably.

"Were you with Grace earlier?"

Cameron shot a glance at his friend. "For a minute," he said and pushed aside the nagging guilt hitting him between the shoulder blades.

"Something's going on with her," Noah said. "She said she's taking some time off work. But she's not talking about why, not even to Evie or our mother. Maybe breaking up with that attorney has something to do with it."

Cameron remembered what she'd said about the suit and sensed she wasn't all that broken up about it. But what she'd said about not belonging—now that, he was sure, had something to do with her return home. Because it was completely *unlike* Grace to say a thing like that. Noah was right—something *was* going on with her. The Grace he knew didn't show vulnerability. She was ice-cool and resilient. At eighteen she'd walked away from him and Crystal Point and moved to New York and had been there ever since, returning once or twice a year at the most. That was the Grace Preston he understood. Not the vulnerable one moment, hotter than Hades the next kind of woman who'd kissed him back like there was no tomorrow.

Wanting her had made every other woman he'd known pale by comparison. And now he knew one thing—he either had to get Grace out of his head for good...or *get* Grace in his bed and in his life.

She was home, on his turf. Maybe he had a shot. The way she'd kissed him gave him some optimism. That kind of response wasn't fake. And he knew Grace. She wouldn't pretend. Whatever was going on with her, Cameron was determined to find out. She'd resist and fight. She'd make things impossible. She'd cut him down with icy barbs and indifference.

Suddenly that seemed like one hell of an interesting challenge.

Cameron's gaze centered on Grace. She was with Evie, talking close. His shirt collar got uncomfortably tight and irritation uncurled in his chest. Because he would bet right down to his boots that they were talking about him.

"So, what happened?"

Grace tried to escape her sister's viselike grip on her wrist but failed. Evie was persistent when she wanted something. She loved her sister and Evie was the one person she could really talk to. But not about this. Not about Cameron.

"Nothing. We were just talking."

Evie's dramatic brows rose. "Well, I imagine you were doing something with your tongues."

Grace flushed and tacked herself at Evie's side to hide from Cameron's view in case he looked her way. Her sister's seven months pregnant belly was a good shield. "I don't want to talk about it."

Evie chuckled. "Oh, no—you don't get out of it that easy. I want details."

"I won't say what…" Grace's response faded on her lips. "Okay," she admitted. "So we might have…"

"Might have?" Evie interrupted without batting a lash.

"We kissed," she whispered into her sister's ear, feeling about sixteen years old. She certainly wasn't about to admit to anything else. "And that's all I'm saying."

Evie hauled Grace into the corner so they had more privacy. "You kissed Cameron?" she squealed. "Oh, my God! I can't believe it."

Neither can I.

"Well, I mean I *can* believe it," Evie said in a wicked whisper. "Did it bring back a whole lot of memories?"

Of course it did. But she wasn't about to say that. Grace regretted ever telling her sister about the three-month relationship she'd had with Cameron—about the kisses and gentle touches and soft moans as they made out in the front seat of his car. Because it brought back other memories as well—the way she'd left, the way she'd run when she'd sensed he was getting serious. It was so long ago. In a different life. Wanting Cameron now was sheer madness. It was champagne that had made her behave so impulsively. And she hadn't been with a man since forever. No wonder she'd acted like she did. She only hoped no one else saw their conspicuous entrance. The last thing she wanted was the Crystal Point rumor mill churning out theories about what had happened between her and the charming and popular Sergeant Jakowski down by the beach.

Everyone liked Cameron. She knew some of what he did in the community—the volunteer work at the surf club, the time he spent with kids from the Big Brothers Big Sisters program. An all-around good guy. Honest, honorable and socially conscious. Grace knew it about him and had always felt like he was rubbing her nose in the fact. Irrational as it was, he made her feel selfish and, worse…self-absorbed. Like her life was meaningless and superficial. He never said it of course, rarely spoke to her unless to demean her fondness for pricey footwear or call her *Princess* in that infuriating way.

"Can I steal my beautiful bride away for a dance?" Scott Jones approached and took Evie's hand.

"Of course," Grace said and smiled when she saw the glow on her sister's face. Evie had found true love with the handsome, California firefighter. "We were done anyway."

Evie smiled. "We'll talk later," she said and allowed herself to be swept away.

Grace remained where she was and studied the crowd for a moment. The usual suspects were in attendance and a few she'd never met before, mostly friends and colleagues of the groom who'd traveled from Los Angeles. She spotted her younger sister Mary-Jayne, or M.J. as she was affectionately called, dancing closely with Gabe Vitali, the best man and cousin of the groom. She was supposed to have been partnered with the outrageously good-looking American, but M.J. had pleaded they swap groomsmen and Grace agreed, unable to refuse her sister's request.

"They make a cute couple."

Grace froze. Cameron had approached and edged alongside her. She glanced at him and he nodded toward M.J. and Gabe. "I'm no judge."

"And yet you're usually so good at it."

It was a dig, but he was smiling so she let it pass. She wasn't about to have an argument with him in front of so many people. "Did you want something?"

"Just to see how you were doing."

Grace raised both shoulders. "As you can see, I'm perfectly fine."

"Good speech by the way."

"Thank you." She took a deep breath. No thanks to him. "I should get back to—"

He laid one finger against her wrist. "I think we should talk, Grace."

Awareness crept along her skin and she tingled where they touched. "I'd rather not."

"So, where are you staying?"

Grace swiveled on her heels to face him. "At Evie's."

"While she and Scott are on their honeymoon?" His brows came up. "Are they leaving you in charge of the B and B?"

The query in his voice was skeptical. "Don't sound so surprised. I'm not totally inept, you know."

He smiled to expose perfectly straight teeth. "I think it's good of you to help out."

She pulled away from his touch, but Grace couldn't ignore the way he watched her and her body was quickly on high alert.

"So, shall we resume our earlier conversation?" he asked.

Grace stepped back. "Don't push it."

"You know, you look really beautiful when your cage is rattled."

"You're an ass, Jakowski."

"And you're hiding something," he replied. "Whatever it is, Grace, you may as well come clean."

Heat crept up her neck and she hated that he could do that. "*If* there was anything wrong, I certainly wouldn't be sharing it with you."

"Your family is concerned about you. Noah thinks you're nursing a broken heart after breaking up with the suit."

"I'm not."

"I know."

He said the words with such arrogant authority that Grace glared at him. "I wish you wouldn't do that."

"Do what?"

"Act as though you know or care. I'll talk to my brother."

"When?"

Grace's skin burned. "When I'm ready."

"You've been home almost a week, seems to me like you would have had plenty of opportunity to tell your family what's going on."

"Stay out of it," she warned.

"Or what?" He chuckled. He was toying with her. As usual. "Ah, *Princess,* you're about as wound up as a spinning top at the moment."

"No thanks to you," she fired back and crossed her arms.

He smiled again. "By the way, you owe me a dance."

Dancing? After what had happened on the beach she had no intention of falling into his arms again. "You don't have a chance of getting me on the dance floor."

"Things have a way of changing," he said and gently took hold of her elbow. "As we discovered earlier."

The kiss. The touching. The insane desire that had taken hold. Of course he'd remind her about it. "Don't imagine for one minute that we'll be repeating that craziness anytime soon."

"Are you sure about that, Grace?"

She stuck out her chin. "Positive."

"Such confidence," he said in that vague, annoying way of his. "So, about that dance?"

She clung to her resolve. "No."

"I could beg and embarrass you."

Grace refused to react. "You mean embarrass yourself. And surely there are other women here you can try to charm the pants off other than me."

He laughed and she hated that a few people looked in their direction. "Is that what you think I'm doing, Grace? Trying to get your pants off?"

She cast him a sharp look. "Try your best, *Hot Tub*."

He grinned at her attempt to antagonize. But she knew he would win out. She'd called him the ridiculous name for a decade because he'd installed a huge spa bath at the house he'd built and her brother teased that it was to impress women. She hadn't liked the idea then. And she liked it even less now.

"Are you throwing down the gauntlet, Grace?"

"Not at all." She managed to pull away and put some space between them. "I'm...tired," she said and shook her head. "Too tired to play games."

"Then tell me what's going on with you. If you do I might be inclined to leave you alone."

Exasperated by his persistent badgering, Grace threw up her hands. "So, what do you want to know?"

His gaze narrowed. "Why you've come back for so long this time?"

"Because this is my home."

He clearly didn't believe that for a second. "Last I heard New York was your home, Grace. Crystal Point was the place you couldn't get away from fast enough."

It was a direct hit. She knew what he meant. Her career was the reason she'd left Crystal Point—the reason she'd put an end to their relationship all those years ago. She'd been overwhelmed, crowded, hemmed in...everything she didn't want to be. Leaving had been her salvation. And her career had panned out exactly as she'd dreamed it would. Until the car wreck that had changed her life.

Grace's back stiffened. "You know why I left. I wanted...
I wanted..."

"Bright lights, big city."

She stilled. Quiet stretched between them, like brittle
elastic. The music seemed to fade and Grace experienced a
strange tightening behind her ribs. "It was never that simple."

"Yes, it was, Grace." His voice was velvet-smooth, his expression unreadable. "You knew what you wanted. What you
didn't. And who you didn't."

She looked into his eyes. It sounded so black-and-white.
But nothing was simple anymore. And she didn't have the
courage to admit the truth—that she'd gone to New York
to make her parents proud and become everything they'd
hoped she would become...or that now she'd come home to
save her life.

Chapter Three

On Sunday morning at her sister's bed-and-breakfast, Grace reorganized the upstairs linen cupboard, alphabetized Evie's cookbooks and by eleven o'clock was sitting on the sofa watching a corny movie on a cable channel.

Anything to take her mind off the job she'd left in New York, the empty apartment that had never really felt like a home and the accident that killed her work colleague. An accident that had altered her in so many ways. Before that awful day she'd been in control of her life and future. There were no question marks. No uncertainty. At least none she was prepared to admit. She had known her trajectory. Her plan.

You knew what you wanted. And who you didn't.

Cameron's words rolled around in her head.

Because there had been the sting of truth in those words.

When they'd dated, when he'd said he had serious feelings for her and wanted to talk about their future together, she'd panicked and cut him down immediately. And as she sat in the lotus position on the sofa and stared absently at the television, Grace remembered what she'd said to him in stunning Technicolor.

"I'm just not interested in anything serious. Especially not with a small-town cop. I'm getting out of Crystal Point as soon as I can. There's nothing and no one that could ever hold me here."

Insensitive and cruel. And a pivotal moment in her life. What if she'd said something else to him? What if she'd had the courage to acknowledge her deepest, secret feelings and fears? And if she hadn't left Crystal Point when she did, would she have felt even more trapped in their relationship, perhaps their marriage, had it ever come to that?

Grace sat back on the sofa and uncurled her legs.

Marriage had never figured in her life. Erik, who was as focused on his career as she was, had never mentioned it. Before Erik, she'd had a three-year relationship with Dennis Collier. The handsome and successful orthopedic surgeon had asked her twice to marry him—both times she'd insisted she was happy with the tempo of their relationship. She worked long hours and kept her own apartment. Toward the end they'd go for days without seeing one another. Eventually Dennis had traded her for a third-year resident at the hospital where he worked. Within six months of their breakup she heard he'd married and had a baby on the way.

The news hadn't torn her up. She'd genuinely cared for Dennis—but knew it wasn't the kind of feeling that could sustain her for a lifetime. There were feelings, certainly… but love? Grace wasn't sure she even knew how to be in love. Long ago she'd run from those feelings, terrified they'd trap her, make her less than whole and dilute her ambition. She'd wanted a career. That's what she'd planned for. That's what her parents expected of her. Not marriage. Not babies. Not Crystal Point. That legacy was left to her brother and sisters.

Noah took over running the family business and Evie was the original Earth Mother. While M.J. waltzed through life as a free spirit, making jewelry and saving the world with her causes. She was Grace Preston—smart, successful... *untouchable*.

Her cell rang, interrupting her thoughts, and she grabbed it from the coffee table.

"Hey, *Princess*."

She bit back a startled gasp and took a deep breath. Strange that Cameron should telephone when her head was full of thoughts of him. "Would you stop calling me that?"

Cameron laughed softly. "I'll do my best. So, how are things?"

"Since last night?" she shot back and ignored the rapid thump of her heart.

He was silent for a moment and Grace could swear he was smiling. "Come down to the surf club this afternoon."

"What?"

"The surf club," he said again. "I want to show you something."

"What kind of something?"

"Something you'll want to see."

Grace colored hotly. The conversation was oddly flirtatious and she was startled by how it made her feel. "I...I don't think so."

"Oh, come on, Grace," he said and laughed. "Live dangerously. You never know—you might like it."

"No."

"You'll miss seeing something great."

Again, more flirting, more...*something*. He was infuriating.

Grace made an unglamorous grunting sound. "Whatever game you're playing, Jakowski, it's not the least bit funny."

"Game?" he said and chuckled. "That's harsh, *Princess*. You need to learn to trust."

He was laughing at her. As always. Her fingers turned white where she gripped the phone. "Jerk!"

She disconnected and wondered why he was the one person who could push her buttons so easily. And then she wondered why she cared that he did.

Her mother came to visit a little later and Grace made some tea and took a spot opposite at the big scrubbed table in the kitchen. Barbara Preston was the übermother. A career teacher, she'd managed to raise four children and work full-time until her retirement a few years earlier.

"So, what's going on, Grace?"

She knew that tone—knew her mother had something to say. "Nothing," she replied and poured the tea.

Her mother made a disbelieving sound and grabbed a mug. "Grace, I know something's up with you. You've been home a week now. And other than at Christmastime every few years, you never stay this long."

Grace looked at her mother. "I'm fine. Just taking a break."

It wasn't exactly a lie. She *was* on a break. A forced break. After the accident, her employer had insisted she see a therapist. Half a dozen visits later the counselor had recommended time off from her hectic job as a finance broker and her life in New York. Grace had resisted until she'd unexpectedly fallen apart one afternoon while meeting a client. Thankfully, the client hadn't been appalled by her unstoppable tears, and instead had called on her secretary, who'd then informed her boss. Another therapy session followed and without any choice but to agree, the week she'd planned to come home for Evie's wedding turned into a month.

"I'm worried about you."

"There's no need," Grace assured her mother. "I was a little burned-out, that's all."

"You're not sick or anything?"

"No," she said quickly. There was no point mentioning the accident. She knew her mother would only worry. "I'm perfectly healthy."

Barbara looked at her and smiled. "Okay, I'll stop smothering. I did think it might have been a man who brought you back home."

In a way it had been. Richard Bennett had been a colleague in the firm where she worked. He was also a devoted husband and father. A forty-nine-year-old man who hadn't deserved his fate.

"There's no man in my life," she said quietly. "And Erik left a long time ago."

"Are you looking for a relationship?"

It was an unexpected question. Her mother never meddled in her love life. And since her family had known of her career ambitions from a young age, her decision to move to New York was never challenged. "You know how I feel about all that."

Barbara sighed and as always, Grace wished she knew how to really connect with her mother. Evie knew how. And Mary-Jayne. They fit in. Grace had always felt like she was watching her family from the outside. Oh, she was loved, she knew that. But being part of things? That was different. She'd never belonged in Crystal Point. New York had embraced her in ways the tiny town never had. Until she'd been forced to abandon that life.

Now she felt as misplaced as she had all those years ago when she'd been sent to boarding school. As a child she'd shown an aptitude for math and music and at twelve had been enrolled into a school that offered a curriculum designed for gifted children. She'd spent six years at that school, coming back only for the holidays. When her high school years were over, Grace had returned to Crystal Point for a few months. It was during that time that she began dating Cameron. Three months later she'd packed her bags and moved to New York.

Sixteen years on and she still didn't know where she fit in.

"Marriage isn't a prison sentence," her mother said gently.

Grace nodded. "I know. But not everyone gets it all. And I'm not the settle down, picket fence type."

"I only want to see you happy."

"I know that, too," Grace replied. "And I am," she said and smiled. Not exactly the truth, but she wasn't about to burden her mother with her problems. She needed to forget. Not dwell.

"Sometimes I think…" Her mother's voice faded for a moment. "I think that you were too young to have left home when you did all those years ago."

"I was strong-willed," Grace said, and managed a smile. "And I wanted to go."

Her mother patted her hand. "I know you did. And your dad and I were so proud of you for having the courage to follow your dreams. And we're still proud, Grace. You always were our shining star."

She'd heard it before. That's why she'd been sent to boarding school while the other Preston children remained in Crystal Point. *Grace is special. Grace is so smart. Grace will have a stellar career in whatever field she chooses.* How often had she heard those words while she was growing up and attending the school? Within six months she'd been pushed up a grade and then spent the following five years as the youngest student in her class. She knew it had cost her parents tens of thousands every year for her tuition. She owed them a lot for giving her the education she'd had. But there were also times when she'd wished she was simply ordinary Grace Preston.

Without the high IQ. Without the pressure to succeed and make good grades.

She'd never told her parent's how she'd felt. There never seemed the right time. To complain would make her ungrateful, undeserving. And once school was over she just wanted to move on from those unhappy years.

When her mother left, Grace changed into designer jeans, high-end mules and a white, immaculately pressed T-shirt. She found a visor hanging on a peg near the back door and positioned it on her head. She needed to walk. To think.

The beach beckoned.

Winter meant fewer swimmers, even though the day was warm and the water temperature would probably be moderate. Grace locked up the private living area upstairs and checked on the single guest who was lazing in the front sunroom. The lone occupant was a gentleman in his sixties who had come to Dunn Inn alone for the first time in ten years, following the death of his wife. Talking with him for a few minutes stretched Grace's emotions and by the time she'd said goodbye and headed outside, her throat was tight and thick. Her nerves were fraught enough and the sad widower somehow pushed her buttons. She took a deep breath and walked across the road. The grassy shoulder led to a long pathway, which ran parallel with the ocean and wound down toward the beach.

Grace followed the trail at a reasonable pace and it took about ten minutes to reach the sandy knolls leading up to the beach. She stalled at the edge of the rise and took a deep breath. The surf club stood to her left.

I didn't come here for this. For him. I'm not going anywhere near that building.

Only…she *was* curious.

Grace took a second, shook her shoulders and walked across the path.

* * *

"There's just no way I can do it!"

Cameron bit back an exasperated sigh as seventeen-year-old Emily Maxwell pulled a pile of books from a battered knapsack. "You knew it was going to be difficult."

"But not impossible," she wailed and dumped the bag at her feet. "I'll never learn this stuff in time."

"You've two weeks before you need to sit that makeup exam, Em," he reminded her.

She rolled her eyes toward the toddler playing on a mat in the corner of the room. "And I've got a two-year-old kid to look after. It ain't gonna happen. It's over."

"How about I ask your grandmother to help with the baby?"

Emily shook her head. "She's got my brothers and sister to take care of. And they're all going out to the farm next week."

Cameron had heard the same story all afternoon. The teenager had been given an opportunity to complete a makeup exam that would go toward her final grade. But she'd talked of giving in to the pressure and Cameron knew he needed to do something to stop her from throwing away her chance at an education. He just didn't know what. Emily was the oldest sister of Dylan. Twelve-year-old Dylan was one of his charges in the Big Brother program sponsored by his station. When Cameron inherited Dylan from the retiring sergeant at the station, he also inherited the teenage mother, her ailing grandmother and two other half siblings. Officially Dylan was his Big Brother charge, but the rest of them were in such dire circumstances, Cameron feared they'd all slip through the cracks and end up separated and in social services. They were a loving family, but down on their luck and needing help.

When Pat Jennings got custody of her grandchildren from her drug-addicted and incarcerated daughter, the town rallied together and raised funds enough for a deposit on a small farm out west. With the house a few months away from being ready for the families' final move, Cameron knew this was Emily's last chance to finish high school. If only she could get past her resistance to study so she could complete the makeup examination. Emily was intelligent, but lacked confidence. She'd missed classes and failed to finish set assignments throughout the year as she juggled single parenthood. It was a heavy load for a girl not yet eighteen.

"You have to find the time to study," he said quietly.

"It's not only the time," she complained bitterly. "The work is just too...well, it's too hard. And I'm not smart enough."

She was. But she clearly didn't believe it.

"I think the best thing at the moment is for you to—"

"Hey, Sarge!" called Dylan as he popped his head around the door. "There's a lady here to see you."

A lady? He looked toward Emily. "Keep studying. I'll be back in a minute and we'll continue this discussion."

"But I—"

"Hit the books," he said and smiled, then turned on his heel.

The second floor of the surf club had recently undergone a complete renovation following a fire four months earlier. Now it was used for Tai Chi classes, the Big Brother program and a couple of other local community events. Today it was a place for Emily to study without interruption while he spent time with Dylan.

Cameron headed down the stairs and came to an abrupt halt when he reached the bottom tread.

Grace.

A jolt hit him behind the ribs. He looked at Dylan, who was hanging off to her left and grinning. "Go and get the fishing gear ready," he instructed and tossed him the keys to his car.

Dylan caught the keys and took off quickly. When he was out of sight Cameron turned his attention to Grace. "Hi."

"Hello."

"You came."

She shrugged a little. "I was walking…I simply happened to… Well, I was nearby and thought I'd come in."

The sensation in his chest amplified. "I'm glad you did." Cameron held out his hand. "Come on up."

She looked at his hand and hesitated. He waited. Grace never acted on impulse. Her actions were always measured. Always in control. She looked immaculate, as usual. Her dark hair was pulled back tightly and caught in a band at her nape. The only anomaly in her seriously fashionable look was the well-worn hot pink visor on her head. She finally took his hand and he instinctively curled his fingers around hers. She didn't resist and followed him up the stairway.

When they reached the landing she withdrew her hand and crossed her arms. "So, what did you want to show me?"

Cameron smiled. "Nothing sinister."

"Not that I'm likely to believe you," she said, raising her perfectly sculpted brows.

He cracked another smile. "Come on, there's someone I'd like you to meet."

Cameron opened the door to one of the two upstairs rooms and beckoned her inside. She tagged after him and he closed the door. Emily looked up from her spot at the desk positioned by the long row of windows. He ushered Grace across the room.

"Emily, this is Grace Preston, a friend of mine."

"Girlfriend?" the teen asked and stood.

"Friend," Grace corrected as she shook Emily's hand. "And I think I just met your brother?"

"Yeah, Dylan," Emily said and laughed. "We look alike."

The toddler in the corner tapped loudly on the plastic drum he was playing with.

"And that's Riley," Cameron explained. "Emily's son."

Grace nodded, frowning a little. He could see her looking at Emily with interest before she glanced at the books on the table. "But it looks as though I'm interrupting you."

"No, you're saving me," Emily replied with a wry grin. "Sergeant Jakowski is a slave driver."

Grace laughed and the sound hit Cameron directly behind the ribs. *Damn.* He wished everything about her didn't affect him like he was a pining schoolboy. "Emily needs to study for a makeup exam in two weeks. This is a quiet place for her to hit the books while Dylan and I go fishing."

"Then I am interrupting you," Grace replied. "I should go."

"No," Cameron said, too quickly. "Stay for a while." He saw her surprised look and fought the color creeping up his neck. But she was here. And he wanted her to stay. "You're handy with the books, right?" he asked and smiled as he pulled out a chair.

Handy with the books was an understatement. Grace was the smartest person he'd ever known. As a child she'd always been top of her class, even before she'd gone to that fancy school. Then she'd headed off to New York to study finance and business. After that he'd heard she'd been headhunted by some of the top brokerage firms in the city.

Grace nodded, clearly still hesitant. "I'm not sure I can—"

"That would be great," Emily said with more enthusiasm than he'd heard from her all afternoon. "I need all the help I can get."

Cameron tapped the back of the chair and spoke. "I'll be back in a little while."

Once Cameron left, Grace sat down. Emily stared at her and grinned.

"So, are you and the Sarge—"

"No," Grace replied quickly and pushed back the heat in

her cheeks. "We're just friends," she said, even if it wasn't exactly true. "We've known one another since we were kids."

And he was the first man I kissed.

Even though she'd developed a silly crush on him when she was twelve, Grace knew she was a "late bloomer" when it had come to boys and sex. While her classmates were pining over pop icons and movie stars, she had her head firmly placed in textbooks or a Jane Austen novel. Being a year younger hadn't helped. She was teased for her bookish ways, her flat chest and seeming lack of interest in any of the boys from the nearby all-male college. By the time her chest arrived she'd already earned the reputation as being stuck-up and closed off from the other girls in her class. And after a while she learned to embrace the isolation from her peers. Making friends lost any appeal and she didn't waste time thinking about boys or romance.

Until the night of her sixteenth birthday.

"That explains why you don't look like his usual type," Emily said and jerked her back to the present. "I mean, they are Gucci jeans you're wearing, right?"

Grace shifted in her seat and took off her visor. She didn't like the idea of Cameron having a *type*. "You know fashion?"

Emily nodded. "I *love* fashion. Not that I can afford anything better than chain-store clothes these days. Riley keeps growing out of his gear quicker than I can buy them. But I would love to have my own store one day. And maybe study design."

Grace pressed her hair back and looked at the textbook on the table. "That's a great ambition. Now, about this makeup exam?"

Emily rolled her eyes. "I've missed a lot of school this year. Nan was helping out with Riley until my half brother and sister came to live with us." The teenager pushed the book toward Grace. "My mother is a screwup. She's in jail.

Her husband died last year. No one knows what happened to *my* dad."

Grace hid her surprise. Teenagers with serious family issues weren't something she had experience dealing with. Unlike Cameron, who she knew spent a lot of time with needy kids like Dylan and Emily. "I'm sorry."

Emily shrugged. "It happens. We're lucky we've got Nan. But she's getting old, you know, and can't do things like she used to. Besides, I have to think about Riley."

Grace glanced at the toddler, still happily playing in the corner. Adolescence, high school exams and a baby? It seemed like a heavy load. "Which is why Cameron wants you to finish high school?"

"Yeah—so I can get a good job or go to college. He's cool, you know…he just nags me a bit sometimes."

Grace smiled. "Well, nagging can be helpful."

Emily laughed. "That's what my nan says. And I guess I know that."

"But?"

The teen shrugged again. "The studying is hard. And I get so tired of being treated differently at school because I've got Riley."

Grace felt the frustration and pain in the girl's voice. She knew firsthand how it felt to be different and then ostracized. "So, how about you show me what you need to study and maybe I can help."

"Are you a teacher?"

"Finance broker."

Emily frowned. "Which means?"

"Which means I'm good with numbers," Grace replied with a wry smile.

She spent the next hour working with Emily. By the time Cameron and Dylan returned, the books were packed away and Riley was asleep in his mother's arms. Emily had asked

Grace to hold the little boy, but she'd resisted. Babies weren't her thing. Making money and math and meetings and work lunches were what she was good at.

Not babies.

Grace didn't have a ticking biological clock. She didn't have some deep-rooted and instinctive yearning to reproduce. She had her career. And it had always been enough.

Being back in Crystal Point wasn't going to change that. Being around Cameron wasn't going to change that either.

"I'll just drop them home," Cameron said as they watched Emily collect her knapsack and haul Riley higher in her arms.

"I should get back to the B and B and—"

"I'll be ten minutes, tops," he said. "Wait here."

Before she had a chance to object, Emily and Dylan waved goodbye and they all disappeared through the doorway. Grace lingered by the desk for a few minutes and got herself all worked up about his high-handed demands. She was just about to head home in protest when her cell rang. It was her boss, Jennifer Mullin-Shaw.

"So, are you relaxing?" Jennifer asked.

Grace was pleased the other woman couldn't see her frown. "Of course."

"And taking the therapist's advice?"

"All of it," Grace assured her. "I'm even watching old movies on cable to relax."

Jennifer laughed and they chatted for a few minutes about mundane things such as the weather and then she gave a brief rundown of her sister's wedding. Minus the part about making out with Cameron on the beach in the moonlight.

"So, you're not dwelling on what happened?"

Grace gripped the phone harder and told a tiny lie. "I haven't thought about the accident at all. I'm feeling…better."

"That's good. I'm pleased you're taking it easy. Give me a call when you're ready to come back to work."

I'm ready now.

But she didn't say it. Instead she ended the call and slipped the cell in her jeans pocket. Her plan to return to the B and B was forgotten when she turned on her heels and discovered Cameron standing in the doorway, arms crossed over his chest, one shoulder propped against the doorjamb.

He looked her over in that slow, infuriating way she was accustomed to. "So, how did it go with Emily?"

She nodded and placed the visor back on her head. "Good. She's a smart girl."

"Yes, she is. Did she tell you about her home life?"

"A little. She told me about her mother and how her two half siblings now live with them and her grandmother."

"Pat took the kids in when her daughter got locked up. Drugs," he explained. "It's been tough for the family. Emily and Dylan's father disappeared years ago and they've lived with their grandmother most of their lives. The father of the two younger kids was killed a few months back. But now they have a chance to start fresh with a new home out near Burdon Creek." He told her how the town had rallied to help the family purchase the small farm.

Grace thought about what he was doing for Emily's family. She tried to think of one selfless thing she done the past year and came up with nothing.

No wonder he thinks I'm shallow. Not that I care one hoot what Cameron Jakowski thinks of me.

"It's good of you to look out for them," she said in a vague way she suspected sounded like some weak attempt to make conversation.

"Someone has to."

Knight in shining armor. Hero cop. All-around good guy. Not the guy for me.

Where did that come from? Grace crossed her arms and

stared out of the window. *Those mindless minutes on the beach the night before, that's where.*

She pulled on her good sense, determined to not think about his arms, his kisses, or anything else to do with the one person who'd managed to get under her skin and make her feel like she was the most self-absorbed woman on the planet. She'd never really cared what Erik thought of her. Or Dennis. Perhaps because she'd always held herself apart and avoided getting too close. But Cameron...he was different. He saw her. Every flaw.

"So, you said you had something to show me?" she asked.

"I did?"

"Mmm-hmm," she replied and tried to dismiss the silly way her pulse raced. But he was hard to ignore in low-rise jeans and a pale blue T-shirt that showed the broadness of his chest and shoulders. And suddenly the air in the room grew hotter, thicker, like a tempting force had swept between them. She'd felt it before and always managed to ignore it. But today she couldn't. He had good looks and charm in bucket loads.

"It's nothing."

She turned her head to glance at him. "Did you get me here under false pretenses?"

"Maybe."

Warmth pushed through her blood. "And now that you have me here, what are your intentions?"

He laughed. "Ah, Grace, you are a confusing and beautiful contradiction."

The compliment part didn't help her determination to not be aware of him. "Then maybe I should leave and put you out of your misery."

"What fun would that be?"

"Who needs fun?" she shot back and managed a tight smile.

"All work and no play, Grace? How's that worked out for you so far?"

"Well enough," she replied.

"Liar," he said softly. "And if I come a little closer you'll be shaking in those three-hundred-dollar shoes of yours."

She drew in a breath. "You really do overstate your charm. If I'm shaking, it's with disbelief that you're so egotistical."

He chuckled and perched his behind on the desk. "You know, Grace, I like you this way...fired up and ready for anything."

Grace raised one brow. "Well, get used to it."

"Don't get me wrong," he said and crossed his arms. "I also like the woman you were last night."

Heat crept up her neck. "Well, don't get too used to *that*."

He laughed and then just as quickly looked serious. "So, tell me about the accident?" He'd heard that part of her conversation with Jennifer? Damn. *Deny everything.*

"It's nothing."

He shook his head. "I don't believe you. I know there's something wrong with you, Grace. I also know you're too proud, or too stubborn, to say what it is because you think it will give me some kind of ridiculous advantage. Tell me," he insisted as his brown-eyed gaze scanned her face. "What accident were you talking about just now?"

She drew in a breath and the truth felt heavy across her shoulders. Grace closed her eyes for a moment. Images jumbled in her head. Lights flashing, brakes screeching, metal crunching...it was over in a flash of a second. And then there had been an eerie quiet, followed by the sound of her own terrified breath.

And suddenly she wanted to tell him everything.

"I was in a crash," she explained quietly, feeling raw and exposed and more alone than she'd ever dare admit. "I was in a car crash."

Cameron responded quickly. "What? When?"

"A couple of months ago."

"Were you hurt?"

She shrugged. Her scars were emotional, not physical. "I dislocated my shoulder and had a few cuts and abrasions. Nothing serious."

Cameron's gaze was unwavering. "It wasn't just a fender bender, though, was it?"

"No."

"It was a serious crash?"

She shuddered. "Yes."

"And you haven't told your family about it, have you?"

"No."

He pushed himself off the table. "Why not?"

Grace's throat tightened. She hadn't spoken of the accident with anyone other than her boss and her therapist. Her work colleagues had stayed off the topic, even when she'd arrived at the office after taking a week off. They knew she didn't do deep and meaningful discussions. They knew she didn't want to talk about Richard's death. "There was no point."

He shook his head. "No point? They're your *family*. You were hurt, Grace, don't you think they had a right to know?"

The heaviness in her throat increased. "I wasn't hurt badly," she said in a defensive tone. *Not like Richard*. "It wasn't worth making people worry."

He frowned. "People? I'm not talking about random strangers, Grace," he said and grabbed her hand. "I'm talking about your family. Your parents. Your brother and sisters."

She tried to pull away put he held her firm. "You don't understand. I can't be like that. I can't let out every emotion I have. I don't have what it takes to…to…"

"To what?" he encouraged so gently the heat in her throat turned into an all-out burn. "To get close to someone?" he asked.

Grace nodded.

He urged her toward him and she jerked as her body pressed against his. "And yet," he said as he curled one arm around her waist. "You feel close now."

Her emotions heaved. "Please don't...don't tease me."

"I'm not teasing," he said so gently her insides contracted. "I promise. But it might help to talk about it."

Grace didn't want his help. She wanted to run back to the B & B. But she didn't move. And instead, she spoke a truth she hadn't shared with anyone. "Okay...here's the truth. After the crash I had a...meltdown," she admitted. "My boss made me come home. It wasn't my choice. I wanted to work through it in New York. I didn't want to come back here. I didn't want sympathy or pity. I didn't want to feel *anything*."

He looked into her eyes. "Does feeling scare you that much, Grace?"

It scared her. It terrified her. If she let herself really *feel* then she would be exposed...vulnerable. *Weak*. "Yes."

He touched her face. "Then I think you're exactly where you need to be."

In his arms? It was the one place she could never be. She shook her head and pulled away. "Promise me you won't say anything. I don't want my parents to—"

"I promise," he said gently and dropped his arms. "For now."

Chapter Four

Later that afternoon Cameron lingered by the table in his mother's kitchen while she stacked plastic containers into two separate carry bags.

"You know, I can cook for myself," he mentioned, and grinned.

"Me, too," his sister Lauren piped up in agreement.

Irene Jakowski gave a look which said she didn't believe either of them. "Humor me and take this anyway."

Which is exactly what they would do. He inhaled the delicious scent of the cabbage rolls. He did love his mother's *golabki*.

"Not too much, please, *Matka*," Lauren patted her flat stomach and used the Polish word for *mother*, which his parents preferred. "Or I'll end up as big as a house."

"Beef and a little mushroom wrapped in cabbage leaves won't add any pounds," Irene said and raised her brows at her youngest child. "Besides, you're too skinny."

"True," Cameron agreed and winced when Lauren's elbow jabbed him in the ribs.

But he was right. His sister looked too thin. Which wasn't a surprise, considering she'd endured a messy divorce a year earlier. He was pleased she now seemed to be pulling through the worst of it.

"The wedding was just lovely, don't you think?" Irene looked at Cameron as she spoke. He knew where it was going. "Evie made a lovely bride."

He was pretty sure Irene had once hoped he'd hook up with Evie, but he'd never felt that way about her. Grace, on the other hand…his mother knew a little of their failed relationship. It wasn't something he enjoyed mulling over.

"The dress looked fabulous," Lauren chimed in to say. His sister and mother owned a bridal store in Bellandale and he knew they'd fitted Evie for her gown. "I knew the off-the-shoulder design was a good—"

Cameron groaned. "If you two are gonna talk dresses I'm outta here."

His mother chuckled. "I only said she made a lovely bride. But all the Preston girls are quite lovely, aren't they? Even Grace, once you get past her prickles."

"Prickles?" Lauren echoed with a frown. "You mean icy barbs. There's no doubt she's beautiful, but she doesn't exactly bring on the warm fuzzies. Not like Evie and M.J." Lauren grabbed the bag their mother passed her way. "Anyway, enough gossiping, I have to get going."

Lauren hugged them both and was gone within a minute.

"I should get going, too," he said, grabbing his keys from the table.

"Your dad won't be back from golf for another hour," she said and grabbed the kettle. "Feel like staying for coffee?"

He glanced at his watch. "Sure."

"Do you also feel like talking about whatever's on your mind at the moment?"

He had to hand it to his mother—she had the female intuition thing down pat. "Not especially."

"Grace, I suppose?"

He looked up. "What?"

"You're always edgy when she's in town. I saw you talking to her at the wedding so I figured there was some connection to your current mood."

Cameron pulled out a chair and sat down. "You're imagining things. And my mood is fine."

Irene shrugged. "How long is she back for this time?"

"I'm not sure."

"Barbara is worried about her," his mother confided. Barbara Preston was Irene's closest friend. "Know anything?"

Cameron ignored the tightness in his chest. He didn't like lying but wasn't about to get drawn into a conversation about Grace, especially when he'd promised to keep her secrets. "Not a thing."

Irene nodded, gave a wry smile and then switched the subject. "So, you're coming to the reunion this year?"

The Jakowski family reunion was an annual event that had been tradition for more than thirty years. "I'll do my best."

"It will make your father happy if you come."

"I know," he said, but doubted he'd attend. He'd missed four of the past five years and this year was shaping up to be no exception. Because even though Franciszek Jakowski treated him like he was his son in every possible way and he loved the other man dearly, when it came to the huge family gathering, Cameron always felt like a fraud.

His mother had married Franciszek when she was just twenty with a three-year-old on her hip. By the time Lauren arrived a few years later he had already been adopted by Franciszek and he was the only father Cameron knew. His biological father had bailed well before he was born, not prepared for teenage parenthood. Irene never talked about him and Cameron never asked. It was only sometimes that he wondered about him, or when faced with the reunion picnic that he felt like he was there by default. Because Jakowski blood didn't run through his veins. He wasn't really part of the four generations of Polish ancestry that was celebrated by his parents and grandparents and uncle and aunts and countless cousins. He was the biological son of a seventeen-year-old misfit who had disappeared off the radar once his teenage girlfriend discovered she was pregnant.

"Please try," he heard his mother say and it quickly got his thoughts back on track.

He drank some of the coffee she'd placed in front of him and smiled. "I will, *Matka,* I promise."

A few hours later he was sitting on the wide timber deck of his double story, four bedroom, two living rooms, way too big to be practical house, a drink in front of him that he hadn't touched. He'd purchased the half-acre block nine years ago and then designed and built the home, of which he only used about one quarter of the rooms.

It was cold out and he heard the sea crashing against the rocks. In the distance he could see the lights from a vessel in the shipping lane, most likely a tanker on its way to collect cargo from the port south of Bellandale. Locally grown sugar cane was shipped out by the ton and the big ships came by weekly during crushing season.

Cattle bellowed in the distance and the sound was oddly comforting. Living in the most northern end of Crystal Point, he had only one close neighbor—an elderly couple who lived in a small house across from his in the quiet cul-de-sac. Cameron liked the solitude and the view. With hundreds of acres of unspoiled pasture behind and the Pacific Ocean to the front, it was an idyllic location.

The dog at his feet yawned and rolled onto its back and it made him smile a bit. The big, goofy mutt had a way of doing that. But the smile on his face didn't last long. His thoughts were full of Grace.

She'd been in a car crash? She could have died.

Life without Grace in it...

The idea made his bones ache. In just twenty-four hours she'd gotten so deep under his skin he could barely think about anything else. He wanted to call her, hear her voice. He stared at the telephone, then grabbed it and his drink and headed inside. Jed hunkered after him and when Cameron started flicking off lights the dog settled on his big mat by the back door.

Once the house was locked up he took a shower and then dropped into bed. The digital clock on the side table blinked ten-thirty at him. Late enough to sleep, he figured and switched off the lamp before he rolled onto his stomach.

Green eyes haunted him instantly.

He grabbed a pillow and punched it a couple of times.

Green eyes and perfectly straight almost black hair.

Cameron flipped onto his back with a groan, determined to not think about her, and failed miserably. Her unexpected vulnerability distracted him, made him forget she was the world's number one ice princess. He shouldn't want her. But he did.

She made him crazy. Still.

And her kisses were like something from out of this world....

The first time he'd kissed her was on her sixteenth birthday. He'd deliberately arrived late to her party to avoid his growing awareness of her whenever she came near. She was too young. Noah's—his best friend's—sister. And despite the odd time he'd catch her watching him when she thought he wasn't looking, she'd barely give him the time of day. Until that night. A darkened doorway and the heady beat of some old song in the background had shifted her usual reserve. A few minutes alone and the temptation of a birthday kiss and he couldn't help but claim her lips. If it hadn't been for a strict voice in his head telling him she was off-limits for at least a couple more years, they might have done more than share a sweet, unforgettable kiss.

A year and a half later he asked her out for real. By then she'd finished school and he was settled into his career as a second-year officer, had wheels and was saving to buy some land where he'd eventually build a house he hoped she'd one day be proud to live in. He'd had plans, ideas, and every one had included Grace Preston. But three months into their relationship she'd said goodbye and headed to New York.

So what the hell am I thinking? Like I want to be on the receiving end of her rejection again.

Was it just sexual frustration that had him feeling like he did? He flipped back onto his stomach. If he kept thinking about how it felt to kiss her, touch her, stroke her beautiful skin, he'd never get to sleep.

Too late.

Cameron rolled again and stared at the ceiling.

He closed his eyes. A busy week loomed ahead. He had a pile of work on his desk, including a few court appearances. One to give evidence against a repeat DUI offender looking to avoid jail time and Cameron doubted the hard-line magistrate would be lenient. The other two involved breaches of domestic violence orders.

He took a deep breath and tried to relax. But when sleep finally came, his dreams were haunted by bright green eyes…

Because she prided herself on being action oriented, Grace had spent most of the afternoon and evening coming up with ways to pull herself from the uncharacteristic funk that had taken hold of her life.

And one thought kept coming back to her.

Cameron.

If he dared breathe a word to her family she would be completely outed.

And one thing Grace knew for certain—once they knew what had happened to her she would be enveloped in their care and compassion and her fraught nerves would surely fracture. She also knew she didn't have the strength for it. It was easier to stay stoic and in control. Easier to act the role she'd played all her life—the supercool and tough-as-nails Grace who would return to New York without anyone guessing she was broken inside.

All she had to do was make sure Cameron kept his mouth shut.

Grace called him again the following morning and when the call went to voice mail, decided to take more action and see him in person. She took Evie's Honda and drove past his house and since his car wasn't there, figured he was at work. So she headed into town.

The police station was easy to find and she scored a parking spot outside. She'd dressed in a black skirt, matching jacket and collared red shirt. The black knee-high boots and patent bag added to the effect she wanted. All business. All control.

When she reached the reception desk, Grace took a deep breath and spoke to the young woman behind the counter. "I'd like to see Sergeant Jakowski."

"Do you have an appointment?"

"No. But I'd appreciate it if you told him I was here."

One name given, a telephone call and a few minutes wait and she had what she wanted. She took the lift to the second level and when she stepped out into the hall found him waiting.

"This is a surprise."

Grace shrugged as she walked toward him. "I called your cell but you didn't pick up."

"So you decided to start stalking me."

She stilled about five feet from him and waited until two uniformed officers passed before responding. "Yes, you look like you're shaking in your boots."

He smiled. "Speaking of boots," he said and looked her over. "They do the job."

"And what job is that?"

"The job of distracting me enough so you can get your own way."

He liked her boots? "You think I'm that manipulative?" she inquired and stopped in front of him.

Cameron opened a door to his left. "I think you're a woman who wants something."

She did. His silence.

"I just came to talk."

He ushered her into the room and closed the door. "So, talk."

Grace looked at him. He filled out his uniform in a way that got her attention. The pale blue shirt fit him perfectly, highlighting his broad shoulders and lean waist. She quickly ignored her wavering thoughts. "I wanted to know if you'll stand by your promise to keep my private business private."

He came toward the desk and sat on the edge. "I'm not about to be a buffer between you and your family," he said with a kind of irritated disbelief. "They're your *family*, Grace. I don't understand your reluctance to tell them about your accident."

"No, you wouldn't," she shot back. "But it's my decision to make."

He crossed his arms. "It's not hard to let people in."

"Now you sound like my therapist," she said and let out a heavy sigh.

"You're seeing a shrink?"

"Counselor," she corrected and quickly realized she'd said too much. "Because the accident was work-related the company was obliged to supply grief counseling to—"

"Whoa," Cameron held up a hand. "Back up a minute. You're seeing a *grief* counselor. Explain that to me."

Grace's skin prickled. "It's normal in these circumstances."

"What circumstances?"

She drew in a breath, steadying herself. "When someone has died."

He took a second to respond. "Someone died? Who?"

"Richard Bennett," she said quietly and felt the intensity of his stare through to her blood. "A work colleague. We were traveling together at the time of the accident."

"Was anyone else in the car?"

"No," she replied. "Richard was driving. We were on our way to meet with a client. But we crashed. It was no one's fault."

"So he died. And you survived?"

She nodded. Her counselor had explained survivor's guilt several times. She'd brushed it off. Ignored it. "The therapist thought I should come home and be with my family for a while. My boss agreed."

"That sounds like good advice."

Grace shrugged. "But unnecessary. I have a job that I'm good at and a life in New York that suits me. I didn't see the need to change that."

"Obviously the people around you did. What about your friends in New York?"

She shrugged again. There were acquaintances and work colleagues. But friends? None who she was close to. The only person who'd visited her after the accident had been her boss, Jennifer. "You know me."

He looked at her for the longest time before he spoke again.

"I do," he said quietly. "And I know your family. They're kind, good people who care about you."

"Precisely why I don't want to alarm them."

"Nice try. What's the real reason?"

Grace got to her feet. "That is the reason. Does it seem impossible that I don't want to worry them? And it's not like I was seriously hurt. I'm fine. Just fine."

His brows came up and he stood and rocked back a little on his heels. "You're a lot of things, Grace...but I suspect *fine* isn't one of them."

Her annoyance spiked. "You don't know anything about it, so I'd rather you didn't try to psychoanalyze me. All I want is your word that you won't say anything to my family, particularly my parents. I'll tell them when I'm ready, and not before."

"You know, I don't think I quite believe you. You're obviously in denial about an incredibly traumatic experience. The best thing you could do is come clean and talk about it."

What a self-righteous jerk. He knew nothing about what was best for her.

"So you won't keep your word, is that what you're saying?"

He rubbed his chin. "I'm not sure keeping my word would be what's best for you."

She clutched her handbag to her side. "Since it's obvious you don't have the decency to respect my wishes and seem to think you have the right to an opinion about my life, I intend to keep as far away from you as possible while I'm back in Crystal Point." She drew in a deep breath. "Or to put it another way—go to hell, Jakowski!"

Then she was out the door and down the corridor as quickly as her feet could carry her.

Of course, in a town as small as Crystal Point, staying away from Cameron was almost impossible.

When she pulled into the driveway in front of her brother's home that evening and saw Cameron's electric-blue sedan parked there, she immediately considered bailing. But she wouldn't have been able to explain that to Noah. Her brother had dropped by the B and B that afternoon to repair a window lock and had invited her to share dinner with his family. Since she still had one guest to attend to, Grace declined dinner and agreed to a coffee visit instead.

Only she hadn't anticipated seeing the one person she wanted to avoid.

She wondered if he'd wrangled an invitation just to irritate her or dropped in without one. It was her sister-in-law who answered the door and invited her inside.

"We've just finished dinner," Callie said as she closed the door. "But I can get you something if you—"

"Oh, I'm fine," Grace assured her. "I've already eaten."

Her brother and Cameron were in the living room. "Grace," Noah said and came around the sofa. He kissed her cheek. He knew she wasn't the hugging type. "Great to see you. Everything okay?"

"Yes." She glanced at Cameron, who was sitting on the sofa. In jeans and T-shirt he looked relaxed and handsome and possessed such an easygoing manner that when he smiled Grace couldn't help but smile back. *Stay on track.* She rattled the bag she carried. "I brought something for the children, I hope you don't mind?"

Noah grinned. "Not at all. I'll round them up."

Her brother left the room and once Callie disappeared to make coffee, Grace glared at him. "What are you doing here?"

"I was invited," Cameron said, smiling as he looked at the bag she carried. "Gifts are a nice touch. I trust you remember the kids' names?"

She frowned. "I'm not that out of the loop. I am their aunt, you know."

"Nice outfit, by the way," he said of her long denim skirt and pale green sweater.

"Spare me the compliments."

He chuckled. "Very…aunt appropriate."

"Are you suggesting I look like a spinster aunt now?"

He laughed again. "Hardly. There's nothing the least bit spinsterish about you, Grace."

"Other than the fact I'm not married?"

"You've still got time to change that."

Grace shook her head slowly. She didn't want to talk about marriage with him. Because despite the denials she knew would come, being around him made her think, imagine. And those kinds of thoughts were pointless. She had her life—it was set. "Marriage is not in my plans. A husband and kids wouldn't mix with my work."

"And you wouldn't consider giving up your career?"

She placed her handbag by the fireplace and didn't quite have the courage to meet his gaze until she'd inhaled a steadying breath. "My career comes first. I'm not the marriage-and-babies sort. I'll leave that to women like Evie and Callie."

He looked at her oddly. "You don't think a woman can have both?"

She raised her shoulders a little. "I've worked with a few women trying to juggle career and family and they always complained how difficult it was. Better to do one, and do it well, than try to divide the time and become mediocre at both."

"That's a rather dim view of things," he said. "What happens when you fall in love?"

"I won't," she said quickly and tried to breathe through the heat rising up her collarbone. "I mean, I've never felt that. I'm not sure I believe it exists."

"I'm sure your brother and Callie would disagree. And

Evie and Scott. Your parents have had a happy marriage, right? Mine, too."

Grace managed a tight smile. "And yet you've managed to avoid it yourself?"

"But I believe in marriage," he said and rested an arm along the back of the sofa.

"Oh, I thought you were too busy carving notches into your bedpost."

He smiled in that sexy way and Grace harnessed all her resistance. "The fact you've been thinking about my bed leads me to believe there's hope for you yet, *Princess*."

"I don't know what—"

"Here we are!" Noah said as the kids rushed into the room. The twins, five-year-old Hayley and Matthew, raced toward her, while nine-year-old Jamie trailed behind. Noah's youngest daughter wasn't a child to be held back and she insisted on hugging Grace and then demanded to know what was in the bag. Grace spread the gifts around and made certain Jamie received his while the twins tore at wrapping paper. The books and DVDs were a clear winner. Once they'd said thank-you, the kids quickly disappeared to their rooms.

"Where's Lily?" she asked of Noah's teenage daughter.

"Studying at a friend's," Callie said as she came back into the room carrying a tray.

Grace shook the bag. "I'll leave this for her."

"It's lovely of you to think about the kids like this," Callie said and passed mugs around.

Grace glanced toward Cameron, and then quickly focused her thoughts. Chalk one up for the closed-off aunt. "My pleasure. I don't get to see them often enough."

"We don't see you enough either," Noah said as he took a spot on the other sofa and suggested she sit down.

She made her way around the sofa and sat beside Cameron. He didn't move and his hand rested only an inch from her shoulder. But she could *feel* him. The connection and awareness was like nothing she'd ever experienced. Grace gripped her mug and drank the coffee. Noah watched her, Callie smiled and Cameron's silence was suddenly deafening.

When he finally spoke she jumped a little. "So, Grace was telling me she'll watch the kids for you next Tuesday."

I was?

Noah looked surprised. "Really?"

"I think that would be great," Callie said and squeezed her husband's knee. "Your parents offered—but I know they'd like to be at the awards dinner."

Awards dinner? She looked at Cameron. There was laughter and direct challenge in his eyes. *Damn his sexy hide.* He was deliberately trying to antagonize her. She managed a tight smile. "I'm more than happy to watch them."

"It's only the twins," Callie explained. "Jamie and Lily want to be there to see their dad get his award."

She feigned knowledge, knew that Cameron was laughing to himself and made a point to settle this particular score with him when they were alone. "What time do you want me here?"

"Six o'clock," Noah said.

They chatted for another twenty minutes and she was grateful her brother didn't question her about New York or how long she intended to stay in Crystal Point. Finally, Cameron got up to leave, said goodbye and offered to walk her out.

Once they were by their cars and out of earshot she glared at him. "What was that about?" she demanded. "Has meddling in my life suddenly become an entertaining pastime for you?"

"More of an *interesting* pastime," he corrected with a self-indulgent grin.

"And clearly volunteering me to babysit is your idea of a joke?"

"Well, you did say your therapist suggested you spend time with your family."

She wanted to slug his smug face. Instead, she drew in a steadying breath. "Thank you for your charitable concern. However, I can arrange my own family time without your interference."

He grinned. "Really? And did you know about your brother's award?"

"Of course," she fibbed.

His brow came up. "Well, in case it slipped your mind, it's a community award. And a big deal. Preston Marine offers traineeships for young people with disabilities. The award is recognition of his work helping these kids."

She knew her brother did that, didn't she? Noah had been at the helm of the boat-building business that had been started by her grandfather for over a decade. Her father had retired a couple of years earlier. A niggling shame seared between her shoulder blades. Was she so busy with her own problems she'd forgotten everything about where she came from?

"Of course," she said again and knew he wasn't convinced.

He came a little closer. "On the other hand, if you don't think you're up to the task of watching the kids, I'm sure they could find someone else."

Grace bristled. "No need for that," she assured him and continued to fight the urge to slap his handsome face. "I'm quite confident I'll manage the task."

He laughed out loud. "Well, that's great to hear, *Princess*. Because the price for my silence has just gone up."

Her blood stilled. "What does that mean?"

"Emily needs a tutor for the next two weeks."

A tutor? "I can't possibly—"

"No lessons," he said, cutting her off. "No silence."

Shock leached the color from her face. "That's blackmail."

"Friendly incentive," he said and grinned. "Besides, Emily likes you."

In truth she liked Emily, too, and even though part of her sensed she would be able to help the teenager, Grace wasn't about to be railroaded. "I'm not qualified to do that."

"You're perfectly qualified," he said and moved closer to open her driver's door.

"I won't do it."

"Sure you will. You fight a good fight, Grace," he said with a kind of arrogant overconfidence. "But not good enough. I'll make sure Pat drops Emily off at Dunn Inn around four tomorrow for her lesson. Good night."

He was close enough that for a second she thought he might kiss her. For a second she actually wanted him to.

But he didn't.

She got into the car and drove off and wondered what had happened to the well-ordered, organized life she'd once had. The life that had been about clients and meetings and skipped lunches and business dinners. Not about tutoring teenage girls, babysitting five-year-olds and dreaming about kissing Cameron Jakowski.

And then, she wondered how she was supposed to want that old life back once she returned to New York.

Cameron stayed away from Grace for the following two days. Mostly because he knew it would drive her crazy. Being the rigid control freak she was, he'd bet his boots she'd want to wail at him some more about being pushed into tutoring Emily. So he gave her a couple of days to work with the teenager without him hovering.

He arrived at Dunn Inn late Wednesday afternoon and found Grace in the downstairs kitchen, preparing things for the evening meal. Of course she could cook. There were a couple of unfamiliar vehicles parked in the circular driveway, indicating guests were in residence. Even working over a stove she was immaculate. Black pants and white shirt and a pristine apron he figured probably wouldn't dare crease, made her look formidable and beautiful.

He remained beneath the threshold and watched her work for a moment.

When she finally looked up and let out a small, surprised gasp, he spoke. "How's the tutoring going?"

"I'm holding up my end of the bargain," she replied and placed a lid on a saucepan. "Emily's a smart girl and I think she'll ace the test with a little more studying."

He walked into the room. "I think so, too."

She frowned. "Is her son's father in the picture? I don't want to ask her directly if the subject is off-limits."

Cameron shrugged. "He took off when Riley was born."

She stayed silent for a moment, looking at him. "Is that why you…"

"Is that why I…what?" he prompted. But he knew what she was thinking. His own parentage wasn't exactly a state secret. Barbara Preston had introduced his mother to Franciszek all those years ago, so they were well aware he was adopted by his dad.

"Nothing," she said tightly and pulled a frying pan off an overhead hook.

"Do you think I'm trying to get over my abandonment issues by helping Emily and Riley?"

"I…don't…know," she said and he noticed she looked a little paler than usual. Maybe she wasn't sleeping? Well, she wasn't the only one. "Are you?"

"I never knew my biological father," he said quietly. "So there's no real issue to get past."

One brow rose. "You don't miss what you've never had, you mean?"

"Exactly. And I help kids like Emily and Dylan because

it needs to be done. Otherwise they could fall through the cracks in social services."

She untied the apron. "I don't know how you manage it, but you always make me feel...feel..."

"Feel what?"

"Self-centered," she said and tossed the apron on the bench. "Selfish. Shallow. Superficial."

At least he was making her feel something. That was a start, right? "Success and beauty don't go hand in hand with being superficial."

She stared at him and the mood between them quickly shifted. His attraction to her had a will of its own and air was suddenly charged with awareness. Her hair was pulled back in a tight ponytail and he had the urge to set it free. Memories of kissing her on the beach only a few nights before rushed back and filled his blood. Her icy reserve had slipped and she'd kissed him back passionately. And he wanted to feel that passion again.

"Don't."

Cameron tilted his head. "Don't what?"

"Don't say I'm...you know."

"Beautiful?" He laughed softly. "No point denying the obvious."

"Like it's all I am."

Cameron moved around the counter. "That's not what I said. But I guess it's easier to think the worst of me."

She turned to face him. "Nothing is easy with you."

He reached out and touched her jaw. When she didn't move he rubbed his thumb across her cheek. "Then let's call a truce."

"A truce?"

"Yes," he said and stepped closer. "And let's stop pretending we don't want each other."

Chapter Five

He wants me.

She couldn't remember the last time a man had said that to her.

Or the last time she'd wanted to hear it. Erik's lukewarm attentions hadn't bothered her because she'd felt the same way toward him. And Dennis was no different. But her feelings for Cameron were different. They always had been. They were there, under the surface, waiting to jump up and take hold. For years she'd been safe in New York—away from him and the connection that simmered between them.

She drew in a tight breath. "I don't have casual sex."

"And you think I do?" he asked and dropped his hand.

Grace raised a brow. "We've already had the conversation about your reputation."

"You shouldn't believe all you hear, Grace."

Yes, I should. It was safer to think of him as a woman-izer. Safer to imagine him making love to someone else. But that notion made her insides contract. *Not that I want him to make love to me.* "I've got three weeks, Cameron. And I'm not going to complicate things by…by…"

"Not everything is so black-and-white."

Grace crossed her arms. "What does that mean?"

"It means you can't put every feeling into a neat little package because you're determined to control everything. The truth is we've been dancing around this for years. I'd rather it be out there and on the table."

She pushed back her shoulders. "I wouldn't. We have a deal—and that's all we have. I want your silence and I'll tutor Emily in return."

He blatantly ignored her. "You haven't got anyone staying here after tomorrow, right?"

"Right," she replied suspiciously. "The place is empty until after Scott and Evie return the weekend after next."

"Good. Pat is taking the kids out to the farm in Burdon Creek this weekend. There's still some work to be done on the place before they can make the move permanently, so I thought you might like to help me give them a hand for a couple of days. Plus you'll get a chance to keep tutoring Emily."

No way. "I can't do that."

"Sure you can," he said and smiled. "It'll be good for you."

"I don't—"

"Just think of all that fresh country air," he said with one brow raised. "Wouldn't that be exactly what the doctor ordered?"

Yes, she thought, it probably would be. But it didn't mean she was about to agree. Spending the weekend with Cameron, in any circumstances, was a complication—and temptation—she didn't need.

"No," she said quietly.

He shrugged, infuriating her. "No weekend, no deal."

Grace felt her control slip away. She thought she had everything settled. A month back in Crystal Point and then she'd return to New York—that was the plan. This wasn't. "More blackmail? Forget it. I'm not spending the weekend with you."

"Emily and Riley will be there. And Pat and the kids. There'll be plenty of chaperones, Grace, so you can relax."

She didn't want a chaperone. She didn't want to relax. "I said no."

"No weekend, no deal," he said again. "Unless, of course, you would prefer to tell your family about the car accident which could have killed you and how you didn't care enough to inform them at the time."

Grace glared at him. "You're an ass, Jakowski. I *will* tell them and you'll have no hold over me."

He grabbed the cell phone on the countertop and held it toward her. "Here you go."

She froze. He knew she wouldn't take the phone. He knew she wasn't ready to tell her family what had happened. One word about the accident and she would also have to talk about her therapist, Richard and the whole awful experience. She lingered over another refusal and considered how hurt her parents would be once they found out the truth.

"Okay," she said resignedly. "I'll go with you. To help out and to tutor Emily," she said with emphasis. "And that's all."

He nodded and stepped back. "I'll pick you up Friday morning, eight o'clock."

Then he dropped the phone back on the counter and left.

The next morning Grace went shopping for new jeans and a couple of polo shirts. Bellandale had a few nice boutiques and she couldn't help splurging on a new pair of fire-engine-red heels that simply screamed "pick me." She also purchased a pair of sensible boots. They were the kind she knew people wore in the country, ankle-length with a square block heel. She walked around the B and B at night in them to try to break in the stiff leather and got mean-looking blisters on her toes as a result.

She also kept up her end of the deal and tutored Emily each afternoon.

"So, you're hanging out at the farm this weekend?" the teenager asked as they ended the lesson on Thursday evening.

Grace closed her laptop. "Yes."

Emily grinned. "Ever been on a farm before?"

"When I was young," she replied. "My grandparents had a small fruit farm and I used to visit sometimes." Not often, though. The farm was more Evie's and Noah's thing back then. Most of her vacations from boarding school were spent in Crystal Point. When her grandparents passed away the farm was sold.

Emily packed her books in her satchel. "So," she said with a curious edge. "You and Sarge—there's really nothing going on between you guys?"

"Not a thing," she said quickly and ignored her flaming cheeks. "Make sure you take your books tomorrow—we can continue with this on the weekend."

"I don't get a break?"

"No chance. One more week at this pace and you'll easily pass the exam."

Emily dropped the bag to her feet. "Not that it will do me much good. It's not like I'm going to get a great job or anything."

"It's not?"

The girl shrugged. "I've got a kid, and even with Nan's help it's gonna be hard to do what I really want to do—which is study fashion design. I work at a coffee place three mornings a week when Nan can watch him. But once she moves to the farm I won't have anyone here. It sucks, but I get why she wants to move. Dylan was getting into a lot of trouble before Sarge came along and he's really looking forward to living on the farm."

"What about day care?" Grace suggested, not really having a clue.

She shrugged again. "I can't really afford it. And I don't want to miss out on Riley growing up. But I want to go to design school, too…" She sighed heavily. "I guess it will work itself out."

Grace felt for the girl. "If design school is where you want to go, then it's exactly what you should do." She smiled gently. "You should follow your dreams, Emily."

Like she'd followed the dreams set out before her. But were they her own dreams? New York. A huge apartment. Designer clothes. A successful career. In the midst of trying to prove herself she'd gotten swept up in wanting what had been expected of her. But the truth was, none of it really satisfied her anymore. The money and fancy apartment were part of the facade that had become her life. When she was younger and ambition had burned in her, Grace hadn't noticed how alone she actually was. Perhaps her failed relationships with Dennis and Erik had amplified that feeling. Or maybe it was knowing both Noah and Evie had found their happily-ever-after that made her question what was really important. And now, more than ever, she didn't know where she belonged.

When Cameron arrived to pick her up Friday morning, Grace was waiting outside the bed-and-breakfast, her Gucci luggage at her heels. She pulled at the lapels of her soft leather jacket and ran her hands down her fine-gauge wool trousers as he eased the big, powerful blue car alongside the curb. It was cold and barely eight o'clock.

He got out and flicked open the trunk. Her heart stopped when he moved around the vehicle. Dressed in jeans and a long-sleeved gray Henley shirt, he looked so good she could barely swallow.

"Morning," he said easily.

Grace walked toward the passenger door and tried desperately to ignore her traitorous feelings. "Be careful with my cases," she demanded with a frosty glare.

He laughed. "Not a morning person, *Princess?*"

Grace opened the car and got inside. What was the worst thing that could happen? She might break a nail or get a few blisters? *I can handle that. I can handle anything.*

She took a deep breath and immediately wrinkled her nose. Something didn't smell quite right. When she heard a strange, almost guttural sound she snapped her neck around and found herself staring into a pair of piercing amber eyes and the most unattractive, jowly, drooling face she'd ever seen.

Grace's breath stopped. *Oh, my God!* The dreadful beast licked his chops and saliva leached from his pinkish, puckered mouth. She jerked her head back to the front and closed her eyes, gripping her hands together.

When Cameron got back into the car she spoke through tight lips. "There's something big and horribly smelly in the backseat."

"That's Jed," Cameron said with a laugh. He started the car and the hideous-looking animal woofed.

The sound reverberated in her eardrum like a trombone. "What is it?" she asked, trying not to think about the terrible smell racing up her nose.

"A dog. My dog."

He had a dog. The biggest, ugliest dog he could find by the looks of things. Grace's only recent experience with animals was her neighbor's Himalayan cat she sometimes watched. Noah and Callie had two dogs, but not like the thing in the backseat.

She glanced at him, determined not to look at the beast in the back. "What kind of dog?"

"Dogue de Bordeaux."

It sounded French. The only French dog she'd seen was a poodle. "It smells."

"He's not an *it*," Cameron corrected as he steered the car in an arc and down The Parade. The road ran the length of the town, a buffer between the narrow parkland and walking track along water's edge and the long row of houses, which ranged from small beach homes to some three-story mansions. "His name is Jed, like I said. And you'll get used to his breath."

"I'd rather not."

Cameron laughed again. "He's a good dog."

"Who needs a breath mint."

"Did you just make a joke, Grace?"

She pushed her handbag to the feet. "Unbelievable, I know. Imagine, me with a sense of humor."

Cameron was imagining a lot of things. Like tugging her perfectly pulled-back hair down for one. There wasn't a tendril out of place. He couldn't see her eyes shielded behind designer sunglasses and wanted to know if they were scorching through him. And the leather jacket fitted like it had been tailored for her. Nothing out of place. Immaculate and beautiful.

She looked at him. "Where exactly are we going?"

"Burdon Creek. It's three hundred and eighteen kilometers west of Bellandale and has a population of one hundred and six. One shop, which is also a gas station, a pub and a post office, and that's about it."

"And the family is happy to settle there?"

"Yes," he replied. "There's a bigger town a few miles up the road where they can get everything they need. It will be good for Dylan. He was a troubled kid when we first met. His father bailed when he was young and his mother had been in and out of drug rehab for years. His two half siblings lived with their father, but he was killed last year in an industrial accident and the kids went back to their mother and Dylan and Emily." Cameron knew how difficult it had been for Dylan to adjust to having his brother and sister living in the small house he shared with his mother, older sister and grandmother. "When his mother was arrested for possession the kids were placed in their grandmother's care. It was her third offense and she got four years' jail time."

"And the children have stayed with their grandmother?"

"Yeah. Pat's a good woman and really wants to give the kids a stable home. But the house she was in only had two small bedrooms. For the past ten months we've been raising money to pull together a deposit so she could buy a home for the kids. A few local businesses came on board and we found the place at Burdon Creek. It needed a bit of work, but most of the structural stuff has been done now. We had contractors volunteer and the past few months they've been traveling back and forth to get the place ready for Pat and the kids."

Grace flipped her sunglasses off and looked at him. "So in between my tutoring Emily what else will we be doing?"

"Painting, moving a bit of furniture, decorating…that sort of thing."

Her perfectly arched brows rose dramatically. "Decorating?"

"I thought you'd be good at it," he said.

"Why?"

He shrugged. "Because you did the decorating for Noah's showroom last year. And you always look like you've stepped off the pages of one of those glossy magazines."

Cameron looked at her and swore he saw a smile tug at the corner of her mouth.

"Is that a compliment?" she asked quietly.

"Absolutely."

"Thank you…I think." The smile grew wider. "But you should know I hired an interior decorator to do my apartment and Noah's showroom. I just supervised."

Cameron grinned. "Looks like you're in charge of moving furniture then."

She laughed delightfully and his insides crunched. It was way too easy being with her like this. He relaxed and pressed a button on the iPod in the center console. Coldplay's unique sound filled the space between them and he wondered for a moment if she'd prefer something else. But she pushed her head back against the headrest, replaced the glasses and closed her eyes. Jed made a weary sound and stretched himself out on the backseat and Cameron headed west.

Grace slept. Not the kind of sleep she got in her bed. This was a deep calm. With the music playing and the soft hum of the motor she was unusually relaxed. Her typical day in a car was driving to and from the office in rush-hour traffic before fighting for a parking space.

She opened her eyes a few times over the following hour or so and watched as the landscape changed. The sugar cane farms were replaced by cattle and pasture and the homes became more infrequent the farther they drove. They didn't speak, which suited her fine and he seemed as content as she was to listen to the music and enjoy the scenery.

The smelly hound in the back didn't stir and she was grateful for that.

Cameron pulled into a roadhouse midmorning, where they refueled and grabbed coffee to go.

"Pat will want to feed us when we arrive," he told her as they walked back to the car. "But if you're hungry we can—"

"I'm fine," she said. "I had a big breakfast." She reached into her handbag and pulled out a small paper bag. "I have muffins for the road."

Cameron grabbed the bag and took a look inside. "You've been holding out on me for the past hour and a half?"

Grace colored. His words smacked of intimacy. And she wondered how she would hold out being with him for the next few days. Because it seemed so incredibly normal to be walking beside him in the morning sunshine.

She shrugged lightly. "I did some baking yesterday. Help yourself."

Cameron took a muffin and ate it in about three bites. "It's good." He unlocked the car and stared at her. He waited until she was in the car before getting in himself. He patted the dog and then wiped his hands on a towel on the backseat. "So, what else can you cook?"

"I just took a Thai cooking class. And I make some mean sushi."

He looked like she'd said rat bait. "Oh. Sushi…I've never tried it."

"It's delicious," she said and clicked her tongue.

His gaze went instantly to her mouth and Grace couldn't stop her lips from pouting ever so slightly. There was something intensely erotic about him looking at her mouth and she felt the sensation right down to the blood in her bones. He turned away before she did, but Grace swore she saw something in his eyes, a kind of raw hunger that turned his irises to a deep chocolate. He cleared his throat and started the engine and she tried not to think about how warm her skin was. Or how much she liked the sensation.

Burdon Creek *was* in the middle of nowhere. It was a quiet, sleepy-looking place that had aura of another time about it. They drove slowly down the one main street and continued past the gas station. The farm was about ten miles from the town center and when they arrived Cameron got out of the car to open the rickety gate.

The house stood at the end of the long gravel driveway. It was old, but she saw where the contractors had worked hard to repair the roof and the large veranda. It needed painting on the outside and the garden was overrun with twisted bougainvillea vine.

There were stables some way from the house and a large machinery shed. A boy in dark overalls was walking across the yard and came over to greet them. It was Dylan, and when they got out Cameron shook his hand.

"I've been feeding the horses," Dylan announced, looking immensely pleased with being in charge of the task.

"The neighbor supplied the kids with a couple of horses for the weekend," Cameron told her as he let the dog out. The big drooling beast made his way around the car and Grace held herself rigid as he pushed against her leg.

"He wants a pat," Dylan told her and came over and rubbed the dog's head. "He always wants pats. Nan said we could get a dog once we get a fence around the house."

"Cam!"

They all turned at the sound of the loud greeting. A sixty-something woman stood on the porch with a walking stick in her hand. She had a mop of frizzy gray hair and a beaming smile. Cameron walked across the yard and hugged the woman close when he reached her. Grace stood still, watching the exchange. She'd never been a hugging sort of person. Even with her family. Of course, it was impossible to avoid it with Evie and M.J., because they were both warm and affectionate, but her parents and Noah seemed to respect her need for personal space.

"Who's this?" the woman asked as both silvery brows rose. "A girl?"

Grace walked across and stood at the bottom of the short stairway. "I'm not really a girl...I'm the decorator."

Cameron laughed and once the introductions were made

Patricia Jennings invited them inside. The house was in various states of repair. Plasterers had been in to replace walls and most of it required painting. There was some furniture scattered throughout certain rooms and the kitchen had received a full renovation.

"Take a seat," Pat invited as they entered the kitchen. "I'll put the coffee on."

Grace sat down while Cameron headed back outside to retrieve their luggage. She placed her handbag on the chair beside her. "Where's Emily?" she asked.

"Putting the baby down for a nap," Pat said and smiled. "I have to say how committed she's become to her studies since you've been helping her. She really wants to finish high school, which isn't an easy task for a young mother. She has had a hard time of it since Riley came along." Pat raised her brows. "I thought of shifting her to a new school but she wanted to stay where she was."

"She's been bullied?"

"A little," Pat replied. "Teenage girls can be cruel."

Grace knew about that firsthand. Her first twelve months at boarding school had been fraught with teasing and isolation. "Are you looking forward to moving here permanently?" she asked, politely making conversation.

Pat turned around, swinging mugs in her hands. "Oh, yes. The kids will love being able to run around and Dylan becomes quite the man of the house when we're here, fixing things and doing chores." Her wrinkled face grew somber. "Maybe he's too grown-up sometimes. We used to be really close. But with the little ones needing me I just don't seem to have the time for him that I used to. I was so worried about Dylan at one stage—but then Cameron came along and he's a changed boy since he's had a man's influence in his life." Her pale blue eyes regarded Grace and she smiled. "Officer Jakowski was a godsend to us. You're a lucky woman."

Grace knew what she meant and quickly set her straight. "Oh, we're not… It's not like that. We're just…"

"Just what?" Pat asked as she poured coffee.

Grace briefly explained how their mothers had been inseparable since they were in their teens, and that Noah was his closest friend. "We've know one another a long time."

Pat nodded, like she suspected there was more to it than that. "It's good of you to come and help us this weekend," she said and brought the coffee to the table. "It's been hard trying to sort through everything, and with the two little ones still missing their daddy I've had my hands full."

Grace couldn't imagine how difficult it had been for the other woman. She looked weary and not in the best of health. But she obviously loved her grandchildren.

"The kids are lucky to have you."

Pat smiled warmly. "I'm the lucky one. When Lynnie…" She stopped for a moment and took a deep breath. "That's my daughter. When she went off the rails this last time I knew I had to do something for the children's sake. Dylan was at such an impressionable age and the younger children needed to be cared for. Their father was killed over a year ago."

"Cameron told me."

Pat tutted. "It was very sad. He's wasn't a bad sort of man. At one time I'd hoped he and Lynnie might have worked things out. But he wasn't prepared to live with an addict. Can't say I blame him." Pat grabbed milk from the refrigerator and placed it on the table. She sat down heavily in a chair and stared at Grace. "You're very beautiful. I can see why Cameron's interested in you."

Grace stopped herself from denying it and put a little sugar in her mug. "It's complicated."

"Life generally is," Pat said agreeably. "I was married for thirty-five years to a good man. When he passed away three years ago I lost the love of my life."

Grace felt a sudden stab of envy. She'd never experienced anything even remotely resembling that. And the look on Pat's face was the same look she saw on Evie's face, and Callie's and her mother's.

True love. When had she become so cynical about it? Her bland relationships with Dennis and Erik hadn't left her brokenhearted. There had been a definite lack of intimacy, both sexual and emotional. She'd lost her virginity to Dennis when she was twenty-two, five months after they'd begun dating. There were no fireworks in the bedroom, though. And in hindsight, very little chemistry between them. Erik had been more sophisticated and more sexually demanding, but that had only created a greater wall between them. Her continued lack of response to him between the sheets had finally made him walk out the door. In some ways she'd been relieved when it had ended.

She remembered the conversation she'd had with Cameron about marriage. It was easy to hide behind the idea that a woman couldn't have it all. And she had told herself she didn't want that time and time again. She had her career and her driving ambition. She wore shoes that probably cost more than the woman sitting opposite her spent on clothes in a year and never let anyone get too close. And that, she realized, was why she'd never felt truly whole. The emptiness had grown bigger as she gotten older, and each year she filled that space with more work, more ambition. She had a half-lived life. But the thought of anything else, anything…more…rattled her to the very foundation of her soul.

"You know, it's the little things that I miss most," Pat said with a soft sigh. "Like how he used to always make that first cup of tea in the morning. Or how he'd mow the lawn and then come inside smelling like cut grass. And we'd play cards every Sunday night." She looked across the table. "There's a lot to be said for the love of a good man."

Grace had no intention of responding to that. Fortunately Dylan and Cameron returned to the kitchen with their luggage and Pat suggested they settle into their rooms. She was surprised to find they weren't going to be in the main house, but in a separate cozy cottage about fifty meters from the mudroom and behind what looked like an old vegetable garden.

Two small children, a boy about four and a girl a couple years older, both with grubby faces and bare feet, raced around to greet them and Pat quickly introduced her other grandchildren, Thomas and Isabel.

"You'll be comfortable here," Pat assured her as they walked across the yard. "This was renovated first, and when we came for weekends we lived here until the house was ready. It used to be a workers' cottage many years ago, when the farm was a working cattle station and before the land was all subdivided."

Grace smiled, walked through the front door and was pleasantly surprised. Although sparsely furnished, it had lovely polished wood floors and high ceilings. It was clean and tidy and inviting.

"You'll have more privacy here than in the house with me and these adorable hellions," she said and gestured to the children zooming up and down the hall making airplane sounds with their arms outstretched.

Pat rounded up the kids and they all left once Grace's bags had been brought into the small hallway, and not before the older woman told them to come back to the main house for lunch in an hour. Once they were gone she turned to find Cameron standing behind her, one shoulder leaning casually against the doorjamb that led into the living room.

So much for chaperones!

"Okay?" he asked.

"It's nice," she replied as she peered into the bedroom off the hall. A large bed filled the room, covered in a crisp white overlay. There was a neat vanity and narrow armoire. She walked across the threshold and turned around. "I'm sure I'll be quite comfortable."

Cameron moved forward and grabbed her bag. "You might want to ditch the leather jacket and change," he suggested as he dropped the luggage into her room. "We'll be painting a little later."

She nodded and cleared her throat. "Um…where are you sleeping?"

He pointed down the hall. "Miles away—so don't fret."

Grace flushed hotly. "I'm hardly fretting."

He smiled and her insides flipped over a little more than usual. He looked good when he smiled, even more handsome. And he had nice hair, she noticed, like the color of beechwood honey. She remembered how it had felt caught between her fingers and the memory made her hands tingle. The smallness of the room created a sudden intimacy and Grace sensed a shift in the mood between them. She stepped back and collided with the foot of the bed. "Well, I'll just get changed."

"Sure," he said and headed for the door, but suddenly he stopped and turned. "What were you and Pat talking about in the kitchen?"

Love…

"The kids," she replied, and placed her handbag on the vanity. "And the house."

"Was she matchmaking?"

"I set her straight," she replied with a shrug. "I told her exactly how we feel about each other."

He looked at her oddly. "I doubt that," he said and then grabbed his bag and headed off down the hallway.

Grace took about twenty minutes to unpack and change into a pair of gunmetal-gray cargo pants and a long-sleeved navy T-shirt and bright red sneakers. She left her hair pulled back in a low ponytail and took off her watch. The last thing she wanted was paint spattered on her Rolex.

When she was done, she took a tour of the small house. There was one bathroom, the kitchen and dining area and the living room. The furniture looked new and the country-cottage print on the sofa and curtains suited the place. There was also a small fireplace and a thick hearth rug in muted greens.

Emily arrived, books in hand, and announced she would be studying in the kitchen in the main house. They chatted for a couple of minutes before she left to start studying.

"Ready?"

Grace turned on her heels. Cameron stood in the doorway. He'd changed, too. He wore a pair of old jeans that had a hole in one knee and white T-shirt that was splattered in places with various shades of paint. Working clothes, she thought, and then felt ridiculously self-conscious in her immaculate two-hundred-dollar cargo pants.

She swallowed hard. "Sure. Let's go."

Once they were outside he suggested a tour of the farm before they headed to the house for lunch. Grace agreed and followed him toward the old stables. Jed rose from his spot on the porch and ambled behind them. The stables were big and old and smelled musty and she wrinkled her nose when they walked through the wide doorway. She picked up another scent immediately and recognized fresh baled hay. It had a sweetish smell and quickly knocked off the old-barn odor.

Through to the other side of the building was a large paddock. Grace spotted two horses happily munching grass. "It's a lovely spot," she said as she crossed her arms over a fence post.

He turned around and half trapped her against the fence. "Is breathing in this fresh air making you feel all country inside?"

Grace didn't move. To escape she would need to press past him. Maybe touch him. She prepped her sharp tongue. "I'm all city—you know that."

"And yet, you're here."

"I was forced into it."

His eyes darkened to the color of melted chocolate. "I'd never force you into anything."

He stepped back and didn't say another word as he began to walk back toward the house. She felt bad. Of course she knew he wouldn't force her to do anything she didn't want to do. That wasn't his way.

"Cameron?" He stopped walking and waited for her to catch up. "I didn't mean anything by that."

He nodded. "Forget it. We should get back."

Lunch was outrageously delicious and filled with more carbs than Grace usually consumed in a month. Fresh baked bread accompanied roast chicken and gravy and a creamy potato dish that was so scrumptious Grace had two helpings. The kids chatted throughout the meal and the littlest one got potato in his hair.

Grace wasn't sure what she felt sitting with the fractured, yet incredibly loving family. Cameron seemed to fit effortlessly within their little group. It made the world she lived in suddenly seem painfully superficial. On the surface she appeared to have it all—career, success, money.

And yet, for more than the first time lately, she wondered what the worth of it all was? At that moment, she couldn't see or feel anything other than a startling realness during the hour she shared with Pat Jennings and her grandchildren. And the man she'd tried desperately to keep out of her heart for so long, but knew she never had.

Or ever would.

Chapter Six

As Cameron watched Grace his chest tightened. She was laughing at something one of the kids said and looked so incredibly lovely he could barely get air into his lungs. He'd never seen her so naturally unguarded. She was still as picture-perfect as always in her pressed trousers and starched T-shirt and there wasn't a hair out of place. But there was something in her expression he hadn't seen before. She smiled at him, as though she knew he was thinking about her. Did she know it? Was it obvious?

"We should get started on the painting," he said.

Grace nodded and stood. "I'll help clean up the dishes first."

"Nonsense," Pat replied. "Leave the dishes to me. I can manage that even with my bad leg. The painting is too much for these old bones. Off you go. I'll make sure the kids don't disturb you."

Cameron stood and left the room and felt Grace's presence in his wake. He headed for the living room and spotted a pile of drop cloths by the entrance. The room was sparsely furnished and had only a sofa and small coffee table.

"Where do you want me?" she asked.

Cameron turned around. Her words sounded provocative and gave his insides a jolt. He grabbed a couple of the drop cloths and held them out to her. "You can place these over the furniture while I prepare the paint."

"Sure," she said as she took them. The painting gear was on the veranda and he headed outside. He stayed for a while to sort through colors and clear his head. When he returned to the living room Grace was sitting on the edge of the sofa. She stood and waited while he placed the paint and brushes by the door.

"What color are we going for?" she asked as she examined the paint lids for swatches.

"You choose," he replied and lifted off both lids.

She looked at the tins and gestured to the warm beige tint. "That one. And I think we should consider a feature wall." She pointed to the long wall opposite the doorway. "Something darker—maybe the rich toffee. If we add a slipcover over the sofa in the same shade it will pick up the color."

He half smiled, intrigued by the interest she showed. "Anything else?"

She bit down on her lower lip for a moment. "Perhaps a lamp—one of those tall ones for the corner. With a low-watt bulb it will cast some nice shadows around the room. And a plush rug for the spot in front of the fireplace. And maybe a couple of pictures for the walls." She raised her brows with a kind of keen excitement. "You know, Evie has some furniture pieces in a storage shed that she hasn't used for years. I think she'd let them go if she knew they were going to a good home."

Her sudden enthusiasm captivated him and Cameron took a deep breath. "I thought you said you couldn't decorate?"

She looked at him. "I said I'd hired a decorator."

"To do what?"

She smiled. "To do what I asked."

He'd never known a woman so determined to do things her own way. "You'll talk to Evie?"

"Yes. In the meantime let's get started."

Cameron started preparing the paint and Grace grabbed a brush. "Do you want to cut in?" he asked as he poured a small amount of paint into a plastic container.

"Sure." She glanced up at the high ceilings. "I'll need a ladder."

That's not all she needed, he thought, looking at her designer clothing and spotless shoes. "There's one outside, I'll get it."

He took off down the hall, silently cursing the way his insides were jumping all over the place. Being near her was making him nuts. He'd be glad when the painting started so the fumes could drown out the scent of the flowery fragrance she wore, which hit him with the force of a jackhammer every time she moved.

He inhaled a long breath and headed for the cottage.

Grace poked the brush into the paint and examined the color. She'd started cutting in the edges around the doorjamb when Cameron returned. He held something out to her.

"Here," he said. "Wear this."

Grace put down her brush and took the garment. She held the soft chambray shirt in front of her and shook her head in protest. "I couldn't possibly—"

"Wear it," he insisted. "You don't want to ruin your clothes. It's an old shirt."

It was an old shirt. But it was incredibly soft between her

fingertips. She nodded and slipped her arms into the sleeves. It was far too big and she rolled the sleeves up to an accommodating length and did the buttons up, but it was surprisingly comfy.

"Thank you," she said and forced herself to not think about how intimate it seemed to be wearing a piece of his clothing.

Cameron grabbed the roller and paint can. "No problem."

She went to speak again but her mouth remained shut. He smiled slightly and awareness rushed across her skin in an all-consuming wave. The white T-shirt he wore did little to disguise his broad shoulders and muscular arms. And his jeans were so worn and faded they amplified the ranginess of his lean hips and long legs.

Grace struggled to drag her eyes away. Everything about him was wholly masculine and she realized at that moment how naively she'd been denying it to herself for so many years. She'd never been attracted to a man the intense way she was attracted to Cameron.

They worked through the afternoon and by four o'clock she was exhausted. Her palms were pink and puckered from the constant pressure of the brush and her neck ached. But despite her pains, Grace was determined to push past her fatigue. She wouldn't give in. Cameron of course, was like a machine. He worked through the break Pat insisted they have, and because she wasn't giving in to her exhaustion, forced Grace to do the same. She quickly took a couple of massive gulps of icy homemade lemonade Pat had brought in on a tray to avoid looking like she was taking a breather, and climbed back up the ladder.

They had music playing softly in the background and the ugliest dog in world was stretched out beside the sofa, snoring the afternoon away.

"We should finish up soon." He'd stopped painting and

came over to the corner where she was propped up on the ladder. He looked up at her and held out his hand. "Come down."

Grace reached out and grasped his hand. He wrapped his fingers around hers and she felt the contact down to her toes. She stepped down the ladder and when her feet touched the floor her legs were strangely unsteady. She placed the container and brush on top of the small ladder and kept her hand in his.

Cameron looked directly into her eyes. "You have paint on your face."

Any other time Grace would have been immediately self-conscious. She usually hated mess and being untidy. But she was reluctant to break the easy mood that had developed between them over the course of the afternoon. "I guess I should go and wash up," she said quietly.

He grazed his knuckles across her left cheek. "I guess you should. It's water-based paint so you don't need to scrub too hard."

"Okay—well, I'll get going and…" Her words trailed off and she moved to pull away. But he didn't release her. "You still have my hand."

He half smiled. "So I do."

"I'll need it back if I'm to get rid of this paint on my face."

He released her immediately. "I'll clean up the brushes and the rest of the gear."

Grace stepped away and pulled her arms around herself. "Okay." She looked around the room. "We did a good job today." She turned to the exposed fireplace and the lovely pale coffee-colored wall framing it. "And it feels good to *do* something good." She gave a humorless laugh. "But I guess you know that already. You've always been generous with yourself." When he didn't say anything she raised a brow. "That was a compliment, not a dig."

Cameron stared at her. "With our history sometimes it's hard to tell the difference."

He was right and Grace experienced something that felt a lot like shame work its way across her skin. "Looks like our truce is working."

"We've gotten off to a pretty good start. No fights, no insults, for at least…" He checked his watch. "Eight hours."

"I've never liked fighting with you," she admitted. "It was just easier than thinking about…about anything else."

"I know."

She didn't respond and left the room as quickly as she could, making for the kitchen. After spending a few minutes with Emily to see how the studying was going, Grace walked back to the cottage.

A shower topped her list of things to do. Grace collected fresh clothes and toiletries and headed for the bathroom. The claw-foot bathtub was the first thing she saw and she was immediately seduced by the idea of a long soak. She quickly popped in the plug and played around with the water temperature. Once the water flowed she added her favorite Dior scented bath foam and stripped off her clothes.

It took close to ten minutes to fill the tub, but finally she slipped into the bubbly water and stretched out her legs. Grace let out a heavy sigh and her body relaxed instantly. She'd had a long, exhausting day and was physically taxed, but had none of the mental fatigue she often experienced as a result of a fifteen-hour stretch in the office.

She rested her arms along the edge of the tub, closed her eyes and leaned her head back. A simple delight. But it felt better than anything had felt for a long time. When was the last time she'd spent the time to really relax? She couldn't remember. Since the accident she'd become even more wound up, more determined to be in control.

She took a deep breath and slipped a little farther down

into the water. A sound caught her attention but she kept her eyes shut. A creak followed, like a door opening. Had she not closed the door properly? *It's probably just the wind pushing the door open.*

Another creak followed. And another. It was the door. And it *was* opening.

Grace clamped her lids tighter. Surely Cameron wouldn't enter the bathroom? But when she finally found the courage to open her eyes, it wasn't Cameron standing by the bathtub.

It was Jed.

The smelly beast had pushed the door open far enough to invade her privacy and was sitting heavily on his haunches, drooling all over the floor. He made a sound, half growl, half whine.

"Shoo!" she demanded, looking around for her towel. It was on the sink where she'd left it. The smelly dog scooted closer and dropped his chin on the rim of the tub. "Go away."

He whined again and showed off his big teeth.

Grace pushed herself back as far as she could go. *I will not panic.* She heard footsteps in the house and quickly pulled herself together. Cameron was back.

"Hot Tub!" she yelled, knowing the nickname he hated would get his attention.

The footsteps grew louder and she heard a tap on the half-opened door. "Grace?"

"You're dog is drooling in my bathwater—get him out of here."

He laughed.

"It's not funny," she protested. "Please get him out of here so I can finish my bath."

Cameron laughed again. She was taking a bath? He hoped the rainwater tanks could support it. He called Jed to come out. The dog didn't come so he called him again. And again.

Damned dog.

"It's no use," she said shrilly. "He's got one paw up on the tub. If he gets in the water I swear I'll…I'll…"

He tried not to laugh and called the dog again. When Jed didn't respond he said, "So, can I come in?"

She was silent for a moment. "Well, yes…okay."

Cameron took a deep breath and pushed the door back. Sure enough, there was Jed, paw up on the rim of the tub, drool oozing from his mouth, and staring at Grace with what was clearly a serious case of puppy love. "He likes you."

Grace scowled at him and ducked down into the water. "Funny. Get him away from me."

"Come on, Jed," he said firmly. "Let's go."

He walked toward the bathtub and kept his gaze centered firmly on the dog.

I will not look at her.

But Jed had his own ideas and sprang up on his back legs, wagging his tail. Any second now, Cameron thought, and the dog would be in the water with Grace. He lunged for the animal and grabbed his collar. Grace screamed. Jed rose up on his back feet and splashed his front paws into the water. Grace moved against the back of the tub and the foamy water sloshed, exposing her creamy shoulders and the unmistakable swell of her breasts and his breath rushed out with a sharp kick.

I am so not looking at her.

But as the bubbles sloshed and rose her body was silhouetted against the opaque water. A body he'd touched that night on the beach. And suddenly looking at her was all he was good for. He glanced at her face and saw her green eyes shining with a kind of hot awareness.

Sex swirled around the steamy room—potent and powerful.

She used her hands to shield the parts she didn't want him seeing and that just kicked at his libido like an out-of-control sledgehammer. He could imagine sliding the soap across her skin, he could almost feel how smooth and slippery...

"Cameron...I...I..."

Grace's voice, barely a whisper, dragged him from his fantasies.

He pulled the dog back, grabbed his collar and with the animal firmly under control he spun him around and headed out of the room. Cameron shut the door and released Jed instantly. The dog scooted off, leaving a trail of wet paw prints in his wake.

Cameron let out a heavy breath, stood outside the bathroom door and rested his forehead against the jamb.

Idiot...

One glimpse of skin and he was done for. He wanted her so much.

And had two more weeks to do something about it.

Grace pulled herself out of the tub once the door clicked shut and hastily grabbed a towel. She rubbed herself dry and pulled on her clothes with less than her usual care.

Cameron Jakowski saw me naked.

Okay, not completely naked but close enough. Close enough that Grace knew that what she saw in his eyes was raw hunger.

She shoved her feet into flat sandals.

No man has ever looked at me like that.

His gaze had scorched her skin like a lover's touch. He'd looked like he wanted take her into his arms and kiss her passionately—right then, right there.

And the knowledge tapped into something inside her. Grace had never considered herself all that desirable. Erik's complaints about her lack of enthusiasm in the bedroom still echoed in her head. Dennis hadn't been as harsh, but she'd sensed his dissatisfaction with her, especially in the latter months they were together.

But those fleeting moments in the bathroom with Cameron made her feel so sexually charged that every part of her skin tingled. The truth pounded through her like the loud beat of a drum.

She wanted to make love with Cameron.

And she knew, without a doubt, that he wanted it, too.

What had happened between them at Evie's wedding should have knocked the truth into her. But she'd spent a week in a kind of hazy denial. And now, all of a sudden, she knew it, felt it, and could almost taste the reality of it. And it scared her. She feared losing control. Of being vulnerable. Because Cameron could do that to her. He'd always made her feel that way. He'd always had a secret, almost seductive power over her.

Grace checked her hair in the mirror and saw it was doing a faux impression of being straight as it fought for release from its ponytail. She tucked some stray pieces behind her ears and grabbed her toiletry bag before she headed from the room.

She dropped her things off in the bedroom and walked through the house. Jed was in the small living room, spread out in front of the fireplace, his deep snoring sounding as if he needed an inhaler. She grimaced at the sight of his pink-and-fleshy gums and then left him to his nap.

In the kitchen she noticed an aluminum tray on the countertop and immediately popped the lid, inhaling the scent of delicious-looking pasta. Obviously from Pat, Grace found the other woman's consideration heartwarming. The clock on the wall read a quarter past seven and her grumbling stomach figured it was soon time for dinner. She popped the tray in the oven and set it to a low heat.

"Hey."

She pivoted on one heel. "I see Pat prepared dinner for us," she said easily. "I've just starting reheating but it shouldn't take long. I thought I would—"

"Grace?"

She took a breath. He stood in the doorway, arms crossed, seeming like he had something to say but wasn't quite sure how to say it. Still wearing the paint-splattered T-shirt and ridiculously sexy jeans he looked so good her traitorous belly flipped over. "What?"

He shrugged. "About before…I want to apologize."

Grace fiddled with a tea towel to do something with her hands. "It was my fault. I should have made sure the door was shut properly."

"That's not what I meant."

Grace cursed the color she knew rose up over her collar. "Oh, well I—"

"Things have changed between us," he said, cutting her off. He ran a hand through his hair and she watched him without taking a breath. "For years we've been skirting around it, avoiding it, pretending that what happened between us when we were young didn't matter. But it does matter, Grace, and it's stopped us from being anything to each other, if that makes sense. We're not friends, we're not enemies…we're not lovers…we're just stuck somewhere in between."

"I can't—"

"I won't pretend I don't want you, Grace. Not anymore."

She stilled instantly. In another time, another life, she would have shot him down immediately. Because now, despite the voice in her head telling her that her life was about to get way more complicated, she wanted him, too.

Even though she knew it wouldn't be enough. She was going back to New York in two weeks. Starting something with Cameron would be madness. It might be mind-blowing. It might be exactly what she needed to help ease the dreadful grief and guilt that clung to her every pore.

But when she opened her mouth, prudence foolishly disappeared and something else altogether came out. "Is that why I'm here?" she asked. "Because you want to get me into bed?"

He took a moment to respond. "Not…entirely."

She couldn't help but smile. Another man might have denied it. But Cameron was too honest to play games. "If that's the case, then I guess we'll just see what happens."

His brows shot up. "And let nature take its course, you mean?"

She dropped the tea towel on the counter. "In a way. I don't see the point in either of us getting worked up over something that hasn't happened—or might never happen."

He stared at her. "So, it *is* mutual?"

She made a job of looking for plates and cutlery to avoid the question. When she'd unearthed both she turned back around and found Cameron still watching her. "Well," she said with a sigh, "I'm hardly the type of woman who lets just anyone put his…I mean…his hand…up my dress." The heat got her then, flaming her cheeks, and she gripped the plates until her fingers were white.

He didn't say anything for a moment. He looked at her though—that look she'd suddenly come to think of as the sexiest look in history. "Okay, Grace. We'll take things slowly, if that's what you want." He muttered something about taking a shower and turned on his heels, and Grace got back to her task before he'd even left the room.

Cameron took a cold shower and did his best to clear the chaos raging through his thoughts. Of course, it didn't work. And by the time he'd dressed, lingered in his room for what seemed like an eternity, and then finally headed back to the kitchen, Grace was still behind the counter, chopping and dicing vegetables for a salad.

He fed the dog and set the table, trying to ignore how ab-

surdly domestic it seemed, moving around the kitchen together, not speaking, but feeling as though they had been
doing it this way for years.

They ate dinner and even opened the bottle of wine Pat
had left in the refrigerator. Once their plates were empty and
the dishes cleared, they were left at the table, lingering over
the remainder of their wine.

She looked different, he thought, then realized it was probably one of the few times he'd seen her without makeup. He
liked it. She looked younger and less uptight. She smiled and
it ignited something inside him. There'd been a kind of easy
camaraderie between them over dinner and he didn't want
that to change, but she looked so fetching with her clean face
and bright smile, he could hardly think of anything other than
hauling her into his arms and kissing her madly.

"You're great with the kids," she said and he got his mind
back on track.

"Thank you," he said. "They're easy to like."

"You'll make a good dad."

Cameron's heart suddenly pounded behind his ribs. Could
she know that's what he wanted? That he was aching for a
family of his own? "One day, I hope so. You know, you're
not bad with kids yourself."

She made a scoffing sound. "I'm a train wreck."

"Emily doesn't think so," he said quietly. "She told me
you've been patient and understanding, but also firm when
she loses concentration."

"Well, she's a good student, despite her lack of confidence.
Did you know she wants to go to college?"

He nodded. "She's got ambition."

"Which isn't a bad thing."

"I didn't say it was."

She fingered the stem of her wineglass. "No, you didn't.
But…"

"But what?" he prompted.

"You didn't always feel that way."

He pushed back in his chair. "You mean about *your* ambition? I was young and had ideas about the kind of future I wanted. Just like you did, Grace. Only mine were small-town and yours were big-city."

She looked at him. "You were angry."

"I was dumped," he said bluntly. "What did you expect? Roses and violins?"

"I guess not. I didn't deliberately set out to...to hurt you." She drew in a tight breath. "In hindsight I shouldn't have started anything knowing how I felt about wanting a career. But I was young and starry-eyed. Even career girls get swept away sometimes."

His heart pumped. "By what?"

Her shoulders rose fractionally. "By romance, I guess. By that first kiss when I was sixteen. By the way you didn't rush me to sleep with you, even though we were dating for a few months."

"I thought we had..." He stopped, remembering how much he'd wanted her back then. "Time."

She looked into her glass for a moment, and then glanced upward. "Well, for what it's worth—I'm sorry for the way I behaved back then. These past couple of months I've had a lot of time to think. It sounds cliché, but there's something life-altering about facing your own mortality. When the car crashed I had about thirty seconds to consider all the mistakes I've made, all the people I've hurt in one way or another. It was a sobering half minute."

"Apology accepted."

She offered a bittersweet smile and stood, scraping the chair back. "We did have a nice three months, though. Life was way less complicated then. Do you think anyone ever suspected?"

Cameron stood and moved around the small table and took hold of her hands. "My mother figured it out. I'm not sure about anyone else. Noah's never said anything to me."

"I told Evie a long time ago," she confessed. "Did you know you were my first kiss?"

He rubbed her hands with his thumbs. "I kinda guessed."

"Was I that bad?"

"Not at all," he said gently. "But you seemed a little surprised."

"I was," she admitted. "At school I was into books and not boys. It didn't exactly make me Miss Popularity. And you'd never shown any interest...I mean, before that night of my birthday."

He chuckled. "Oh, I was interested. But you were too young and my best friend's sister."

"So what changed that night?"

"Seeing you standing in the doorway," he said and reached up to twirl a lock of her hair. "When I arrived everyone else was by the pool, but you were inside, and alone. You looked beautiful in that little blue dress. Before that I just..." He shrugged and smiled. "I just wanted you to grow up quick so I could kiss you like I'd imagined doing so many times."

He bent his head and kissed her softly. It wasn't like the night on the beach. This kiss was gentler, sweeter somehow. He wasn't sure how long they stood like that—just kissing, just holding the back of her neck tenderly with his one hand while the other lay against her hip. Grace gripped his arms and held on, and he enjoyed the feel of her mouth against his own and the soft slide of her tongue.

When the kiss ended Cameron laid his forehead against her. "Well," he whispered hoarsely. "That seems pretty natural to me. Good night, Grace," he said softly and released her. "Go and get some sleep. I'll lock up."

She rocked on her heels. He knew sleep wasn't what either of them wanted. But he was offering her an out and he knew she'd take it.

She said good-night and walked from the room without saying another word.

Chapter Seven

Cameron didn't sleep more than two hours. With Grace only meters away down the hall he lay awake most of the night and stared at the ceiling. When he'd finally had enough of fighting the sheets he swung out of bed and got dressed. It was just after seven and he could hear Dylan in the yard with his little sister. Cameron looked out of the window and spotted Isabel racing around her brother as he snuck out from the chicken pen clutching a basket in his hands. His sister gave him no peace as he crossed to the house and it made Cameron smile. Lauren had been like that, he remembered fondly. Six years younger, his sister had hung from his every word when they were growing up.

He was still smiling as he left the room, then headed for the kitchen once he'd let Jed outside. Cameron made coffee, drank a cup and was just rinsing off the utensils when he heard a curse. A very loud curse. He stood still and waited. Then it came again.

Grace's voice was unmistakable. But the words coming out of her mouth were unlike any he'd heard from her before. He took off past the living room and headed for the hall. The profanity started again and he stalled outside her bedroom.

"Grace," he said quietly as he tapped on the door. "Are you all right?"

Nothing for a moment, then a clipped, "Yes…fine."

"You sound like you're in—"

"I'm fine, like I said," she insisted. "I'm just having a little trouble with my… I forgot to bring something to this forsaken place, that's all. Can you please leave me alone?"

"Sure," he said, grinning to himself. "I've made coffee."

"Whatever," she mumbled and he heard the frustrated banging from behind the shut door.

Something was up, but he didn't press the issue. He walked back to the kitchen and opened the refrigerator, mulling over the contents. When nothing took his fancy he shut the door and reached for a glass, and then stopped dead in his tracks. Grace stood in the doorway.

And she looked thunderous. "Don't say a word," she warned.

Cameron bit back the urge to smile. "About what?" he asked innocently.

Both her hands snapped up to frame her head. "About this!"

Now he smiled, because he couldn't help himself. Her hair, usually so straight and severe, bounced around her face in a mass of wild curls. Untamed and out of control, she'd never seemed more beautiful in her life. "It looks—"

"I forgot my straightener," she said with a sniff.

"What?"

"Hair straightener," she replied. "My flatiron. And now I have to deal with this *mess*."

He laughed then and she didn't like that one bit. "Your hair looks fine," he assured her. "It looks pretty."

She plucked at a few strands. "It's not pretty. It's not fine," she retorted, then let out a long breath. "You think I'm over-reacting?"

Cameron raised a hand. "Don't accuse me of thinking."

That made her laugh and she clutched her fingers together. "No one has seen me like this since…well, I can't remember the last time."

"You look good," he said and passed her a cup. "Drink up. We've got work to do."

She took the coffee and patted her stomach. He noticed she was wearing his shirt again. He liked that. "I'm hungry. Feed me first."

Cameron's libido did a leap. The mood between them seemed oddly playful and it made him think about fisting a handful of that glorious hair and kissing her neck. "I make a mean batch of scrambled eggs," he said and begrudgingly pushed back the idea of kissing her. "Feel like risking it?"

She nodded, perched on a bar stool and sipped her coffee. "I'm game."

He got what he needed from the refrigerator and began cooking while Grace quietly drank her coffee and stared at the linoleum countertop. She looked like she had something on her mind and he wondered if she'd spent the night staring at the ceiling like he had. After a while she put the cup down and linked her hands together.

"Why did you kiss me last night?"

Cameron stopped whisking eggs and stared at her. His chest tightened. "Because I wanted to. Because you're beautiful." He smiled. "The usual reasons."

"You know I'm leaving in two weeks?"

"Yes."

"And you know I'd never move back?"

Cameron put the eggs aside. "You wouldn't?"

Grace shrugged. "I don't belong in this world, Cameron. I don't belong in *your* world."

"Is that your way of letting me down gently?" he asked, and noticed her green eyes were suddenly luminous as she looked at him. "Even though you're not denying there's an attraction here?"

"But when a relationship is only based on strong physical—"

"Were you in love with the suit?" he asked quickly. "Or the doctor?"

"No."

"Have you ever had an intimate relationship just for the sheer fun of it?"

Her gaze narrowed. "I don't believe in casual sex."

"I'm not talking about something casual, Grace. I'm talking about having a relationship without laying down a whole lot of ground rules."

"I don't do that," she said hotly.

Cameron's brows shot up. "You don't?"

"Okay, maybe I do," she replied. "I like to be in—"

"In control," he said, cutting her off. "Yeah, I get that about you, Grace. But sex shouldn't be about control. It should be fun."

She glared at him. "Just because I take things seriously, that doesn't make me an uptight prig. I know how to have fun. Maybe my relationships with Dennis and Erik weren't all fireworks and passion. And maybe I did insist on separate apartments and avoided having them stay over because I'm too independent about have to be in control of *everything*. Maybe I'm all that and more...but it doesn't mean I'm sex-starved or frustrated or that I'm going to jump into the nearest bed I can find."

If I had any sense I'd forget all about her.

But he was all out of sense when it came to Grace.

"I wasn't suggesting you should," he said and bit back a grin. "Just, to not dismiss the idea entirely."

She shrugged. "I'm not good at relationships. I'm not good with people. With men. I always seem to make them leave." Her hands came to her chest and she held them there. "Do you know that I've only ever trusted three men in my whole life," she said softly and with such rawness his insides constricted. "My father, my brother..." She let out a long sigh. "And you. I know it probably hasn't seemed that way."

"No," he said. "But things often aren't what they seem."

"Like what?" she asked.

"Like the way I've always felt about you, Grace."

The words hung in the room. She didn't say anything else as they sat down for breakfast. They ate the eggs in a kind of forced silence. Grace offered to wash up and he didn't argue as he headed off. He'd said too much. Admitted too much. Her silence was like a swift slap in the face. It was a rejection. Again.

He was accustomed to it.

Don't you ever learn, Jakowski?

He left the room, mumbling something about paintbrushes and getting started on the painting.

By eight-thirty Grace headed for the main house. Pat was in the kitchen and greeted her with a broad smile.

"The kids are in the stable," the older woman explained. "Waiting for kittens to be born. A stray arrived last time we were here and I didn't have the heart to call animal welfare." She looked at Grace. "Did you sleep okay?"

Grace patted down her curls. "Yes, thank you. The cottage is very comfortable."

"But small," Pat said, grinning. "Too small and snug for

one old lady, four kids and a baby. But for you and Cameron—I imagine snug would be good."

Grace's cheeks flamed. "Like I said, we're not—"

"I know what you said," Pat said cheerfully and plopped a tea bag into a cup. "But I also know what I see. Even the bravest man might be afraid of letting his true feelings show," Pat said quietly. "If he believes he's going to get hurt."

Like the way I've always felt about you...

That was just it. He had let his feelings show.

And it terrified her. For years she'd handled his antagonism and sarcasm—that was easy. That she could combat with insults of her own. This was something else. Knowing he had feelings for her, still had feelings for her, made it impossible to keep denying her own feelings...the ones that were madly beating around in her heart.

The back door opened and Dylan entered excitedly. Cameron soon followed. He glanced at Grace and then turned to Pat. "Looks like rain in the distance."

"Rain?" Pat's expression widened. "Wouldn't that be lovely? We need a downpour to fill up the rainwater tanks. What I'd give for something more than the two-minute shower I have every time we're here."

Grace looked at Cameron, instantly mortified when she remembered the luxurious soak in the tub she'd had the afternoon before. She hadn't considered water preservation. She'd only given a thought to herself. His eyes were dark as he watched her, as if he knew her thoughts. Shame raced across her skin. What hadn't he said something to her?

"I'll have one-minute showers from now on," Grace told Pat. "You can use my saved minute for your bathtub."

Pat grinned broadly. "You're a sweet girl, Grace." Her crinkled eyes zoomed in on Cameron. "You shouldn't let this one go in a hurry."

Cameron smiled and leaned against the doorjamb. "I'll see what I can do."

It was a highly inflammatory thing to say and Grace's skin warmed immediately. "We should get started on the painting," she said and avoided the curious look on the older woman's face as she took a step. "I'd like to work with Emily this afternoon."

"The main bedroom needs doing," he said. "We can start there."

She didn't say another word and swiveled on her heels. In the main bedroom seconds later, she saw that Cameron had already moved the furniture to the center of the room and covered it with a drop cloth.

"Grace?"

He was behind her and she turned immediately. "What color today?" she asked, ignoring the thunderous beat of her heart behind her ribs. "Perhaps a pale—"

"Grace," he said again and with more emphasis. "We've got another two days here—so let's not get hung up on what I said earlier, okay?"

She shrugged. "It's forgotten already." She picked up a can of paint and thrust it toward him. "Let's start."

He took the paint and grabbed her hand before she could escape. "There's no need for you to be afraid of me."

"I'm not," she refuted.

"You're shaking."

Was she? Grace looked at her hands. The quiver was undeniable. "Let me go."

"Not until you tell me what's wrong."

"I can't," she said and tried to pull away. "I can't talk to you."

"Grace?"

It was too much. Too much honesty. Too many feelings were emerging and she had no idea how to handle it...or to handle him. She shouldn't have said anything. She should have worked on getting through the next two days without getting involved. But she lay awake for half the night, thinking about him…thinking about his kiss, his touch, and how suddenly it was the one thing she wanted more than anything else.

And it couldn't be.

She wasn't cut out for a relationship with him. She was going home in two weeks. Back to New York and everything familiar.

Grace took the brush and headed for a corner. She turned around and faced him, her back to the wall. "I just want to get through the weekend."

"Is being with me such a hardship?" he asked quietly.

"No," she admitted and looked sideways. "Which is exactly my point." Grace twirled the brush between her fingers. "I'm not going to sleep with you."

He looked tempted to smile. "I don't remember asking you to."

She plucked at the sleeve of the shirt that had become incredibly comfortable against her skin. She had the silly thought she might just keep it after the weekend was over.

"But you said…"

"I said what?" he queried. "That I want you?"

She exhaled. "Yes."

"So, I want you. It doesn't have to mean the end of the world, Grace," he said quietly. "It doesn't have to mean anything."

"Good," she said and pushed back her shoulders. "Because it doesn't." Grace turned on her heels, determined to ignore him and pretended to focus on painting.

Three hours later, and without more than half a dozen words said between them, the room was finished. Lunchtime loomed and Pat stuck her head in the doorway just as Cameron was pulling drop cloths off the bed, and told them to come to the kitchen. Grace ducked past the older woman, muttering something about washing up first and he didn't stop her.

He headed off to do the same once the bedroom was back in order. But he didn't find Grace in the cottage. She was outside with Isabel, examining a low branch on a citrus tree, which was weighed down by its fruit. He stood by the cottage steps and watched the exchange. With her hair down, her jeans spattered with paint and his old shirt hanging loosely off her shoulders she looked so incredibly lovely his chest felt like it would implode. Only Grace could do that to him. Only ever Grace.

Isabel laughed at something Grace said and she pulled a piece of fruit off the tree.

She really is good with kids.

But she didn't want them. That should have sent him running. Because he wanted children. The damnable thing was, he wanted to have them with Grace.

It took ten minutes to clean up, switch T-shirts and head back to the main house. He'd heard Grace come inside and head for the bathroom and left her to wash up as he made his way back to the main house. When he walked into the kitchen he quickly picked up that something was wrong. Pat and Dylan stood opposite one another and both faces were marred with a stricken look.

"What's up?" he asked as the back screen door banged behind him.

"It's Thomas," Pat said quickly, looking ashen. "He's gone missing."

Cameron stepped forward. "Missing? How long ago?"

Dylan shrugged his bony shoulders. "I'm not sure. Could be an hour or more. I thought he was with Isabel in the stable."

"Isabel was the last person to see him?" Cameron asked. Another shrug. "Dunno."

"Let's ask her, okay?"

Pat called the girl to come into the kitchen. Isabel couldn't remember when she'd last seen her brother and Cameron's instincts surged into overdrive. "We'll look around the house first," he assured Pat. "In all his favorite spots."

Grace entered the room and he told her what was happening.

"I'll help you look," she said and headed directly back out through the mudroom.

Fifteen minutes later, after every possible hiding place had been exhausted around the perimeter of the house, and they called his name repeatedly, Cameron knew they needed to widen the search.

"You head next door," he told Dylan. It was about one mile to the nearest neighbor and Cameron knew the boy would cover the ground quickly. "Grace and I will cut across the back paddock and head east. He can't have gotten too far. You stay here with the girls," he said to a worried Pat. "And call me if he comes back. Also, call the local police station and alert them to what's going on—tell them we're coordinating a search and you'll get back to them within the hour if we need help."

While he gave Dylan instructions he noticed Grace packing a small bag with water and cereal bars she'd found in the pantry. Within minutes they were outside and winding their way past the stables and through the barbed-wire fence.

"Any idea where he might be?" she asked as he held the wire apart while she slipped through.

They both stood and stared at the endless miles of pasture ahead of them. "Just a hunch he'd head this way. He knows not to go near the road because Pat has drummed road safety awareness into all the kids. This way seems logical."

She nodded. "Could he get far ahead of us?"

"Possibly. If he's just walking and not distracted." He raised his hand in an arc. "We'll keep about thirty meters apart. And watch for holes in the ground. I don't want you breaking any bones."

She nodded and walked off, creating space between them. And then they started walking, tracking across the undulating ground, looking for signs, anything that might indicate a little boy had come wandering this way. They were about ten minutes into it when his phone rang. When he finished talking and slipped the phone back into his pocket he noticed Grace had moved toward him a little.

"Who was that?" she asked in a loud voice.

"Fish," he replied.

She frowned. "What does that mean?"

"It was Pat," he explained. "Apparently Isabel remembered Thomas saying he was going to find a fish for the cat. Cats like fish, right?"

"I'm not sure I'm following you."

Cameron pointed toward the horizon. "There are three water holes on this property."

She flipped her sunglasses off her nose. "Do you think he might have—"

"I'm not sure," he said quickly and started walking again. He could see Grace's concern in the narrowing of her features. "Don't worry—he'll be fine."

She nodded. "Okay. Let's pick up the pace."

They did so quickly and thirty minutes later came across a small dam. Cameron checked for footprints and found only those belonging to cattle and the tracks of a lone wallaby.

"Nothing here," he said and trudged back up the side and onto the flat.

"That's a good thing, right?" Grace asked and passed him a bottle of water from the small backpack she'd brought with her. "If he's not here he might be on his way back. Maybe he's home already?"

Cameron forced a smile at her optimism and took the water. "Maybe. Let's keep going, though. The closest neighbor in this direction is about another three kilometers from here."

Five minutes later he heard from Pat again. He told her to call the neighbors and say they were on their way and to contact the police again and keep them updated. His phone crackled and faded as he rang off.

"Reception's gone for the moment," he said to Grace as they headed off again. "From now on we just keep walking and looking."

She nodded and turned away. But not before Cameron saw the fear in her expression. He felt it, too, although he wasn't about to admit that to Grace. They continued their trudge across the undulating landscape and didn't speak, but the tension between them was unmistakable. A shared tension brought on by the building threat that they wouldn't find Thomas—that he was lost, injured or worse.

Cameron spotted the familiar rise of another water hole ahead. A few cattle bellowed in the distance and he saw Grace hesitate on her feet as she walked. He doubted she'd ever been anywhere near a cow. He picked up speed and called the little boy's name. Grace quickly did the same and within seconds they were both jogging. She was faster than he'd imagined, even over the rough terrain. He stayed pace with her and somehow they ended up side by side, moving swiftly across the grass, avoiding stones and dips in the ground. He grabbed her hand and her tight grip seemed to push them harder and faster. Finally they reached the water hole and took long and hard steps up the embankment, sinking slightly in the unsteady clay underfoot.

"Cameron!"

Grace's voice echoed across the water as they both crested the rise. He saw Thomas immediately, on his belly, facedown in the murky water. He was at the water's edge in four strides and pulled the sodden, unconscious little boy into his arms, praying that they'd reached him in time.

Chapter Eight

Grace heard a scream and realized it was her own terrified voice. Cameron trudged up the embankment with Thomas in his arms as she dropped the backpack.

Panic coursed through her blood. She'd felt that panic before. The accident and Richard's death came rushing back into her thoughts. She tried to shake off the memory, tried to act normally, tried to stop her knees from failing.

Take a breath...one...two...

Slow breathing helped whenever she experienced that rush of adrenaline, that same dreaded coldness whispering across her skin. Usually it happened when she was alone at night, or about to drift off to sleep...then the darkness wrapped her up and for a while she was back, trapped in that car, praying... hoping that someone would find her.

"Grace?"

Cameron's voice jerked her back into the present and she quickly pulled herself together as he laid the child on the ground. Thomas looked ghostly pale and she dropped to her knees beside him.

Her voice cracked when she spoke. "Is he breathing?"

Cameron shook his head and rolled the child over to clear water from his airway.

"Try my phone again," he barked and pulled the phone from his pocket as he turned Thomas onto his back again. "The nearest hospital is half an hour away so get an ambulance to meet us at the farm."

Grace grabbed the phone and hit the emergency number. Thankfully, there was a signal and she quickly made the call, ensuring an ambulance was on its way to the house. Time stretched like elastic, and what was seconds seemed like an eternity. She watched, horrified and fascinated as Cameron performed CPR and encouraged the child to breathe in between puffs of lifesaving oxygen. Finally Thomas spluttered and drew in a long gasp of air. She touched the boy's muddy hair soothingly as his breathing steadied. He opened his eyes and croaked out a word she couldn't understand. With instincts she hadn't known she possessed, Grace comforted Thomas and told him it would be all right. Cameron rocked back on his heels and closed his eyes and Grace touched his arm.

"You did it," she said, squeezing a little. "He's okay."

Cameron nodded and let out a long breath. "Let's get him home."

She nodded. "He's cold," she said, touching his pale face. Grace pulled a sweater from the small backpack and quickly threaded Thomas's arms into the sleeves and then took off her own jacket and tucked it around his small body. She rubbed his hands together for moment then looked toward Cameron. "Let's go."

She watched as he lifted the child effortlessly and held him against his chest. He walked back to the house as quickly as possible, and too emotional to speak, Grace followed. Pat and the rest of the children were waiting by the fence when they arrived and she heard Cameron's palpable sigh of relief at the sight of the ambulance in the driveway. Two medics were instantly on hand and rushed forward to take Thomas from Cameron's arms. Within minutes the little boy was wrapped in a thermal blanket and received the necessary attention from the officers.

Pat came to Grace's side, tears in her pale eyes. Without thinking, Grace braced one arm around the older woman's shoulder and held her tightly. Cameron spoke with the officers as they loaded Thomas into the vehicle.

"You should accompany him," Grace said to Pat. "Cameron will go with you. I'll stay here with Emily and the kids."

Pat nodded as tears welled and fell. "Thank you."

Minutes later Grace watched the ambulance skim down the gravel road following closely by Cameron's sedan. She hadn't said anything to him as he'd left. She hadn't needed to. The realization they could communicate with simply a look filled her blood, her skin, her very core.

She gathered the children and headed back to the house. Dylan seemed unusually quiet and she ushered him into the kitchen with the girls and Jed at their heels and made a quick meal of ham-and-cheese sandwiches. After they'd eaten Isabel raced off to her bedroom, too young to fully comprehend what had happened to their brother, while Emily went to bathe Riley and put him to bed. Dylan however, lingered by the sink. Aware that the boy was grappling with his emotions, Grace suggested a makeshift game of cards to help distract him until he chose to talk about how he was feeling.

It took about thirty minutes.

"Do you think he'll be okay?"

Grace dropped a card onto the table and chose another. "Of course he will."

"I should have watched out for him." He looked downward. "I wasn't watching. I wanted to muck around with the horses. I didn't want to get stuck watching the kids again. I forgot about him. I forgot and he disappeared. If Nan finds out she'll be really angry."

She heard the panic and pain in Dylan's voice and felt the need to comfort him. "I dropped my little sister on her head once," she admitted and looked at him over her cards. "I was supposed to be looking after her while my mother was outside. We were twirling…but I got dizzy and dropped her."

"You *dropped* your sister?"

"Mmm-hmm."

Dylan's eyes widened. "Did you get into trouble?"

"Big-time," she replied. "For about ten seconds—until my mother realized how upset I was. She knew I didn't mean it. Just like your grandmother will know you didn't mean to forget you were supposed to watch Thomas. It just happened."

He looked instantly relieved. "Do you think so?"

"For sure."

Dylan managed a little smile. "Thanks, Grace—you're the best."

A strange tightness constricted through the middle of her chest and she took a deep breath. When she heard a movement from the doorway she snapped her neck around. Cameron stood at the threshold.

"You're back?"

"Not for long," he said and came into the room. "Pat wants the kids to go to the hospital."

The blood leached from her face. "Is Thomas—"

"He's fine," Cameron assured her, and Dylan, who had jumped up in his chair. "No permanent damage. He's awake and he wants to see Dylan and the girls. I said I'd drive them back into town and they'll stay overnight at a motel. I'll pick them up tomorrow."

"I should get some things together for Isabel and tell Emily," she said as she stood and pushed the chair out. "She'll need to get Riley's booster seat for your car."

"That would be great. Come on, Dylan, let's get you ready." He went to turn, but then halted. "I should be back in a couple of hours."

Grace watched as Dylan scooted from the room and followed Cameron up the hallway. She gathered some fresh clothes for Isabel and then helped her change into jeans and a long-sleeved T-shirt.

Emily took some time gathering Riley's things together and Grace helped pack his baby bag.

"I feel bad," Emily said as she pulled on her jacket. "I've been wrapped up in taking care of Riley and studying. I haven't spent much time hanging out with the rest of the kids."

Grace patted the teenager's arm. "You can only do what you can," she said and picked up the bags. "Come on, your grandmother is waiting for you."

She stayed by the front steps as Cameron organized everyone into his car and packed their small bags into the trunk. He waved goodbye and drove off.

And now I'm alone.

Well, not exactly. Jed had ambled from his spot on the veranda and followed her back inside. Strangely, she didn't mind the company and allowed him to sit by her feet when she returned to the kitchen table. She shuffled the deck of cards and busied herself for a while with a game of solitaire. Once she was done Grace closed up the house and headed back to the cottage. She took a shower and the hot spray eased some of the tension tightening her shoulders. Now conscious of water shortages, she lingered for mere minutes, then changed into sweats and sat on the sofa in front of the television.

And quickly, like a runaway train, it hit her.

Thomas could have died.

For those few terrifying minutes she'd thought he wouldn't make it.

Fear closed her throat over and Grace sucked in some much needed air. She clutched her arms over her chest. Her lids dropped heavily as a familiar chill rushed over her skin. *I'm so cold.* She remembered that feeling. She remembered the fear and the helplessness. She remembered thinking she was going to die. And she remembered Richard's lifeless body, twisted and battered, beside her.

Jed groaned. She glanced at the dog. He pulled himself up, suddenly on alert. Grace quelled the unease narrowing through her blood. She heard a car door shut. Cameron. She got to her feet and rushed to greet him by the front door.

"He's fine," Cameron said as he walked across the threshold.

Grace clutched his arm. "Thank goodness."

"I need to feed the horses and then I'll hit the shower," he said and ran a weary hand through his hair. "Give me half an hour."

Grace released him and watched from the doorway as he walked back outside. The dwindling sun was all but gone when he returned to the cottage and headed for the bathroom. She fed the dog in the small mudroom and remained in the kitchen. Dinner would be pretty hit-or-miss, she realized when she opened the refrigerator. She pulled a couple of cans of soup from the cupboard and popped the contents into a saucepan to heat. Cameron came into the kitchen just as she had finished toasting thick slices of sourdough bread.

"You've been busy," he said as he passed the counter and saw the bread and green salad she'd prepared.

"It's not much," she said, feeling faintly embarrassed.

In low-slung faded jeans, white T-shirt and bare feet, he looked sexy and tempting.

Grace's skin warmed thinking about it and she turned back to her task.

"Do you need some help?" he asked and braced his hands on the edge of the counter.

She glanced sideways and avoided thinking about how his biceps flexed. "I'm good. So you said Thomas was doing well?"

"They want to keep him in for a couple of nights to be sure. But he's awake and talking."

She stopped what she was doing and looked at him. "Thanks to you."

"I wasn't alone," he said and stole a cucumber slice from the salad bowl.

"I didn't do much."

He leaned forward and crossed his arms. "You were there, Grace. You helped me do what needed to be done. You kept him warm," he reminded her. "And you comforted Dylan."

Her eyes widened. "You heard that?"

"About how you dropped Mary-Jayne on the head?" He grinned. "I heard. Explains a lot."

Grace laughed for probably the first time that day. And it felt good. "Poor M.J.," she said and returned to stirring the soup. "I love her dearly, you know."

"I think you have a great capacity for love, Grace," he said quietly. "You just don't show it."

The spoon rattled in the saucepan and she turned fractionally, avoiding his brown eyes. "Too hard."

"To admit you're human?"

She felt his questioning stare in the small confines of the kitchen. "Human? Am I? I've been called a lot of things."

"By me?" he prompted gently. "I guess that's true. We've said a lot of things to one another over the years."

"I deserved it," she said and stirred the soup some more.

"It's not like it isn't the truth. I know what I am. I know what people think of me."

"And what's that?"

"Oh, you know—that I'm a workaholic ice princess. Everyone has their place in a family, I guess. In mine, M.J. is the lovable one," she said. "Evie's the sensible one. And I'm the…smart one."

"And beautiful."

She shrugged and continued to stir.

"And talented in the kitchen. And good with kids." He looked at Jed lolling by the back door. "And dogs."

"Shocked even myself with that one," she said and spooned soup into two bowls. "Who would have thought?"

He grabbed the bread and salad, followed her to the table and sat down.

"I'm not fooled, Grace."

Grace slipped into a chair and looked at him. Really looked. Her heart—the same heart she'd tried hard to wrap in ice for so many years was suddenly pounding behind her ribs—and she was melting. The power he had over her—the power she'd denied because she was terrified of being vulnerable to him, of giving herself, of losing herself…suddenly that power made her want him even more.

She sighed out a breath. "Today I…I thought Thomas was going to die."

"Me, too."

"If he had…" The words caught, lingered, and then disappeared.

"But he didn't. He's safe. And so are you."

She looked up, emotion clogging her throat. Had she truly felt safe since the accident? Almost losing Thomas had brought all those memories back to the surface. And yet, being in the kitchen with Cameron, she somehow didn't have the usual emptiness in her heart.

"I feel safe now."

Cameron stilled. There was something incredibly vulnerable about Grace in that moment. He wanted to race around the counter and haul her into his arms. But resistance lingered. He couldn't be sure what she was feeling. And the idea of rejection suddenly waved like a red flag in front of him.

"I'm glad you feel safe with me."

She shrugged lightly. They ate in silence, but the tension in the room was extreme. Once the food was consumed and the plates taken care of, Cameron made his way to the sofa in the living room. She followed and stood by the fireplace.

"Are you joining me?" he asked and sat down.

She hesitated. The modest lamp in the corner gave enough light to see the wariness in her expression. "I should...go."

"Go where? To bed?" He checked his watch. "A little early for that, don't you think?"

A sigh escaped her lips and he watched her perfectly bowed mouth for a moment. Like everything about her face it was a thing of pure beauty. "I just thought—"

"Safe with me one minute, afraid of me the next. What's really going on with you, Grace?"

"I'm not afraid of you," she replied.

"Then sit down."

She took a few steps and dropped onto the sofa. "Okay, I'm sitting."

"Good," he said. "Now, talk."

She shook her head. "There's nothing to—"

"There is," he said, cutting her off. "I can see it in your eyes."

"Maybe I'm just upset over what happened today. I'm not made of stone, you know. If that little boy had—"

"But he didn't," Cameron said. "And we've already established that you're safe and sound here. So, talk to me," he insisted and rested an arm on the back of the sofa.

"What about?"

"Whatever's on your mind."

"Nothing is," she said and twisted her hands together.

Cameron pushed some more. "You could tell me about the crash and what happened that day."

Her breath caught. "I don't want to talk about it."

"Maybe you don't want to. But I think you need to."

"I have a shrink for that," she said and crossed her arms. "I went to counseling. I talked about *it* in exhausting detail and six sessions later I'm…I'm here."

"Here?"

"Home," she said quickly. "Crystal Point."

"I've never heard you call Crystal Point home before."

She shrugged. "My therapist thought being here would be good for me. I've told you all this already."

There was so much bite in her words Cameron knew she was holding back. "But you didn't say why?"

"I was in a car wreck."

"And your friend died?"

"Richard was a colleague," she said in a whisper. "And again, I've told you what happened. We were driving out to meet with a client and the car ran off the road. Richard died and I survived."

Cameron considered her words. "What happened then?" he asked and shifted to face her.

Her green eyes glittered. "We crashed and were trapped inside. That's the whole story."

Cameron wasn't convinced. "And how long were you trapped inside?"

She looked at him and shook her head. Shutters came up and a second later she stood.

"Grace?"

She shook her head again and headed for the fireplace. Cameron watched, mesmerized and confused, and he quickly pulled together his thoughts. Silence stretched between them, fueling the growing tension in the room. When he finally stood and took a few steps toward her, she was holding her arms tightly around her waist. He said her name again.

"I can't go back there," she said quietly and kept facing away. "I can't go back there with you."

"Back where?"

She shuddered. "To the crash. To that time. I'm trying to forget, not remember. I'm trying to get those days out of my head and—"

"Days?" he asked, cutting off her words. "What do you mean? How long were you in that car, Grace?"

She turned and faced him, eyes shining. She looked lost and he fought the urge to haul her into his arms. "Two days," she whispered.

Cameron stared at her. "You were trapped for two days? You and Richard?"

She nodded faintly. Very faintly. And Cameron's curiosity and instincts surged. Pieces of the puzzle fell into place. He recognized fear and grief in her haunted expression. And he knew that look from the years of police work and of dealing with victims of trauma.

"Richard was dead, wasn't he?"

"I said that already."

Cameron pressed on. "I mean he was dead when the car crashed. And you were alive?"

She took a second. "Yes."

"And there was nothing you could do for him, was there?"

Her lips trembled. "No."

Realization quickly dawned. She'd spent two days trapped inside a wrecked car with a dead man. No sweet wonder she was as closed up as a vault. The walls she'd erected around herself, the shadow of unhappiness in her eyes, her reluctance to let her family know the truth—it made perfect sense. "Grace." He said her name gently. "Has your counselor talked to you about post-traumatic stress disorder?"

She shuddered out a breath. "I'm not crazy."

"Of course you're not," he said and took a step closer. "But when someone has an experience like you've had it's quite normal for—"

"I'm perfectly fine," she said, cutting him off. "And I don't need analysis from your police officer's handbook."

Cameron took hold of her hand and urged her toward him. "Grace, I'm not analyzing you. I just wish you'd told me earlier."

"Why?" she asked, but didn't pull away. "So you can get inside my head and work me out?"

"So I could help you," he said gently.

"I don't need help. I'm not about to fall apart."

"Maybe you should," he suggested. "Maybe falling apart is exactly what you need."

She didn't move for a moment and uncertainty clouded her expression. Cameron remained still and waited. Her eyes filled with tears that slowly spilled over. Her skin looked pale in the lamplight. And she'd never seemed more beautiful. He wanted to soothe her, hold her, kiss her. But he checked himself.

"I can't. I have to fight it. I have to fight…you."

He touched her face. "No, you don't. We're not at war anymore."

"You don't understand—I need to stay strong," she said. "It's all I know."

"There's strength in admitting you're scared, Grace," he assured her and wiped the moisture from her cheek with his thumb. "And there can also be strength in tears. Resisting your grief and fear won't help you move on from the crash. It will only magnify the guilt you feel because you survived."

Grace choked back a sob. *How could he know that?* Months of guilt and anguish pressed between her shoulders. She dropped her head against his chest as his arms came around her.

"I was glad," she admitted as emotion tightened her throat so much she could barely swallow. Grace forced more words out. "I was happy and I shouldn't have been. I didn't have the right to be happy...not when Richard was...was gone."

Cameron stroked her back tenderly. "It would have been relief, Grace. And a perfectly rational reaction."

She shook her head against him. "No. I was *happy,* really happy." She shuddered as fresh tears burned her eyes. "We were trapped inside. I couldn't get out of my seat. Richard was...he was next to me and I knew he wasn't breathing and there was so much blood. But when I knew I was alive and not seriously hurt I started laughing hysterically and I couldn't stop and it—"

"That's not happiness, Grace," he insisted. "It was relief, like I said. You went through a traumatic experience." He grasped her chin, tilted her face and gently kissed her forehead. "You *should* be glad you survived. And thinking that doesn't make you a bad person."

More tears came, hard racking sobs that pushed up from deep inside her. She couldn't stop them. The tighter he held her, the more emotion came to the surface. For months she'd kept it all inside. Even with her therapist she'd held back, afraid to fully let her feelings show. Now, like never before, she felt like telling him everything.

When Cameron led her back to the sofa and sat down she followed and settled beside him. Without a word he turned her toward his chest and rested one hand over her hip, while the other stayed firmly on her shoulder.

"Grace, what happened during those two days, when you were stuck in the car?"

She wiped tears off her cheeks and looked at him. "The client we were to see lived in an isolated place. There was poor phone reception so we didn't know that the client was ill and had actually cancelled the meeting. Because of that, no one knew that we hadn't arrived for our appointment. We weren't reported missing until about thirty-six hours after the crash. It was Richard's wife who reported us missing when he hadn't called her the next day."

"And?" he prompted.

She shuddered. "It was a deserted road and a small animal had rushed out in front of us. Once we crashed, the car flipped onto its side and I couldn't open any of the doors to get out. And I couldn't find my phone so there was no way to contact anyone or call 911. So, I waited and just hoped that wild animals or dehydration wouldn't get me before I was found. And all that time Richard was…" She stopped and swallowed a heavy lump of emotion. "He was strapped in by the seatbelt and I was underneath. I couldn't climb over him. I couldn't do anything. And I kept thinking…why me? Why did I survive? If the car had landed a foot or so over, the passenger side would have hit the tree. But it didn't. It crushed the driver's side and the car rolled and it all happened so fast Richard didn't stand a chance." She sucked in a deep, painful breath. "He was a good man. His family grieved for him so much."

"That's to be expected."

Her shoulders grew heavy. "I know. And I know these things are random and happen and there's no way of controlling it…but still, I can't help wondering. In a split second someone lives and someone dies. There's really no sense to be made."

Cameron touched her hair and her heart contracted at his gentleness. "I think that every time I'm on duty and attend a motor vehicle accident. Your feelings are real, Grace. But if your friend died on impact there's nothing you could have done. It wasn't your fault."

Logically, Grace knew he was right. Her therapist had said it often enough. But the feelings lingered. Fresh tears filled her eyes and she blinked and more truths tumbled out.

"Richard's wife came to see me when I returned to work. She said she was collecting the rest of his things from his office, but I knew that wasn't the only reason." Grace took a long breath. "She stood in the doorway and stared at me... and somehow I knew what she was thinking. She looked around at my office, saw there weren't any photographs on my desk or anything in the room that might indicate that I meant something to someone, and I could feel her resentment. I felt such *guilt* in that moment that I couldn't speak. I couldn't talk about Richard, I couldn't express my sorrow for her loss. He was a man with a loving family and so much to live for, and I was just...I was...*me*—work-obsessed, closed off, friendless."

The truth was raw and painful and her whole body ached, inside and out.

"I don't think I've ever felt as alone as I did in those few minutes," she admitted with a sob. "An hour later I fell apart in front of a client and my boss made me take some leave and see a therapist. My treatment was to come home." She shrugged and didn't bother to wipe the tears from her cheeks this time.

"You don't need validation for surviving the crash, Grace. Not from your family, me or anyone else."

She couldn't pull back the agonized groan that escaped her lips. His insight both scared and soothed her. Her feelings were jumbled and when he moved closer the words she wanted to say somehow disappeared. His mouth hovered near hers. She pushed forward and their lips met, softly, because she wasn't sure she should do it. Part of her longed to kiss him over and over and try to erase the pain and guilt in her heart. And part of her wanted to run. Because she'd run from her feelings for Cameron since she was eighteen years old.

She pulled back and broke the contact of their lips. "I shouldn't have done that."

"I didn't mind."

She sighed heavily. "I know. And that's why I shouldn't have done it. I also shouldn't have told you what happened. It's my problem and—"

He kissed her hotly and the rest of her denials faded. Grace wasn't sure how long the kiss lasted. When he stopped she was breathless.

"Then why did you tell me?" he asked. "If for no other reason than you needed to talk about it to someone."

"Because you—"

"Does my wanting you frighten you that much?"

Her heart stilled. Had she ever really been wanted? By Dennis? By Erik? Had she really wanted them in return? A resounding *no* rang out in her head. She'd only wanted a career. Not love. Not sex. Not a home and family. Just work. And now, she was as vulnerable as she'd ever been, with the one man who could make her forget she had a life waiting for her back in New York.

"I can't," she admitted hollowly. "I just can't. Not with you."

His brown eyes absorbed her as he twirled strands of her hair between his fingers. Finally, he shifted in the seat. "You should get some sleep."

Grace stilled. "I'd like to stay here for a while, if that's okay?"

"Sure," he said and stood. "Good night."

As she watched him walk from the room, Grace knew that as confused and tired as she was, all she really wanted to do was fall into Cameron's strong arms and stay there for the night. And maybe longer.

Chapter Nine

Cameron flipped on his back and stared at the ceiling. Sleep was out of the question. He managed to waste about an hour or so before he got up, pulled on jeans and a T-shirt and padded down the hall.

Grace was asleep on the sofa and he covered her with a knitted blanket hanging over the back of the love seat in the corner. She looked exhausted and he lingered for a moment, considering everything she'd told him. Without her secrets and frosty reserve she seemed achingly vulnerable and it pierced his heart.

He wanted her.

He loved her.

And she was so messed up he should ignore every feeling he had. Because he was going to get his heart smashed. Again. She was leaving in two weeks. She didn't want a relationship with him. She didn't want marriage or kids. She'd spelled it out many times.

Dumb ass.

He longed for the impossible.

She stirred and he quietly left the room and headed for the kitchen. He pulled a glass from the cupboard and filled it with water. *I need to chill out.* Not that he needed any more thinking time. He'd been thinking about Grace all his adult life. She was why he'd never settled, never made a commitment with any of the perfectly lovely women he'd dated.

I just can't. Not with you.

That was plain enough.

It should have worked like a bucket of cold water over his feelings, his longings and his libido.

"Oh—sorry. I didn't realize you were still awake."

He looked up. Grace stood in the doorway.

"Thirsty?" he asked.

She shook her head. "I didn't mean to disturb you."

"That's okay. I couldn't sleep."

She glanced at the clock on the wall which had just ticked past eleven o'clock. "I guess I crashed out for an hour or so."

"You must have needed it," he said and came around the counter.

Grace hesitated by the doorway. "Cameron," she said with a shaky breath. "I wanted to thank you for listening earlier. I've never really talked about the crash or Richard before."

"No problem."

"And about what I said…I meant…I meant that I…"

As her words trailed off he leaned against the counter and shrugged. "You can't force feelings Grace, I get that."

She shook her head. "That's not it."

Cameron's heart surged forward, battering against his chest. "Then what?"

"It's why I left," she said on a breath. "Why I couldn't be what you wanted back then. I knew you were getting serious and the plans I had didn't include Crystal Point or settling down."

"So you left for New York and didn't look back?"

"Yes," she replied. "And in two weeks I'll be going back there. You know that, right?"

"Sure."

"So, if anything happened it would—"

"Anything?" he prompted.

Cameron uncrossed his arms and pushed himself off the counter. As he moved the air between them shifted on some invisible axis. Hotter somehow, even though it was obviously cool outside. And thicker, like a gust of something sinfully seductive had blown into the room.

She sucked in a breath. "I want…I want…"

"You want what?"

Her green eyes glittered. "I want to…*feel*."

Cameron kept his head. As beautiful as she was, as inviting as she was, he needed to be sure of her. "You know, you've had a pretty harrowing day. And bad days can make for impulsive decisions."

"I'm never impulsive."

"You were on the beach last weekend," he reminded her.

She shrugged a little. "So, despite what people think, I'm a normal woman with a normal woman's needs."

"I know you're a woman, Grace," he said quietly. "But today was hard—not only did Thomas almost die, you talked about the crash that almost took *your* life. When emotions come out like that, feelings can get…misdirected." He took her hand. "The thing is, if you want comfort—I can give you that. If you want sex—I can give you that, too. But tomorrow, I'll still be me. And you'll still be the same woman who wanted to get away from Crystal Point."

She moved closer. "Tomorrow isn't tonight. But if you don't want me I'll understand and—"

"Grace," he said, cutting her off. "Of course I want you." He ran his fingers through his hair. "I'm not made of stone. Do you think I haven't been imagining what it would be like to make love to you every minute of every day?"

She smiled. "Then make love to me. Please."

Cameron blinked twice and wondered if he were dreaming. She looked so beautiful. And startlingly vulnerable. He found some life in his legs and moved across the room.

"You're sure?" he asked.

She nodded.

He gripped her hand and she curled her fingers around his and turned, urging him forward and down the hall to her bedroom.

Once there she released him and stood beside the bed. Cameron's heart hammered. He'd imagined this moment countless times—even when they'd pretended to hate one another. And now he was with her, in her bedroom, standing barely a foot apart.

"But you're not sure about this, are you?" she asked and twisted her fingers together. Grace was nervous.

So am I.

"I'm sure," he replied and took her hand in his. "Only, I'm still me, like I said. I'm still a small-town police officer—and it's what I'll always—"

She reached up and placed two fingers against his mouth, cutting off his words. "I was eighteen and foolish when I said that. Who hasn't said stupid things in their life that they regret?"

She had a point. He regretted many of the things he'd said to Grace over the years. The digs, the antagonism—foolishness to hide behind so he didn't have to face his feelings for her, and the rejection he'd felt. But he wanted her so much. And right at that moment, the risk of getting his heart broken was worth it.

He took her hand and urged her forward, cupping the back of her neck with his other hand. "There's no going back once we do this, Grace."

"I know."

Without another word he drew her close and took her lips in a deep, drugging kiss. She groaned low in her throat and gripped his shoulders, holding on as breath and souls mingled. Kissing Grace was like nothing on earth.

Need for her spiked and his arms tightened around her waist, settling on her hips. Her sweatshirt fell off one shoulder and the bra strap went with it. He trailed kisses down her jaw and neck. The scent of her skin was powerful to his senses and he felt all the blood in his body rush to his groin.

Go easy...go slow.

She said his name and ran her fingers through his hair. Her eagerness spiked his desire. "Take this off," he muttered against her shoulder, tugging lightly at her sweatshirt.

"You first."

Obliging instantly, he released her for a second and pulled his T-shirt over his head and tossed it on the floor. Her palms came to his chest and the touch sent his blood soaring. He kissed her again, hungry for the taste of her. Her mouth opened and she rolled her tongue around his, softly at first, almost tentative and it made him smile.

Grace pulled back, all eyes and swollen lips. "You're laughing?"

"No," he said gently and grasped her chin. "Just thinking how good it feels to be with you like this."

She nodded and stepped back, then grabbed the hem of her sweatshirt and slipped the garment off in one fluid movement. Cameron watched, absorbed by the evocative look in her eyes. The white lace bra pushed her breasts upward and his hands tingled. He wanted to touch her breasts so much he ached. But she was calling the shots at that moment and he didn't mind one bit.

She discarded the top and rested her fingers on the waistband of her sweatpants. It was both excruciating and erotic to watch as she slowly slid the sweats past her hips and over her thighs. They dropped in a puddle at her feet and she pushed them out of the way with her foot. The white lace briefs were quite modest and unbelievably sexy.

She stepped back again and sat on the edge of the bed. When he moved toward her she pushed back farther onto the mattress. Cameron rested a knee on the bed and looked down at her lying against the white quilt. Her dark hair fanned wildly around her face. Her body was curved and toned, her skin smooth. A tiny diamond glittered from her pierced navel and seemed oddly at contrast with the controlled, serious woman he'd always believed her to be.

"You are so beautiful." Cameron moved beside her and grasped her shoulder. "And incredibly sexy," he said as he ran his fingertips down her arm.

"Really?" She took hold of his hand as he curved his palm over one hip. "Cameron," she said, suddenly too serious. "Just so you know…I'm not very good at this."

He stilled. "This?"

"This," she said again, quieter, like she had some terrible secret. "I'm not very responsive. I mean, I like the idea of… making love. But when I'm with someone I sort of shut down. I think there's something wrong with me. I'm only telling you because I don't want you to think it's something you've done. Or didn't do," she added quickly.

A feeling akin to pain pierced his chest. How could she possibly think that? "The suit?" he accused. "He said that? He said there was something wrong with you?"

She nodded. "And before that. Dennis said—"

"How about we don't worry what the suit or the doctor

or anyone else has said to you." He grabbed her hand and brought it to his lips. "Can you feel that?"

She nodded again.

He traced his tongue inside her palm. "And that?"

"Yes," she whispered.

"Do you trust me, Grace?"

Her breath caught in her throat. "I do."

"So, trust me now," he said quietly. "Trust this. Trust *us*...."

He looked into her eyes, saw her agreement and then kissed her. For a while, kissing was enough. She gave her mouth up to him, responding to each slant, every breath and each time he took her bottom lip between his. He threaded his hands through her beautiful hair, loving the way the wild curls got caught between his fingers.

The need to love her right, to pleasure her unselfishly, had never seemed more important. Her hands were on his chest and her soft caress burned through him. He kissed her and reached for the back of her bra, flicking the garment apart. He felt her smile beneath his mouth and then she shifted her shoulders free of the white lace.

He looked at her breasts, wanting nothing more to worship them...and more...worship her. Tonight. Forever. When he cupped one breast and closed his mouth over her nipple he thought he might die a slow, agonizing death. Pleasure and pain ripped through his middle, arrowing downward, making him so hard so quickly, he wondered if he would pass out.

He said her name against the luscious peak and groaned when she pushed toward him. Her hands were in his hair, over his shoulders, his neck, everywhere, like she couldn't get close enough, touch enough, feel enough. He caressed her skin, finding the places she liked. When his fingers reached the band on her briefs she stilled and drew in a sharp breath.

"Relax," he whispered against her mouth. "And trust me."

* * *

Grace looked into his eyes and nodded with a hazy kind of surrender. She did trust him. Completely. More, she realized as he efficiently dispensed with her underwear, than any man she'd ever known. And for the first time in her life, without questioning why, she gave herself up to feel…to really feel… like she'd always longed for in her secret dreams.

His hands were magic over her skin, his mouth hot and demanding, yet also gentle as he coaxed response from her. She gave it willingly and wound her tongue around his as their kisses deepened, touching his chest, his strong, smooth shoulders. And she waited for what she suddenly craved, she waited for his intimate touch. None of her usual apprehension rose up—instead, Grace let go of her insecurities and fell apart in his arms.

He knew how to touch her, knew where, as though he'd been touching her forever, and beyond. While he stroked her, while his skillful fingers drew narcotic pleasure along her every nerve ending, he continued to kiss her mouth. He took her bottom lip between his teeth and suckled gently. When the tempo of her breathing changed he released her mouth and looked down into her face. His eyes were dark, clearly aroused, and she lost all her inhibitions beneath his penetrating stare. Grace spiraled, she flew, her blood fired as every part of her raced toward a shattering climax so intense, so wondrous, she couldn't stop herself from saying his name, over and over.

She came down slowly, breathing in tiny gasps of air, floating on a steady wave of aftershocks. Her eyes burned. No tears, she told herself. Not now.

"See," Cameron said quietly, kissing her jaw, her chin, and the delicate spot below her ear. "Nothing wrong with you at all."

The tears she'd tried to deny suddenly filled her eyes and

she blinked, desperate for him not to see them. Too late. He wiped the moisture from her cheek with his thumb.

So vulnerable, so exposed, Grace felt the rawness deep down to her bones.

"Sorry," she whispered and moved to turn her head away.

Cameron grasped her chin. "For what? Feeling pleasure?" He touched her bottom lip. "Don't ever be sorry for that, Grace."

"For being so emotional," she explained, hot with embarrassment. She was naked and exposed while he remained half-clothed.

"Making love is emotional." He rubbed her lip again. "Or at least, it should be."

He was right. And she wanted it to be that way. She also wanted his clothes off.

Grace moved her hands to the top snap on his jeans. "My turn," she said, pushing past her awkwardness. "Take these off."

It took barely seconds and finally he lay beside her, skin touching skin, arms entwined. In the dim lamplight his tanned body looked bronzed and amazing. Grace touched the soft hair on his chest with her fingernails. She felt his arousal press against her belly.

"Okay?" he asked and traced one finger along her arm.

She nodded and leaned toward him. "Kiss me."

For the next hour he did more than simply kiss her. Cameron kissed and stroked her, using his hands and mouth to drive her toward the pinnacle of pleasure once again. When his tongue dipped in her navel and played around with the tiny piercing she had there, Grace almost bucked off the bed. *Who would have thought*... He groaned low in his throat and offered encouragement when she touched him, kissed him, although there was nothing particularly practiced about her technique.

And then, when Grace thought she could crave nothing else, want nothing more, he passed her the condom he'd placed on the bedside table. She sheathed him quickly, if a little unsteadily, and waited, poised for his possession as he moved over her. He took his weight on his elbows and watched her.

This is it. Some faraway voice spoke to her. *This is what I've been waiting for. This night. This man. This feeling.* And as he entered her slowly, Grace knew a sense of completion she'd never experienced before. He stayed still for a moment and she remained lost in his eyes.

When he moved, Grace moved with him. When he kissed her, she kissed him back. When he smiled against her mouth, she returned the gesture. Two people, somehow fused by more than making love. The pace between them quickened. More need, more urgency, more passion, she thought, from some dreamy place, as her body began the throb with a heady longing once again. She linked her arms around him, holding on, kneading wanting fingers into his back. And finally, when they could take no more, they came together in a white-hot frenzy of release.

When it was over, when the pleasure receded and their breathing returned to something resembling normal, Cameron eased his weight off her and lay at her side.

He grabbed her hand and held it against his chest. "Still okay?"

Grace let out a breath. "Yes."

"No regrets?"

"Not yet," she replied honestly. "Thank you."

"For what?"

"For being so…" Her words trailed as an unusual lethargy seeped across her skin. "So sweet."

"Sweet?" He echoed but she knew he was smiling. "Damned with faint praise."

Grace shifted closer. "It's high praise, actually."

"Okay then." He sat up and swung his legs off the bed. "Back in a minute."

He left the room and Grace stretched her body. She closed her eyes, only to be roused a couple of minutes later when Cameron returned and quickly shuffled her underneath the covers before he got back into the bed.

He reached for her, wrapping her in his arms once he'd flicked off the bedside lamp. "Get some sleep, Grace."

Grace sighed contentedly and pressed herself into his chest, trailing her fingertips up and down his rib cage. She closed her eyes again and listened to the steady rhythm of his heart as she drifted off to sleep.

When she awoke the following morning, Grace was alone. The digital clock on the table read half past seven. She could hear movement around the cottage. A door closed and Jed's familiar whine echoed from the kitchen where he was clearly searching for food.

Footsteps came up the hallway moments later and Cameron rounded the doorway with a cup in his hand.

"Coffee?" he asked as he came into the room.

Grace pulled herself up, conscious to not let the sheet slip past her breasts. Silly, she supposed. He'd seen all of her there was to see. But she couldn't suppress the niggling anxiety that began to knock steadily behind her ribs.

"Lovely," she said as cheerfully as she could. Morning-afters were not her specialty.

But Cameron clearly had no problem with them, she realized when he sat on the edge of the bed and passed her the cup. Lots of practice, no doubt. That thought didn't go down well either. He looked casual and relaxed. He wore the jeans she'd practically ripped off with her teeth the night before and nothing else. The top snap was undone and she stole a glance at the line of soft hair arrowing downward from his belly button. Color rose up her collarbone and she quickly sipped the coffee. "Mmm, good. Thank you."

"I have to go into town this morning to pick up Pat and the kids," he said easily. "If they release Thomas it'll take two trips so I might be gone awhile. But later, we could do something together."

Grace looked at him over the rim of the cup. "Didn't we already?"

He smiled and Grace knew he was remembering how they'd made slow, seductive love again just before dawn broke. "I guess we did."

"What did you have in mind?" she asked, trying to push aside the images in her head and the memory of his kisses. "And does that mean we get the day off today?"

"For sure. You've earned it."

Her eyes popped wide. "I have?"

"For yesterday," he explained, grinning. "And Friday you worked hard. I was thinking we could take the horses out."

"Horses?" Her smile disappeared as she placed the cup on the bedside table. "I don't really do horses."

He shrugged and grinned. "Okay, what would you like to do instead? We could go into town and have lunch if you'd prefer that?"

Her smile returned. He was being very sweet and she decided to make an effort and expand her horizons. "Actually, horseback riding sounds like fun."

He looked skeptical of her sudden turnaround. "You're sure?"

"Positive."

He kissed her soundly. "Great. So, what about breakfast?"

Grace groaned. "Are you always so chipper in the morning?"

Cameron laughed and grabbed her free hand. "Depends what I've been doing the night before."

"Sex puts you in a good mood?"

He rubbed the underside of her wrist. "You put me in a good mood."

They both laughed out loud. "I do not. Most of the time we seem to be working out new ways to insult one another."

"I like this much better," he said and brought her hand to his lips and kissed her knuckles.

"Me, too."

He took a moment to respond. "And if I said I wanted more—would that send you running?"

More what? Sex? "I told you I don't do this casually."

His gaze narrowed. "And I do? Is that your implication?"

"Well, I—"

"Did it feel casual to you, Grace?"

She shook her head. "Not at all."

"Last night I asked you to trust *us,* Grace. Whatever you think of me, you must know I would never make love to you unless it was *real.*"

Did she know that? Is that why her heart hammered so loudly? *I'm afraid.* In the cold light of day, with passion abated and only truth between them, Grace was forced to examine what she knew was her own truth. Somehow, the lines had blurred. The antagonism had gone. The feigned dislike had disappeared. She'd made love with Cameron and had felt love in that moment. From him. From herself.

He smiled and then proceeded to make love to her all over again, wringing the last vestiges of response from her, driving Grace toward some place where only pleasure existed.

Pat and the kids returned midmorning. Thomas was being kept another night at the small community hospital, and according to his grandmother was doing remarkably well.

She remained in the kitchen with the older woman and Emily for a while, sharing tea and talking about the children.

They discussed the upcoming trail ride and Grace did her best to hide her nerves. But Pat wasn't fooled.

"You'll be fine," Pat assured her and tapped her hand. "Cameron won't let anything happen to you."

Grace warmed from head to toe. "I know."

It was well before lunch when Cameron came into the house. She hadn't seen him since he'd picked up Pat and the kids. Instead, he'd been outside tending to the animals with Dylan and doing some minor repairs on the paling fence near the chicken run. She wasn't sure if Pat sensed a change in their relationship. But Grace could feel it with every fiber in her body.

"Are you ready to go?" he asked when he appeared in the doorway.

Grace nodded. "Although I need to get my cap."

Pat moved across the kitchen and grabbed a hat off a peg near the door. "Take this," she offered. "Much better to keep the sun off your face."

Grace took the battered wide-brimmed hat which looked like one her sister-in-law, Callie, often wore. "Er—thanks."

By the time they reached the stables Grace was so nervous her hands were sweating. The horses, both tacked and tied up, seemed huge and ominous.

"The hat," he said, motioning to the object in her hand. "You actually need to put it on."

Grace looked at the hat. It was old and shabby and she had no inclination to put it on her freshly washed hair. In fact, she had become accustomed to her new, all-natural hairstyle. "Oh, I don't think—"

"Wear the hat." He took it from her and plonked it on her head. "I insist."

Grace caught his smile and was just about to playfully protest again when his phone rang. He answered the call and spoke for barely a minute. When he was done he was frowning.

"Something wrong?" she asked.

"Lauren."

His sister. "Is there a problem?"

He shrugged. "Nothing much. Come on, let's get going."

It took a few minutes, but Grace was finally in the saddle. It was one of the Western types, so at least she had a horn to hang on to. And she was pleased the horse appeared to have a calm temperament and good manners.

"I haven't done this for twenty years," she told him.

"You'll be fine," he assured her. "Just follow me."

Clearly an accomplished rider, he reined his mount to the left and headed through an open gate behind the stables and into a wide pasture. It was a picture-perfect late-autumn day. The sky was clear blue, the air crisp and clean. The ground was reasonably flat and grassy with the occasional outcrop of rock and thankfully Grace's horse followed Cameron's. After a few minutes she'd convinced herself to loosen up. And she liked watching him. As with everything he did, he looked relaxed and confident.

"Where did you learn to do this?" she asked as they steadily walked.

"My mother's folks owned a farm out west. I'd go there during school break."

How little she knew about him. A memory clicked in. "They're both gone now?"

"Yeah," he replied. "They died within a few weeks of one another. After fifty years of marriage they couldn't bear to be parted I guess."

It was a romantic notion. Fifty years together—as companions, lovers, friends, parents…what an incredible legacy to leave behind. It softened something inside her and being with Cameron got her thinking. He wanted her like she'd never been wanted before. He'd whispered words against her skin, drawn pleasure from every part of her and given her the confidence to let go of her inhibitions. And now, as she rode with him in the afternoon sunlight, for the first time in her life Grace wondered if she actually could have it all.

Chapter Ten

"So, what did your sister want?" she asked, shifting her mind from images of them making love and imagining happily-ever-afters. Her question sounded impossibly nosy and she was surprised when he answered.

"Giving me a lecture."

Grace immediately tensed. Did his sister know they were together? Was that why Lauren had called her brother? The horse sensed her tension and responded by breaking into a trot. She caught her balance and rose from the saddle every second beat before collecting the reins and easing the gelding back.

Cameron was beside her in a flash. "Are you okay?" he asked and lightly grabbed one of her reins.

"I'm fine." Grace took a breath. "A lecture about what?"

He released the rein. "My mother wants to know if I'm going to the Jakowski family reunion."

Grace had a vague recollection that his entire extended

family got together every year. "Oh, right. It's tradition for you to all meet once a year?"

"Yep."

Grace tilted her hat back. "Well, it should be a good day."

"Maybe."

She pulled back fractionally on the reins. "Isn't it usually?"

He shrugged. "I haven't been for the past few years."

Grace eased the horse to a halt. Cameron took a few more paces to stop and then turned the toffee-colored gelding around. Head to head, the horses nuzzled one another.

She stared at him. "But isn't the day a big deal for your parents? And all your other relatives, like your grandparents and cousins and such?"

"I guess."

Grace took a deep breath. She sensed his energy changing. He didn't want to talk about it. However, she did. "Let's stop for a while," she suggested. "There's a spot over there near those trees. We can tie the horses up."

Without waiting for him she clicked the horse forward and trotted toward the trees. Once they were both dismounted she handed the reins to Cameron and waited for him to securely tether the animals.

She found a rock beneath the shade of a tree and watched as he retrieved two small water bottles from his saddlebag. Once he joined her she spoke.

"Tell me why you don't go. And tell me the truth."

Cameron didn't want to admit to anything. "It's complicated."

She took off her hat and raised her brows. "That sounds like something I'd say. You don't do complicated. So, 'fess up."

He smiled at her words. This was a new Grace. A little playful, even though she regarded him with serious eyes. He liked it a lot. But he wasn't quite ready to admit the truth.

"I'd rather not talk about it."

"Too bad," she shot back.

Cameron sucked in a frustrated breath. "Because it's a *Jakowski* family reunion."

She stared at him. "And?"

"And I'm not a... I'm not really a Jakowski."

It was the first time he'd said the words out loud. In the past he'd been asked the same question and always used excuses like work commitments, or lack of time. But he wouldn't lie to Grace.

And she asked another hard question. "Because you were adopted by Franciszek?"

Relentless, he thought and inhaled. "Yes."

"Do you actually believe he regards you as anything other than his real son?"

He shrugged. "I never said it was rational."

She grabbed his hand and Cameron felt the connection through to his blood. Her nails tapped on his palm. "You were what—three years old when he married your mother? So that's thirty-three years of being your father. Not that I'm an expert on parenting, but I don't imagine he'd be anything other than incredibly proud to call you his son."

He knew she was right...in his head. But the last time he'd attended the family reunion he'd realized he was the only one there not related by blood, aside from respective spouses. The extended Jakowski clan was large and traditionally Polish, where bloodlines and birthright were important. And that blood didn't flow through his veins. It was why he wanted his own family, his own children.

And Grace, he knew, did not.

"Like I said, not rational."

She linked their fingertips. "You know, you don't hold back telling me what I should do—my family not knowing about the accident as an example. So, here's a little of that back at you—you *should* go. Because they're your family and they love you. If that's not enough, then go out of respect for Franciszek, who loved you enough to want to call you his son and give you his name. And out of respect for the man you have become."

Shame hit him squarely between the shoulder blades. She was right. So right. He knew he hurt his parents by not attending. He had a sudden idea. "Would you go with me?"

"Go with you?" she echoed. "Like a…date?"

"Yeah…my date. My friend." *My girlfriend.* He felt about sixteen years old just thinking it.

She managed a wry smile. "I'll…think about it."

When he leaned forward and kissed her it took about five seconds for Grace's brain to kick in. He cupped the back of her neck as she returned the kiss, tasting her lips for the longest time. Finally they pulled apart. She was breathing hard, taking deep puffs into her lungs.

"Let's keep going," he suggested and pushed away the thoughts she had of lying down on the soft grass and making love with him. "The horses will get restless if we stay here."

She nodded, grabbed her hat and stood. Within minutes they were back in the saddle and headed east. They stayed out for a couple of hours, mostly walking through fields that belonged to an adjoining landowner.

When they got back to the farm she left the horse in his care and returned to the cottage.

Grace had blisters on top of blisters. Horseback riding. A great idea—*not*.

She ached all over and as she peeled off her jeans she grimaced at the red and angry blisters formed on the insides of her calves. She figured the ones on her behind would be worse. Just how was she supposed to rub the aloe vera there?

Pat had chopped off a leaf from the overgrown plant by the house when Grace had hobbled from the stables.

"Are you okay?"

Cameron stood in the doorway of her bedroom. His eyes briefly darted to the unmade bed before returning to her face. To his credit he didn't stare at her near-naked bottom half. Her sensible skin-colored briefs disguised little. She pushed the jeans aside with her feet. "Fine."

He nodded and looked like he was doing his best not to smile. "Need any h—"

"Fine," she muttered. "Like I said."

He pulled something from his back pocket and held it out to her. "Balm—for the sore spots," he explained. "Only use a little, it's pretty powerful stuff."

Grace took the tube. "Thanks."

Once he left she sank onto the bed. She needed thinking time.

They were lovers. Did lovers spend an afternoon riding horses, laughing together, enjoying one another's company? Did lovers attend family gatherings like the one he'd asked her to attend with him? Grace was more confused than ever. In the past she'd always been well into a relationship before having sex. Making love before making any kind of commitment. And her history of commitment was one of *noncommitment*.

Their differences seemed suddenly insurmountable. She had a life in New York...Cameron's life was clearly in Crystal Point. She was desperate to regain her edge again, to go back to work and be successful. Cameron wasn't career driven in the same way. She knew he liked being a police officer and was exceptionally good at it—but it didn't define him. And he wanted the kind of woman she could never be.

She showered, hoping to clear her thoughts, and then applied some balm before she changed into gray-and-pink sweats. Her hair seemed to have a life of its own and framed her face in a mass of curls. No makeup. All natural. It felt right in so many ways. And that was the core of her growing dilemma. Her two worlds were clashing. And she didn't know which one would claim her.

"Hungry?" Cameron asked when she walked into the kitchen.

He'd also showered and changed into loose-fitting jeans that sat low on his hips, and a white tank shirt. "Yes. What's on the menu?" she asked as her gaze lingered on his broad shoulders.

He held up a casserole dish. "Just have to heat it up. You could set the table."

She did the task quickly and grabbed sodas from the small refrigerator. As she moved around the room Grace was again struck by how normal it all felt. She couldn't remember ever experiencing such a strong sense of companionship with anyone before.

During dinner and the few hours that followed they talked, laughed and made out for a while on the small sofa. Grace relaxed in his arms as they watched television and sipped coffee. Afterward he took her to bed and made gentle love to her.

They planned to leave midafternoon Monday, which still gave them a couple of hours in the morning for Cameron to continue painting while she spent some study time with Emily. Cameron took Pat to the hospital to collect Thomas at nine o'clock, and while he was gone she and Emily abandoned the books and roped Dylan into helping them with the decorating. By the time Cameron returned she was rinsing out brushes by the back door.

"You're done?" he asked, staring down at her from the top step.

Grace craned her neck around. "I'm done."

"Good job. We'll leave after lunch if that's suits you?"

"Of course. I need to clean up and pack first."

By one o'clock Grace found herself deep in Pat's full arms. The older woman was returning to Crystal Point the following day with Emily and the other children. "Make sure you stay in touch. I know my granddaughter is thriving at her schoolwork with your help." Pat made her promise to stay connected. "It's been wonderful having you."

Grace blinked at the hotness in her eyes. In just days she'd become unexpectedly attached to the harried-looking woman and her grandchildren. "I will," she assured her. "Thank you for having me—I've enjoyed being here."

She said goodbye to the children, lingering with Thomas, who was still a little weak from his ordeal, but assured of a full recovery. She made a date with Emily for a brief lesson on Tuesday afternoon, mindful that she'd agreed to watch Noah's kids that evening. Jed lay on the backseat as Cameron stowed their bags in the trunk and then they were on their way. She watched as the kids waved frantically when they drove off and Grace swallowed the hard lump in her throat.

The return drive took a fraction over three hours. The familiar sight of the Pacific Ocean as Cameron crested the road heading into Crystal Point was unusually comforting to her. He pulled up outside the B and B. Five minutes later her bags were upstairs and they were staring at one another across the small lounge room.

"Everything okay?" Cameron asked perceptively.

Grace nodded. "Of course."

"Scott and Evie will be back next week, right?"

She nodded again. "Monday. I'm looking forward to seeing Evie."

He rubbed his hands together. "Well, I guess I'll talk to you soon."

The mood seemed too casual. Too polite. He wasn't suggesting they continue to see one another. He wasn't suggesting anything. In fact, he looked as though he couldn't get away from her quick enough. "Sure."

He left without another word.

Grace spent over an hour with Emily on Tuesday afternoon. They talked about the previous weekend and Thomas's accident. Emily told her Cameron had visited Pat that morning to check on them. She didn't respond to the information—and didn't admit that she hadn't heard from him at all since he'd dropped her off the day before. Once she was certain the teen had a study plan for the rest of the week, she showered, pulled on jeans, a collared pale blue T-shirt and navy zipped sweater and headed for Noah's house. She was surprised by how happy the kids were to see her, and then remembered the gifts she'd given them last time and was touched when Hayley made her promise to read the book that she said was now her favorite.

It also struck her how nice it was to be an aunt. She'd never really taken the time to get to know her brother's kids. Her trips back to Crystal Point were usually short and infrequent and she always brought work with her. This time was very different. So many new experiences were filling places in her heart—places she was only now prepared to admit were empty. Even the time she spent with Emily had its own reward. The teenager was doing so well with her studies and Grace knew she'd ace her upcoming exam. Thinking she had played a small part in that made her feel good about herself. And genuinely happy for Emily. She'd even made some inquiries about fashion design school for her.

"There's food in the refrigerator. And we shouldn't be too late," Noah told her. Dressed up in a suit her brother looked handsome, and she told him so. "Thanks for doing this."

"My pleasure," she said and straightened his tie. "Have fun."

Callie came into the living room, stopped and stared at her. "You know, your hair looks good like that."

She'd forgotten to straighten her hair that morning. "It's my holiday hair," she said and pushed her curls back. Once she was back in New York, once she was back in her apartment, everything would return to normal.

Then why does this feel normal, too? Why did a weekend with Cameron and Pat and the kids feel like a glove that fit my hand perfectly?

"The twins haven't been in the bath yet," Callie told her. "But they are under strict instructions to behave."

Bath? Right. How hard could it be? She put on a smile. "No problem. Enjoy the night."

"Thanks again," Noah said as he kissed her cheek and then quickly ushered his family outside.

Five minutes later the twins announced they were hungry for dinner and Grace was just about to herd them into the kitchen when the doorbell rang. She told the kids to stay in the living room and went to the front door.

Cameron stood on the threshold. "Hey."

Her stomach flipped over in that way she'd become used to whenever he was near. "What are you doing here?" she asked, letting him into the house.

He shrugged. "I got you into this babysitting gig," he said with a grin. "I thought you'd like some backup."

She couldn't help the smile that tugged at the corners of her mouth. Couldn't help remembering what had happened between them over the weekend. Couldn't help wanting more. Which made it one massive complication.

Grace nodded. "You prepare dinner and I'll get them into the tub."

He gave a lopsided grin. "Good luck."

"What does that mean?"

He chuckled and followed her into the living room. "Don't turn your back."

"My back? I don't under—"

"Uncle Cameron!"

The kids were clearly delighted to see him and when he swung Matthew high in the air the little boy laughed hysterically. Hayley wasn't about to be excluded and clamored for attention. He hauled them both in his arms for a moment and zoomed around the room making *vroom vroom* noises. Grace stood by the doorway. He really was remarkable with children and as she watched him an odd and unfamiliar feeling bunched down low in her belly.

Children had never figured in her life agenda.

Love had never figured either.

She sucked in a breath. *Love.* Impossible. She wasn't about to fall in love. Not in Crystal Point. And not with Cameron. It was just sex. A holiday romance at best. She'd been vulnerable and sought comfort in his arms. Only a fool would think it was more than that. Only a fool would want more.

And only a fool would be mad at him for not calling her for the past thirty-six hours.

"You know where the kitchen is," she said to him and then put on her best serious aunt face. "Come on, you two. Bath time."

They groaned as Cameron set them on their feet and raced around the room for a minute before she was able to usher them down the hallway. By the time she got them into the bath, washed, dried off and changed into pajamas, nearly an hour had passed. The kids had thrown water at her when she tussled with them about washing their hair and Matthew wailed about the soap in his eyes. At the end of it she was wet and short on patience.

"Everything all right in here?" Cameron asked from the doorway of the twins' bedroom.

"Everything's peachy," she lied and finished buttoning Matthew's pajama top. "How's dinner looking?"

"All set," he replied and held out his arms for Hayley. "How do my famous cheese-and-bacon hot dogs sound, kids?"

Her niece raced toward him and climbed up. "Yay, Uncle Cameron."

Good old Uncle Cameron. Grace set her teeth together. The man could obviously do no wrong. She smiled extra sweetly and by the look on his face he knew, damn him, that she was close to tossing a shoe in his direction. "Let's go."

"After you," he said and stepped into the hall so she could pass.

Despite her determination to not like his cooking, she had to admit the hot dogs were the most fabulous she'd ever tasted. They were so good, in fact, she ate two.

Later, once the kids had their fill, Cameron took them off to tuck them into bed with a book for half an hour before they had to go to sleep. It gave Grace a chance to clean up the kitchen and put on a pot of coffee.

He returned twenty minutes later, didn't look the least bit harried and she pushed back a stab of resentment. He did everything with a kind of casual ease she suddenly envied.

"Is it exhausting being good at everything?" she asked when he perched against the counter.

His expression narrowed. "Is that a dig, or a question?"

She poured coffee. "I'm not being snippy."

"Really?" He took the mug she offered. "You know, there's no angle to getting along with people. You just do it."

She raised a brow. "You mean *you* just do it."

"Well, it doesn't help that you've got a Back Off sign stamped on your forehead." He grinned and then drank some coffee. "You've handed things pretty well this past week. You certainly got along with Pat and the kids."

"Strangers aren't as complicated as family or…"

"Lovers?" he suggested when her words trailed off.

Grace looked into her mug. "I was going to say *friends*. But I guess we've changed those boundaries now."

He looked into her eyes. "Friends? I'm not sure we've ever been that, Grace. But we can try…if that's what you want."

The thing was, she wasn't sure what she wanted. They'd crossed a line and she wondered how she'd ever face him when she returned to Crystal Point in the future. What would happen when he married and had children? It's what he wanted. And even though those plans had never figured into her own life, Grace knew it would be painful to see him settled with a wife and children.

Because…

Because her feelings had somehow become muddled. What she wanted had never seemed so unclear. She looked at him and felt his stare through to the blood in her veins.

If only…

If only I was a different kind of woman.

"Grace?"

"Sometimes I wish…I wish things were different."

"Things?" he prompted and placed the mug on the table.

She drew in a shaky breath. "Me. I wish *I* was different."

He stilled. "Why?"

"Because then I wouldn't want to run so far away from you one moment, and run straight toward you the next."

Cameron fought the urge to haul her into his arms. Her admission hit him squarely in the chest. Her behavior confused him. No surprise there, he figured, as women had been confusing men since the dawn of time. He'd spent two days wondering if he'd made the biggest mistake of his life by making love with Grace. Because now he wanted her more than ever.

"I guess you need to decide which one you want to do more."

She stared at her feet. "That's not helping."

"Do you think I'm going to make this easy for you?"

She looked up. "I'd hoped you would."

"Not a chance."

"Even though we both know the odds of this working out are…are…" She stopped and quietly drew in some air. "I live in New York and you live here. And despite this…this attraction between us, I don't want what you want."

Cameron edged toward her. "How do you know what I want?"

"Because I just know," she said on a breath. "You want to settle down and have a family and I've never—"

"Never is a long time, Grace," he said, moving closer as he cut off her words.

She put down her mug and backed up against the counter. "You want me to be blunt? Here it is—I don't want children," she said and he heard the rattle in her voice. "And you do."

"Aren't you jumping the gun a bit, Grace?" he teased. "There's a whole lot of other stuff that comes before having babies."

"I know that it's—"

"Like marriage," he said quietly. "And spending more time together than one weekend."

He watched, fascinated as her cheeks bloomed with color.

"But I thought—"

"You thought what?" he asked, cutting her off. "That I want more from you? You're right, I do. But only if you want to give it. I can't help wondering why you are so determined to *not* have a baby?" he asked and looped a hand around her nape.

She met his gaze. "Because a baby and a career don't mix. And since my career would always come first, that's no way to raise a child. I don't have that built-in *baby* gene like Evie or my mother."

He rubbed her neck softly. "So, never?"

"Never. Like I said."

"Then I guess we're doomed," he said and kissed her.

She sighed against his mouth and moved closer. Cameron gently pushed her back against the counter and cradled her into the crook of his shoulder. She fit so perfectly and was made for his arms, but he held back the words he wanted to say.

She's not ready...

And there was no guarantee she ever would be.

"I'm gonna miss doing that," he said and trailed his mouth to her cheek. "A lot."

She trembled. "I have to go back to New York. I'm not staying here."

"So you said," he whispered against her ear.

"I meant it."

Cameron nuzzled her neck. "But you're here now."

She made a sound, half groan, half sigh. "You're trying to confuse me..."

"I'm not trying to do anything," he said and nibbled her lobe. "Other than make out a little." Cameron found her mouth again and kissed her soundly. "But since I'm on the night shift for the next few days I really have to get going," he said, and pulled back. "I'll see you Saturday, around eleven."

She shook her head. "Saturday?"

"We have a date, remember?"

"A date?"

"The Jakowski family reunion picnic," he said and figured he had to get away from her as quickly as possible. Otherwise he might be tempted to do a whole lot more than kiss her neck. "You said you'd come with me."

Her brows shot up. "I said I'd think about it."

He half smiled. "And?"

"And…it's probably not a good idea," she replied. "It might give the impression that we're…you know, sleeping together."

"We *are* sleeping together."

"Really?" She crossed her arms. "I don't know about you, but I've been sleeping alone this week."

Cameron tried not to laugh. She was mad at him. Good. At least she was feeling *something*. "Missing me, then?" He let the words hang in the air for a moment.

"Not at all."

Her resistance made him ache for her, "Sure you are," he said and grabbed his keys. "I'll see you Saturday, eleven o'clock."

She still looked like she wanted to bail on their plans, but she nodded. "Okay… Saturday."

Then he left.

On Saturday morning Cameron picked Grace up from the B and B. True to his word, he hadn't called her. It hadn't been easy. But he'd done some serious thinking.

She was leaving in a week and he was running out of time. He knew she was fighting it…fighting him. She didn't want babies. She didn't want a relationship. She didn't want to stay in Crystal Point.

And yet, they had an incredible connection. He felt it deep within his bones. It *was* the kind of connection that could last a lifetime…if only she would let it.

Grace wasn't exactly smiling when he pulled up. She got into the car and strapped on the seat belt.

"I thought you might have stood me up," he said.

"A deal is a deal."

"Still mad at me?"

She looked straight ahead. "Jerk."

He laughed. "Well, it promises to be an interesting day.

How are things going with you?" he asked. "Told your folks yet?"

"No," she replied. "But it's you we're here to work on today, remember?"

He remembered. Cameron had a knot in his stomach thinking about it. He would much rather take Grace home and make love to her all afternoon. "I remember."

She frowned and then her mouth was slowly drawn into a smile. "You could have called."

"But we're doomed, remember?"

She shifted in her seat. "I'm here now," she said, reminding him of his words a few days earlier. "And still here for another week."

"Does that mean you'll be wanting my attention?"

"Jerk," she said again and crossed her arms. "I've changed my mind about you. You're as impossible as always."

He grinned. He loved that about her. Loved that she had so much spirit.

When they arrived at the park he spotted his parents' sedan and knew his mother would hyperventilate once she saw him with Grace.

"Everything okay?" Grace asked as he walked around the back of the car.

She smiled and he was quickly bedazzled. "I'm good. Just waiting for my mother to ask what my intentions are."

"And what will you tell her when she does?"

Cameron's hand stilled on the picnic basket he was pulling from the backseat. His three weeks were nearly up and the words he wanted to say remained unspoken. But he knew he needed to get them out soon. He had a plan and he was going to stick to it. He grabbed the basket and closed the door. Grace had insisted they stop at the only organic deli in town and he watched as she organized the bewildered-looking girl behind the counter and pulled together a gourmet hamper.

He gazed at her as she collected a blanket and her bag, and admired how incredible she looked in a skirt, blouse and a bright red button-down sweater. His heart rate rose instantly.

"I'll tell her we've stopped hating one another," he said when she reached him.

"I never hated you," she said and stopped beside him. "Not really."

He touched her hand. It was their first touch in four long days. "No?"

"It was easier than facing the truth." She shrugged. "What can I say. I'm a coward."

Cameron squeezed her fingers. "You survived for two days alone and hurt in that car wreck. One thing you're not, Grace, is a coward."

She gave a brittle laugh. "It was only afterward that I fell apart."

"Which doesn't mean you lack courage."

Her eyes glittered and she pulled her hand away. "Yes, well…we should get going."

The reunion was in full force. About seventy relatives had turned up and tables topped with bright checkered clothes and crockery had been set up beneath a pair of giant trees. Away from the barbecues a group of children played and he spotted his father knee-deep into a game of Twister with a few of his great-nephews.

He saw his mother at one of the tables, sorting through plates and cutlery. She looked up as he approached and he knew the exact moment she realized Grace was at his side. Her surprised stare turned into a genuine wide smile.

She came around the table and hugged him close. "Good to see you here. Your dad will be pleased."

Guilt twinged between his shoulders. It had been four years since he'd shown his face at a Jakowski reunion. "Yeah. I brought—"

"Grace," his mother said, moving from him to take Grace's hand. "Wonderful to have you here with us. You look lovely as always."

"Thank you, Rennie."

All of the Preston siblings called Cameron's mother Rennie, rather than using the more traditional aunt label, which was often given to older, close family friends. "I believe you're looking after the B and B until Evie and Scott return from their honeymoon next week?"

"That's right."

"And Trevor?" Irene asked of Evie's sixteen-year-old son.

"He's staying with his grandparents up north for another week."

Cameron saw his mother's brows go up. "How lovely that they have a grandson to visit them."

He shook his head. "Two minutes."

Irene gave an innocent look. "What?"

"Two minutes before you pull out the no-grandchildren card." He smiled. "You're slipping, Mother."

He could see his mother's mind working in overdrive. Could see her mentally planning weddings and baby showers and happily-ever-afters. He placed the basket on the table and tried to ignore the sudden acceleration of his heartbeat. Because he'd imagined them, too. By the time Lauren sidled up beside him, his mother had ushered Grace toward an adjacent table of relatives and was introducing her to a few of his cousins and their spouses.

His sister pinched his arm. "Just checking that you haven't turned to stone."

He frowned. "What?"

Lauren's brows snapped up. "I couldn't believe my eyes. Of all the women I would ever expect you to be with, she isn't one of them."

Cameron held on to his temper. "She has a name. And I thought you liked the Prestons?"

Lauren shrugged and her blond hair bounced around her face. "I like Evie and Mary-Jayne. And Noah," she said, and then let out a breath. "And Grace, I suppose. Don't mind me. I wallow in self-pity a lot these days. It keeps me company."

"Sorry, kid," he said and rested an arm around her shoulders. "I know you've had it tough."

"That's still no excuse for being mean," Lauren said, then squeezed him back. "Even if I have always thought one look from those green eyes could turn a mortal man to stone."

He grinned. "She's not what you think."

Lauren's eyes glazed over. "People rarely are, I guess. But I thought you hated each other."

"Nope."

Cameron stayed at Lauren's side, but his gaze moved to Grace. As she mingled with his relatives he realized nothing fazed her. The boardroom, his bedroom...a park filled with Jakowskis. She was effortlessly confident, supremely adaptable and worked the crowd as though she had known everyone for years. But he'd seen the other Grace, too—the haunting, vulnerable woman who'd fallen apart in his arms.

"Whoa," Lauren said and tapped his shoulder. "That's a look I haven't seen before." She made a face. "You really do like her?"

"I really do like her."

I love her. And he figured his sister had probably worked that out, too.

Chapter Eleven

Grace allowed herself to be paraded around on Irene's arm. After they'd done the rounds of most of the relatives and spent a few minutes talking with a somewhat breathless Franciszek, they headed back to their table.

"Do I have you to thank for getting Cameron here today?" Irene asked as she pulled lids off plastic containers filled with assortments of cold chicken, potato and green salads and delicious-looking coleslaw.

Grace smiled and pulled a tray of cheese and smoked ham from the basket they'd brought. "He wanted to be here."

"That's sweet," the older woman said. "Although not exactly true. I know my son. But I'm grateful to you for making him see sense." She sighed. "He thinks I don't know why he avoids coming. But I do."

"I'm not—"

"My husband loves him just as much as he loves Lauren." Grace managed a smile. "I think he knows that."

"I hope so. Is Cameron hoping you'll distract me?" Irene asked and smiled. "You might encourage me instead." She paused and then quickly got straight to the point. "Are you dating again?"

Again? So she did know about their past relationship. "Not exactly."

"Sleeping together?"

Grace's skin burned and she dropped her gaze. "Well, I—"

"Your mother is my closest friend, Grace," Irene said quietly. "If you and my son are involved then I'd like to know about it."

"We're...just..." She shrugged helplessly. "I don't know what we are for sure."

Irene tapped her arm. "I know Cameron. And I know you. I hope it works out the way you both want."

But we both want different things.

When they sat down for lunch she was seated between Cameron and his uncle Henryk. Unsurprised to discover Cameron could speak Polish, Grace laughed as she stumbled over the pronunciation of words he tried to teach her. He placed a hand on her thigh under the table and didn't move it for the entire duration of the meal. The awareness between them had been building all morning and so had her need for him. His desire for her made her feel both safe and scared and connected to him in ways that had her heart beating madly.

Later, while Cameron walked off to speak with his father, Grace remained with Irene and Lauren and helped clear away the leftover food. She knew both women were curious about her relationship with Cameron. When Irene wandered back to the car to grab a wicker hamper, Lauren stepped beside her.

"So, you and Cameron, huh?"

Grace placed the lid on a half-eaten tub of pasta salad. "Am I in for an interrogation? If so, I already had one of those from Rennie."

Lauren raised both brows. "You're both of age. You can do what you like."

"But you don't approve?"

"I love my brother," Lauren said quietly. "And I wouldn't want to see him get attached to someone who's not going to hang around."

Like you.

The other woman didn't have to say it. Everyone knew her life was in New York.

Everyone knew she'd never settle for a life in Crystal Point.

"I don't want that either," she said and stacked the tub into a basket.

"I hope so," Lauren said, clearly acting protective of her only sibling. "I know we've never really gotten along. But for Cameron's sake we should probably make an—"

"I'll fold the tablecloths," Grace said, desperate to shut down the conversation. She looked around for Cameron and found he was on his way toward them. She drew in a relieved breath, grabbed the brightly colored cloth from the table and started folding.

He joined them and sidled up beside her. "Everything okay?"

Grace glanced at Lauren, who'd now moved to the other side of the table packing up picnic chairs. "Fine."

"I'll take you home when you're ready."

She glanced at her watch, saw that it was after four and figured there was little point in lingering. She certainly didn't want to answer any more questions from Lauren or Rennie. Grace nodded and he took a few minutes to say goodbye to his family while she finished packing. By the time they were back in the car and on their way to Crystal Point it was half past the hour.

He was quiet and she wondered about his mood. It was hard to tell. Their relationship had changed so much in the past two weeks. The old Cameron she knew and was prepared for. She'd always handled the insults and sarcasm. But now things were different.

When they pulled into the driveway at the B and B the silence between them was deafening. He grabbed the basket from the backseat and headed to the side of the house and toward the door that led to the private living area upstairs. The sensor light flicked on and she pulled out the keys. Once inside, he followed her up the stairs and into the kitchen and adjoining living area.

He placed the basket on the counter before spinning around to face her. He looked tense. Maybe angry.

"Is everything all right?" she asked quietly.

"Sure."

She twisted her hands together. "So, today wasn't too bad."

"You're right, it wasn't." He was unreadable, impenetrable. The only sign that he was feeling anything was the tiny pulse beating in his cheek.

"Would you like coffee?" she asked, desperate for conversation.

He moved across the room and hovered in the doorway. "No, thank you."

Inside the small room the tension between them escalated instantly. He returned her stare, blistering and intense, and so hot it almost burned through to her very soul.

Her breath caught as realization hit. It wasn't anger that held him from her, kept him distant. It was something else. Something she'd only glimpsed once before—the time when she'd been in the bathtub. Since then, every time he'd looked at her, touched her, kissed her, she'd felt his restraint. He'd always handled her gently, as though he sensed her lingering inhibitions. Every touch had been for her—her pleasure, her needs.

This, she thought as her blood pumped with urgent anticipation—this was desire, raw and powerful. This was need generated from long days apart. This was another level, another place, another kind of connection she'd never experienced before.

He wants me.

"Cameron...I—"

"Come here."

She stilled at the sound of his softly spoken command, felt the heat in the room rise up and sweep through to her bones. The only sounds were her heels clicking over the tiled floor as she stepped toward him.

He reached for her, moving one arm around her waist as he drew her close. "I've missed you." His mouth hovered an inch from hers. "So much."

"I've missed you, too."

He fisted a handful of her hair and tilted her head back. When he kissed her, hot and hard and deep, Grace pressed against him. Her blouse got crushed in the onslaught but she didn't care. All she felt was him...his hands, his mouth, his tongue demanding hers. She gave herself up, felt his surging need and matched it. Grace dug her hands into his shoulders as he swiveled around and trapped her against the door frame. She moaned low in her throat, wild with need and an aching hunger for him that boiled her blood. He managed to push her sweater off her shoulders in between kisses and toss it aside. Her blouse gave way beneath his fingers as buttons popped. She didn't care. She wanted his hands on her skin. She wanted him around her, over her, inside her.

Once the blouse was gone her bra was next. Cameron tugged at the straps and pushed them down over her arms. Her breasts rose up to meet his mouth and his hot breath against one nipple, then the other, drove her beyond coherent thought. Her skirt and briefs were quickly dispensed with and Grace gasped as he picked her up rested her against his hips. She wrapped her legs around him and rocked, felt his arousal and rocked again.

She waited while he snapped the top button and zipper on his chinos. Then he was inside her, plunging deep, taking her on a wild ride. Grace wasn't sure where he got the strength to hold her as they moved together, but with one hand braced against the door frame and the other around her hips, he supported both their weights. Pleasure built, skin burned on skin, and when it came she let herself go. Driving, aching, seeking the release she craved, Grace clung to him as they came together in a shattering wave of white-hot bliss.

It seemed an eternity before their breathing returned to normal. When he finally released her and set her on her feet, Grace realized that while she was completely naked, except for her bra settled around her waist, he was still fully clothed. He didn't release her, though. He tucked her head beneath his chin, steadying her with one arm, the other still rested against the door frame.

"Where's your bedroom?" he asked hoarsely after a moment.

Grace motioned down the hall and within a second he lifted her again and held her against his chest. Once in her bedroom he placed her gently by the foot of the big bed. She stayed perfectly still as he discarded his clothes. The lamplight dappled the hard contours of his shoulders and arms and she thought how she'd never seen a more beautiful man in her life. Longing rose up and hit her directly in the solar plexus.

Grace pressed against him. "Cameron…"

"I want to make love to you."

She sighed out a breath. "Isn't that what you just did?"

Cameron grasped her chin and tilted her head back. "That wasn't so much making love as it was my need for you."

"And mine for you," she admitted on a whisper, coloring hotly. "I've never done anything like that before."

He rubbed her cheek. "I'm sorry. I don't usually let that part of my anatomy do my thinking."

Grace bit her bottom lip and smiled. To be desired so completely, so urgently and with so much unabashed passion was highly erotic. For the first time in her life she completely rejoiced in her sexuality. He gifted her immeasurable pleasure and she suddenly longed to return that gift. She wanted him to feel what she felt—complete abandonment, total trust and mind-blowing ecstasy.

She pulled back and linked their fingertips. "Come with me," she urged and led him into the bathroom.

When she flicked on the jets of the double shower spray and pulled him into the open cubicle he raised both brows inquiringly. "What did you have in mind?"

Grace laughed, pushed him gently against the tiled wall and circled her palms over his pectorals. "Whatever I want," she said, kissing a trail from one small budded nipple to the other.

Laughter rumbled in his chest. "Throwing down the gauntlet, Grace?"

She nodded and kissed lower. He was already aroused, already hers to take. "And if I am?"

He raised his arms and braced against the wall. "Whatever you want," he invited softly.

Grace smiled and eagerly took up the challenge. Tenderness and desire transcended through her fingertips, her lips, and her tongue. He offered her moans of encouragement, and when he could take no more, when she felt his control slip, Grace gave him all she could. In that moment she had the power, the potency in her touch to bring him to his knees as release claimed him, and she held him through the pleasure, giving him her strength and the feelings that were in her heart.

* * *

Four hours later Cameron was in the small kitchen making scrambled eggs.

Which look as scrambled as my brain at the moment.

Grace sat on the other side of the counter on a stool, wrapped in a fluffy robe, sipping a glass of wine. With her hair mussed, her eyes a kind of hazy green and her lips the color of cherries, she looked delectable. She smiled at him over the rim of her glass.

"Pleased with yourself, are you?" he asked as he stirred the eggs.

A dreamy look washed over her face. "Hmm?" She shrugged and the robe opened, showing the hint of cleavage.

Cameron did his best to concentrate on the cooking and not her exposed skin. "You know exactly what I mean."

She smiled again, deep and alluring. "It's no secret to you that I've had a fairly repressed sex life." She put down her glass. "Until now."

It was quite the admission. "Why?"

She shrugged again. "Control, I guess. I could close off and only give the parts of myself I was certain wouldn't make me vulnerable."

Cameron pulled the eggs off the heat. "Being vulnerable isn't weakness, Grace."

"I'm starting to realize that."

He came around the counter, grabbed her hands and swiveled the stool ninety degrees. "Can you let go of your control long enough to think about your future?"

His heart pounded as he spoke. He'd had days to plan what he wanted to say to her. But the moment he'd picked her up that morning it confirmed what he wanted to do. What he'd planned to do since they'd returned from Burdon Creek.

"My future?" The tremor in her voice was unmistakable.

"Our future," he said and moved between her legs, pulling her close.

She drew in a long breath and tilted her head. "I don't understand what—"

"Grace," he said as his heart thundered and Cameron took as much air into his lungs as he could. "I've spent the past sixteen years denying what I feel and I—"

"Cameron, I think we should—"

He place two fingertips against her lips. "Let me finish," he said gently. "I have to say this, Grace. I've been working out ways to say this to you for the past week. For a long time I've been pretty casual about how I viewed relationships. I didn't allow myself to get seriously involved with anyone. I kidded myself that I didn't want anything permanent, or any woman to mean more to me than some good times and sex. But that's not really what I want."

She stared at him, unmoving.

"At Evie's wedding everything changed." He touched her cheek and ran a thumb along her jaw. "All those years of fighting and insults and antagonism…it was as though I'd woken up in a reality where none of that stuff existed. And now I want permanent, Grace. And I want it with you," he said, cradling her hips intimately. "These past couple of weeks I've felt an incredible connection with you. Tell me you felt that, too?"

"I did," she whispered. "I do."

His grip tightened. "Then let's not waste that feeling, Grace. A lifetime ago I let you go even though I knew it was the last thing I wanted. And before I had a chance to tell you how I really felt about you." His thumb moved over her cheek and he smiled. He stroked her face one more time before he reached into his pocket and withdrew a small box. "I love you, Grace. Marry me?"

The world tilted on an axis and Grace felt like she was falling. She didn't, though. He was there, in front of her, holding her against him. His brown eyes were dark and rich. He flicked the box open and Grace saw the most perfect ring, a brilliant white diamond surrounded by superbly cut emeralds.

"The green stones are the same color as your eyes," he said and watched her as she continued to stare at the box. When she didn't move he spoke again, slower this time. "But if you don't like it we can change the—"

"I like it," she said quickly and drew in a sharp breath. "I really do." Emotion clogged her throat. And the *yes* she wanted to say so much danced around in her head. "But… Cameron…I…I…"

He pulled back, suddenly pale as he put space between them. "Are you saying no?"

Grace wobbled on the stool and then slid to her feet. "No… Yes… I mean, I'm not saying… I'm just saying—"

"You're saying what?" he asked, cutting her off.

"It's just so unexpected," she said quickly. "So fast…"

"Fast? We've been dodging around this for years. I love you…I'd hoped you loved me back."

Grace pushed back her shoulders and slowly moved across to the living room and sat on the sofa. Cameron remained by the kitchen, a trillion miles away.

"Please, come and sit down," she said and tied the robe tighter.

He nodded, came across the room and sat beside her. Grace took a breath, the longest she could. She wanted to touch him. She wanted to feel the safety of his arms around her. Instead she stared at the jewelry box he still held in his left hand.

"I know how hard that must have been to say," she said quietly. "And if I wasn't leaving next week, things might be different. But I—"

"So we can make them different, can't we?"

Another breath. Another dose of steadying oxygen in her

blood. "How? I have a life in New York. And a career I can't simply discard."

He stayed silent for a moment, absorbing her words. "Okay…you have a career. We'll work around it."

She met his eyes. "How can we do that? Your life is here. My life is there. And we both want different things." Grace grabbed his hand and the jewelry box lay between their palms. They were connected by a ring that part of her desperately wanted, but another part of her knew she couldn't take. "We both know what kind of wife you want, Cameron. One who lives in Crystal Point, for starters. And one who wants to settle down and raise a family with you. That's not me. That won't ever be me." Emotion burned her eyes. "I'm sorry. But I've never pretended to be anything other than who I am. I just can't be that kind of woman."

Despite knowing he was getting exactly what he should have expected, Cameron felt like he'd been punched in the gut. He pulled air into his lungs. "And that's it?"

Her hand moved off his. "I know it's not what you want to hear."

Cameron jumped up and the ring he bought her rolled to his feet. He left it there. "No, it's not."

She looked at the small velvet box and picked it up, holding it for a moment before she placed it on the low glass table in front of her. "My career has always been all I am. And I have to go back and prove to myself that I can do it again. For the first time in months I feel strong enough to do my job properly. Please try to understand."

He did understand. She was rejecting him. Again.

"Ambition above all else?" he asked, pulling a tight rein on his hurt and disappointment.

"Of course not," she replied. "But I've not made any secret of that fact that I intended to go back."

Cameron experienced a strange pain in the middle of his chest. She'd made up her mind. She was leaving. He'd lost her. Again.

"And tonight, Grace? Is it your way of saying goodbye? Chuck in some last-minute hot sex before you pack your bags and leave everything behind?"

"I'm not that—"

"What?" he shot back abruptly, cutting her off. "Cold?"

She looked instantly wounded and Cameron's insides burned with a hollow pain. He didn't want to upset her... not intentionally...but he was angry and disappointed and plain old hurt.

"You think I'm cold?" she asked in a quiet voice. "After everything we've... After tonight and every other time we've been together?"

"Don't confuse sex and love, Grace."

She stood up quickly. "What do you want me to say to you? That I'm torn...of course I am. This is the hardest decision I've ever had to make."

Annoyance began to weave down his spine. "Really? It seems fairly cut-and-dried."

She wrapped her arms around herself. "I didn't lie to you. I didn't make any promises. You know how I feel about marriage and children. I've worked hard to get the career I wanted. And now...now I have to prove that I can do it again without falling apart like I did after the accident." She sucked in a long, heavy breath. "I don't expect you to understand... you've never failed at anything."

I've failed to get your love.

"Of course I have," he said roughly.

"I mean you've never failed to be anything other than yourself," she said tremulously. "Last weekend with Pat and her grandchildren, I really saw you for the first time. I saw that you're funny and charming and incredible with kids and so unbelievably comfortable in your own skin. Wherever you go, you belong."

Cameron stilled. "I'm not sure what that has to do with you turning down my proposal."

"Everything. Nothing. It's just that you know who you are. And I'm a slightly neurotic, overachieving control freak who has never really belonged anywhere except in the life I've made in New York. Whenever I come back here it reminds me of how different I am from everyone else. Most of my life I've felt as though I have been stuck in between worlds."

He knew that about her and his heart lurched. "Then, how about we meet somewhere in the middle?"

She took a shuddering breath. "How can we? In the middle there's an ocean."

"It's just geography, Grace."

"It's more than that," she refuted. "It's about you being an important part of this community. And the kids like Dylan and Emily—they need you. I could never ask you to change or give up being part of that. Just like I can't change what defines me."

Cameron took four steps forward and reached her. He grasped her shoulders and molded the bones beneath his hands. He wanted to kiss sense into her. He wanted to love her until they weren't sure where she began and he ended.

"That's a cop-out, Grace. This isn't about the job or anything other than the fact you're scared to death to really feel something for someone. That's why every relationship you've had has been lukewarm. You chose the doctor and the suit because they didn't threaten your little safe world where you don't have to let yourself be seen for who you really are."

The truth hit Cameron with lightning force.

"I get it now," he said, releasing her. She shuffled back slightly. "I finally get why you came back. It's not about the car crash or your friend's death or because a therapist told you to spend time with your family. You simply don't want anyone to work out that you're not perfect. But now you've regrouped, right? You have your strength back—you've faced what happened in the accident and you want to dive straight back into that life. And by doing that you can once again turn your back on this place and everyone in it."

"I didn't turn my back on Crystal Point," she snapped, emotion bared in her eyes. "I was *sent* away."

He stilled. "What?"

"I was sent away," she whispered this time as she sank back onto the sofa. "To school."

"School? You mean—"

"I mean boarding school," she said, cutting him off. "I mean to a place where I didn't know anyone and where I was put in a class higher than my age because I was considered too smart, too advanced for my normal grade. A class where I was first tormented and then ignored for being younger and smarter…and different. And I'd come home for holidays and my family would all be here—this fabulous tight-knit unit— a unit I wasn't really part of. I was told how lucky I was to be getting such an amazing education. And they were right. I did get the best education possible." Tears glittered on her lids. "But when school was over and I came back I felt so out of place…so distant. That's why I couldn't stay."

The question he'd pondered a thousand times came out. "So it wasn't because of us?"

"No." She shook her head. "It was never about that. In so many ways you were the only reason I wanted to stay." She took a long, steadying breath. "But I knew you were getting serious and I got scared."

"Scared of what?" His insides crunched. "Of falling in love?"

"Of failing to be…more," she admitted unsteadily. "Of not living up to the expectations of my parents, my teachers…

and even myself. I had to live the life that had been planned for me. If I didn't, it meant it would have been a waste to send me to that expensive school. And I couldn't do that to my parents. But when I came back…"

He knew what she meant. "I got in the way?"

She shrugged. "I left quickly because I didn't want to get in any deeper."

His back straightened. "And still don't, clearly."

She held the velvet box in both her hands. "Please don't be like this. We can have tonight…tomorrow…"

"You know," he said quietly, resignedly, "I've pretty much loved you since you were sixteen years old. But I'd just joined the police force and I knew you weren't ready for a relationship. So I waited a couple of years—waited until you were old enough. When you came back from school and we started dating I thought it would lead to a life together. But you told me then that nothing would keep you in Crystal Point—especially not a small-town police officer. So I guess things haven't changed all that much." He took a deep breath and tried to not think about how much he ached inside. "Goodbye, Grace."

Without another word he turned around and walked out of the room. And out of her life.

Chapter Twelve

When Evie and Scott arrived home on Monday, Grace heaved a sigh of relief.

Her flight back to New York was booked and although she was glad to have a few more days to spend with her sister, she also wanted to go home. *And New York is my home.*

She thought Evie looked exhausted and told her so. They sat together in the kitchen, sipping the peach iced tea her sister had begged for.

"I'm fine, honestly," Evie insisted and patted her bulging belly. "Just tired from the trip home. I did nothing but relax and get pampered by my lovely husband while we were away."

"You've popped out," Grace said as she looked at her sister's stomach. "And still a month to go."

"Three weeks," Evie replied. "I wish you were staying until then."

Grace drank some tea. "I have to get back to work. So, tell me about the honeymoon."

Evie grinned. "Everything?"

"Well, not *everything*."

Her sister laughed. "It was romantic in a mostly non-amorous kind of way." Evie rubbed her palms across her abdomen. "What about you? What did you get up to while we were away?"

I made love with Cameron Jakowski. Again and again. Oh, and I got a marriage proposal, too.

"Not much," she lied then explained about babysitting Noah's kids and tutoring Emily.

"Babysitting?" Evie's steeply arched brows rose significantly. "Really?"

"Don't look so surprised."

Evie smiled. "I'm delighted, not surprised. The twins are adorable. Notorious at dinner and bath time, though."

"Mmm…well, I had a little help."

"Help?"

Grace drew in a breath. "Cameron stopped by. He cooked dinner while I was on bath duty."

"Cameron did?" Evie's eyebrows went up again. "And?"

Grace shrugged as the weight of her suddenly complicated life pushed down heavily on her shoulders. "And we had dinner and then he left."

"That's not what I meant. What else has been going on with you two?" her sister asked with way too much intuition. "And don't bother denying it. After what happened at the wedding I wouldn't be surprised if—"

"I slept with him."

Evie's green eyes almost popped out of her head. "Oh—I see. And what else?"

She took a few seconds before she told her sister of the weekend at Burdon Creek, Thomas's accident and briefly mentioned how she and Cameron had become close.

"But why did you agree to go in the first place?" Evie asked.

She wasn't about to admit to Cameron's little bit of blackmail. "To help Emily."

Her sister clearly wasn't convinced. "Another thing I don't understand. Since when have you been a math tutor?"

Grace met her sister's gaze. "She needed help to pass a makeup exam. I'm good with numbers."

"I know that. You're the smartest person I've ever met. But you don't usually get…involved…with what other people are doing."

Now Grace raised a brow. "Is that a nice way of saying I'm a self-absorbed neurotic with little time for anyone other than myself?"

Evie smiled. "Well, I might not put it exactly that way."

"But the gist is the same? Yes, I know what I am. I know what people think."

Evie smiled again and drank some tea. "Well, who cares what others think. I love you for who you are. We all do."

Grace swallowed a thick lump in her throat. Shame and guilt pressed down on her shoulders. She felt like such a coward. She'd returned to Crystal Point and then run from the truth. As she had done over and over. If she was to be with her family and try to heal the disconnect she'd felt most of her life, then she needed to really *be* with them. She needed to let them in and admit she was scared and vulnerable and hurting.

She needed to tell them about the accident.

Cameron was right. Thinking about him brought a deep, hollow pain to her chest. His words resonated in her head over and over.

I love you, Grace. Marry me.

He loved her. It was the first time a man had ever said that to her. And the first time she'd ever wanted to say it back.

"What?"

Evie again, looking way too intuitive. Her sister could be relentless when she wanted to know something. "It's nothing." She took a deep breath. "I'd like to go to our parents' tomorrow night. There's something I need to tell you all."

Then she could go home.

"I hear she's leaving next week."

Cameron sat in the kitchen of his parents' house. His mother stood on the other side of the granite counter, looking at him over the rim of her reading glasses. Irene Jakowski always got straight to the point.

"So I believe."

"And you're letting her go?"

He ignored the jabbing pain at his temple. "Let's not do this."

"I didn't raise a quitter. I raised someone who became the kind of man who goes after what he wants."

Until I got my heart crushed.

"I can't make her feel something she doesn't," he said flatly and stared into the coffee mug in front of him.

Irene tutted impatiently. "If you want her you should fight for her."

"I also can't fight against her ambition," he replied and pushed the mug aside. "She's made it pretty clear what's important in her life."

"Cameron," his mother said, gently this time. "The Grace I saw at the picnic didn't seem too interested in her career. She couldn't keep her eyes off you. You're made for one another—you always were. Besides," Irene's eyes grew wide and she smiled. "I want grandchildren. With Evie's baby coming soon, Barbara will have six little angels and I don't have any. Soon I'll have nothing to talk about with my best friend."

Cameron smiled at his mother's sense of drama. "I didn't realize you were so competitive with Barbara Preston."

"Of course I am," she replied with a laugh. "What else do you think we want to talk about? Kids and grandkids are our staple diet of conversation. At least, it would be if you decided to settle down and supply me with some."

"Maybe you should try your luck with Lauren?"

"Hah," his mother scoffed. "Your sister has convinced herself she's a man-hater after that fiasco with what's-his-name. You, on the other hand, have an opportunity to be with a perfectly lovely girl who just happens to be the daughter of my best friend."

"Since when did you become the president of Grace's fan club?" he asked, trying to diffuse his mother's enthusiasm.

"Since I realized that you're in love with her."

He wasn't about to deny it. Irene Jakowski could see a lie through thick fog. "She's made her choice."

She took a breath. "And when did you become so black-and-white? You negotiate and work through problems every day in your job with those troubled kids you help. You don't give up on them—you don't give up on anyone. What about Dylan? Isn't he another example of keeping faith in what you believe? You wanted to help him and you did. You helped that entire family get back together. Don't the same rules apply in your own life?"

Her point had biting accuracy. "It's not the same thing."

Irene took off her glasses. "Oh, I see…bruised that monumental ego of yours, did she?"

"I don't see what—"

"You're as bad as your father. Did you know he dithered around for months before he asked me out and when I said I had plans he didn't bother to ask me again? I waited three weeks and then I asked him. Then I stood him up just to make a point. He got mad for about two days and then came back groveling. And he proposed marriage three times before I finally accepted him. Good thing, too."

"Is there a point to this?"

"My point," she said slowly, "is that women, even the most complex women, like to be wooed. Chased, pursued...call it whatever you like."

"And if she turns me down again?"

Irene grinned. "Go woo some more."

Cameron laughed for the first time that week. Irene Jakowski always said what she thought. Woo her? But he knew his mother was right. He had quit. Grace had announced her intention and he'd bailed, he'd walked off to lick his wounds in private.

Fat chance of that in this family.

He wanted to see her again. He wanted to hold her again. But he knew Grace...he knew the more he pushed the more she would resist.

"She's going back to New York," he said flatly.

"So, follow her."

Cameron stood and pushed the chair out. "I have to go," he said and grabbed his keys. "Thanks for the coffee." His kissed his mother goodbye and left.

Grace was incredibly touched by the support she got from her family when she told them about the accident, Richard's death and her ensuing breakdown. They sat quietly and listened as she spoke of the two days she was trapped inside the car and the fear that she would die before she was found.

"Why didn't you say something earlier?" It was Noah, her most practical sibling, who spoke.

"At first I was in shock about what had happened. And then...I was embarrassed that I'd fallen apart," she admitted and looked up from her spot on the big sofa. "Anyway, I apologize for shutting everyone out."

"Grace," her mother said and grasped her hand, patting it gently. "Even though you live thousands of miles away, you're still very much a part of this family. If you had called we would have been there for you."

Of course they would have. In her heart she knew that. But the feelings of disconnect she had from when she was sent to boarding school had caused her to close up like a vault. But right now, more than ever before, Grace knew she was loved. Everything Cameron had said was true. Grace could have wept. "I know," she said and managed a tight smile. "And thank you for understanding."

Except when she drove Evie back to the B and B, she couldn't miss the deliberate silence from her sister.

"Okay," Grace said as she pulled into the driveway and turned off the engine. "Say what's on your mind."

"Is there any point?" Evie asked and let out an exasperated breath as she unclipped her seat belt. "I can't quite believe you, Grace. Maybe our parents and Noah and M.J. were too stunned to say anything back at the house—but I'm saying it now—what gave you the right to exclude us so deliberately? You could have been killed. One of us should have been there—heck, we *all* would have been there if you'd only said something. A phone call. Even an email. Would that have been so difficult?"

"No," she replied softly. "You have every right to be angry."

Evie touched her arm. "I'm not angry. I'm...hurt. Don't do it again, Grace. Don't treat us like we don't matter."

Grace was about to apologize again when Evie winced. "What is it?"

"Nothing," her sister assured her and then touched her belly. "Only, I'm thinking the backache I've had today isn't backache."

"What do you—"

"I think I'm going into labor," Evie said on a rush of sharp breath. "You might want to go inside and tell my husband. And also tell him not to forget my bag," she added.

Grace was out of the car with lightning speed.

Sure enough, Evie did go into early labor. Grace stayed at the hospital through the night and was the first person to be told that her sister had given birth to a healthy baby girl.

Evie's husband, Scott, emerged from the birthing room to give her the news.

"They're fine," he said and ran a weary hand though his hair. "The baby is three weeks early, and she's…she's…" He stalled and took a deep breath. "Perfect."

"Congratulations," Grace said and found herself in the middle of a huge bear hug.

She didn't pull away. The old Grace would have balked at hugging anyone, let alone her brother-in-law. But she'd changed. Her prickles were…well, less prickly.

The ice princess had finally begun to thaw.

She left the hospital and headed back to the B and B to shower and change and give the new parents some time with their baby. But that afternoon she returned for a visit with her sister and took only minutes to be persuaded to hold the baby, who had been named Rebecca.

"She's so beautiful, Evie," she said, holding baby Rebecca close. A tiny tuft of dark hair stuck out above the top of her soft pink wrap and Grace touched her head gently.

Evie sighed contentedly and pushed back against the pillows. "I know. I can't believe she's finally here."

"And there were no complications during the birth?"

"Not one. She was eager to come into the world. Although I'd forgotten how tiring the whole thing can be. It's been sixteen years since I had Trevor."

Grace looked at her niece and smiled warmly. "Well, you did great. And Scott?"

"Poor darling." Evie's face lit up. "I sent him home to get some sleep. He's mesmerized by how perfect she is and has been staring at her for most of the day."

"He's a first-time father so I guess that's to be expected." Grace glanced at her sister and smiled. "It's really good to see you so happy."

Evie nodded and adjusted the front of her nightgown. "What about you? Do you truly believe going back to New York will make *you* happy?"

With her emotions bubbling at the surface the last thing Grace wanted to do was break down when Evie was experiencing so much joy. She put on the stiffest face she had. "It's where I live."

"That's not exactly an answer. Is it what you want?"

What I want? Grace didn't know. Holding the baby brought up so many feelings, so many longings. Her womb was doing a whole lot of uncharacteristic backflips and she suddenly found herself doing the unthinkable—actually imagining having Cameron's baby. The very notion brought heat to the back of her eyes.

"I wouldn't be doing it if I didn't think it was for the best."

Evie's mouth twisted. "I know you better than that. What exactly happened between the two of you?" her sister asked. "And don't just tell me you slept with him. There's more, I know it."

Grace touched Rebecca's face and marveled at the softness of her skin. She drew in a shaky breath and told her sister the truth. "He proposed."

Evie's huge green eyes bulged. "Cameron asked you to marry him?"

"Yes."

"And what did you say?"

Grace pushed back the emotion in her throat. "I said I was going back to New York."

"You turned him down?"

"I...guess I did." The pain of the words struck deep and Grace gathered her composure. "We can't have a relationship when we live in different countries, let alone a marriage."

"You could stay," Evie suggested. "Or you could ask him to go with you."

Grace didn't bother to hide her surprise. "His life is here."

"And yours is in New York? Yeah, yeah, I get that. I just don't understand why there can't be a middle road."

"Because...because there just can't. Cameron's life is in Crystal Point—his job, all the work his does with kids... I would never ask him to change who he is."

"And you won't change for him?"

She shrugged.

"Do you really hate Crystal Point that much?" Evie asked.

"I don't hate it," she replied quickly. "I just don't...fit in."

"Look at you," her sister said gently. "You're holding your niece like she is the most precious thing in the world. And for the past two weeks you've been running the B and B, baby-sitting Noah's kids and helping a young girl pass her exams. Does that paint a picture of someone who doesn't *fit in?*" Evie sighed. "You know, love is sometimes about compromise. You do love him, right?"

Grace pushed back tears and looked up, denial hanging on the edge of her tongue.

Evie's gaze narrowed. "Well, even if you won't admit it, I'll bet my boots you do."

Her gaze dropped immediately. "You know I—"

"Don't let anyone know what you're feeling...ever?"

The old Grace would have jumped all over her sister's words. But Evie was so right it hurt through to her bones. "I guess I don't," she admitted, thinking about the small velvet box in her handbag. She'd carried the ring with her since the night he'd asked her to marry him. Sometimes she opened the box to look at it, never quite having the courage to put the ring on her finger—afraid that if she did she would be forever changed.

"Like I said," Evie continued, "compromise. And sometimes one has to give and one has to take. It's not a competition, Grace, I mean to see who has to change the most…it's just the way it is. When Scott moved his life from California to Crystal Point he did it with an open heart. He did it because he *loved* me. And I am grateful for that every single day."

Grace touched the baby's soft hair. "But you had this beautiful girl on the way," she reminded Evie. "That's a big incentive for anyone."

"Love is enough, Grace. You just have to let yourself believe it."

I'm not that brave—I wish I was. Grace snuggled Rebecca against her chest and inhaled the sweet baby smell. She was a wondrous thing and she couldn't get enough of her soft hair and rosebud mouth. All her adult life she'd insisted that children weren't in her future. And now, as she held the newborn infant, Grace experienced a longing so deep and so acute her heart actually ached.

There was a brief knock on the door and Evie invited whoever it was to enter.

Grace almost hyperventilated when the door swung open and Cameron strode across the threshold. He stopped when he saw her and the flowers in his hand dropped to his side. He looked at Grace and then the baby she held in her arms.

The room spun momentarily. Her breath caught, making a sharp sound which echoed around the walls. Grace's heart surged. She hadn't seen him in what seemed like an eternity. In that time she'd experienced every emotion possible—from despair to anger and then a deep wrenching pain. And as he watched her with blistering intensity all of those sensations pulsed through her blood. Time stalled, drawing them both into a moment of acute awareness. With the baby held against her, Grace knew what he was thinking.

This could be our child one day.

A hollow ache rushed through to her bones. Her womb rolled, taunting her with the possibility of what *could* be. Like a speedy camera she saw it all so clearly—the home, the children and the happiness she'd always been afraid to want.

"Hey, Evie," he said, breaking the contact between them as he walked toward her sister, kissed her cheek affectionately and handed her the flowers. "Congratulations on your new addition."

Evie was appropriately grateful and glanced at Grace. United in loyalty, she recognized her sister's questioning look. Grace forced tears back and concentrated on the baby while Cameron and Evie spoke. She couldn't look at him. She was raw. If he said a word to her Grace knew she could break down and cry. And that wasn't an option. Not in front of Evie. And not in front of him.

Dressed in uniform, he'd obviously come straight from work. He looked so attractive and she was struck with images of how she'd often imagined stripping his blues off.

She stiffened when he approached and admired the baby from barely two feet away. The familiarity of him assailed her senses. His hair that she loved running her fingers through. His broad shoulders and arms which had somehow become a safe haven. Everything about Cameron made her want… made her need. She took a steadying breath as she stood.

"Cute kid," he said easily. But Grace wasn't fooled. His shoulders were tight, his jaw rigid. She knew he was hanging by the same thread she was. The temptation to run into his arms became a powerful force and it took all her will to keep a rein on her emotions.

Grace had placed Rebecca in her mobile crib when Evie spoke again.

"Would you like to hold her?" her sister asked Cameron.

His hand immediately rested on the pistol holstered at his hip. "Not while I'm wearing this," he said evenly. "I'll wait until she's home."

Evie nodded. "Well, I think I might take a little walk," she announced suddenly. "I need to stretch my legs. Look after Grace and my angel for a few minutes, will you, Cameron? I'll be back soon."

Grace watched as Evie shuffled off the bed, touched the sleeping baby on the cheek for a moment and then quietly left the room.

"That was subtle," he said once the door closed.

Grace swiveled softly on her heels. "You know Evie."

He raised both brows inquiringly. "You told her about us?" he asked. "I'm surprised."

Grace shrugged and moved across the room to stand near the window. "She's my sister. I tell her things."

He looked instantly skeptical. "You didn't tell her about the accident until yesterday, though, did you?"

"You know about that?"

"Your mother called mine. Mine called me."

Grace shrugged. "Well, everyone knows now, so no more secrets." From the window she spotted a view of the neighboring parklands and tried to concentrate on the scene and not think about how messed up her thoughts were.

Silence stretched like elastic.

"Do you know what I thought when I came into this room and saw you holding the baby?"

She didn't turn. Didn't move. Rebecca's soft breathing was all she heard. And the dreadful silence that grew in decibels with every passing second. She knew exactly what he'd thought. Because she'd thought it, too.

Cameron spoke again. "I thought how beautiful you looked holding the baby. And then I wondered how could I get you to stay? How could I get you to change your mind and give this…give us, a chance?"

Grace turned around and faced him. "You can't."

"I know, Grace," he said, keeping his voice low.

Her heart lurched forward. But she wouldn't break. "I'd like us to still be…friends."

"Friends? You're kidding, right? Since when have we ever really been friends?"

She drew in a shaky breath. "We could try," she whispered.

Cameron stepped toward her. He reached up and touched her cheek. "I don't want to be your friend, Grace. I want to be your lover and your husband and the father of your children. I want you to be the first person I see when I wake up in the morning. I want it all, as scary as that sounds to you. But that's what love is, Grace…having it all, wanting it all."

She nodded, although she wasn't sure how. "Cameron, I—"

"But I know that's not what you want."

Grace closed her eyes. It would be easy to fall under the spell of his gentle touch, his comforting voice. She opened her eyes again when he released her and met his gaze head-on as he stepped back. The growing distance quickly pulled them apart.

"I want…" Her voice cracked. *Like my heart is cracking.* "A part of me…a part of me does want those things." She looked at the baby and experienced a sharp longing so severe she had to grip the edge of the crib for support.

"But?"

She swallowed hard and stared at Rebecca. "But my career—"

"Comes first? Yeah—I got that, Grace."

"No one gets both," she said quietly, suddenly numb.

He didn't say anything. The tension coursing through him was palpable and vibrated around the room. Grace longed to touch him, to reach for his face and hold him between her shaking hands. It had been so long since they'd touched and her skin ached with the need to feel the heat of his body. But she didn't move. Didn't dare ask him to take her in his arms.

What if we never touch again?

"In your world…I guess not," he said quietly.

The door opened and Evie walked back into the room. She hesitated for a moment, clearly sensing the tension in the room, and then plastered on a big smile.

"How's my girl?" she asked cheerfully and walked across to the crib. "Did she miss me?"

Grace pulled her composure together. "She's been a perfect angel." She touched Rebecca's tiny head for a moment before she grabbed her handbag. "I'll head off." She hugged her sister close, hanging on for as long as she could, feeling Evie's innate strength and unquestioning love. "I'll see you soon."

Evie nodded. "Sure."

She didn't look at Cameron. If he saw her eyes, if he were to look deep within her he'd know she was on the brink of a meltdown. She took a gulp of air, said goodbye to her sister and muttered another in his direction and left the room. And she didn't take another breath until she was halfway down the corridor.

Evie Jones's stare made it clear to Cameron that he was in for an earful. He tried to ignore it. "Your daughter is beautiful, Evie," he said and stepped around the mobile crib. "No doubt Scott is—"

"Can I ask you something?" she queried, cutting him off, hands firmly on hips.

He took a second to respond. "Ah—okay."

"Are you really in love with my sister?" she asked bluntly. He stilled. "Well, I—"

"Because if you are," she said, cutting him off again, "you've a strange way of showing it."

Cameron had always liked Evie. But he wasn't about to get into a conversation about his feelings for her sister. Even if he understood Evie's motives and natural loyalty toward Grace. "She's made her choice."

Evie harrumphed. "Looks like you have, too," she said with bite. "To act like a jerk, I mean."

Why was it that all the women around him seemed to be dishing out insults and advice? First his mother, now Evie. "What did Grace tell you?"

"Enough," Evie replied. "And I know my sister. Better than you do, by the looks of things."

Cameron reined in the irritation weaving up his spine. "I know she wants her career more than...more than anything else."

"Rubbish," Evie scolded, not holding back. "What she wants—what she's always wanted, probably even before she knew it herself—is you."

It was exactly what he wanted to hear. But Cameron wasn't about to get sucked in by Evie's romantic notions. "I know you're trying to help, but—"

"What I'm trying to do," she said, making no attempt to stop interrupting him, "—is understand why you've given up on her so easily."

That got his attention. "And what exactly do you suggest I do, beg her to stay?"

Evie blew out a weary breath and looked at him intently. "If that's what it takes."

Cameron swallowed hard. "I can't do that."

"Even if it means you could lose her forever?"

I've already lost her. It was a ridiculous conversation. "I thought I'd done enough when I asked her to marry me."

"She's scared of...feelings," Evie said with a sigh.

"I know she is," he said and pushed back the pain behind his ribs. "But I can't do any more."

Evie didn't look surprised by his words. "Can't? Or won't?"

"She made her choice."

"I see. So this is about pride?" Evie asked.

Heat rushed through his blood. "It's about knowing when I'm beat."

She'd rejected him again and he wasn't about to go back for another dose. Not now. Not ever.

Chapter Thirteen

New York greeted her with same bright lights and never-ending energy that she remembered.

Grace holed up in her apartment for three days before she pulled herself together, dressed in her best power suit and hightailed it back to her office. Her assistant had a stack of emails, files and interoffice memos waiting for her. There was enough work to keep her busy for the next two months, including weekends.

At least I won't have time to think about anything else.

Or anyone.

Or someone.

She pushed herself all day and when her boss came into her office around four carrying two foam cups of coffee, Grace closed down her laptop and stretched her shoulders.

"So, how was the vacation?" Jennifer Mullin-Shaw asked as she passed her the coffee.

Grace had worked for Shapiro, Cross & Shaw for eight

years. Jennifer had been made partner fifteen years earlier and was the epitome of a committed, successful career woman. For many years Grace had wanted to emulate the other woman. She wanted to be a partner one day. She wanted the money and prestige and to be respected among her peers the way Jennifer was. A couple more years and she knew she'd get there.

"It was fine," she said and drank some coffee.

"And you're feeling better?"

"Fine."

Jennifer, always business, nodded. "So, you're fine? Ready to get back to work?"

Grace pointed to the computer. "I've enough to keep me busy for the next few months."

Jennifer sank into the chair opposite her and looked over the rim of her cup. "There's a spot opening up. Kurt's moving to Chicago. Better salary, bigger office. Interested?"

Grace straightened. Five weeks ago she wouldn't have hesitated to say yes. Five weeks ago she wanted the bigger office and better salary.

Five weeks ago she wasn't prepared to admit she was hopelessly in love with Cameron Jakowski.

"Of course," she said with as much enthusiasm as she could muster.

"It means more high-profile clients," Jennifer said as both brows came up. "Which equates to longer hours and pretty much means you can say goodbye to your personal life. Are you ready for that?"

"Sure."

Jennifer nodded and stood. "Good. I'll talk to Jim and Harris," she said of the two other partners in the firm. "And we'll make it official next week. Congratulations, you've earned this."

Grace got to her feet. "Thank you."

The other woman headed for the door, but turned before she crossed the threshold. "Are you sure you're okay, Grace? You seem distracted."

"I'm fine," she assured her. "Just a little jet-lagged."

"Well, I'm pleased the vacation did the trick for you. It's good to have you back."

As she watched Jennifer disappear her insides were strangely empty.

Grace could barely believe it. A promotion. A new office. She'd arrived at the pinnacle of her chosen profession. It was everything she'd worked toward. *I'm back. I made it.* She should have been jumping through hoops.

Instead, she had a hollow spot in the middle of her chest that seemed to be getting deeper and deeper each day. Five weeks ago she'd returned to Crystal Point, broken and afraid. Miraculously, she'd healed those wounds and made peace with her guilt and fear. Life moved on. *She'd* moved on.

And still the hollowness prevailed, settling behind her ribs, making her remember how she got to be standing alone in her office. And what she'd left behind. In the window Grace caught her own reflection. The black suit, killer heels, perfectly straight hair. All she saw was a stranger, a facsimile of a woman she'd once been.

I have the career I've always wanted. I have the life I've always wanted. It's here, for me to take.

And yet…another life now beckoned. A life she missed. And suddenly she longed to be that woman again. The woman who'd felt like she was really part of her family for the first time. The woman who'd helped Emily ace her makeup exam and who'd spent a crazy weekend with Pat Jennings and her adorable grandchildren. The woman who'd left her hair to create its own curly madness and loped around in paint-stained clothes. And the woman who'd experienced such an acute connection with Cameron she could barely draw breath without remembering how it felt to lie in his arms.

She'd been so determined to not feel anything and to not be derailed, but as she looked out the window, Grace knew she was the world's biggest hypocrite. Because she'd told Emily it *was* possible to have it all. In that last week during their tutoring sessions she'd spouted speeches about having both a career and a family. A career and a personal life.

Do as I say, not as I do.

Memories bombarded her. Bathing the twins. Sharing tea with her mother. Jed loping beside her. Emily looking so proud of her achievements. Holding Evie's baby. And Cameron.

The man I love.

The man she'd always loved. Even at eighteen. Or sixteen, when he'd kissed her for the first time. And through the years where their relationship had been fraught with insults and goading and so much simmering tension.

And he's in love with me, too.

The city below made noises she couldn't hear from the lonely spot in her ivory tower. And as if a great wave of peace had washed over her, Grace knew exactly what she wanted.

She packed the laptop into her case and flung it over her shoulder, grabbed her handbag and jacket and left the room. A few minutes later she tapped on Jennifer's office door and was quickly beckoned inside.

"Grace?" The other woman looked at her bags and jacket. "You're heading off?"

She took a deep breath and a smile curved her mouth. "Actually…I'm going home."

"I can't believe I passed that exam."

Emily's excitement was great to see and Cameron nodded. "I told you that you would."

"I know," she said, and shrugged. "You and Nan both believed I could do it. And Grace."

His back stiffened. It was hard to hear her name. Harder still to not think about her twenty-four hours a day. "Just keep hitting the books and you'll get a good final grade."

"Good enough to go to night school I hope," Emily said cheerfully and bounced Riley on her knee. "Grace made some inquiries for me when she was here."

"She's special, that one," Pat said from her spot at the table and looked directly at him. "But I guess you know that already."

Cameron had dropped Dylan home after the Big Brother meeting and stayed for coffee. He hadn't planned on every part of the conversation being about Grace. "I've organized the moving truck for next Tuesday," he told Emily, ignoring Pat's question as politely as he could.

"Great," the teenager said. "I can't wait to get my own place." She quickly patted her grandmother's hand. "Not that I don't like living here with everyone, because I do. But it will be awesome for Riley to have his own room. And once I get my driver's license I can come and see you all in Burdon Creek every few weeks."

It was a good plan, and one he'd help see through to fruition. They were a strong family, despite the challenges they'd faced, and Cameron knew they'd be okay.

"You know," Pat said and stirred her tea. "I hear New York's quite the place to visit."

He didn't miss the point. "I'm not much for big cities."

No, he was small town. Grace was big city. Oil and water. He should have known better, right? In some ways he knew he'd been waiting for her rejection since that night on the beach. And she hadn't disappointed. His pride took another battering. So he'd bailed.

In every other part of his life, in every other part of himself, Cameron was rational and reasonable. He forgave, he compromised, and he fought for what he believed in. But this was different. Because he'd told Grace he loved her and she hadn't said the same. She hadn't admitted anything. She'd made him hurt and he felt that hurt through to the marrow in his bones. It was excruciating, soul destroying. He was a small-town police officer and that wasn't enough.

His love wasn't enough.

He wasn't enough.

Just like he hadn't been for his father.

Cameron's breath suddenly twisted like a knot in his chest. Damn. There it was—the real reason he'd let her go without a fight. In a way it was the same reason he worked so hard to be a good man...to prove his worth. To override the loss of the father who hadn't wanted him. That's why Grace's rejection when they were young had affected him so deeply. Because he'd felt like he wasn't worthy, like he wasn't enough to have her love. Then resentment and dislike had kicked in and he'd spent the next fifteen years behaving like an incomparable ass.

Until she'd come back and he'd realized that he still loved her, still wanted her, and more. He needed her. Like the air he breathed. Like water he drank. Grace was in his blood, his heart, his soul. And he missed her perfectly beautiful face.

But what could he do? Pat's idea was out of the question. He wasn't about to hightail it to New York to face the blunt force of another rejection—no matter how much he wanted to see her.

Only a crazy man would do that, right?

Grace was back in Crystal Point. It was late Sunday afternoon when she pulled her rental car outside her parent's home. There were several other cars out front, including the familiar sight of Cameron's electric-blue Ford sedan. She knew from Evie that her mother had organized a party to celebrate Rebecca's arrival.

I can do this, she thought as she headed through the front door.

She heard the party coming from the back patio area and made her way down the hall. Grace found her mother in the kitchen and dropped her bag on the counter.

Barbara swiveled around instantly. "Grace!" she exclaimed, quickly looking her over, clearly taking in Grace's disheveled appearance as she came around the counter. "What are you doing here? Are you okay?"

Grace accepted her mother's warm embrace and held on. When she pulled back the other woman's expression was one of deep concern. "I've been so foolish. And so blind."

Barbara frowned slightly. "What do you mean?"

Before she could reply heels clicked over tiles and they both stepped back. Irene Jakowski walked into the kitchen and came to a stunned halt. "Grace...you're here?"

Grace swallowed a lump in her throat. "Yes," she whispered.

Irene smiled warmly. "Good girl."

She managed a smile and her breath came out as a shudder when she looked toward the doors that led outside. "Is... is he..."

Irene nodded and squeezed her arm. "He is."

She took a few steps forward. "Thank you."

Barbara Preston watched her daughter walk outside and turned to her best friend. "What was that all about? What does it mean?"

Irene grinned broadly. "I think it means that one day you and I will probably be sharing grandchildren."

Cameron had walked through the family room and onto the back patio when he heard someone call Grace's name.

Stupid. He heard her name everywhere. On the street. On the television. In his dreams.

But this caught his attention. He stopped in the doorway and looked around.

And there she stood.

Like a vision. A beautiful vision with her hair curling wildly around her face. She wore jeans and an old shirt. *His* shirt he realized after a microsecond. *She's wearing my shirt. She's here and she's wearing my shirt.* His heart almost burst through his chest.

The dozen or so people on the patio all stilled. And stared. She stared back, from one to the next. And then she found him with her gaze. In that moment no one else existed and his mind soared with a hazy kind of hope. He fought the urge to go to her, staying back, head spinning.

She's here.

Cameron's gaze flicked to the group of curious people watching her...taking in her hair and clothes and the faintly expectant expression on her face. She did look different than the Grace they were used to. They were used to the usual perfection of her immaculate clothing and straight hair. Funny, but she always seemed perfect to him. His mind was bombarded with memories—Grace in the morning, her hair spread out on his pillow. A sleepy Grace who couldn't keep her eyes open as they watched television together. Grace coming apart in his arms when they made love.

"Can I...can I talk to you?" she asked hesitantly, looking only at him.

The twenty feet between them suddenly seemed like a huge divide—especially with their respective families watching on the sidelines. Maybe he should have suggested they go inside. But he didn't want to move...he didn't want to shift the incredible contact throbbing between them.

"Okay...talk."

Her eyes widened and glittered. She wouldn't do this in front of her family. Or would she? He tried to be cool and rested one shoulder against the doorjamb and watched as she swallowed hard.

"Here?"

Cameron nodded. "Here."

She glanced at the sea of curious faces watching their exchange and shook her head fractionally. Cameron looked across the patio and saw Evie nodding, almost prompting her sister to continue. He watched and panic rose when she stepped back. She turned on her heels and walked toward the door to the house. His mother was there. As was Barbara Preston.

After a moment she turned again, back to him. Relief pitched in his chest when he saw strength in her eyes.

"You were right," she said quietly and crossed her arms over his paint-splattered shirt. "About me. About everything."

Cameron waited, breathless.

"I *have* always wanted to be perfect," she stressed, looking at him. "But after the accident I was so far from that. I was out of control. I felt weak, like I'd lost my edge. It was as if I'd been cut off at the knees."

"And?" he asked, trying to appear casual even though his insides were jumping all over the place.

"And I came back here to refocus. I had to prove that I could be that person again—the one who was ambitious and strong and successful—because that's who I'd been raised to be. That's what defined me. I knew I had to take back my life and not be afraid, and not feel so wretchedly guilty that I'd survived and someone else had died." She drew in a deep breath. "So, I *did* refocus. Then I went back to New York and got a promotion the very day I returned to work." She drew in another breath, shakier, short. "And it would have been a great job."

Cameron straightened and pushed himself off the door. *"Would have?"*

She nodded. "I quit."

More gasps echoed around the patio. Cameron could barely get his words out. "You quit? Why?"

He saw her lip tremble and watched, both fascinated and agonized as her green eyes filled with tears.

"Because I didn't want to make the biggest mistake of my life." Her voice quivered, almost breaking. "So, I quit, like I said. Which means I'm unemployed." She raised her shoulders and dropped them heavily. "I've decided I'm going to work for myself now. Freelance. I'll get a few clients and who knows…" She blinked at the wetness threatening to fall. "All I know is that I can do that anywhere. I can do that…here."

Cameron harnessed his feelings. They weren't done yet. He had to know more. He had to know how she really felt. "And will that be enough?" *Will I be enough? Will we be enough?*

Grace nodded. "I've been incredibly stupid. And afraid. And dishonest with myself. And with you," she added. "I want things. I want all those things we talked about. I do want my career…but I want everything else, too. I want a home and a family and…and who says a person can't have b-both?" She hiccupped and clasped her arms tightly around herself.

"I guess it depends how much you want them."

She nodded. "I want them badly enough to stand here and make a complete fool out of myself right now."

Cameron bit back a grin. She *was* making a fool of herself. A beautiful, perfectly adorable fool. "And you're doing that because?"

Grace drew in a breath and glanced at the stunned, silent people standing on the edge of the patio. Emotion choked her eyes, her heart and her skin. They were her family and she wasn't being judged as weak or foolish or any of the things she'd always feared.

"Because…" she said shakily and let the tears come, over her lids and down her cheeks. "Because when I'm with you I'm the best version of myself. And I'm…just…so much in love with you."

There it was. Her heart laid out for everyone to see. She ignored the shocked gasps from the sidelines. Ignored everything and everyone except Cameron.

He hadn't moved. But he looked deep into her eyes. Into that place made only for him. Grace tried to smile, hoping to see love and acceptance and forgiveness.

"Say something," she whispered.

He grinned. "You're wearing my shirt."

Grace unhooked her arms and touched the fabric. "It was all I had of you."

"It's not all you have, Grace." He smiled broadly and she saw the love in his expression. "Whatever I am, with every part of who I am…you've always had every bit of my heart."

Relief and love and gratitude flowed through her and she kept crying, but they were happy tears she was proud to show. "So, will you ask me that question again? Because if you do, I'll promise to get the answer right this time."

He laughed softly and looked toward the people staring at them, all stunned by what they had heard. Except Evie, who was smiling the biggest smile and holding her baby against her chest. And Irene Jakowski, who looked at Grace as though she had just hung the moon.

He nodded. "I'm asking."

Grace laughed, happiness radiating through her. "And I'm saying yes."

His smile reached right into her heart. "Then get over here," he beckoned softly.

She took about two seconds before she raced across the patio and flung herself into his arms. For the first time in her life she didn't give a hoot what anyone thought of her. She didn't care that some of her family were now looking at her as though she'd lost her mind. Serious, overachieving, humorless Grace was gone. She didn't want to be *perfect*. She simply wanted to love this incredible man who'd somehow managed to love her too despite her prickly, icy reserve.

He kissed her then, right there, in front of the world, and Grace gave up her heart, her soul, her very self, and kissed him back.

"Am I the only one who didn't know about this?" Grace heard Noah ask in an incredulous voice. She also heard Callie's "no, dear," and smiled beneath the pressure of Cameron's kiss.

Finally they pulled apart. He smiled and gazed down at her. "Let's get out of here," he suggested and grasped her hand. "So I can do this properly."

Grace took a deep breath and vaguely heard him excuse them both. Within less than a minute they were inside the house and he pulled her down onto the sofa in the living room.

"I don't think poor Noah is over the shock," she said, laughing.

Cameron molded her shoulders with his hands and looked into her eyes. "He'll get used to the idea," he assured her. "Once we're married."

"Married?" she echoed dreamily.

He looked panicky all of a sudden. "You did agree to marry me, didn't you?"

She nodded. "Yes. But you'll need this to make it official," she said and pulled the ring he'd offered her weeks ago from her pocket. "It really is beautiful."

"You kept it?"

She nodded. "Of course I did. I've been carrying it with me everywhere."

"Does it fit?" he asked and took the ring from her fingertips.

Grace shrugged. "I'm not sure. I didn't dare try it on. I wanted to…so much."

Cameron smiled deeply and grabbed her left hand. "Where it belongs," he said as he easily slipped the ring onto her finger. "Now and forever, Princess."

Grace's heart did a flip. Hearing him call her Princess was the most wonderful thing she'd ever heard. "I'm so sorry, Cameron. For every time I made you feel like I didn't want this…that I didn't want *us*. I'm sorry for being the foolish girl I was at eighteen who didn't have the sense to see what was right in front her. And I'm sorry for being so self-centered that I—"

"Grace, I—"

"Let me finish," she said and placed a gentle finger against his mouth. She moved her hand to his cheek and held him there. "You are, without a doubt, the most amazing man I have ever known. You're strong and honest and honorable and so incredibly kind. To love you…to be loved by you… is truly humbling."

"That's very sweet, Grace," he said and kissed her softly.

"I'm not sweet at all," she defied as their lips parted. "And you know it. In fact, you probably know me better than anyone."

"I know you're in my heart, Grace. I know I love you more than I ever imagined I could love anyone."

"I love you, too," she said and experienced a swell of love so deep, and so rich, it tore the breath from her throat. "For so long I've been afraid to truly feel anything. I had my career and let that define me…I let that be all that I was. But I was hollow inside." She gripped his hands. "You saved me," she said quietly. "You saved me when I came back and didn't know how tell my family about the accident. You saved me by letting me tutor Emily, which showed me how good it feels to really do something for someone else. And you saved me every time you held me and made me feel less broken. When I think of how close I came to making the wrong choice…" She shuddered.

He brought her hands to his lips and kissed them softly. "You're here now. We're here now. That's all that matters."

"But I—"

"No buts," he insisted and smiled. "Although now is probably a good time to talk about the flight I just booked to New York."

Grace's eyes filled with more tears. "You…you were coming to see me?"

He smiled warmly. "Of course. To see you—or to bring you back—or live there with you. Either way, Grace, being apart from you was never an option."

"But you didn't say anything like that before."

"I'm an idiot," he said flatly. "And too proud to admit I was afraid of rejection. You knew that," he said as he touched her face. "You asked me why I help kids like Dylan and I wasn't honest with you. I don't think I really understood why until the other day. All my life I've felt like I had to somehow make up for my biological father running out on me and my mother, as though in some way it would make the hurt go away." He clutched her hands and his voice broke with emotion as he said the words. "And it stopped me from being truly grateful for the father I have."

"You do have a good father," she assured him.

He kissed her softly. "I know. And, Grace, if you want to go to back to New York, if you want that promotion, then we'll go—together. And if you want to stay in Crystal Point, we'll stay."

Grace closed her eyes for a moment. When she opened them again he was watching her with blistering intensity. "I want to stay," she replied. "I want to marry you and live in your house. I want us to take Jed for long walks along the beach. I want to share our life with our families. I want to be at your side in this community and help kids like Dylan and Emily. And one day soon, I want to have your baby."

He raised a brow. "You want kids? You really do?"

What she wanted had never seemed clearer. "I really do."

He kissed her. Long and sweet and filled with love. "I love you, Grace, so much."

She smiled, remembering what Pat had said to her.

There's a lot to be said about the love of a good man.

Yes, Grace thought as she pressed against him, there certainly was.

* * * * *

MAROONED WITH THE MAVERICK

BY
CHRISTINE RIMMER

Christine Rimmer came to her profession the long way around. Before settling down to write about the magic of romance, she'd been everything from an actress to a sales-clerk to a waitress. Now that she's finally found work that suits her perfectly, she insists she never had a problem keeping a job—she was merely gaining "life experience" for her future as a novelist. Christine is grateful not only for the joy she finds in writing, but for what waits when the day's work is through: a man she loves who loves her right back, and the privilege of watching their children grow and change day to day. She lives with her family in Oregon. Visit Christine at www.christinerimmer.com.

For my dad.
I love you, Dad.
And miss you so much!

Chapter One

At 2:10 in the afternoon on the Fourth of July, Collin Traub glanced out the great room window of his house on Falls Mountain and could not believe what he saw in the town down below.

He stopped stock-still and swore under his breath. How could the situation have gotten so bad so fast? He probably should have been keeping an eye on it.

But he'd been busy, his mind on work. And it was later than usual when he stopped for lunch and came upstairs.

To *this*.

He could kick his own ass for not paying more attention. It had to be about the wettest day on record in Rust Creek Falls, Montana. The rain had been coming down in buckets since yesterday morning. And Rust Creek, which ran northeast to southwest through the center of town, had been steadily rising.

Collin had told himself it was no big deal. The creek

had good, high levees on either side, levees that had held without a break for more than a hundred years. He'd never doubted that they would hold for another hundred.

And yet somehow, impossibly, sections of the levee on the south bank were crumbling. Through the thick, steady veil of rain that streamed down the windows, he watched it happen.

The levee just...dissolved, sending foaming, silvery swaths of water pouring through more than one breach. It was a lot of water and it was flowing fast and furious onto the lower-elevation south side of town.

People were going to lose their homes. Or worse.

And the water wouldn't be stopping on the edge of town, either. South of town lay Rust Creek Falls Valley, a fertile, rolling landscape of small farms and ranches—and any number of smaller creeks and streams that would no doubt also be overflowing their banks.

The Triple T, his family's ranch, was down there in the path of all that water.

He grabbed the phone off the table.

Deader than a hammer.

He dug his cell from his pocket. No signal.

The useless cell still clutched in his hand, Collin grabbed his hat and his keys and headed out into the downpour.

It was a hell of a ride down the mountain.

One-third of the way down, the road skirted close to the falls for which the mountain was named. The roar was deafening, and the pounding silver width of the falling water twice what he was used to seeing. He made it past without incident. But if the rain kept on like this, the road could easily be washed out. He'd have himself a real adventure getting back home.

But now was not the time to worry over coming back.

He needed to get down there and do what he could to help. He focused his mind on that, keeping his boot light on the brake, giving the steering wheel a workout, as he dodged his 4x4 F-150 around mudslides and uprooted trees, with the rain coming down so thick and fast he could hardly see through the windshield. Now and then, lightning lit up the gray sky and thunder boomed out, the sound echoing off in the distance, over the valley below.

Lightning could be damned dangerous on a mountain thick with tall trees. But with the rain coming down like the end of the world and everything drenched and dripping, a lightning strike causing a forest fire was probably the last thing he needed to get anxious over today.

Water. Rivers of it. That was the problem.

There were way too many spots where the streams and overflowing ditches had shed their contents across the narrow, twisty mountain road. He was lucky to make it through a few of those spots. But he did it.

Fifteen endless minutes after sliding in behind the wheel, he reached Sawmill Street on the north edge of town. He debated: go right to North Main and see what he could do in town, or go left over the Sawmill Street Bridge, skirt the east side of town and make tracks for the Triple T.

The rest of his family was three hundred miles away for the holiday, down in Thunder Canyon attending a wedding and a reunion. That made him the only Traub around.

His obligation to the family holdings won out. He swung left and crossed the Sawmill Street Bridge, which was still several feet above the raging water. With a little luck and the Almighty in a generous mood, that bridge might hold.

The Triple T was southeast of town, so he turned south at Falls Street until he caught sight of the miniature lake that had formed at Commercial and Falls. He saw a couple of swamped vehicles, but they were empty. He swung left again. Having been raised in the valley, he knew every rutted dirt road like he knew the face he saw when he looked in the mirror to shave. Collin used that knowledge now, taking the higher roads, the ones less likely to be flooded in the troughs and dips, working his way steadily toward the ranch.

About a mile from the long driveway that led to the barns and houses on the Triple T, he crested a rise and, through the heavy curtain of pouring rain, saw another vehicle on the road ahead of him: a red Subaru Forester moving at a dead crawl.

He knew that Subaru. And he knew who was behind the wheel: Willa Christensen, the kindergarten teacher.

In spite of everything, the pounding, relentless rain and the flooded road and the pretty-damned-imminent danger, Collin grinned. Since a certain evening a little more than four years before, Willa had been running away from him—and no, he hadn't been chasing her.

Yeah, he had something of a reputation. People called him a skirt chaser, a player, the Traub family bad boy. But come on. He had better things to do with his time than sniff around after a woman who wanted nothing to do with him. And since that night four years ago, Willa took off like a shot whenever she saw him coming. Collin found her frantic efforts to get away from him pretty comical, if the truth were known.

His grin faded. She shouldn't be out in this mess. The way she drove—so cautious, like some nervous old lady—she was way too likely to misjudge a flooded spot, to get all flustered and stomp the brake and end up trapped in the waters that swamped the low sections of the road.

He knew where she was headed. The turnoff to the Christensen Ranch wasn't far past the one to the Triple T.

But the way she was handling her vehicle, he didn't like her odds for getting there in one piece.

Collin readjusted his priorities, skipping the turn to the Triple T, staying on her tail.

The rain came down harder—if that was possible. He had the wipers on high, beating fast and hard across the windshield. *Thwack thwack thwack thwack.* Even on high, they could hardly keep up with the sheer volume of water falling out of the gunmetal-gray sky.

Lightning flashed, a jagged spear of it striking a twisted oak on a rise up ahead. The red Subaru in front of him lurched to a stop as the old oak crashed to the ground, smoke trailing up in a shower of sparks. Thunder boomed across the valley as the Subaru inched forward once again.

Every dip in the road held a churning miniflood. Each time Willa drove that little red station wagon down into a trough, Collin held his breath, sure she wouldn't make it through the swirling waters streaming across the road. But each time, she surprised him. She drove steadily forward at a safe, even crawl. And each time, the swirling water had to surrender her to higher ground. He went through in her wake, gritting his teeth, letting out a long breath of relief when he made it clear, too.

The sick ball of dread in his gut tightened to a knot when she suddenly hit the gas—no doubt because she'd finally realized that he was the guy in the pickup behind her. Instead of taking it slow and steady as she had been, watching the bad spots on the streaming, rutted road in front of her, suddenly she was all about getting the hell away from him.

"Damn it, Willa," he muttered under his breath, as if she might actually hear him. "Slow the hell down...." He leaned on the horn to get her to ease off the accelerator and watch the next dip. It looked pretty deep down there.

But the honking only seemed to freak her out all the more. She must have lead-footed it right to the floorboards. The Forester shot forward—and then took a nosedive into the water rushing across the low spot in the road.

It was bad. Deeper than he'd realized. As the vehicle leveled out, she was up to her side windows in churning brown floodwater.

And going nowhere. She'd swamped it.

Collin hit the brakes. The pickup came to a stop several feet above the flood. He shoved it into Park, turned off the engine, kicked down the parking brake and jumped out, hitting the rain-slick road at a run. Instantly drenched to the skin, with the rain beating down like it wanted to flatten him, he reached the churning water and waded in.

The Subaru was already drifting, picked up by the current and, half-floating, pushed toward the lower side of the road. The water was too high to see the danger there, but Collin knew that the bank at that spot dropped off into a ditch. A deep ditch. If the Subaru went over the edge, he'd have a hell of a time getting Willa out before she drowned.

She'd been raised in the valley, too. She knew what waited at the edge of the road. Inside the station wagon, she was working the door latch, trying to get it to open. She shouted something at him and beat on the window.

He kept slogging toward her, though the water seemed to grab at him, to drag him back. It was like those dreams you have where you have to get somewhere fast and suddenly your legs are made of lead. It seemed to be getting deeper, the pull of the swirling current more powerful, second by second.

Half stumbling, half swimming, while the Subaru slowly rotated away from him as it drifted ever closer to the shoulder and the ditch beyond, Collin bent at the knees and launched himself at the driver's door.

He made it. His fingers closed around the door handle. He used it to pull his feet under him again.

"You push, I'll pull!" he yelled good and loud.

She just kept pounding on the window, her brown eyes wide with fright.

He hollered even louder than before, "Push, Willa! Count of three."

She must have heard him, must have finally understood. Because she pressed her lips together and nodded, her dark, pulled-back hair coming loose, the soft curls bouncing around her fear-white cheeks. She put her shoulder into the door.

"One, two, three!" He pulled. She pushed. The door didn't budge.

"Again! One, two, three!"

The miracle happened. The Subaru rotated just enough that the current caught the door as he yanked the handle and she threw her shoulder against it. The damn thing came open with such force it knocked him over.

He went under. The door hit him in the side of the head. Not all that hard. But still.

Trying to be a hero? Not the most fun he'd ever had.

Somehow, he managed to get his waterlogged boots under him and pushed himself upright, breaking the surface in time to see his hat spinning away on the current and Willa flailing, still inside the Subaru as the water poured in on her through the now-open driver's door.

Wonderful.

He went for her, diving through the open door, grabbing for her and catching her arm. He heard her scream—or she tried to. The water cut off most of the high-pitched sound. It kept pouring in, beating at them as it filled the cab.

They had to get out and get out now.

He pulled on her arm until he'd turned her, faceup, and

then he caught her in a headlock. Okay, it wasn't delicate. It wasn't nice and it sure wasn't gentle. But with his arm around her neck, at least he could turn and throw himself out the door. She grabbed his arm in both her hands, but by then, she seemed to have caught on to what he was trying to do. She wasn't fighting him anymore. She was only holding on as tight as he was.

He squirmed around to face the open door. The water shoved him back, but at least the rotation of the vehicle kept the door from swinging shut and trapping them inside. He got his free hand on the door frame, knees bent, boots braced on the side of the seat. Another hard push and they were out just as the Subaru went over the bank into the ditch.

The weight of the vehicle going under sucked at them, but Willa slipped free of his hold and started swimming. Since she seemed to be making it on her own steam, he concentrated on doing the same.

Side by side, they swam for the place where the road rose up out of the ditch. His boots touched ground. Beside him, she found her footing, too—for an instant. Then she staggered and went under.

He grabbed her again, hauling her up, getting one arm around her waist. Lightning tore another hole in the sky and thunder boomed as he half carried, half dragged her up and out of the racing water.

She coughed and sputtered, but she kept her feet moving. The woman had grit. He had to give her that. He kept hold of her, half-supporting her, urging her to the high side of the road and up the hill far enough that they were well above the water and reasonably safe.

They collapsed side by side onto the streaming ground as the rain continued to beat down on them, hard and heavy, never ending. She turned over, got up on her hands and knees and started hacking and coughing, spitting up water. He dragged in one long, hungry breath after another and pounded her back for her, helping her clear her airways so she could breathe. When she was finally doing more breathing than hacking, he fell back on the ground and concentrated on catching his own breath.

Lucky for him, he just happened to turn his head and glance in the direction of his truck about then. The water *had* risen. Considerably. It was maybe two feet from his front wheels now.

He turned to the waterlogged woman gasping beside him. "Stay here. Do not move. I'll be right back."

Swearing low and with feeling, he lurched upright and beat feet on a parallel track with the road. When he got even with his truck, he half ran, half slid down the hill, raced around the rear of the pickup and hauled himself up into the cab. The key was still in the ignition—and the water was lapping around his front wheel wells by then.

He turned it over, released the brake, put it in Reverse and backed to the top of the last rise. Once there, he slammed it in Park again and jumped out to see how things looked behind him.

Not good. The road was flooded in the previous trough. Water in front of him, water behind. The truck was going nowhere until the water receded.

Fair enough. He got back in and parked on the shoulder. Taking his keys with him that time, he left the truck and locked it up.

Then he looked for Willa.

She was gone.

Chapter Two

A moment later, Collin spotted her.

She was on her feet and slogging up the long slope of the hill. He knew then where she was headed. There was a big, weathered, rambling structure way at the top—the Christensen barn.

"Willa, what the hell?" he yelled good and loud. "Hold on a minute!"

She didn't pause, she didn't turn. Her hair plastered to her head, and her little white T-shirt and snug jeans covered with mud and debris, she just kept on putting one boot in front of the other, heading up that hill.

He was powerfully tempted to let her go.

But who knew what trouble she'd get herself into next? If something happened to her, he'd end up with a guilty conscience for leaving her all by her lonesome. Plus, well, he didn't have a lot of options himself, at the moment. The floodwaters were all around.

And it might be July, but the rain was a cold rain and the

wind was up, too. He needed shelter to wait out the storm and the barn had walls and a roof. It was better than nothing. Willa was going to have to get over her aversion to him, at least until there was somewhere else he could go.

With a grunt of resignation, he climbed the hill after her, tucking his head down, putting one foot in front of the other, as the water streamed over him and his boots made sucking sounds with each step he took.

He caught up to her maybe twenty yards from the barn. She must have heard the sloshing of his boots at last.

She stopped, her arms wrapped around herself to control the shivers that racked her, and whirled to confront him. "Collin." She tipped her head up and drew her slim shoulders back. Water ran down her cheeks, into her wide mouth and over her chin.

He could see her nipples, hard as rocks, right through her T-shirt and her bra. "What, Willa?"

"Thank you for saving my life."

"Hey." He swiped water off his nose. Not that it did any good. "No problem. Can we move it along? It's pretty damn wet out here. I'd like to get in that barn."

She gripped her arms tighter around herself. "I would like for you to go away and leave me alone."

"Oh, you would, would you?"

"Yes. Please."

He raised his arms out wide, indicating all of it—the never-ending storm, the floodwaters surrounding them, the cold wind and the flash of bright lightning that lit up the sky again right at that moment. The thunder rumbled. He waited for the sound to die away. "Exactly where do you suggest I go, Willa?"

She flung out a hand. "What about your truck?"

He folded his arms across his chest and simply looked at her.

Her shoulders sagged and she let out a low cry. "Oh,

fine. All right. You can come in the barn. Just…fine. Okay." And she turned around again and continued walking.

He fell in behind her.

The barn loomed ahead. When they reached it, she undid the latch and slipped in. He went in after her, pulling the door to, latching it from within.

The barn had another door on the far wall. Someone must have left the latch undone, because that door stood wide-open. It was probably not a bad thing in this situation. The Christensen livestock needed more than a run-in shed on a day like today and the animals had found what they needed through that wide-open door.

The rambling space was wall-to-wall critters. There were cattle, goats, some chickens and several cooing pigeons. Carping blackbirds perched in the rafters. A couple of pigs snorted beneath one of the two windows and somewhere nearby a barn cat hissed and then yowled.

A dog barked. Collin spotted a muddy white Labrador retriever. The dog was headed for Willa.

She let out a happy little cry. "Buster! There you are!" She dropped to a crouch and opened her arms. The dog reared up and put his front paws on her shoulders. Whining with excitement, he licked her face with his sloppy pink tongue. "You are such a bad, bad dog," she crooned in a tone that communicated no criticism whatsoever. "Hey, now. Eww." She turned her head away from Buster's slobbery attentions and saw Collin watching her.

"Nice dog." He'd had a great dog named Libby who'd died the winter before. She'd been sixteen, with him since he was eleven and she was an ugly pup, the runt of the litter wanted by no one—but him.

"Down, Buster." She rose again and tried to brush the mud and water off her soaking wet shirt and muddy jeans.

It did zero good. "Technically, he's my dog," she explained, "but he's always loved it here on the ranch, so he lives here more than with me. He was supposed to be staying with me in town, though, while my parents and Gage are in Livingston for the big rodeo." Gage Christensen, her brother, was the town sheriff. "That dog just will not stay put. He keeps running off to get back here." A shiver went through her. She wrapped her arms around herself again.

"You're freezing," he said. It came out sounding like an accusation, though he didn't mean it that way.

"I am fine." She shivered some more. Her hair was plastered on her cheeks and down her neck. She swiped at a soggy hunk of it, shoving it back behind her ear. "Just fine." She scowled at him.

Whoa. For a minute there, she'd almost seemed friendly—but then she must have remembered that she hated his ass. She turned her back on him and started weaving her way through the crush of horses and cattle. The Lab followed her, panting happily, wagging his muddy tail.

It should have been warmer in there, with all the steaming, milling livestock. But it really wasn't. How could it be, with that far door wide-open and both of them soaking wet? He slapped the bony butt of a little red heifer who'd backed in too close. She let out a cranky "moo," and ambled away—not far, though. There wasn't really anywhere to go.

He found a hay bale against the wall and sat on it as he pondered what he ought to do to make things a little more comfortable. He hesitated to go over and shut the other door. The smell of wet livestock and manure would get pretty strong if he did that.

As he considered what to do next, he watched the dripping brown-haired woman who had spent the past four years avoiding him and now happened to be stuck with him until the rain ended and the floodwaters receded.

Willa was keeping busy shivering and ignoring him, wandering from steer to goat to barn cat to bay mare, petting them all and talking to them low and soft, as though she had a personal relationship with each and every four-legged creature on her family's place. And maybe she did.

She'd always been a fanciful type, even way back when they were kids. He knew this from actual observation.

Collin had run wild as a kid. He was the youngest, sixth of six boys, and his mom was worn-out by the time he came along. She didn't have the energy to keep after him. He went where he wanted and came home when he felt like it. He wandered far and wide. Often, he found himself on Christensen land. Now and then, he'd run into Willa. She would be singing little songs to herself, or making crowns out of wildflowers, or reading fairy-tale books.

She'd never seemed to like him much, even then. Once she'd yelled at him to stop spying on her.

He hadn't been spying. A kid wasn't spying just because he stretched out in the tall grass and watched a neighbor girl talking to herself as she walked her big-haired brunette Barbie doll around in a circle.

Collin tried to get more comfortable on the hay bale. He scooted to the wall, leaned his head back against the rough boards, closed his eyes and tried not to think how cold he was, tried not to wish he'd grabbed a snack to take with him when he'd run out of the house. His stomach grumbled. He ignored it.

It would have been nice if he could drop off to sleep for a little and forget everything. But no such luck. He would just start to doze when a fit of shivering would snap him awake and he would realize anew that they were smack-dab in the middle of one hell of a disaster. He hoped that no one in town had drowned, that the hands and the animals on the Triple T were safe. He couldn't help wondering how much of both the town or his family's ranch would be left standing when the floodwaters receded.

And how much of the state was affected? What about Thunder Canyon, where his family had gone? Were they underwater, too?

Eventually, he gave up trying to sleep and opened his eyes. Willa stood at the window that faced southwest, the one not far from where two spotted pigs were snorting over an upturned bucket of feed. With the white Lab at her feet, she stared out through the endless curtain of the rain. He rubbed his arms to try and warm up a little and knew she must be staring at her parents' place. The Christensen house was about level with the barn, on high ground, atop the next hill over.

He knew he was asking for more rejection to try and talk to her, but he was just tired and dejected enough to do it anyway. "The house should be safe," he said. He didn't mention her brother Gage's house, which was down the slope of the hill behind her parents' place. It wouldn't be visible from Willa's vantage point, which was just as well. As Collin remembered, it was a ways down the hill and probably already below the rising waterline.

She surprised him by replying. "Yes. I can see it. It's okay, for now...." She sounded strange, he thought. Kind of dreamy and far away. She had a few scratches on her arms. And a bruise on her cheekbone. But like him, no serious injuries. They'd been very fortunate. So far. She added, "It's all so unbelievable, don't you think? Like maybe this isn't even actually happening. Maybe I'm just dreaming it."

"Sorry, Willa." He meant that. He *was* sorry. "I think it's really happening."

She sent him a glance. For once, her mouth didn't pinch

up at the sight of him. "I lost my phone." A shiver went through her and her teeth chattered together. "Do you happen to have yours with you?"

"It's in my truck, I think. But there must be towers down. I was getting no signal when I tried using it at a little after two."

Willa sighed and turned back to the window. "Life is so…fragile, really, isn't it? I mean, you go along, doing what you need to do, thinking you're taking care of business, that you're in control. But you're not in control, not really." Outside, lightning flared. Thunder rolled out. "Anything could happen," she said. "It could rain and rain and never stop…." Her lips looked kind of blue, he thought.

He really needed to come up with a way to warm her up a little. Rising, he began to work his way around the barn, looking for a blanket or a tarp or something.

Willa kept talking. "Oh, Collin. I keep thinking of the children in my class last year. And the ones in our summer school program. I can just close my eyes and see each one of their sweet, smiling faces. I hope they're all safe and dry. Our school, the elementary school? It's on the south side of town. That's not good news. And my house is on the south side, too…."

He pushed a goat out of the way as he came to a spot where the wall jogged at a ninety-degree angle. Around that corner was a door. He opened it. "Willa, there's a tack room here."

She sighed again. "Yes. That's right. And a feed room over there." She put out a hand in the general direction of the other shut door farther down the wall. And then she started in again, about life and the flood and the safety of her friends, her neighbors and her students.

Collin took a look around the tack room. There were the usual rows of hooks holding ropes and bridles and bits. He was a saddle maker by trade and he grinned at the sight of one of his own saddles racked nice and neat, lined up with several others on the wall. There was a window. And another door, allowing outside access.

The floor in there was wood, not mixed clay and sand as it was out in the main part of the barn. And the walls were paneled in pine.

And then he saw the stack of saddle blankets atop a big cedar storage trunk. He went over and grabbed one. Shooing out the goat that had followed him in there, he shut the door and made his way through the milling animals to Willa.

She didn't even flinch when he wrapped the blanket around her. "Thank you."

He took her by the shoulders. "Come on. Let's go...." She went where he guided her, back through the cattle and horses and goats, with the dog right behind them. He let the dog in the tack room with them, and then shut the door to keep the rest of the animals out. There were a few hay bales. He sat her down on one and knelt in front of her.

She frowned down at him. "What are you doing?"

He held her gaze. "Don't get freaky on me, okay?"

She looked at him in that pinched, suspicious way again. "Why not?"

"You need to get out of those wet clothes. There are plenty of blankets. You can wrap yourself up in them and get dry."

"But...my clothes won't dry."

"It doesn't matter. Right now, *you* need to get dry."

She considered that idea—and shook her head. "I'll take off my boots and socks. I'll be all right."

He decided not to argue with her. "Fine. You need help?"

"No, thank you." All prim and proper and so polite. "I'll manage."

"Are you thirsty?"

She gaped at him. "Thirsty?" And then she let out a wild little laugh. "In this?" She stuck out a hand toward the water streaming down the lone window.

"Are you?"

And she frowned again. "Well, yes. Now that you mention it, I suppose I am."

He rose. "I'll see if I can find some clean containers in the barn. We can catch some of the rainwater, so we won't get dehydrated."

She blinked up at him. "Yes. That makes sense. I'll help." She started to rise.

He took her shoulders again and gently pushed her back down. "Get out of your boots and shoes—and wrap this around your feet." He held out another blanket.

She took it, her gaze colliding with his. Holding. "What about you?"

"Let me see about setting out containers for water. Then I'll grab a few blankets and try and warm up a little, too."

Half an hour later, he had his boots and socks off. They'd pushed four hay bales together and spread a blanket over them. Side by side, wrapped in more blankets, they passed a bucket of water back and forth.

When they'd both drunk their fill, there was still plenty left in the bucket. He set it on the floor, where Buster promptly stuck his nose in it and started lapping. "You don't happen to have a nice T-bone handy, do you, Willa?"

She chuckled. There wasn't a lot of humor in the sound, but he took heart that at least she wasn't staring blindly into space anymore. "Plenty on the hoof right outside that door." She pointed her thumb over her shoulder at the door that led into the barn.

He scooted back to the wall for something to lean against. "Not that hungry yet."

"I didn't think so." She scooted back, too, settling alongside him, and then spent a moment readjusting the blanket she'd wrapped around her feet. "There." She leaned back and let out a long breath. "I believe I am actually beginning to thaw out."

"That was the plan." Outside, the rain kept falling. The sky remained that same dim gray it had been all day. "Got any idea what time it is?"

"I don't know. Six, maybe? Seven?" She sounded... softer. A little sleepy. That was good. Rest wouldn't hurt either of them. "Won't be dark for hours yet...."

He was feeling kind of drowsy, too, now that he wasn't chilled to the bone anymore and most of the adrenaline rush from the various near-death events of the day had faded a little. He let his eyelids droop shut.

But then she spoke again. "It's really very strange, Collin, being here with you like this."

He grunted. "This whole day has been pretty strange."

"Yes, it has. And scary. And awful. But, well, that's not what I meant."

He knew exactly what she meant. And why was it women always had to dig up stuff that was better left alone? He kept nice and quiet and hoped she wasn't going there.

But she was. "Maybe this is a good chance to clear the air a little between us."

"The air is plenty clear from where I'm sitting."

"Well, Collin, for me, it's just not."

"Willa, I—"

"No. Wait. I would like a chance to say what's on my mind."

He didn't let out a groan of protest, but he wanted to.

And she kept right on. "It was very…humiliating for me, that night at the Ace in the Hole." The Ace was on Sawmill Street. It was the only bar in town. People went there to forget their troubles and usually only ended up creating a whole new set of them. "It was my first time there, did you know? My twenty-first birthday." She sounded all sad and wistful.

He'd known. "I think you mentioned that at the time, yeah."

"Derek had just dumped me for a Delta Gamma." Straight-arrow Derek Andrews was her high school sweetheart. They'd graduated the same year and headed off to the University of Idaho together. "Collin, did you *hear* me?"

"Every word," he muttered.

"Did you *know* it was over between me and Derek?"

"Well, Willa, I kinda had a feeling something might have gone wrong with your love life, yeah."

"You led me on," she accused. "You know that you did." He'd seen her coming a mile away. Good-girl Willa Christensen, out to find a bad boy just for the night. "And then you…" Her voice got all wobbly. "You turned me down flat."

"Come on, Willa. It wasn't a good idea. You know that as well as I do."

"Then why did you dance with me all those times? Why did you flirt with me and buy me two beers? You acted like you were interested. More than interested. And then, when I tried to kiss you, you laughed at me. You said I wasn't your type. You said I should go home and behave myself."

He'd had some crazy idea at the time that he was doing her a favor, keeping her from doing something she wouldn't be happy about later. But with Willa, no good deed of his ever went unpunished. And was she going to start crying? He hated it when a woman started crying.

She sniffled in her blankets, a small, lost little sound. "I still can't believe I did that—made a pass at *you.* I mean, you never liked me and I never cared much for you and we both know that." That wasn't true—not on his part anyway. Far from it. But he wasn't in the mood to dispute the point at the moment. He only wanted her not to start crying—and he thought maybe he was getting his wish when she squirmed in her blankets and grumbled, "Everyone knows how you are. You'll sleep with anyone—except *me,* apparently."

Mad. Now she was getting mad. As far as he was concerned, mad was good. Mad was great. Anything but weepy worked for him.

She huffed, "I just don't know what got into me that night."

He couldn't resist. "Well, Willa, we both know it wasn't me."

She made another huffing sound. "Oh, you think you're so funny. And you're not. You're very annoying and you always have been."

"Always?" he taunted.

"Always," she humphed.

He scoffed at her. "How would you know a thing about me the last four years? Since that night at the Ace, all I see is the backside of you. I come in a room—and you turn tail and run."

"And why shouldn't I? You are a complete tool and you never cared about anything or anyone in your whole life but yourself."

"Which is girl talk for 'You didn't sleep with me,'" he said in his slowest, laziest, most insolent tone.

"You are not the least bit clever, you know that?"

"You don't think so, huh?"

"No, I do not. And it just so happens that I'm *glad* we never hooked up that night. You're the last person in the world I should ever be sleeping with."

He tried not to grin. "No argument there. Because I'm not having sex with you no matter how hard you beg me."

"Oh, please. I mean just, simply, *please*." She sat up straight then. Dragging her blankets along with her, she scooted to the edge of the hay bales, as far from him as she could get without swinging her bare feet to the floor. Once there, she snapped, "You do not have worry. I want nothing to do with you."

He freed a hand from his blankets and made a show of wiping his brow—even though she wasn't looking at him. "Whew."

"In case you didn't know, it just so happens that I have a fiancé, thank you very much."

"A fiancé?" That *was* news to Collin. The information bothered him. A lot—and that it bothered him bugged him to no end.

"Yes," she said. "Well. Sort of."

"Willa, get real. You do or you don't."

"His name is Dane Everhart and he's an assistant coach at the University of Colorado. We met at UI. We've been dating on and off for three years. Dane loves me and knows I'm the one for him and wants only to marry me and, er, give me the world."

"Hold on just a minute. Answer the question. You're saying you're engaged?"

She fiddled with her blankets and refused to turn around and look at him. "Well, no. Not exactly. But I *could* be. I promised to give Dane an answer by the end of the summer."

He stared at the back of her head. Her hair was a tangle

of wild, muddy curls from her dip in the floodwaters. It should have looked like crap. But it didn't. It looked like she'd been having crazy good sex with someone—and then fallen asleep all loose and soft and satisfied.

And why the hell was he thinking about sex right now? Was he losing his mind? Probably. A few hours trapped in a barn with Willa Christensen could do that to a man, could drive him clean out of his head.

He sat up, too, then, and sneered, "You're in love with this guy, and you're not going to see him until *September?*"

"So? What's wrong with that?"

"Well, I mean, if you're in *love* with him, how can you *stand* to be apart from him? How can *he* stand to be away from you?"

"You wouldn't understand."

"Are you in love with him, Willa?"

She squared her slim shoulders. "I just *told* you that you wouldn't understand."

"That's right. I wouldn't. If I loved a woman, I'd want her with me. Where I could touch her and be with her and hold her all night long."

Willa gasped. She tried to hide the small, sharp sound, but he heard it. "Oh, please. As if you know anything about being in love, Collin Traub."

"I said if I *was* in love."

"Well. Humph. As it happens, Dane has gone to Australia until the end of the month. He gets only a short summer break before practice begins again. And do you know how he's spending his limited free time? I will tell you how he's spending it. At a special sports camp. He's helping Australian children learn about American football. Because he's a good man, a man who *cares* about other people. That's how he is. That's *who* he is…"

There was more. Lots more.

Collin let her heated words wash over him. The point, as far as he saw it, was that she hadn't answered the main question. She hadn't come out and said, "Yes. I'm in love with Dane Everhart."

He felt absurdly satisfied with what she *hadn't* said. She could rant all night about the wonderfulness of this Dane character while talking trash about *him*. At least she was acting like the Willa he'd always known. At least she was full of fire and vinegar and not shaking with cold, shock and fear anymore.

Collin smiled to himself, settled back against the wall and closed his eyes.

Chapter Three

Willa felt Collin's presence behind her acutely.

But she didn't turn to him. She sat on the edge of the pushed-together hay bales and stared resolutely out the tack room's one window as waves of never-ending rain flowed down the glass.

She finished what she had to say about Dane. "It just so happens that Dane would have liked to have taken me with him. But he was going to be very busy with the Australian children and I had things I could be doing here at home. We have summer school at Rust Creek Falls Elementary, in case you didn't know and I…" Her voice trailed off.

Collin hadn't said a word for a couple of minutes, maybe more. Had he fallen *asleep,* for heaven's sake?

She wouldn't put it past him. He was such an exasperating, impossible man. Always had been. And no doubt always would be.

So why am I starting to feel ashamed of myself?

Willa's cheeks were flaming. She tucked her chin down into the scratchy saddle blanket he'd wrapped around her. At least he couldn't see her embarrassment at her own behavior—not as long as she didn't turn and face him.

Which she was not going to do right now, thank you very much.

Stretched out on the floor by the hay bales, Buster huffed out a long sigh. Willa bent down and scratched him on the head. His tail bounced happily against the rough plank floor.

She gathered her blankets close again. All right, she probably shouldn't have gone off on Collin like that. No matter how humiliating her history with the guy, he'd been there when she desperately needed him. He'd saved her life a few hours ago, at no small risk to himself.

Plus, well, she hadn't really been honest while she was getting all up in his face just now, had she? She hadn't bothered to mention that she had serious reservations about her and Dane. Dane was the greatest guy in the world and he did want to marry her, very much. But Rust Creek Falls was her home and he wasn't about to give up his wonderful career at CU. And more important than geography, Dane somehow didn't quite *feel* like her guy.

Whatever her guy *should* feel like. She wasn't sure. She just had a certain intuition that Dane wasn't it.

And worse than her doubts about her future with an ideal man like Dane, well, there was that longtime *thing* she'd had for Collin—oh, not anymore. Of course not. That night at the Ace in the Hole had put an end to her ridiculous schoolgirl crush on the town bad boy. But before that night she used to fantasize about him now and then.

Or maybe even more often than now and then.

She used to wonder what it would be like if bad-boy Collin were to kiss her. Or do more than kiss her…

Not that it mattered now. None of her past silliness over Collin mattered to anyone. It had been a fantasy, that was all. *Her* fantasy. He'd never been the least interested in her. He'd made that painfully clear on the night he led her on and then laughed in her face.

And really, after all that had happened today, her four-year grudge against him for not having sex with her was beginning to seem nothing short of petty. She really needed to let the past go. She needed to be…a bigger person than she'd been so far about this. She needed to be a *better* person.

And she needed to start doing that now.

Willa cleared her throat. "Um. Collin?"

He shifted a little, back there against the wall. "What now, Willa?" His voice was scratchy and deep. Lazy. What was it about him? He just always made her think of wrinkled sheets and forbidden passion.

In a purely impersonal, objective way, of course.

"I, um, well…"

"Come on. Spit it out."

She made herself say it. "I'm sorry, okay?" She hauled her blanket-wrapped legs back up on the hay bales and wiggled around until she was facing him again. He lay sprawled under his blankets, his head propped against the wall, his eyes shut, his eyelashes black as coal, thicker than any girl's, his full mouth lax and lazy, just like his voice had been, the shadow of a beard on his cheeks. A curl of that impossibly thick black hair of his hung over his forehead. She clutched her blankets tighter to keep from reaching out and smoothing it back. "I shouldn't have jumped all over you like that. I shouldn't have called you a tool. That was…small-minded and mean-spirited of me, especially after all you've done for me today."

He didn't say anything for a minute. And he didn't open

his eyes. Again, she wondered if he'd dropped off to sleep and she had to resist the urge to reach out and shake him. But then those bad-boy lips curved upward in a slow smile. "So you don't think I'm a tool, then?"

"Um. No. No, of course not. I shouldn't have said that. I'm sorry. I am."

"And you think maybe you could stop racing off like your hair's on fire every time you see me coming?"

A fresh wave of embarrassment had her cheeks flaming all over again. But what did it matter? He couldn't see her blush. His eyes were shut. Also, she truly wanted to make amends. "Ahem. Yes. Fair enough. I will do that. I will stop avoiding you."

"Well, all right then. I accept your apology." He patted the empty space beside him. "Stretch out. Try and get some sleep. I'm thinking we're going to be busy when the rain stops and the water goes down."

His words brought reality crashing back down on her. She hung her head. "Oh, Collin. It seems like it's never going to stop. I know my brother's house is already underwater. And what if it just keeps rising, what if we—?"

"Shh." He reached out and clasped her arm through the thick wool of the blanket. His grip was strong. Sure. It made her so very glad that he was here with her, that she wasn't huddled in the family barn all alone, waiting out the endless storm. "Don't go there." His voice was calm and firm. "There's no point."

She lifted her head. His eyes were open now, steady on hers. Shamelessly, she pleaded, "Tell me that we're going to be okay, that Rust Creek Falls will be okay, that we'll make it through this, come back better and stronger than ever."

He didn't even hesitate. He told her what she needed to hear. "We will. Just watch. Now come here. Come on..." He lifted the blanket that covered him.

She didn't think twice. She went down into the shelter of his offered arm, resting her head on his shoulder. He was so warm and big and solid. He smelled of mud and man, which at that moment she found wonderfully reassuring. He fiddled with the blankets, smoothing them over both of them.

Willa smiled to herself. All those crazy teenage dreams she'd had about him. And here she was, damp and dirty, bruised and scratched up, lying practically on top of him, grateful beyond measure to share a pile of saddle blankets with him. The world seemed to have gone crazy in the space of a day. But right now, in Collin's arms, she felt safe.

Protected.

She closed her eyes. "I didn't realize until now how tired I am...."

He touched her hair, gently. Lightly. "Rest, then."

She started to answer him, but then she found she didn't have the energy to make a sound. Sleep closed over her. She surrendered to it with a grateful sigh.

When she woke, the light was different.

Sun. It was sun slanting in the window—and the window faced east. That meant it had to be morning, didn't it?

Also...

She was lying on a man. Collin. He had both arms wrapped around her and his cheek against her dirty, snarled hair. Her head was on his shoulder, one arm tucked in against her side.

Her other arm rested on Collin, which was perfectly acceptable, given the circumstances. But the hand that was attached to that arm? That hand was exactly where it shouldn't be.

And where it shouldn't be was hard.

Blinking, not quite putting it all together as reality

yet, Willa lifted her head from his shoulder and blearily squinted at the morning light. Outside, faintly, she could hear birds singing.

Without moving her hand away from his very definite, very thick and large hardness, she looked down at him. Because, seriously. Could this actually be happening?

It was.

And he was awake. He gazed up at her with the strangest, laziest, *sexiest* expression. "Mornin'."

She puffed out her cheeks as she blew out a slow breath. And then, with great care, she removed her hand from his private parts and whispered, "The sun's out."

He nodded. "The rain's stopped. It stopped hours ago." He was playing along with her, pretending the contact between her hand and his fly had not occurred. Which was great. Perfect. Wonderful of him.

She backed off him onto her knees, dragging the blankets with her, and shoved her hair out of her eyes. "You, uh, should have woken me."

"Uh-uh." He reached out and clasped her shoulder, a companionable, reassuring sort of gesture that made tears clog her throat. She swallowed them down. And he said, "You needed your sleep and so did I. I woke up in the middle of the night and it was quiet. I knew the rain had finally stopped. I thought about getting up, but then I just closed my eyes and went back to sleep."

Buster was up, making whining noises, scratching at the door that led outside. "I should let him out...." He took his hand from her shoulder. She wished he hadn't, that he would touch her again, hold on tight and never, ever let go. But he didn't. And she pushed the blankets aside, swung her legs over the edge of the hay bales and stood up. Barefoot, she went and pulled the door open. Buster went out and she scolded, "Don't run off, now." And then she lingered in the open doorway, staring up at the sky. Blue as a newborn baby's eyes. She glanced back over her shoulder at Collin.

He was sitting up, bare feet on the floor. He had a case of bed head every bit as bad as hers, and he was kind of hunched over, his elbows on his knees. "Come on," he said gruffly. "Put your boots on," He raked his fingers back through all that thick, every-which-way hair. "We'll see if the water's gone down enough that we can get across the ravine to your folks' house."

They put on their damp socks and boots and pulled open the door that led into the main part of the barn.

"Needs a good mucking out in here," Collin said. Did it ever. Most of the animals had wandered off, out into the morning sunshine, leaving a whole lot of fresh manure behind. "You supposed to be taking care of the place all by your lonesome while your folks and your brother are off at the rodeo?"

She shook her head and named off the neighbors who'd agreed to look after things and feed the stock until the family returned. "But I'm guessing they probably all have their own problems about now." At least it was summer and grazing was good. The animals wouldn't starve if left to their own devices for a few days.

Instead of slogging through the mess on the barn floor to one of the outer doors, they ducked back into the tack room and went out through the exterior door there. Buster was waiting for them, sitting right outside the door, acting as though he'd actually listened when she told him not to wander off.

Willa scratched his head and called him a good dog and tried to tell herself that the jittery feeling in her stomach was because she hadn't eaten since lunch the day before—

not rising dread at the prospect of how bad the damage was behind the barn on the next rise over, and along the roads that crisscrossed the valley. And in town…

"It's a beautiful day," she said, tipping her head up again to the clear sky. "You'd almost think yesterday never even happened."

"Hey."

She lowered her gaze to him. Even with his hair sticking up on one side and a smudge of dirt at his temple, he still looked like every well-behaved girl's naughty, forbidden fantasy. "Hmm?"

His dark eyes searched hers. "You okay?"

And she nodded and forced her mouth to form a smile.

On the other side of the barn, the two pigs from the night before were rooting around near the water trough. A rooster stood on a section of busted-down fence and crowed as Willa stared across the ravine at her parents' house.

The house was untouched by the flood, though the water had gotten halfway up the front walk that was lined with her mother's prized roses. Her dad's minitractor lay on its side at the base of that walk. And a couple of steers had somehow gotten through the fence and were snacking on the vegetable garden in the side yard.

Below, in the ravine, the water had receded, leaving debris strewn down the sides of the hill and up the one on which the house sat. There were tree trunks and lawn chairs down there, boulders and a bicycle, a shade umbrella and any number of other items that looked bizarre, scary and all wrong, soggy and busted up, trailing across the pasture. Willa turned her eyes away, toward the road.

And saw her red Subaru. It had drifted past the ditch and lay on its side in the pasture there. It was covered in mud.

"Guess I'll be needing a new car." She tried to sound philosophical about it, but knew that she didn't exactly succeed.

"Come on," he said. "Let's go check out the house. Watch where you put your feet in that ravine."

Buster and the two pigs followed them down there. They picked their way with care through all the soggy junk and knotted tree roots. It was going to be quite a job, cleaning up. And she knew that all the other ranches in the valley had to be in a similar state, if not worse. Her family still had a barn and the house, at least. And as far as she could see, there were no animals or—God forbid—people lying broken amid the wreckage down there.

When they reached the house, they skirted the downed tractor and went up the front steps. She'd lost her keys. They were probably still stuck in the ignition of her poor Subaru. But her mom had left a house key where she always did, in the mouth of the ceramic frog by the porch swing.

They went inside. The power and phone were both out, but still, it all looked just as it had the last time she'd been there, the white refrigerator covered with those silly smiling-flower magnets her mother liked, some of them holding reminders to pick up this or that at the store. There were also pictures of her and her brother and a few recipes her mom was meaning to try. In the living room, the remote sat on the magazine table by her dad's recliner and her mother's knitting bag waited in its usual place at the end of the fat blue sofa.

Her childhood home. Intact. It seemed a miracle to her right then. And she wanted to cry all over again—with a desperate, hot sort of joy.

Collin turned on the water in the kitchen. It ran clear,

but they both knew that the flood could have caused contamination of any wells in its path.

She said, "We have wells for the stock. But for this house and Gage's place, we have a water tank that taps an underground spring higher up on this hill. The floodwaters wouldn't have reached that far. So the water here, in the house, is safe."

"That's good. A lot of valley wells are going to need disinfecting. Any source of clean water is great news."

She nodded. "And in town, they get water from above the falls. So they should be all right, too, shouldn't they, at least on the north side of the creek?" He shrugged. She knew what he was thinking. Who could say what they would find in town? And what about his family's place? "I know you probably want to head over to the Triple T...."

"Yeah. But let's check out your brother's house first, and then see about getting something to eat."

Gage's house. She realized she didn't want to go there.

But she did it anyway. And she was glad, again, for Collin's presence at her side. The house was locked up. They looked in the windows. It was bad. The waterline went three feet up the walls, but the moisture had wicked higher still in ugly, muddy little spikes. Gage's furniture was beyond saving, soggy and stained, the stuffing popping out.

"Can we get to the propane tank?" Collin asked. "Better to be safe than sorry when it comes to a possible gas leak." She showed him the way. They were able to turn it off from outside. Then he said, "Come on. There's nothing more we can do here right now."

They went back to her parents' house and found plenty to eat in the pantry. She filled Buster's food bowl and the hungry dog quickly emptied it. After the meal, she took the perishables out of the fridge and put them in a bucket in the front yard. The two pigs went right to work on the treat.

By then it was still early, a little after seven. Collin suggested they make use of the safe water source and take showers before they left. There was just no way to guess the next time they'd have a chance to clean up a little. As at Gage's place, the tank was heated by propane, so they even had hot water.

Willa chose from some of her own old clothes that her mom had stored for her in a box under the stairs. She got clean jeans, a fresh T-shirt and a pair of worn but sturdy lace-up work boots to wear. For Collin, she found an ancient purple Jimi Hendrix Experience shirt that belonged to her dad, a pair of her dad's boots that were a pretty decent fit, and some trusty bib overalls. She also gave him a towel, a toothbrush, shave cream and a disposable razor. He took the guest bathroom. She used the master bath, and she made it quick.

Still, as she stood before the steamy bathroom mirror wrapped in one of her mother's fluffy towels, combing the tangles out of her wet hair, she couldn't help but think that Collin was just down the hall in the other bathroom, possibly naked.

Or if he wasn't by now, he *had* been a few minutes ago.

She caught her lower lip between her teeth and glared at her own reflection. "Get your mind off Collin naked," she told her steamy image in an angry whisper. "Seriously. You should get help, Willa Christensen."

And that struck her as funny, for some reason. The idea that she needed counseling over Collin Traub. She laughed. And then she pulled herself together and pinned her still-wet hair into a knot at the back of her head.

A few minutes later, they were out in the kitchen again, deciding what to take with them when they left.

She didn't tell him so, but he looked sexy even in overalls. He'd used the razor she'd given him and his dark stubble was gone, his hair still wet, but minus the dried mud from the flood.

Before they left, they filled a couple of gallon-size plastic containers with water. She stuffed a backpack with a few personal items. Her mom had a key to Willa's house in town and she took that, since hers was lost somewhere in her mud-filled car. She also grabbed a leash and a plastic container of food for Buster. She would have grabbed her dad's first aid kit, but Collin said he had one in his pickup.

"You want to wade out to your car?" Collin asked her. "See if maybe we can find your purse or your keys?"

It was way out there in the middle of that muddy field. And it didn't look promising to her. "We just got dry boots," she reminded him. "Let it go."

Collin didn't argue. She figured he was probably anxious to get to the Triple T.

They locked up the house again and headed for his truck, which waited at the top of the road where he'd left it. Buster hopped in the back and they climbed in the cab.

His cell was stuck in one of the cup holders. He tried it. "Still no signal."

Willa hooked her seat belt. He started the engine, pulled a U-turn and off they went.

It took them over an hour to get to the Triple T. The roads were washed out in several places and they had to find a way around the trouble spots. There was soggy, broken stuff strewn randomly wherever the water had risen, not to mention swamped, abandoned vehicles. Willa tried to take heart that they were all only *things*.

Collin played the truck's radio for news. Roads and bridges were out everywhere. Any number of small towns on the western side of the state from Butte north had sustained serious damage. A third of the state had been designated a disaster area and there were constant warnings—about staying off the roads as much as possible, about exercising caution in flooded buildings, about the danger of snakes and the hazards of rats. About steering clear of downed power lines.

At the Triple T, all the buildings were above the waterline and undamaged, but there would still be one heck of a cleanup to deal with. The hands who'd been taking care of the place were there and safe. Willa told them how to get into her parents' house to get fresh water for the next day or so, until they could disinfect the wells. They said they would check the stock for her as soon as they'd dealt with the animals on the Triple T.

Once Collin seemed satisfied that the hands had things under control, he said, "We should get going, go on into town."

She caught his arm before they got in the cab.

He stopped and turned to look at her. "Yeah?" His skin was so warm under her hand. Smooth flesh, hard muscles beneath. She felt suddenly shy with him and jerked her hand away. He frowned. "What's the matter?"

"I, well, I was just thinking that I'll bet you really want to go back up the mountain to check on things at your place. You could just drop me off when we get to Falls Street and I can hitch a ride in."

He stuck his fists into the front pockets of her dad's overalls and tipped his head to the side. "What the hell, Willa? I'm not leaving you alone on the street."

His words warmed her. But still. She really did need to stop taking advantage of his kindness to her.

Kindness.

Incredible. She'd been so busy judging him as a heartless, undisciplined sex maniac for all these years, she'd never had a clue what a softy he really was. She shook her head. "Oh, come on now. It's Rust Creek Falls. We both know I'll be perfectly safe."

"We don't know what's going on since last night. And I don't want you wandering around alone."

"Collin, I would hardly *wander*. And I know everyone in town, so I won't by any stretch of the imagination be alone."

"I'm coming with you. I want to be with you when you check on your house." He said the words in a cautious tone. They both knew where her house was: directly in the path of the water. She was already resigned to the fact that it had to be flooded and was hoping that at least some of her clothing and furniture might be salvageable.

"Honestly, I can handle it. I was pretty shell-shocked yesterday, I know. But I'm over that. I'm ready to face whatever comes. You don't have to worry about me."

He was scowling now. "Why are you trying to get rid of me?"

She fell back a step. "But I'm not. I just thought…"

He caught her arm with his calloused hand. It felt so good, his touch. And his grip was so strong. "What?" he demanded. "You thought what?"

She looked up at him, at his smoldering dark eyes and those lips that seemed like they were made for kissing a woman and she wondered what he would do if *she* kissed *him*. The idea made her feel both embarrassed and giddy. She almost giggled.

"Willa," he demanded. "What is going on with you all of a sudden?"

Now she was thinking about earlier that morning. About waking up with her hand where it shouldn't have been—about how he'd been turned on.

Get real, Willa. Just because he became aroused didn't

mean he was dying to have sex with her in particular. It was simple biology, and she needed to remember that.

And if he wanted to keep on being kind to her, well, maybe she'd just let him. Maybe she'd just go right on taking advantage of Collin Traub and enjoying every minute of it. "Nothing is 'going on' with me. I just wanted to make sure I wasn't taking advantage of you."

"You're not."

"So…you don't mind going into town, then?"

"It's not about minding. It's what I planned to do. People will need help. They'll need every able-bodied man."

"And woman," she reminded him.

"Right." He had the good sense to agree.

She pressed her lips together to keep from grinning up at him like some addled fool and said, "Well, fair enough, then. I was just, um, checking."

He seemed to realize suddenly that he was gripping her arm—and let go. "Checking." Now he looked suspicious.

She put on her most innocent expression. "Uh-huh. Nothing wrong with checking, making sure you're okay with what's going on."

"If I'm not okay, you'll know it."

"Well, then, I'll stop checking."

"Good. Can we go now?"

She had that silly urge to grin again. Must be the stress of all she'd been through since yesterday. Yeah. Right. That must be it.

The trip into Rust Creek Falls was as booby-trapped with obstacles as the ride to the Triple T had been.

There was the smell of smoke in the air. It wasn't just from wood fires in stoves and fireplaces. They heard the sirens, saw the roiling smoke in the distance. On the south side of town, some homes had caught fire. Willa prayed her house wasn't one of them—and then she put her house out of her mind and prayed that no lives were endangered by the fires.

Other travelers were on the road by then, most of whom they recognized. Everyone seemed to have somewhere important to go. People waved and honked, but nobody pulled over to talk about what they'd been through or exchange information about the disaster. Collin had the radio on. All the way there, they listened to advice on how to deal with the aftermath of the Great Independence Day Flood.

When they finally got to Falls Street on the southeastern edge of town, they had to circle around and take other roads farther east and then work their way back in. It was nothing but mud, pools of water, swamped, abandoned vehicles and way too much debris south of the creek. The buildings they saw before they turned east were still standing, but bore the telltale signs of water damage within.

Eventually, they reached Sawmill Street and turned west again. The water level was way down from flood stage and the bridge appeared intact. Collin pulled the pickup to the shoulder before they crossed it. They both got out to have a look, to make sure that crossing would be safe. Buster jumped out to follow them.

But then a couple of pickups came rolling across from the town side. Behind the wheel of the second truck was a rancher they both recognized, Hank Garmond. Hank owned a nice little spread at the southwestern edge of the valley.

He pulled to a stop. "Willa. Collin. I see you're both in one piece and still breathing. Could be worse, eh? I'm headin' back to my place. We still got a house, but we lost the barn and sheds. Haven't started counting cattle yet. I just stopped in at Crawford's to try and get a few supplies to tide us over." Crawford's General Store, on North

Main, was a town landmark. The store sold everything from basic foodstuffs to farm supplies, hardware and clothing. "Shelves are already lookin' pretty bare in there."

Collin asked, "How bad is it?"

"In town? Power's out, and all the phones. North of the creek is okay, from what I heard. No flooding, the water supply unaffected. South is not lookin' good. Commercial Street Bridge is washed out. There's damage to the Main Street Bridge. People are bypassing it. We still got this bridge though." He pointed a thumb back over his shoulder. "Praise the Lord for small favors." *Very small favors,* Willa couldn't help thinking. True, it was pretty much what she and Collin had thought it would be, but somehow, to hear Hank confirm their suspicions made it all the more horribly real. "And then there's what happened to Hunter McGee." Hunter McGee was the mayor.

"What?" Willa demanded.

"Tree fell on that old SUV of his. So happened he was in the SUV at the time."

Willa respected Mayor McGee. He was a born leader, a real booster of education and had planned and promoted several school-related fund-raising events. "My Lord," she cried. "Was he hurt?"

"The tree fell on the hood. Not a scratch on him." Hank resettled his hat on his head and Willa felt relief. But then Hank added, "Must have scared the you-know-what right out of him. He had a heart attack."

Willa put her hand over her mouth. "Oh, no…"

"Oh, yeah. It was over real quick for Mayor McGee."

"Over?" Willa's heart sank. "You—you mean he's…?"

Hank nodded. An SUV and another pickup came across the bridge. The occupants waved as they drove by. Hank said somberly, "They took him to Emmet's house. Emmet pronounced him DOA." Emmet dePaulo, a nurse-practitioner, ran the town clinic. "Clinic's flooded, in case you were wondering."

Willa and Collin exchanged grim glances. They weren't surprised. The clinic was south of Main. "Emmet and a couple of his neighbors waded in there and saved what equipment and supplies they could first thing this morning. Luckily, Emmet had a lot of his medical stuff stored on the second floor and the water didn't make it that high. He's set up an emergency clinic at his house, for now."

"They got the volunteer fire guys out on search and rescue?" Collin asked.

Hank shrugged. "Can't say. I ain't heard of anybody dead, hurt bad or stranded…'ceptin' Mayor McGee, I mean. Rest his soul. But I did hear that some county trucks brought in salvage-and-rescue equipment and sandbags yesterday before the levee broke. This morning, the town council put together an emergency crew to patch up the places where the water got through. So that's taken care of for now. And you can just have a look at the creek. Water level's back to normal range."

Collin gave a humorless chuckle. "Yeah, one good thing about breaks in the levee. They tend to bring the water level way down."

"That they do," Hank concurred. "Plus, there's no rain in the forecast for at least the next week. So we're unlikely to have a repeat of what happened yesterday—oh, and the town council called a meeting at noon in the town hall to talk cleanup and such. Wish I could be there, but I got way too much cleanup of my own out at my place and I need to get after it. Bought the bleach I needed, at least. I can disinfect my well." Hank tipped his hat.

"You stay safe and take it slow on the road, Hank," Collin said.

"Will do. You keep the faith, now." The rancher rolled on by.

Collin put his arm around her. "You're lookin' kind of stricken, Willa."

She leaned into him, because she could. She needed someone to lean on at that moment. And Collin was so solid. So warm. So very much alive. "I'd been letting myself hope that at least no one had died—and I really liked Mayor McGee."

"I hear you. Hunter was a good man and this town could sure use him about now." He pulled her a little closer in the shelter of his arm and turned them both back to the pickup, Buster at their heels. The dog jumped in back again and they got in the cab.

As they drove across the bridge, Willa tried not to dread what might be waiting for them on the other side.

Chapter Four

It didn't look so awfully bad, Willa told herself as they drove along Sawmill Street. In fact, there on the northern edge of town, things seemed almost normal. Willa spotted a couple of downed trees and some flattened fences, but nothing like the devastation they'd witnessed coming in.

When they turned onto Main Street going south, they saw that the Crawford store parking lot was packed, people going in—and coming out mostly empty-handed. She supposed she shouldn't be all that surprised. It wouldn't take long to clear out the shelves of emergency supplies if everyone in town and most of the valley's ranchers showed up all at once and grabbed whatever they could fit in a cart.

The Community Church had its doors wide open. People sat on the steps there or stood out under the trees in front. Most of them looked confused. And lost.

"Shouldn't the Red Cross be showing up any minute?" she asked hopefully. "And what about FEMA and the National Guard?"

Collin grunted. "With a lot of the state in this condition, the phones out and the roads blocked, we'll be real lucky if a few supply trucks get to us in the next day or two." And then he swore low. "Isn't that the mayor's SUV?" The old brown 4x4 was half in, half out of the town hall parking lot. It had definitely come out the loser in the encounter with the downed elm tree. The tree lay square across what was left of the hood. The driver's door gaped open. A couple of boys in their early teens were peering in the windows.

"That's just too sad," Willa said low. "You'd think they'd want it off the street."

"Damn right." Collin muttered. "A sight like that is not encouraging." He hit the brake—and then swung a U-turn in front of the library, pulling in at the curb.

"Collin!" Willa cried, surprised. "What in the…?"

He shouted out the window at the two boys. "Hey, you two. Get over here."

Both boys froze. They wore guilty expressions. But then they put on their best tough-guy scowls and sauntered to Collin's side of the truck. They were the older brothers of a couple of Willa's former students and when they spotted her in the passenger seat, they dropped some of the attitude and mumbled in unison, "'Lo, Ms. Christensen."

She gave them both a slow nod.

One of them raked his shaggy hair off his forehead and met Collin's eyes. "Yeah?"

As he'd already done several times in the past eighteen hours or so, Collin surprised her. He knew their names. "Jesse. Franklin. Show a little respect, huh?"

Jesse, who was fourteen if Willa remembered correctly, cleared his throat. "We are, Mr. Traub." *Mr. Traub.* So strange. To hear anybody call the youngest, wildest Traub *mister.* But then again, well, the Traubs were pillars of the

Rust Creek Falls community. Some of that probably rubbed off, even on the family bad boy—especially to a couple of impressionable teenagers.

Franklin, who was thirteen, added, "We were just, you know, checkin' things out."

Collin leaned out the window and suggested in a just-between-us-men kind of voice, "You two could make yourselves useful, do this town a real big favor...."

The two boys perked up considerably. "Well, yeah. Sure," said Jesse.

"How?" asked Franklin.

"Head on up to the garage. See if Clovis has a tow truck he can spare." Clovis Hart had owned and run the garage and gas station at Sawmill and North Buckskin for as long as Willa could remember. "Tell him the mayor's SUV is still sitting in the middle of Main Street with a tree trunk buried in its hood and lots of folks would appreciate it if Clovis could tow it away."

The boys shared a wide-eyed look. And then Franklin said, "Yeah. We could do that."

"You want me to take you up there?"

"Naw," said Jesse, puffing out his skinny chest. "We can handle it ourselves."

"Good enough, then. Thanks, boys—and tell Clovis he probably ought to bring a chain saw for that tree."

"We will." The two took off up Main at a run.

"That was well done," Willa said, and didn't even bother to try and hide the admiration in her voice.

Collin grunted. "Maybe, but do you think they'll make it happen?"

"You know, I kind of do. They're good kids. And this is a way for them to help. And you know Clovis."

"Yes, I do. Clovis Hart respected Hunter McGee and he won't like it that the car Hunter died in is sitting on

Main with the hood smashed in for everyone to stare and point at."

She glanced toward the dashboard clock. It was 10:45 a.m. "So what do we do now?"

"I was thinking we could go and see how your house made out...."

She glanced over her shoulder, out the back window, past a happily panting Buster, at the Main Street Bridge. Someone had put a row of orange traffic cones in front of it to warn people off trying to use it. And one of her brother's deputies was standing, arms folded, in front of the pedestrian walk that spanned one side. "It doesn't look like they're letting folks cross the bridge."

Connor glanced over his shoulder, too. "We could try heading back to the Sawmill Street Bridge, then going on foot along the top of the levee until we get to your street."

"That could be dangerous...I mean, with the breaks in the levee and all. We would have to go carefully, and we don't know what we'll find if we manage to get to my house. It could take hours and we would miss the noon meeting Hank mentioned. I do think we should go to that."

Collin faced front again, his big shoulders slumping, and stared broodingly out the windshield back the way they had come. "You know who'll be running that meeting now Hunter's gone, don't you?"

She did. "Nathan Crawford." Nathan was in his early thirties, a member of the town council. Everyone expected him to be mayor himself someday. He and Collin had never liked each other. It was as if the two had been born to be enemies. Nathan was as handsome and dynamic as Collin was brooding and magnetic. Collin had always been a rebel and Nathan considered himself a community leader.

Rumor had it that five or six years back, Nathan's girlfriend, Anita, had gone out on him—with Collin. Word was Anita had told Collin that she and Nathan were through. But apparently, she'd failed to inform Nathan of that fact. There'd been a fight, a nasty one, between the two men. Some claimed Collin had won, others insisted Nathan had come out the victor. After that, the two had hated each other more than ever.

Plus, there was the old rivalry between their two families. Nathan was a Crawford to the core. The Crawfords not only owned the general store, they were also as influential in the community as the Traubs. And for as long as anyone could remember, Crawfords and Traubs had been at odds. Willa didn't really know the origin of the feud, but it seemed to be bred in the bone now between the town's two most important families. Traubs didn't think much of Crawfords. And the Crawfords returned the favor.

She spoke gently, but with firmness. "I really think it's important that everyone who can possibly be there attends that meeting."

He put his arm along the back of the seat and touched her shoulder, a gentle brush of a touch. She felt that touch acutely. His dark eyes sought hers—and held them. "So you want to go to the meeting first and then decide what to do about getting to your place?"

She smiled at him. "I do. Yes." Right then, a Rust Creek Garage tow truck came rumbling toward them down the street.

"I've got a chain saw in my toolbox in the back." Collin got out to give Clovis a hand.

At ten past two that afternoon the town hall meeting was still going on.

Collin sat next to Willa and wished he was anywhere but there. He was getting hungry, for one thing. And he figured the rest of the crowd had to be hungry, too.

The big multipurpose meeting room was packed. They had a generator for the lights, but there was no air-conditioning, never had been in the town hall. As a rule, it didn't get that hot in Rust Creek Falls. But with all the bodies packed in that room, it was hot now.

Tired, frightened, stressed-out townsfolk had taken every chair. More people stood at the back or along the side walls. There were children, too. People didn't want to let their kids out of their sight at a time like this. And kids got restless when forced to sit or stand in one place for too long.

Babies were wailing and small voices kept asking, "Daddy, when can we go?" and "Mommy, is this over yet?"

There were a lot of big talkers in town and every one of them was insisting on being heard. Plus, that jerk Nathan sat up there on the hall stage with the other useless members of the council and kept banging the mayor's big hand-carved oak gavel for order.

All right, it was true. A lot of people thought the world of Nathan Crawford. And maybe, if Collin were being fair about it, he'd admit that Nathan had a few good qualities. However, when it came to most Crawfords, and Nathan in particular, Collin just plain didn't feel like being fair.

Nathan had the council in his pocket, naturally. They all looked at him like he was wearing a damn halo or something, like he was the one sent down from heaven to single-handedly fix everything that had gone so completely wrong since the day before.

"Everyone, your attention!" Nathan boomed in that smooth baritone that made people think he knew what he was talking about. "We all have to work together here. As I've said before, though phone, internet and TV are temporarily out of commission, we have the radio system at the sheriff's office and we are in communication with

DES—that is the state office of Disaster and Emergency Services. They are well aware of what is going on in Rust Creek Falls and the valley. And, unfortunately, in far too many other communities in western Montana. The good news, however, is that everything is under control and moving along."

Somebody in the crowd made a rude noise.

Nathan banged the mayor's gavel some more. "If we could all just be patient for a little bit longer, we will get these teams firmed up, so we can all get going on the cleanup right away."

Collin knew he should keep his mouth shut. His plan had been to get through the meeting, help Willa deal with the probable ruin of her home and then pitch in wherever he was needed. But Nathan and the council had their priorities turned around. And while there were plenty of people willing to go on and on about the difficulty of the situation and how much they wanted to help, nobody else seemed ready to tell the council they were putting the cart before the horse.

He got to his feet. Beside him, Willa startled and looked up at him, wide-eyed. She did amuse him, the way she always looked so worried about what he might do next. He sent her a glance that he meant to be reassuring. Her eyes only got wider. So much for soothing her. He faced front and waded in.

"I'm sorry. Nobody's speaking up about the real issue here and so I suppose I'm going to have to be the one. Nathan, cleanup is not the issue yet," he said good and loud. "First, we need to get teams into the flooded areas and see who needs help there. We need search and rescue and we needed it hours ago."

A chorus of agreement rose from the crowd. Apparently,

others thought there should be a rescue effort. It was only that no one had been willing to stand up and say it out loud.

Nathan banged his gavel. He looked at Collin the way he always did: as though he'd just crawled out from under a rock. "Order. Please, everyone. I already explained. We have the volunteer firefighters out searching for trapped or injured survivors."

"One team, you're saying? With how many men on it?"

Nathan didn't answer either question. Instead, he went right on with his argument. "Those men are trained for this and know what they're doing. We don't think it's a big problem. No one has reported anyone missing."

"And how're you going to know if someone's missing?" Collin demanded. "People can't call. The phones are out. There can't be more than a third of the people in the valley here at this meeting or hanging around Main Street. Where are the rest of them? Trying to clean up what's theirs? Off to Livingston for the rodeo, or down in Thunder Canyon with the rest of my family? Or trapped on the upper floors of their houses, wondering why no one's come looking for them?"

"But we *are* looking. And I honestly do not believe—"

Collin didn't even let him get started. "And you didn't answer my first question. How many men are out on search and rescue, Nathan?"

Others spoke up then. "Yeah! How many?" someone demanded.

"Not enough, that's how many!" answered another.

Nathan's face had gone a deep shade of red. "People, please. Order!"

Collin stuck his hands into the pockets of Wayne Christensen's overalls and waited for Nathan to stop pounding that gavel. Once he did, Collin answered the question himself. "I'm guessing about nine. Nine men to cover the whole of this town and the valley. Have I got that right?"

"Nine strong, able men who are trained in effective search and rescue," Nathan insisted, his face even redder than before.

Collin kept after him. "It doesn't matter how good they are. Nine men are not enough. We need to put every able-bodied adult on the search until we've made a circuit of all the homes and ranches in town and in the valley. It shouldn't take more than the rest of today and tomorrow, if we get a move on. After that, we can change our focus to salvage and cleanup."

Down the row from him and Willa, one of the Crawford men called out, "Sit down and shut up, why don't you, Traub? Let them that knows what they're doing make the decisions here."

"Yeah," said another voice. "We don't need the likes of *you* tellin' us what to do first."

And that was when Willa shot to her feet beside him. At first, Collin thought she would grab his arm and beg him to stay out of it.

But it turned out he'd misjudged her. "I feel I must add my voice to Collin's," she said in that prim schoolmarm way of hers that never failed to get him kind of hot. "We have no idea how many people might be trapped in their homes or their barns. There are bound to be collapsed buildings. People could be buried in the rubble, praying they'll be rescued before it's too late. We've already lost Mayor McGee."

"Bless his soul," said a woman's voice.

"Amen," said another.

Willa wasn't finished. "Search and rescue is the first job. And we need to give it everything. We can't afford to lose one more precious life in Rust Creek Falls or the valley."

And Collin added his voice to hers. "We've got to save our *people* before we worry about our property."

The room erupted in whistles and applause. People shouted, "By God, he's right!" and "Search and rescue!" and "Collin's said it!" and "Listen to the schoolteacher!"

By the time the clapping finally stopped, even Nathan had seen the writing on the wall. He did what he had to do and went along. "The council, as always, seeks to understand and take action according to the wishes of our citizens. We will call in the nine trained men and reassign them as team leaders."

Willa leaned close and asked softly, "Call? The phones are out...."

He whispered back, "They'll have handheld radios—walkie-talkies."

"Oh. Right..."

Nathan was still talking. "For today and tomorrow—and as long as is needed—those nine leaders will head the teams in our search-and-rescue efforts. Volunteers, seek out a leader. Marjorie?"

Marjorie Hanke, the council member to Nathan's right, stood, picked up a pointer and smacked it against the map of the county that hung behind the council table. The map had already been divided into sections for the proposed cleanup teams. "Team one, section one—and so on," Marjorie announced. "We've been fortunate in that rubber boots, heavy rubber gloves and necessary tools have already been trucked in and will be provided to each of you. Please wear the boots and gloves at all times when searching in mud or standing water. Be on careful lookout, everyone, for vermin of all persuasions. Floods bring out the rats and displace the snakes. Thank you, Nathan." With a nod, she set down the pointer and took her seat again.

Nathan wrapped it up. At last. "Getting around in the flood areas isn't easy, but we are able to truck in supplies from Kalispell for those in need. The Ladies Auxiliary of the Community Church has set out a meal on the church lawn while we've been busy with our meeting here. If everyone will file outside in an orderly manner, Pastor Alderson will lead us in a prayer, after which we will share a late lunch. By then, your team leaders will have returned—and the search for missing survivors can commence."

Chapter Five

Buster, leashed to a railing outside the town hall, whined and wiggled in greeting when Willa went to collect him. She took a minute to pet him and praise him for being such a good dog.

Collin got her pack from his pickup for her and then he walked across the street to the church at her side. When her friend and fellow teacher, Paige Dalton, waved and called her name, Willa quickly looked away and pretended she didn't hear.

No, it wasn't nice of her to treat a friend that way. But she wanted a few more minutes with Collin. Soon, he would be off with one of the search teams. And then he would probably want to go up the mountain, to check on his house. There would be no reason, once he left with the searchers, for them to be together anymore. The time had come when they would go their separate ways.

She would always be grateful to him—for saving her

life in the flood, for helping her make it through those awful first hours trapped in the barn. But she felt a bit wistful, too. For most of that day, it had almost seemed as though she and Collin were a team, ready and able to do what needed doing, fully capable, between them, of handling whatever challenges might arise. It had been a strangely heady feeling.

She wished she didn't feel so sad suddenly. But already, she was looking back longingly on the afternoon and evening before, and at the morning just passed. In retrospect now, it seemed hard to believe that she'd held a grudge against him for four long years. Her recent ill will toward him seemed something from another lifetime—from someone *else's* lifetime. She simply didn't have it in her to feel bitterness toward him now.

Now, she could almost view the flood and its immediate aftermath as some sort of lovely, exciting adventure story come to life, an adventure starring the two of them— which was way too self-absorbed of her and she knew it. This was no adventure story. This was a bona fide real-life disaster. People she cared about were losing everything.

Including herself, if you came right down to it. She wasn't holding out a lot of hope for the condition of her house. And what about all of her stuff? She had so many treasures—her favorite velvet sofa pillow, the fairy-tale books she'd collected since childhood, that spindly inlaid table she proudly displayed in the front hall…

The list was endless. What would be left of the things that she loved?

She ordered herself not to go there. Her belongings might be precious to her, but they *were* only things and she needed to remember that now.

At least she had flood insurance, as did Gage, thank God. Whatever condition her house might be in, there would eventually be money to repair or rebuild. Many people in town and in the valley couldn't afford flood insurance. They could end up with nothing.

Collin nudged her arm. "You're wrinkling up your forehead. What's the matter?"

She tugged on Buster's leash as he dawdled, sniffing at the curb. "Just worrying, I guess."

"Stop." He gave her one of those sexy bad-boy grins of his. "We're going to get fed. It's something to be happy about."

At the church, the ladies auxiliary had been busy. They'd set up rows of tables out on the lawn. And they'd even thought of people's pets. Thelma, Hunter McGee's mother, gave her a bowl of water for Buster and a couple of dog biscuits. The older woman looked pale, Willa thought, and her eyes were swollen and red-rimmed.

Willa wrapped her in a hug and whispered, "He will be greatly missed."

Thelma sniffed and forced a brave smile. "We must soldier on," she said, and bent to give Buster a pat on the head.

Everyone remained standing while the pastor said a short prayer. He praised the stalwart heart and fine leadership of their lost mayor and asked that the people of Rust Creek Falls might find the strength they needed to endure this difficult time. At the last, he blessed the food.

"Amen," they all said softly, in unison.

It wasn't a fancy meal, but when you're hungry, the simplest food can be so satisfying. They had chicken salad sandwiches, chips, apples, oatmeal cookies and all the water they could drink. Collin sat next to her. They didn't talk. They were too busy filling their empty stomachs.

The volunteer firemen started coming in, muddy and looking tired. They washed up in the church restrooms and grabbed sandwiches, which they ate standing up. People rose from the tables and surrounded them, eager to join their teams.

Collin leaned close to her. He smelled faintly of her dad's shaving cream, which made her smile. He muttered, "I meant what I said before. Finish eating and we'll find a way to get to your house. I can join a team after that."

She set down her cup of water. "Thank you, but no. You said it yourself in the town hall just now. The search for survivors has to come first."

He looked at her, a probing sort of look. That dark lock of hair had fallen over his forehead again the way it tended to do. More than ever, she wanted to smooth it back.

But she didn't. Instead, she took a bite of her cookie and downed her last sip of water.

"You sure?" He looked doubtful.

"I am, yes. First things first."

Willa assumed she would end up watching the little ones while their mothers and fathers went out on the search-and-rescue teams. People knew she was good with their kids and trusted her with them.

While Collin went to join a search team, she asked Mrs. McGee about pitching in with child care. Thelma told her to check in with the church nursery. The older woman also volunteered to look after Buster for the rest of the day.

"He's a nice dog," Thelma said, her tone bright and cheerful, endless sadness in her eyes. "Taking care of him will be no trouble at all."

Willa thanked her, gave her another quick hug and ran up the steps into the church, headed for the nursery in back.

Paige caught up with her in the sanctuary. "Willa. I've been so worried about you. The whole south side is flooded. Your house, is it…?"

"I don't know. I haven't been there since it happened. I left to check on the ranch and track Buster down before the levee broke. On the way, my car got swamped."

"Oh, my Lord. But you got out all right…."

"Thanks to Collin Traub." Willa brought her friend up to speed on how Collin had saved her from the flood. "My car's a total loss. And we ended up waiting out the rest of the storm in the barn."

"I don't know what to say. It's awful. But I'm so glad you're okay."

"Yeah. Still breathing and all in one piece—and the barn and my parents' house are fine."

Paige asked hopefully. "Gage's place?"

Willa bit her lip and shook her head. "Bad."

"Oh, Willa." Paige held out her arms.

Willa went into them and held on tight. "It's all so scary…"

"Oh, I know, I know." Paige pulled back, took Willa by the shoulders and gazed at her through solemn, worried brown eyes. "Collin, huh?" she asked gently.

Willa wasn't surprised at her friend's cryptic question. Paige was one of the few people in town who knew about that awful night at the Ace in the Hole *and* about Willa's longtime crush on the Traub bad boy. Willa had told her friend everything on one of those Friday nights they shared now then—just the two of them, watching a romantic comedy on DVD, a big bowl of popcorn between them. Paige could keep a secret. She would never tell a soul.

Willa realized it was time to admit that she'd let injured pride cloud her judgment in a very big way. "I was all wrong about him." There was no one else nearby, but she kept her voice low just in case. "I mean, so what if he turned me down once? It's not that big of a deal. He's a good guy, someone anyone would want at their back in a crisis."

"Well, I can see that, but still…" Paige let the sentence die unfinished.

Willa reminded her friend, "Paige, seriously. The man saved my life yesterday and he was right there, sticking by me all night and this morning, too, when we had to face all the damage."

Paige put up both hands. "All right. He's a hero. You've convinced me." And then she shrugged. "I'm not surprised, really. I always believed there was a good guy underneath all that swagger." Like Willa, Paige knew the Traub family well. She'd even been in love with a Traub once—Collin's brother Sutter. It hadn't worked out for them. Now Sutter owned a stable in the Seattle area. He didn't come home often, and when he did, he never stayed long. "So…" Paige hesitated.

Willa tried not to roll her eyes. "Go ahead."

"Are you and Collin together now?"

Together. With Collin. The thought made her cheeks grow warm. She hastened to clarify, "No. It's not like that. He helped me out when I needed a hand, that's all. He helped me a lot and I'm grateful to him."

"Right." Paige gave her a knowing look. "And there *is* still Dane to consider."

Willa felt instantly guilty. She hadn't given Dane Everhart a thought since last night, when she'd made a big show of throwing the poor guy in Collin's face. "I told you. I really don't think it's going anywhere with Dane—and yes, when he proposed marriage, I should have said no right then and there. But Dane is so sure that he and I are a good match. And he's so charming and confident and… I don't know. We get along, but it's never been anything romantic."

Her friend said softly, "But Dane would like it to be."

Willa gulped and nodded. "It's so completely...*Dane*, to decide to marry me and refuse to take no for an answer. But in the end, he'll have to face facts. He's just not the guy for me."

Page coaxed, "But Collin is?"

"No. Really. Come on, Paige. I said it was nothing like that with Collin."

"But you *always* liked him—and not in that friends-only way that you seem to feel about Dane."

Willa lowered her voice even more. "It was a crush that I had on Collin, a teenage crush, that's all—and stop looking at me like that."

"Like what?"

"Like you think I'm lying to myself."

"Did I say that?" Now Paige was looking way too innocent.

"You didn't have to. And you've got it all wrong. It's just that Collin and I have patched up our differences and we're on good terms now." Okay, she'd spent the previous night in his arms, but only because it had helped them keep warm. And she wasn't even going to *think* about that moment in the morning when they first woke up. Uh-uh. She was just wiping that moment clean out of her head.

"So you and Collin are friends, then?"

Friends? With Collin? It kind of felt that way, but maybe it was just the flood and all they'd been through since yesterday. She had to be careful not to read too much into it. He was off helping with the rescue effort now. When he returned, there would be no reason for him to seek her out. Their future contact with each other would be casual: saying hi when they passed each other on the street, stopping to chat now and then when they ran into each other at the store or the doughnut shop. "I don't know. We're... friendly, okay? We're getting along."

Paige's soft mouth tipped up in that warm smile that always made Willa so glad to be *her* friend. She chuckled. "Honey, you sound confused."

Why not just admit it? "Okay. Yeah. I am, a little…"

"You come and stay at my house tonight." Paige lived on North Pine, well north of the flooded area. "We'll have a nice glass of wine and I'll set you straight."

Willa laughed, too. "Uh-oh."

"Seriously. I want you staying with me as long as you need to. And don't you dare go out and stay at the ranch alone now. You need to be with a friend."

Willa felt suddenly misty-eyed. "Thanks, Paige."

Paige leaned closer. "And I have to say, I like it that Collin stood up in the meeting and got everyone to see that we need to put all our effort on searching for survivors first."

"Yes—and that reminds me. Are you helping with child care? I was just going to the nursery to see if they need me."

Paige caught her arm again. "I guess you didn't hear. The older ladies are taking care of the kids. Women our age in good shape, they want pitching in with the rescue effort. Come on. We'll get ourselves on a team."

Three people were rescued that day: two disabled shut-ins marooned upstairs in their flooded houses, and a rancher, Barton Derby, who lived alone and whose barn had collapsed on top of him. The team leaders kept in communication on their handheld radios and passed on the news when someone was found.

Barton Derby had compound fractures to both legs and had to be taken to the hospital in Kalispell, a long drive with so many of the roads badly damaged or still flooded. The word was that Derby survived the trip without incident.

The two shut-ins were physically unhurt, just very hungry and frantic over the damage to their homes. Willa and Paige's team leader told them that Thelma McGee, who owned a big house on Cedar Street, had taken them both to stay with her until other arrangements could be made.

For Willa and Paige's team, the triumphs were small. They pulled two foundering heifers from a pond, contacted old Barrett Smith, the local vet, to treat an injured horse and brought a frightened cat down from up a tree. Mostly, though, they made the circuit of the houses and outbuildings in their section of the search map and found the owners in residence doing their best to deal with the thousand and one challenges the flood had dumped in their laps.

The teams began returning to Main Street at dusk. The phones and electricity were still out, but there was food in the church multiuse room for anyone who needed it. Makeshift dormitories had been set up in the town hall and Masonic Hall for those who had nowhere else to go.

Paige came with Willa to the church, where they ate with their team by the light of kerosene and battery-powered lanterns. Once they had food in their stomachs, she nudged Willa. "Come on. Let's go to my place and get some rest..."

Willa hesitated. She would have loved a shower and to settle into that nice, big bed in Paige's guest room. But somehow, she couldn't do it. "I think I'll just get a cot in the town hall."

"Willa. Why? I want you to come and stay with me."

"And I love you for that. But I just can't..." It seemed important right then to stick with the other people who had been dispossessed. She wanted to stay close to the center of things, at least for the first night or two, until the search for survivors was finished and she could be certain that everyone in town and in the valley was safe and whole, with food in their bellies.

"You're sure?" Paige brushed her arm, a companionable touch.

Willa nodded. "Yeah. It just…feels right, to stay with the others for now."

So Paige gave her a hug and promised to be back for breakfast before the search began again in the morning. Then she asked around to see who needed lodging. She took Buck and Bella McAnder and their two little girls home with her. The McAnders lived a few houses down from Willa, on South Broomtail Road. All over the north side of town, people were doing that, taking in families who lived south of the creek.

So far, Collin had yet to appear for dinner. Once Paige was gone, Willa checked out the team sign-up sheets that were posted on the wall right there in the church multiuse room. He'd joined Team Three, headed by Jerry Dobbs. It was the team that had rescued Barton Derby.

Team Three came in a few minutes later. Collin wasn't with them. She knew she ought to leave it alone. If he'd been injured in the search, she would have heard about it. There was nothing to worry over.

But then, well, she just *had* to know for sure that everything was okay with him. She approached Jerry Dobbs and asked if he knew where Collin might be.

"A real asset to our team, that Collin," Jerry said. "Without him, we might not have gotten Bart out from under his barn. People can't help but get scared around piles of unstable materials. Some held back, afraid to pitch in. Or worse, some were *too* brave and not careful enough. Collin reassured the scared ones and kept an eye on the chancetakers. The man's a born leader, levelheaded and calm and encouraging to others in a crisis. Plus, he's in top shape and light on his feet."

Willa didn't especially like the sound of all that. Had Collin put himself in danger to get Barton out? It would be just like him, after all. "Yes," she said, and tried to sound cheerful. "Collin Traub has no fear."

Jerry nodded. "And I think he mentioned something about stopping over at the Triple T to see how they were getting along out there."

She should have known. Of course he would have to go see how the hands at the family ranch were managing. She thanked Jerry, shouldered the pack she'd been dragging around with her all afternoon and walked over to Thelma's to get Buster.

By then, Thelma had a houseful of visitors. She'd made room not only for the two rescued shut-ins, but also for a couple of young families who owned houses on the south side of the creek.

"I'll be over at the church for breakfast tomorrow," Thelma said, as Buster sat on the step, cheerfully panting, cocking one ear and then the other, glancing from Thelma to Willa and back again. "I'll be happy to take Buster then. He's been a comfort, I have to tell you. He likes to stick close to me, but he's not in the way."

"He's a good dog," Willa said fondly. Buster made an eager little whining sound in response. "Just don't let him out unsupervised or you never know where he'll head off to."

"I won't," Thelma promised. "I'll keep him close."

Willa thanked her again and said good-night.

In the town hall, the generator was still going strong. It seemed so bright in there compared to the lantern light at Thelma's and in the church. The chairs in the meeting room had been folded up and stacked against the walls.

Rows of narrow cots waited for her and about fifty other people whose houses were in the still-restricted area south of the creek. She was a little anxious that Buster might not be allowed in. But it wasn't a problem. Marjorie Hanke, the councilwoman assigned to supervise sleeping arrangements in the hall, told her that as long as he behaved himself he could sleep beside Willa's cot.

Collin wasn't there. Disappointment tried to drag her down, which was ridiculous. The man had his own life, after all. He had things he needed to do. He could be staying at the Triple T for the night, or over at the church getting something to eat, or possibly bedding down in the other makeshift dormitory in the Masonic Hall. He might even have headed up the mountain to his house.

She truly hoped he hadn't been foolish enough to do that. Not in the dark. After the storm, there was no telling what condition that road would be in.

It was very annoying. He was so unpredictable. A person hardly knew what he might do next.

And really, she needed to stop thinking about him. She needed to be grateful that he'd saved her life and glad that she'd gotten past her issues with him—and let it go at that.

She leashed Buster to a leg of the cot and took her turn in the bathroom, washing up as best she could in the sink. Marjorie was passing out baggies containing personal grooming supplies to those without, but Willa had her own. She'd raided her mother's medicine cabinet for soap, deodorant and a toothbrush, and she'd also thought to grab an old pair of lightweight pink sweatpants, flip-flops and a clean T-shirt from the box under the stairs.

Back in the meeting room, people were settling in, getting as comfortable as possible for the night. When everyone had finished in the restrooms, Marjorie turned off all the lights, save one. She left it on low, for a night-light.

Willa lay back, stared at the dark ceiling overhead and felt certain she'd be awake half the night, worrying about her parents and Gage, who were probably going nuts, wondering what was happening at home. She knew she would end up lying there, eyes wide-open, obsessing over the extent of the damage of her house. She was positive that she would have to firmly remind herself not to get all worked up over the tragic death of the mayor, and not to think about Collin, who surely would not have been so foolish as to head up the mountain in the dark of night.

But strangely, within minutes of zipping up her borrowed sleeping bag, her eyes had drifted shut. With a sigh, she turned on her side, tucked her hand under her cheek, and let sleep steal all her worries away.

The double doors to the town hall meeting room were shut when Collin arrived. He eased through them soundlessly.

Marjorie Hanke, in a cot by the door, sat up and pointed to an empty one a few feet away. Collin whispered a thank-you and tiptoed to the unoccupied cot. It wasn't that far from the door, which was great. He had a big plastic bag full of stuff for Willa and a pack for himself. Both of those, he stowed under the cot.

A couple of rows over, he heard a low, familiar whine. A tail thumped the floor: Buster. So Willa *was* sleeping here. He considered going over there and making sure she was all right.

But come on. His creeping close and peering down at her wouldn't help her in the least.

Uh-uh. If he went to her, he wouldn't be doing it because she needed him right now. It would be because he wanted to see her, plain and simple. In the space of one night and the morning after, he'd found it all too easy to get used to having her around. All too easy to wish she might *stay* around.

He liked her.

Always had, though he knew she used to think he didn't.

Maybe he liked her too much. He needed to keep a rein on himself because he knew that nothing was going to come of his liking Willa Christensen more than he should. She was a nice girl. She had a college-graduate Mr. Good-Guy boyfriend off in Australia, a boyfriend who'd asked her to marry him.

There was no way Collin fit into that picture.

Someone coughed. A cot squeaked as someone else turned over. At the other end of the room near the stage, somebody was snoring. Collin should shuck off his boots, stretch out on the cot and try to get a little sleep. Morning would come way before he was ready for it.

Too bad he didn't feel all that much like sleeping. He moved silently back to the doors and slipped through again. Swiftly, he crossed the dark front hall and let himself out into the cool of the night.

On the steps, he sat down, drew his legs up and wrapped his arms around his knees. It was a clear night, a sliver of the waning moon hanging above the distant mountains way across the valley. He stared up at that moon and tried not to think about the woman sleeping in the dark hall behind him, tried not to think about that morning, when he'd woken up with her soft, pretty little hand on his fly. A bad, bad idea, to think about that. Thinking about that would only get him all worked up all over again.

He heard a faint sound at his back, the squeak of heavy hinges as the door opened behind him. Buster nuzzled his shoulder. He threw an arm over the dog and scratched him behind the ear as the door squeaked shut. The latch clicked.

Willa. He could feel her, hovering there behind him in

front of the door. He was way too glad she'd come out to find him.

"Go back to bed, Willa," he said lazily, not turning to look at her, keeping his gaze front, on that sliver of moon. "How many times do I have to tell you? I'm not having sex with you."

Willa laughed, a low, slightly husky sound, one that seemed to skim the surface of his skin, raising goose bumps as it went. Raising more than goose bumps if he was going to be honest about it. He drew his knees up a little tighter so she wouldn't see how she affected him.

"You are impossible," she said in a voice as low and husky and full of good humor as her laugh.

He shrugged. "So I've been told."

And then she came and sat on his other side, so he was sandwiched between her and her dog. It wasn't a bad place to be. Not bad at all.

She said, "Buster's happy to see you. He woke me up when you came in."

"Sorry."

She leaned toward him a little, nudging him with her shoulder in a way that felt downright companionable. "Don't be."

He stroked the dog's big white head. "He's a great guy." The dog turned, tongue lolling, and gazed at him adoringly. "And so good lookin'."

Willa chuckled again. "Oh, yes, he is."

He still hadn't looked at her. Mostly because when he did, he knew he wouldn't want to look away. "What about you, Willa? You happy to see me, too?"

"I am," she answered in a near whisper. "Yes." She was quiet. He could feel the warmth of her along his side. She smelled of soap and toothpaste—and something else. Something that was simply Willa. Kind of green and fresh and a little bit lemony. Who knew the smell of soap and lemons could get a man worked up? She spoke again. "I was kind of worried you'd tried to go up the mountain to your place."

"Not in the dark."

"Good."

"I went to the Triple T. They got the wells disinfected and are hoping to be using the water by tomorrow or Sunday. Most of the stock survived. And they're busy with cleanup. I stopped in at Clay's house and borrowed a few things—clean jeans and boots, a couple of shirts." Third-born of his five brothers, Clay had recently married. He lived down in Thunder Canyon now, but he still owned a house on the Triple T. "Then I went over to your family's place, just to see if things were okay there."

"You didn't have to do that."

"Willa. I wanted to."

A silence from her, then, "Thank you."

"I used the guest-room shower again. And I left your dad's clothes in the hamper. Hope you don't mind."

"I don't mind at all. How was it there?"

"Better."

"Really?"

"Yeah. The neighbors and the hands from the Triple T had been there. The pigs are back in their pen and the chickens are in the coop. Looked like they even made a start on the cleanup."

"That's good," she said. "Really good. I'm grateful."

He did look at her then. She was staring out toward the moon, the curve of her cheek so smooth in the dim light, her pretty lips slightly parted. She wore a different T-shirt from the one she'd had on earlier, pink sweatpants with white trim and a worn-down pair of flip-flops.

She kept her gaze on the moon, and that was fine with

him. Gave him more time to look at her. He took in everything about her. Her toenails were painted. In the dark, it
was hard to be sure of the exact color. Maybe purple. Like
plums. He stared at them for a time. When he looked up,
she was watching him. "Did you get something to eat?"

He nodded. "I had some stew at the Triple T."

Those cute dimples of hers tucked themselves in at the
sides of her mouth as she smiled. "Jerry Dobbs says you're
a natural leader, that they might not have saved Bart Derby
if not for you."

"Well. You know Jerry, heavy on the 'go, team, go.'"

"I think you're being modest, Collin." Her big brown
eyes gleamed at him.

He felt an odd little pinch, a heated tightness in his
chest. Also, in his borrowed jeans. "Modest? Me? Not a
chance."

Buster got up and wandered down the steps to lift his
leg on a tree trunk. When he started sniffing the ground,
moving toward the street, Willa called to him. "Buster.
Come." He came right back and plopped down where he'd
been before.

Collin said, "I filled a bag with clothes from that box
under the stairs at your folks' house, in case you need
them. I left it back in the hall, under my cot. I brought
jeans and shirts and underwear, too." There had been little
lace panties and a bra and several pair of socks. "Not that
I noticed the underwear or anything..."

"As I recall, it was pretty frayed, that underwear. But
I'm grateful to have it at this point." She groaned, lowered
her head and put her hand over her eyes. "I can't believe
I'm sitting here discussing my old underwear with you."

"Hey." It was his turn to bump her shoulder with his.
"What are friends for?"

She looked up and into his eyes, all earnest and hopeful, suddenly. "We are, aren't we? Friends, I mean."

He wanted to kiss her. But he knew that would be a very bad idea. "You want to be my friend, Willa?" His voice sounded a little rough, a little too hungry.

But she didn't look away. "I do, yes. Very much."

That pinch in his chest got even tighter. It was a good feeling, really. In a scary sort of way. "Well, all right then. Friends." He offered his hand. It seemed the thing to do.

Her lower lip quivered a little as she took it. Her palm was smooth and cool in his. He never wanted to let go. "You better watch it," she warned. "I'll start thinking that you're a really nice guy."

"I'm not." He kept catching himself staring at that mouth of hers. It looked so soft. Wide. Full. He said, "I'm wild and undisciplined. I have an attitude and I'll never settle down. Ask anyone. Ask my own mother. She'll give you an earful."

"Are you trying to scare me, Collin Traub? Because it's not working."

He took his hand back. Safer that way. "Never say I didn't warn you."

She gave him a look from the corner of her eye. "I'm onto you now. You're a good guy."

"See? Now I've got you fooled."

"No, you don't. And I'm glad that we're friends. Just be straight with me and we'll get along fine."

"I am being straight." Well, more or less. He didn't really want to be her friend. Or at least, not *only* her friend. He wanted to be *more* than her friend. But sometimes a man never got what he wanted. He understood that, always had. Sweet Willa Christensen was not for the likes of him. But right now, he just needed to look out for her, take care of her a little. Make sure she got through this hard time all right. He added, "And I've been thinking."

"About what?"

"The things that need doing."

She braced an elbow on her knee and dropped her chin in her hand. "Such as?"

"I'm guessing we'll finish up the search for survivors by around noon tomorrow. Meet me at the church when your team comes in. One way or another, we're going to get to your house tomorrow."

Her smooth brow furrowed. "What if they won't let us into the area?"

"You worry too much. They'll let us in. They pretty much have to."

"Not if they don't think it's safe."

"At some point, people are just going to go in anyway. The whole town has pitched in, put their own problems aside to search for survivors. It's not right to expect them to wait forever to get to their homes. Nathan and the rest of them have to take that into account or they'll have trouble on their hands."

"Collin…"

"Your face is all scrunched up again. Relax."

"It's only that I feel kind of bad, to keep on taking advantage of you like this."

"Don't," he commanded gruffly.

She just couldn't let it go. "But I know you need to get up to *your* place."

"My place is fine."

"But you can't be sure."

"Willa. We're going to your house and we're going tomorrow."

"I'm only saying that you don't have to—"

He put up a hand. "I know I don't have to. And you don't

have to worry. It's pretty much impossible to take advantage of me. If I say I'll do a thing, it's because I *want* to do it." And when it came to the woman beside him, well, what he wanted was to do whatever she needed. He added, just to make himself sound tough and uncompromising, "I don't do anything because I think I *have* to. Life is too damn short for that."

Chapter Six

It all went as Collin had predicted, which only made Willa more aware of how completely she had once underestimated him. He understood so much, really. About people. About the way things worked.

The nine teams searched for four hours the next day, covering the rest of the valley and the flooded area south of the creek in town. They found a couple of stranded pets and more cattle that had to be pulled from muddy ponds, but no people in need of rescue.

Willa's team was out at the far western reaches of the valley. They finished up the search of their section by a little past noon and returned to town, where everyone had gathered at the church for the midday meal. Willa sat with Paige and the rest of their team.

Collin sat at another table, his team around him. He glanced up and saw her and gave her a nod that she took to mean he still intended to take her to her house.

Her heart kind of stuttered in her chest and then re-commenced beating a little too fast. Partly because trading meaningful glances with Collin excited her more than it should. And partly because it was happening at last: she would see her house again. She sent a little prayer to heaven that it wouldn't be too bad.

While they ate, Nathan Crawford got up and gave a speech. He thanked everyone for the great job they were doing. He praised Rust Creek Garage for having plenty of gas to share with the searchers and the foresight to own a generator so that the pumps were still working. He said that state and county workers were on the job around-the-clock, trying to get services back online and roads and bridges repaired.

He advised, "If you have family members who were out of town for the holiday and you're wondering why they haven't returned—please don't be overly concerned. The governor has declared a state of emergency and asked that people try and stay off the roads, many of which are badly damaged. Bridges are out all over the western half of the state. It's just going to take a while to get all our services back up and running and for people to get back home."

Nathan also reminded them that the next phase was cleanup. "I hope many of you will pitch in with the community effort, that you'll donate your time if you can spare some. But we're suspending our teams for the rest of the day and all day Sunday so that everyone can handle personal business. Those who live south of the creek will have a chance to visit their homes." The floodwaters had sufficiently receded, he added, and gas and water mains to the damaged areas had been shut off for the time being. The town council realized that people had to be allowed back in to begin to assess the condition of their property.

"Please use the Sawmill Street Bridge only. Follow the newly posted signs for the safest route to your property."

Next, he got to the hazards, which were many. "Please, please, be extra careful about entering buildings. Proceed with caution. If you see a downed wire or pole, keep clear and remember to report it." He reminded them all to wear boots and gloves and watch out for dangerous animals displaced by the flood. "Also, take note. Any buildings roped off with yellow tape have already been determined to be unsafe for entry. We've done our best to personally warn all of you whose houses are in that condition, but the priority until now has been rescuing the stranded. There are assuredly buildings that should have been roped off but haven't yet. Please. Don't approach any houses that are taped off. Search-and-Rescue Team One reports that our elementary school is badly damaged and possibly structurally unsound. So, also, we ask that you stay away from the school and the school grounds."

Willa's heart sank at that news. Beside her, Paige made a low sound of distress. Were they going to lose the school?

That would hit hard. If they had to rebuild, how long would it take? They only had two months until the start of the next school year.

Nathan ended by saying that dinner would be served at six and thanking the charitable organizations that had come through with donations of food and supplies. Then Pastor Alderson got up and invited them all to a brief Sunday service after breakfast the next morning, a service that would include a final farewell to Mayor McGee.

A funeral. Willa sighed. Lately, life was just packed with sad and difficult events. But then again, it was important to give people a chance to pay their respects and to grieve.

She glanced toward Collin again. But he'd already left

his table. She thought of last night, of sitting out on the front steps of the town hall with him. That had been so nice. Just the two of them and Buster, alone under the sliver of moon.

She almost wished she could go back there now, just run away from reality and all the everyday grimness of surviving the worst flood in the history of Rust Creek Falls. Run away and sit out under the moon with Collin, forever.

Even if they were just friends.

"You ready, Willa?" His voice, behind her. A little thrill pulsed through her.

Beside her, Paige frowned. "Ready for what?"

She pushed back her folding chair and gathered up the remains of her meal to carry to the trash and recycle stations. "Collin's taking me to see my house."

Paige looked at Collin. He gazed coolly back at her. "How are you, Collin?"

"Just fine, Paige. You?"

"Wonderful," Paige said in a tone that could have meant anything. She turned her gaze to Willa. "Shall I come with you?"

Willa shook her head.

"Are you certain?"

"Yes. But thank you. I'll be fine."

"You be careful."

"I will. Don't worry."

They got into Collin's truck and he paused before he started the engine. "Where's Buster?"

"Thelma's keeping an eye on him."

"Good. Safer for him if stays at Thelma's until this is done."

She nodded her agreement and he pulled the truck out into the flow of traffic, most of which was going where they were going. Her neighbors were as eager as she was to see firsthand how their homes had fared.

They followed the signs across the Sawmill Street Bridge, down Falls Street and then west on Commercial. They had to move at a crawl, even though road crews had already been hard at work. Fallen trees, utility poles and flooded vehicles had been cleared from the roadway. But the streets themselves were badly damaged, the pavement erupted and broken apart in places, pools of standing water and puddles of mud everywhere, some as big as ponds. The buildings that lined the street had not fared well. Some were partially collapsed and roped off with yellow tape. Yards were still cluttered with household items and who knew what all.

Fires had taken out a whole row of houses on South Pine. A few of them were burned all the way to the ground.

At Main, they passed the elementary school. It was still standing, at least, though sections of the roof had fallen in. There was no way to tell from the street how bad the damage might be.

For Willa personally, the moment of truth came much too soon. They turned onto South Broomtail and pulled to a stop at what was left of the curb in front of her one-story bungalow.

She had to stifle a gasp of dismay at what she saw. Like all the other yards on the street, hers was a mess, strewn with a bunch of mud-caked stuff she couldn't even identify. The roof on one side of her front porch sagged alarmingly. The porch itself was empty. Her white wicker chairs and cute little spray-painted metal folding tables topped with potted geraniums were nowhere to be seen. And the cosmos and columbines, the boxwood hedge and the rows of mums and Shasta daisies she'd so lovingly planted along her front walk? If they were still there, she couldn't recognize them under the layer of mud and trash.

Collin reached over and took her hand. She wove her fingers good and tight with his. It helped—his warm, strong grip, the calloused flesh of his palm pressed to hers. The contact centered her down, reminded her again that she *could* get through this, that she wasn't alone.

He said, "You can wait for the insurance people, let them tell you what can be saved. I can turn this truck around and get us the hell outta here. You don't have to try and go in there."

She gripped his hand tighter. "What was that you said last night? About not wasting any part of your life doing what you think you *have* to do?"

"So don't. We'll go." He tried to pull his hand from hers.

She held on. "I mean, I *want* to go in. I...need to go in, Collin."

"Look at that porch roof. It could be dangerous. Someone on one of the county crews should have roped it off."

"I'm going in."

"Willa, it's not safe."

She hitched up her chin and stared straight in his eyes. "I have to. I do. I don't agree with what you said last night. Some things, well, a person does just *have* to do."

Collin tried to think of a way to talk her out of it. But she had that look—so solemn and determined. When Willa got that look, there was no changing her mind.

Maybe he could bargain with her a little. "Just let me go in first, okay? Let me make sure that it's safe."

She still had his hand in a death grip. "Great idea. You can get killed instead of me."

"Willa. I'm not going to get killed—and if you think

that it's too dangerous, well, why are we even talking about going in?"

"It was a figure of speech, that's all. I'm sure it's all right. We can go in together. But you're not leading the way. I won't have it. Do you understand?"

In spite of the very real danger in the situation, he wanted to smile. "You know you sound like an angry schoolmarm, don't you?"

"Well, I *am* an angry schoolmarm. And you'd better not cross me right now, Collin Traub."

He put on his most solemn expression. "No, ma'am. I wouldn't dare."

She let go of his hand and he wished that she hadn't. "Here." She passed him his heavy black rubber gloves. He put them on and she put on hers. They were both still wearing their waterproof search-and-rescue boots. "All right," she said. "Let's get it over with."

They got out and picked their way through the piles of broken, muddy junk in the yard. The smell was pretty bad—like spoiled food and smelly socks and other things he decided not to concentrate too hard on.

"Look," she said, and pointed. "One of my wicker porch chairs. Right there—and look over there. Isn't that a slow cooker?"

He only shrugged. The things she pointed to were unrecognizable to him.

The mud-caked porch creaked in an ominous way when they went up the steps. But it held. One front window was busted out, the other crisscrossed with cracks.

She reached for the door—and then she dropped her hand and laughed. "The key…"

For a moment, he knew relief. She'd forgotten the key. Good. But then she reached into her pocket and came out with it. She stuck it in the lock and gave it a turn.

The door swung inward.

It wasn't anything he hadn't expected. Mud everywhere and water wicking halfway up the walls. The same rotting, moldy smell as in the yard.

They went through the small entry hall and into the living room, where he doubted that any of the furniture could be saved. The large picture window on the side wall had cracked from corner to corner. The fireplace was full of mud.

"My grandmother's clock," Willa said in a tone of hope and wonder. It was on the mantel, a brass carriage clock, untouched. She went over to it, and gathered it into her arms. "It's an antique. A mercury pendulum clock." She glanced up and met his eyes. Hers were suspiciously misty. "Hey. It's *something*...."

They moved on, first to the kitchen and then down the short hallway to the bedrooms and the single bath. It was bad, all of it, every room full of mud. There wasn't much worth saving.

But there were some pictures on the walls that were good as new, and some stuff in the kitchen, dishes and such in the higher-up cabinets. And the things on the counter, too: a red toaster, cutting boards, some glass figurines on the windowsill. He suggested that they try and see if they could scare up some boxes to put the stuff in.

Willa shook her head. "And put the boxes where?"

He wanted to offer his house, but he hadn't made it up the mountain yet, and he knew she'd only argue that she couldn't impose on him. He thought of Paige. He didn't like what had gone down with Paige and his brother Sutter, but he knew Paige was a good woman at heart and a true friend to Willa. She would store Willa's stuff for her in a heartbeat. But then Willa would only give him some other excuse as to why that wouldn't work. "We'll haul them out to your parents' place. How's that?"

She clutched the brass clock like a lifeline and said primly, "That would take the rest of the day. And they are just *things,* after all."

"They're *your* things. And you need to get them out of here." He asked gently, "And what else are we gonna do with the rest of the day?"

"Other people might need our help and we should—"

He didn't let her get rolling. "Need our help doing what? Saving *their* things? We're doing this. Deal with it."

Her lower lip was trembling and her eyes were more than misty now. "I can't... I don't..." He felt a tightness in his chest at seeing her cry. She sniffed and turned her head away. "Oh, this is ridiculous. I have so much to be grateful for. There is no point in my crying over this. My crying will not change a thing...." A tight little sob escaped her.

"Come on. Come here." He reached out his rubber-gloved hands and pulled her close. "It's all right."

"No. No, it's not. I loved this house. I loved my little red Subaru."

"I know," he soothed. "I understand."

"I...I keep telling myself how it doesn't matter, that what matters is I'm alive and in one piece and so is most everyone else in town. But then I think of my...my treasures. My fairy-tale books, my favorite velvet pillow...I want them back, Collin. I want my *things* back."

"Shh, now. I know you do. There's nothing wrong with that. It's natural. Don't be so hard on yourself...."

"Oh, I am being such a big baby...." Sobs shook her slim frame.

He held her. He stroked her back. She curved into him, fitting against him as though she was made to be in his arms. For that moment, he forgot about everything. It all just…receded: her ruined house, the smell of mud and mildew, her grandmother's clock poking into his belly. There was only the woman in his arms. He held her and rested his cheek on her soft hair and waited.

Eventually, she pulled back enough to gaze up at him. Her nose was red and her eyes were puffy and she was so beautiful that his chest got tight all over again. He wished that…

But no. It was never happening. He wasn't going there. No way.

She sniffed. "Well. This is embarrassing."

He took her lightly by the upper arms. "You okay now?"

She sniffed again. "My nose is red, isn't it?"

"Your nose is beautiful."

"Liar."

It all seemed…strange and scary, suddenly. For a moment there…no. *Uh-uh. Not going there,* he reminded himself for the second time. He put on a big, fake smile and asked, "What do you say we go find those boxes?"

It took the rest of the day to scare up the crates and boxes, pack up what was salvageable and drive it out to the Christensen place. Her dad had a storage area off his work shed. They put it all in there.

By then, it was past time for the community meal back in town. They'd planned ahead and brought clean clothes with them so they could take advantage of the chance for hot showers. As before, he took the hall bath and she took the one off her parents' room.

She came out of her parents' bathroom, her brown hair still wet, smoothed back into a knot at the nape of her neck, smelling like flowers and rain and lemons, better than any woman he'd ever known.

And he'd known a lot of them—well, not in the past

couple of years. After he hit twenty-five or so, all that chasing around had begun to seem kind of pointless. But back when he was younger, he'd lived up to his rep as a player. Then he'd been out to have himself a good time every night of the week.

And not one other woman back in the day had ever smelled as good as Willa did right then.

They raided the pantry. As they ate canned stew, crackers and peaches, Willa said how happy she was with the cleanup around the ranch.

"They've done a lot," she said, "in just a couple of days."

Her car was still out there on its side in the pasture and probably would be until she could call her insurance guy or the FEMA people and have it towed away, but the animals were back in their proper pastures and pens. The neighbors were making sure the stock got fed.

They headed back to town at a little after eight, stopping off at the Triple T for a few minutes on the way, just to check on things. In Rust Creek Falls, they went to Thelma's to get Buster, and then they returned to the town hall for the night. There were several empty cots. Some people had found neighbors to stay with and some had gone to live with out-of-town relatives for a while.

Marjorie Hanke turned out the lights at eleven. Collin still felt wide-awake, so he got up and went outside to sit on the steps under the sliver of moon.

What do you know? He wasn't out there five minutes before Buster was nudging up against him on one side and Willa was dropping to the steps on the other.

He almost teased her about how he wasn't having sex with her. But no. Sex seemed a little dangerous to speak of now, something he couldn't afford to joke about.

And then she kind of leaned against him and said,

"Aren't you going to tell me to keep my hot little hands to myself?"

There was nothing he would like better than her hot little hands all over him. However, that was not going to happen, as he knew damn well and kept constantly reminding himself.

He kept it light, meeting her eyes, teasing, "I know I can count on you to do the right thing."

She didn't reply. There was one of those moments. They looked at each other and neither looked away. He would only have to lean in a few inches to capture that mouth of hers, to feel her lips against his.

Finally.

At last.

But he didn't. Apparently, he had some small amount of self-control left.

He thought of the boyfriend, the one who had asked her to marry him. He reminded himself that it was only an accident of fate that had her sitting next to him on the town hall steps at a quarter of midnight on July 6. And somehow, he managed to turn his head and stare at the moon again.

She said, very softly, "Remember when we were kids? You used to spy on me.…"

He chuckled. "I had a lot of free time on my hands. And I never thought of it as spying."

"You would watch me when I had no idea you were there. That's spying, Collin Traub. I would look up—and there you would be, staring at me."

He gave her a grin. "You're getting mad about it all over again."

She frowned—and then her brow smoothed out. "You're right. I am. And that's silly. It was years ago. It's like that night at the Ace in the Hole. Better to just let it go." She tipped her head sideways and studied him. "You were so different from your brothers...."

"Yeah, well. My mom was tired when I came along. She had five boys already. Boys are exhausting. They need discipline and supervision. Mom did a good job of that with the rest of them. But she kind of gave up on me. I ran wild."

"I remember," she said wryly.

He elaborated with some pride, "I broke every rule and climbed every fence and spied on you when I knew it would freak you out. I also used to like to tease the bulls."

"Well, that's just plain asking for it."

"Yeah, it is. I guess I had an angel on my shoulder, though. Because somehow, every time I got in the pasture with one of the bulls and danced around shouting and waving my arms, I managed to jump the fence before I got gored."

She was shaking her head. "What were you thinking?"

"That it was fun! I mean, I liked it, being known as big trouble just waiting to happen. I got blamed for everything, sometimes for things I didn't even do. And it kind of got to be a point of pride for me that not a day went by I didn't get grief for some crazy, dumb-ass behavior or other."

She was looking at him again, her eyes shining brighter than the stars in the clear night sky overhead. "So you became known as the family troublemaker, the one no one could ever depend on."

"Because I *am* the family troublemaker that no one could depend on."

"But you're not," she argued. "Just look at you lately, standing up for what's right in the town meeting, getting a couple of kids to make sure the mayor's car was towed off Main Street the day after he died, saving Barton Derby from under the wreckage of his barn...."

"My *team* saved Bart Derby, the mayor's car was not a big thing—and you stood up in that meeting, too."

"What about rescuing me when I would have drowned, and then looking after me during the storm? And what about afterwards, too? What about today, at my house, when you held me while I cried and promised me it was going to be all right?"

"It was what you needed to hear right then."

"Exactly. Honestly, Collin. I don't know what I would have done without you since the flood." She'd better stop looking at him like that. If she didn't, well, he was going to grab her and plant one on her.

"Don't make a big thing out of it, okay?" he heard himself mutter.

"But it *is* a big thing."

"No, it's not...."

"Yes, it is!" She got that bossy schoolteacher look. "And that does it. I'm not sitting still while you minimize all the good you've done. I'm going to tell you how I see it."

"Uh-oh."

"You listen to me, now...."

He tried not to groan. "What will you do if I don't?"

She put her hand on his arm, apparently to hold him there by force. He felt that touch from the top of his head to the tips of his toes—and everywhere in between. "You are a born leader, Collin. This town is going to need a new mayor and I keep thinking that you could be the right man for that job."

Mayor? She thought he should be *mayor?* He couldn't help it. He threw back his head and laughed out loud. "Willa, okay. We're friends now and everything. But you don't know what you're talking about."

"Oh, yes, I do. I am onto you, in a big way."

He grunted. "No, you're not. You're making something out of nothing."

She pursed up her mouth at him. "When you're finished blowing me off, you just tell me. And then I will share my insights with you."

There were a whole bunch of sarcastic comebacks to that one. But for some unknown reason, he didn't use any of them. Probably because he did kind of want to hear what she had to say. "Okay, fair enough. Hit me with it."

"I will. Ahem. So you grew up a wild child, undependable. And as it so often happens in a small town like ours, people get it in their heads what a person is like and that's it, that's just the way it is. No one ever thinks to look at that person differently, to take a chance on depending on him, to expect more than misbehavior. There's a local perception and no one ever tests it. The perception becomes the reality."

"Took psychology at UI, did you, Willa?"

She gave him her sweetest smile. "And I'm not even at the good part yet.... Where was I? Oh, yes. So in the meantime, you're keeping busy fulfilling everyone's low expectations of you. And, as you said yourself, you find that not having anyone expect much of you is actually kind of fun. Because you can do what you want. You're not stuck like all your brothers, bearing up under the weight of everyone's high estimation of your sterling character. You actually have the freedom to live exactly as you please and you never have to worry about letting anyone down."

He could easily become annoyed with her. "Think you got me all figured out, don't you, Willa?"

She didn't back off. "To a degree, yes. You are adventurous and bold, with no desire to settle down. So naturally, in your teens, you become the town heartbreaker.

You do a lot of experimenting with women. Because, as you said, it's fun."

He'd heard about enough. "Come on. You're getting into dangerous territory here. You know that, right? Next you'll be digging up that night at the Ace again, getting all up in my face for not taking you up on what you were offering."

She put her hand on his arm again. He wanted to jerk away—and also to grab her and kiss her senseless. "No. Honestly. I'm over that." And then she smiled. So sweet and open, that smile. He realized that he definitely wanted to kiss her more than he wanted to get away from her. "Even if I am probably the only woman you ever turned down."

He almost told her that wasn't true, but then she'd just say he was bragging. "Seriously. Where are you going with this?"

She tipped her head to the side, frowning a little the way she did when she was thinking something over. "Hmm. I guess I'm just trying to make you see that being defined by other people's low expectations of you isn't really working for you anymore."

"And you know this, how?"

"I'm not blind, you know. I've been around you a lot the past few days. And what has been a tragedy for Rust Creek Falls has brought out the best in you. After all that's happened and all the good you've done—all the good you *will* do in the coming days, you're not going to be able to go back."

"Go back where?"

"To the way things were before the levee broke."

"Believe it or not, I happen to like the way things were."

"Maybe you did. Before. But it won't be enough for you now."

"You have no idea what's enough for me, Willa." He

ached to reach for her. Reach for her and pull her close and kiss her until her head spun and she let him do whatever he wanted with her, until he finally got a taste of what she'd been tempting him with since before he was even old enough to know what temptation was.

She just wouldn't stop. "You've started to expect more of yourself and that is a wonderful thing. Why can't you admit that?"

It was the tipping point. He couldn't stop himself. He reached out and grabbed her by the shoulders good and tight. And then he growled at her with all the frustrated heat and hunger he was trying so hard to deny. "I don't need you telling me how I feel or where I'm going."

She blinked at him and her big eyes got bigger and her mouth looked so soft and surprised he only wanted to cover it with his and stick his tongue inside. "But, Collin. I was only—"

"*Don't,* all right? Just don't." With great care, he straightened his arms, pushing her away from him. Then he let her go.

"Collin, I…"

He stood up. That was pretty damn stupid. He was as hard as a teenage kid caught thumbing through *Playboy.* All she had to do was look and she would see it.

Too bad. He wasn't hanging around to watch her reaction. He mounted the top step, hauled the door wide and went in, pulling it firmly shut behind him.

Chapter Seven

Willa had trouble getting to sleep that night. She felt awful. She knew that she'd gone too far. Yes, she did honestly believe she'd only told Collin the truth about himself.

And really, not a thing she'd said to him had been bad. Some men wouldn't mind being called a born leader. Some men would be pleased to hear how wonderful they were.

But not Collin, apparently.

And all right, well, maybe she'd laid it on a bit heavy. She'd turned her inner schoolmarm loose on him—and not the good, patient, understanding and gentle schoolmarm.

The other one. The bossy one who knew what was good for you and was bound to tell you all about yourself whether you wanted to hear it or not.

Had she wrecked their new friendship?

Oh, she did hope not. Because she really, really liked being his friend. She liked it more than she should, probably. With a guy like Collin, well, a girl could get really confused as to where she stood with him.

On the floor by her cot, Buster whined in his sleep. She reached her hand down to him, ran her fingers over the smooth, warm crown of his big head. He woke enough to press his wet nose against her palm and then settled back to sleep with a sweet chuffing sound.

She thought of all the good things Collin had done for her since the flood, of the way he'd held her that afternoon, so tenderly, so kindly, in the muddy ruin that had once been her home.

No. He was a real friend to her now. Too good a friend for her to lose him just because she'd presumed to lecture him about his life.

In the morning, she would apologize. And everything would be all right.

He wasn't there for the community breakfast in the morning and he didn't come to the church service after the meal.

Willa sat with Paige and wished he was there. She worried that he *wasn't* there because she had pushed his buttons and made it necessary, somehow, for him to prove what a tough, bad guy he was—too bad to show up for Sunday services and give Willa a chance to say she was sorry.

The choir sang of sweet comfort and the pastor quoted inspirational sections of scripture, verses meant to be uplifting in hard times. He gave a sermon on sacrifice and the meaning of community. He talked about how the Lord was with them and that each and every one of them was proving their worth and their goodness by their deeds in this time of trial.

And finally, when the sermon was over, Pastor Alderson led them in a prayer for Mayor McGee and the service became a farewell for Thelma's only son.

People stepped up with vases full of flowers, picked wild or from their own gardens. The choir sang the songs that Hunter had liked best, a couple of country-and-western love songs, "Red River Valley," a Bob Dylan ballad and some other songs Willa hadn't heard before.

It was during one of those other songs that she sensed movement at the end of the pew. She glanced that way.

Collin.

He wore clean jeans and a white shirt and his face was smooth from a recent shave. Had he made it up to his house on the mountain, then? He caught her eye, just for a moment. He didn't smile. But he wasn't scowling, either. She could have stared at him forever.

But she didn't. She forced her eyes front again while he made his way along the pew toward her. He muttered soft apologies as their neighbors slid their legs to the side, giving room for him to pass. Shelby Jenkins, a friend who sometimes worked as a substitute teacher at the elementary school, was sitting on her left.

She heard Collin whisper, "S'cuse me, Shelby..."

Shelby slid over and he took the empty space next to Willa. He smelled of soap and aftershave and her heart just lifted up when he settled in beside her. She couldn't even look at him right then, there were so many strange and powerful emotions chasing themselves around inside her. She had a dopey smile on her face, she just knew it, a totally inappropriate expression for a funeral.

He did that thing—that thing they'd started when they sat out on the town hall steps in the evening—leaning to the side in her direction, nudging her so gently with his shoulder.

She had to press her lips together to keep from letting out a silly squeak of pure joy. Because he wasn't all that mad at her, after all, evidently.

Because now she knew that everything between them would be all right.

The service continued. Pastor Alderson invited folks to stand and a say a word or two, to speak their testimony on the life of Hunter McGee.

In the front pew, Thelma stood first. Her voice only shook a little as she spoke of how proud she was to be Hunter's mom, as she told a little story about his boyhood, about his dreams for Rust Creek Falls, about how his one true love had died too young and he'd never known the joy of fatherhood, but he had loved Rust Creek Falls. It had meant the world to him that the people of his town had elected him their mayor.

When Thelma was finished, others stood, one at a time, taking turns, telling about growing up with Hunter, about the many ways that he'd helped them or made their lives richer, somehow. Each of the town council members took a turn, with Nathan Crawford going first. Willa had thought she might speak, but then it turned out that the things she would have shared were already said. She felt content to let it be.

The testimonies went on for over an hour. Until finally, one of the older Daltons sat back down after speaking of how Hunter had pitched in to help repair the Masonic Hall. There was a silence in the chapel. Willa thought that the sharing was done.

But then Collin shifted at her side. She blinked and looked over at him as he rose to his feet. He looked a little nervous, she thought, and so very handsome and dear.

Everyone turned and watched him expectantly. As a rule, Collin Traub didn't speak out in public, but Willa knew they all had to be remembering his impassioned arguments in the town hall the other day and eager to hear whatever he might contribute now.

Collin cleared his throat. "I just want to say that Hunter McGee was a man we all thought of as a friend. He had a way about him. He was wise and he was patient, too. But he had a killer sense of humor and that gleam in his eye that let you know he didn't judge you and he wanted only the best for you, no matter how big a troublemaker you might happen to be." Collin paused then, and glanced around with an abashed sort of expression.

People grinned and a few even chuckled.

Collin continued, "Somehow, Hunter always managed to get to the heart of an issue without ever choosing sides. He had a rare sort of fairness in him and a willingness to help. Yes, he's gone to a better place now. But at the same time, it seems to me that he's still here with us in spirit, that he's working beside us now, in this tough time when we need men like him the most. We haven't really lost him." Collin fisted his hand and laid it against his heart. "He's right here." He raised his hand and touched his temple. "And he's in here, too, in all of us. We can remember all he showed us about how to live and work together. And we can be grateful that we have his fine example to carry us forward as we work side by side to rebuild this town."

Collin sat back down.

There was a silence. Somebody murmured, "Oh, yeah."

And someone else said, "Tell it, Collin."

Several more "Oh, yeahs" and one or two "Praise Gods" followed.

Collin turned and looked at Willa, which was when she realized she was staring at him. He gave her a scowl, mouthed, *What?*

She only shrugged and faced front again and tried not to feel smug that he had just proved the truth in what she'd said to him the night before.

* * *

Outside after the service, Thelma embraced Collin and laid her hand gently on the side of his face. "Such a fine young man," she told him softly. And then she raised her lacy handkerchief to dab at her wet eyes.

A couple of the Dalton men clasped his shoulder as they filed out of the chapel. Willa observed all this and tried really hard not to feel too self-righteous about the things she'd said the night before. He really was a born leader, but what he did with that talent had to be of his own choosing.

Paige touched her arm. "I'd ask you to come sit with me for lunch, but I have a feeling you've got plans."

Willa gave her a hug and they parted. Buster whined at her, eager to be released from the iron bench where she'd leashed him. She went over and got him, crouching to pet him and make a fuss over him for being so good during the long church service.

"Rumor has it the church ladies are serving pizza for lunch today," Collin said from behind her.

Buster whined and wagged his tail in greeting and Willa's heart seemed to do a sort of forward roll under her breastbone. She asked, without turning, "Does the rumor mention pepperoni?"

"Yeah. Pepperoni and sausage, too." He dropped to a crouch at her side. Buster wiggled closer to him and head-butted his hand. Collin scratched the dog behind both ears and Buster lolled his tongue in doggy bliss.

Willa felt terribly shy suddenly. She stared at his hands as he petted her dog. "I, um, should walk Buster first...."

"Hey."

Her throat had a big lump in it. She gulped it down and made herself meet those low-lidded black eyes. "Hmm?"

"We okay, you and me?"

She remembered that she was going to apologize. "I lectured you. I shouldn't have done that. I'm sorry."

"You got nothing to be sorry for." His voice was low and more than a little rough. The sound of it sent a warm, lovely shiver running underneath her skin. He added, "You got a right to your opinion."

"But, well, you did get mad."

He smiled then, one of those slow smiles of his, the kind that used to make all the girls back in high school sigh and fan themselves. "So then, *I'm* sorry. I had no right at all to jump all over you for telling the truth as you see it." He kept on looking at her, a deep look that made her whole body feel sensitized, excited. Wonderfully alive. "Forgive me?"

That lump was back in her throat again. She gulped a second time to clear it. "I do. And yes. We're okay."

"Whew."

She felt her mouth tremble into a smile that answered his. "Did you go up to your house, then?"

"No. I'm hoping I'll get to that tomorrow. This morning, I went out to the Triple T and had breakfast with the hands. They got the wells in working order, so I had a shower, too." He swept upward and she stood, too. "Let's walk this dog," he said.

"Good idea."

"The park? We can let him run."

"Perfect."

After lunch, the governor dropped in—literally—in a helicopter.

The chopper landed in the middle of Main Street and the governor emerged, waving and smiling, trailed by a guy in a FEMA vest and another, more muscular fellow in dark glasses. Waving as he went, the governor ran up and stood on the town hall steps, where the town council members waited. He shook hands with each of them.

And then he gave a little speech—more of a pep talk, really. He said the same things Nathan was always saying: that road crews and the power and telephone companies were working around-the-clock to get the roads open and services back online. He asked everyone to sit tight until services were restored and, whenever possible, to stay in the Rust Creek Falls Valley until the roads were declared safe for travel.

He praised their spirit of independence, their ability to roll up their sleeves and do for themselves. Since the good people of Rust Creek Falls seemed to be managing better than most in the stricken areas, he could see that the Red Cross and the National Guard wouldn't be needed there—not at that point anyway.

After the governor spoke, the FEMA guy talked about the services FEMA offered and the progress of the cleanup. And then, with more smiling and waving, the three visitors ran back and boarded the helicopter and off they went.

Collin leaned close and said in her ear, "Wasn't that inspiring?" She gave him a look and left it at that. And then he said, "I was thinking we could try and see what we can salvage from Gage's house."

She wanted to grab him and hug him—for being so generous, for thinking of her poor brother, who had to be worried sick about now and was no doubt moving heaven and earth to get back to town. "Yes. Please. Let's do that."

The church ladies had several boxes they could spare. So she and Collin put them in the back of his pickup and headed for the ranch, where they worked until after five packing up things at Gage's and putting them with Willa's boxes in her father's work shed.

They made it back to town in time for dinner at the

church. As they ate beans and rice with ham, Nathan got up and proudly announced that cell phone service was restored. He reminded them of the places that had generators where they might charge their batteries. People applauded the news—and then hurried off to find the phones they'd stopped carrying around with them for the past three days.

In the pickup, Collin called his mother first. Willa had run out with him and ended up sitting in the passenger seat beside him as he nodded and listened, and seemed to be having trouble getting a word in edgewise. He kept trying to tell his mom what had happened there at home, but Ellie Traub had never been the quiet type. As soon as he started talking, she would get going again and he ended up mostly saying, "Yeah. Okay. All right. That's good, Mom. Really…"

When he finally said goodbye, he reported to Willa that his mom, his dad and his brothers were fine. "They got the rain down there in Thunder Canyon," he said, "but flooding was minimal. Mom says they're willing to wait a few more days until the governor gives the go-ahead. But if the okay doesn't come soon, they're heading for home." He added that the people of Thunder Canyon were already talking about ways to help Rust Creek Falls with flood cleanup and the rebuilding that would follow.

And then he handed her the phone. "Go on. Call your folks."

Again, she had a really strong urge to hug him. But instead she started dialing.

Lavinia Christensen cried when Willa said hello. "We've been calling and calling," she sobbed. And then she wanted to know why Willa wasn't calling from her own cell.

Willa explained that she'd lost it in the flood. "This is Collin's cell."

Her mother sniffled. "Collin *Traub?*"

"Yes." She cast Collin a warm glance. "He's been great to me, Mom. Wonderful." Collin sent her one of those *knock-it-off* looks when he heard her praising him. She pretended not to notice.

Her mom was kind of sputtering. "Well, I, ahem. The Traubs are good people."

"They certainly are—and if you need to reach me, just call this number. Collin will make sure I get back to you until I can get a phone of my own."

"I...I will. Yes. Of course."

Willa assured her mom that she was all right and that the ranch house was fine and so was the barn. She said that most of the stock had survived the flood and the neighbors had all pitched in to keep the animals fed and to clean up the mess. Her mom cried some more when she heard the bad news about Willa's house and Gage's place.

It turned out her folks were still in Livingston, waiting for news that the roads were clear. Gage, however, had set out for home.

When Willa called him, she had to explain all over again that he should call her on Collin's phone for the time being. He started quizzing her about Collin.

She cut him short. "What about you? Where are you now?"

He said he'd been held up three times so far with washed-out bridges and roads, but he wasn't giving up and had spent each night since the flood in a different town. Willa got teary eyed then and told him about the condition of his house—and hers. Her brother said he loved her and not to cry and he would be there as soon as he could. He said he'd visited the sheriff's stations in the towns where he'd stayed and used their radio systems to contact his office. So he'd known that she was all right and he'd been told of the death of Hunter McGee.

When he mentioned Mayor McGee, Willa started crying all over again. She'd been dry-eyed at the funeral, but there was something about her brother's voice. She could tell that the mayor's death had hit him hard. Collin hauled a box of tissues from the glove box and passed it to her. She grabbed one and wiped at her streaming eyes.

When she hung up with Gage, she gave the phone back to Collin. He turned on the pickup so he could hook up his car charger and then, with the phone plugged in, he called a couple of his brothers in Thunder Canyon and then his brother Sutter, in Washington State.

When he hung up, he said in a tone that dared her to argue, "I think a lot of Sutter. He's a damn good man."

Willa only nodded. There were people in town who didn't approve of the stand Sutter had taken when their older brother Forrest went off to fight in Iraq. And then there was the way he'd broken Paige's heart. But still. Willa had always liked Sutter and if he and Collin were on good terms, well, that was just fine with her.

Collin narrowed those almost-black eyes at her and his full mouth curved down at the corners. "You got something on your mind, Willa, you ought to just go ahead and say it."

Willa answered sweetly, "You love your brother. There is nothing wrong with that."

That evening, the number of citizens requiring emergency shelter was a third what it had been the first night. FEMA had brought in some trailers that day for people to stay in temporarily. And more people had either left town to stay with relatives or moved in with friends. A lucky few had discovered that the damage to their homes wasn't bad enough to keep them from moving back in.

Willa and Collin stayed in the town hall again that

night. After the lights were out, she took Buster and went to join Collin under the stars.

"Been waiting for you," he said when she dropped down beside him.

A little thrill shivered through her at his words and she had to remind herself not to be an idiot. It wasn't a man-woman kind of thing between them. They were friends. Good friends, amazingly. But that was all. He wasn't interested in her in *that* way and he never had been.

She wrapped her arms around her knees and rested her chin on them. "Are you still planning to go up the mountain tomorrow?"

"Yeah. In the afternoon. It should be fine up there. The generator automatically kicks in when the power goes out, so what's in the fridge and the freezer stays cold. I've got a freezer full of food I'll bring down and donate to the church kitchen."

She stared at him, thinking how smoking hot he was—because, hey, even if they were just friends, there was no law that said a girl couldn't look. She could get lost in those eyes of his. And even in the darkness, his hair had a shine to it. And it was so thick.

That night four years ago, at the Ace in the Hole, before he laughed at her and told her to get lost, they'd danced to a couple of slow numbers together. She remembered so clearly the feel of his hard, hot shoulder beneath her hand. His lips had looked soft and dangerous, both at once. And the scent of him: incomparable, a heady mix of aftershave, man and something temptingly wild. The rush of blood through her veins had been dizzying. And she would never forget her powerful desire to slide her fingers upward, over the hot flesh of his neck and into that thick, crow-black hair of his.

He asked, "Do I have dirt on my nose?"

She chuckled, the sound surprisingly husky to her own ears. "No. Why?"

He held her gaze as though he never planned to look away. "You're staring at me."

Right. She supposed that she was. She went on staring and told him way too dreamily, "Buster and I are going with you."

"Going with me where?"

"Up to your house tomorrow."

Those thick inky brows drew together. "It's not a good idea."

Too bad. He wasn't talking her out of it. But for now, she played along. "Why not?"

"The road up there is bound to be a mess. It could be dangerous."

"All the more reason you shouldn't go alone."

"You're going to protect me, are you?"

She braced her chin on her hand. "I am. Absolutely. You're a big, tough guy and all, I know. But even tough guys sometimes need a little help."

The way he was looking at her now, she could almost imagine that he did think of her *that* way. Which probably meant she was being an idiot again. But so what? There were a lot worse things than being an idiot. A girl could live her whole life without ever getting her fingers into Collin's black hair. That would be sad. Immeasurably so.

Now he was looking stern. "It's not a good idea."

"You already said that."

"I'll probably end up staying up there overnight."

"So? I'll take the sleeping bag from my cot. It will be fine."

He seemed a little insulted. "I have a guest room—and believe it or not, it has a bed in it, complete with sheets and blankets and pillows."

"Wonderful. So it's settled."

He wasn't going for it. "I told you. You need to stay here."

"We'll see...."

"I mean it, Willa. You are not going up the mountain with me."

The next morning, Collin rejoined his team.

Before he left to help with cleanup down in the area around the flooded clinic, Willa told him that she and Paige and some of the other teachers had been asked to reconvene summer school. Since the day would be a clear one, they would hold their classes in Rust Creek Falls Park. On rainy days, classes would be hosted by some of the parents—and a few of the teachers, as well.

When he came in for lunch in the church, he returned a call from his mom, one from his brother Clay and another from Sutter. Then he made calls to a few top CT Saddles customers. He apologized for the fact that he would be filling their orders late. They'd all heard about the flood and told him not to worry, to stay safe and take his time.

Willa wasn't there at the church for lunch. He ignored the little curl of disappointment in his chest when he didn't see her. Every day he was with her, it got easier to let himself think that there was more going on between them than friendship.

There wasn't. Once things got back to normal, her bigshot boyfriend would show up. She would realize what that other guy could offer her and she would end up with his ring on her finger. Which was the way it should be. Willa deserved the best.

Dolly Tabor, one of his teammates on the rescue-turnedcleanup crew, had kids in summer school. She mentioned that the church ladies were delivering the school lunches to the park.

So, great, he thought. Willa was having lunch with the kids in the park.

He asked Dolly, real casual-like, when summer school would be over for the day. Dolly said at three.

Collin made his plans accordingly. He knew Willa and he knew her ways. She thought she was going up the mountain with him. And there was more than one good reason why he couldn't let that happen. For one thing, the trip up there was likely to be hazardous. He wasn't putting Willa in danger. And then, if they ended up stuck at his place for the night, well, that would present a whole other kind of danger.

It was one thing to be alone with her for an hour out on the town hall steps at night, or while they worked side by side hauling stuff out of her brother's flooded house. It was another thing altogether to spend the night with her at his place, just the two of them, alone on Falls Mountain.

Uh-uh. That would be asking for the kind of trouble they weren't going to get into together. He had to face reality here. He'd done what he could to help her through the worst of it after the flood. Her family would be back in town any day now. From what she'd said about Gage working his way north, her brother could be home already.

Collin needed to start getting a little distance from her. He had to stop spending so much time with her, had to give up those nighttime talks out on the town hall steps. He needed to stop kidding himself that it was innocent, that they were just hanging out, joking around a little before turning in.

It wasn't innocent—not for him anyway. Every night it got harder to keep his hands to himself. If he didn't get some distance, he would end up making a move on her.

He knew she really wanted to be his friend and all that. But he wanted more than friendship and where was that going to go? He liked his relationships with women to be simple—and short.

Nothing with Willa was simple. So he would put an end to it, make sure it never even had a chance to get started. She would be hurt and probably angry with him for taking off up the mountain without a word to her. But too bad.

It was for the best.

He got Jerry Dobbs aside and said he was heading up to his place. Jerry clapped him on the back and told him to be careful on the road up there.

Across the street at the town hall, he collected the plastic bag full of clothes and personal items he'd left under his cot. Marjorie Hanke was there, so he told her he wouldn't be needing the cot anymore.

And that was it. He was free to get the hell outta town.

He shouldered the bag and headed for his truck in the parking lot in the back, feeling more down than he should have, wishing things could be different and calling himself ten kinds of fool to want a thing he was never going to have—and wouldn't know what to do with anyway.

He almost tripped over his own boots when he caught sight of Willa. She was leaning against his rear wheel well, Buster on one side, her bag of stuff and backpack on the other.

Chapter Eight

She had her arms folded across her middle and her head tipped to the side. The early-afternoon sun brought out bronze highlights in her coffee-colored hair. She gave him a slow once-over. "I knew it."

He glared at her, trying his best to look pissed off. "You knew what?"

"You were just going to sneak away without even telling me. That's not very nice, Collin."

"I did tell you. I told you last night."

She tightened her arms around herself and pressed her lips together. "And I told you that I was going with you." She pushed off the wheel well and stood up straight. "So here I am."

His bag of clothes rustled as he let it slide to the pavement. He was actively ignoring the rapid beating of his heart, the ridiculous surge of happiness that was blasting all through him.

She really did want to go with him. She wasn't letting him get away without a fight.

But so what? He needed to focus on the goal: to get her to give up this insanity and go back to the park. "No. It's a bad idea. And aren't you supposed to be over at the park teaching summer school?"

"Shelby Jenkins is helping out. She took over for me."

"But you—"

"I'm going, Collin. Don't mess with me on this."

How in hell could he do the right thing if she kept pushing him to screw up? A voice in the back of his mind kept chanting, *She wants to come, she wants to come.* And the bad-acting idiot inside him kept whispering, *Man, if it's what she wants, why not?*

He ground his teeth together. "I wasn't planning to come back until tomorrow."

"That's okay. I've got my stuff. And you've got a guest room. It's all good."

"I thought you had summer school."

"I told you, Shelby's helping out. I explained to her that I was going up the mountain with you and we might not make it back until later tomorrow. She'll take my kids for me. I'm covered."

"Get real, Willa. You go up the mountain with me and spend the night, the whole town will be talking when you come back down. The Traub bad boy and the kindergarten teacher. I can hear them all now."

She laughed. Like it was funny. He watched the dimples flash in her pink cheeks and he thought about licking them. "I'm sure they're already talking. We've practically been joined at the hip since the flood. And in case you've forgotten, we spent a whole night together in my dad's barn and the world didn't come to an end."

In case he'd forgotten? He would never forget. Especially not what had happened in the morning. His fly. Her hand. Sitting there on the edge of that hay bale, willing the humiliating bulge in his pants to go down. He strove for calmness and reasonableness. "We had no choice then. It was the barn or drowning. This—you and me, up the mountain together? That's a clear choice."

Her mouth had pinched up tight. "What is going on with you? Suddenly you're acting like it's 1955 or something. Like you're worried about my reputation, which is excellent and unimpeachable, thank you very much."

Unimpeachable? She really did talk like a schoolteacher sometimes. Which got him hot. Real hot. But he wasn't going to think about that. "It's a very small town, Willa. People here are conservative. You know that as well as I do."

She just wouldn't back down. "You're making way too much of this. Everyone in town knows me and respects me. No one has—or will—judge me for being your friend." In her excitement, she unfolded her arms and waved them around. "In fact, Crawfords aside, this town happens to think the world of *you,* in case you haven't been paying attention."

"That doesn't mean they won't gossip."

"Oh, please. You never cared about people talking before."

"I care now."

"I don't believe you. Here's the way I see it. If you really don't want me along, if you're sick of having me around and you want to get rid of me, that's one thing. If you just *have* to have a little time to yourself, well, okay. I can accept that. But all this other stuff you've been handing me about my reputation and how it's 'a bad idea,' how I should be over at the park instead of with you, well, you can just stop that, Collin Traub. You can just…get a little bit straight with me. Please." And with that, she blew out a hard breath and flopped back against the wheel well again, folding her arms across her chest once more.

"Crap, Willa." He folded his own arms. He told himself that this argument was over and he'd won it. Because she'd just given him the out that he needed. He only had to say he didn't want her with him, that he preferred to be alone. He only had to lie to her.

Which he had no problem doing, under the circumstances. After all, it was for her own good.

Buster whined and stared up at him hopefully. And Willa simply waited.

He opened his mouth and said, "Fine. Get in the truck."

Willa had always loved the drive up Falls Mountain. It was paved only a part of the way up, but when the pavement ran out, the dirt surface was well tended and the ride reasonably smooth—or at least, it always had been until the flood.

The narrow road proceeded in a series of switchbacks under the tall evergreens. Now and then a switchback would lead out onto a rocky point before doubling back. You could park your vehicle and stroll to the edge and gaze out over the whole of the Rust Creek Falls Valley below, a beautiful sight that never failed to steal her breath away.

And then, two-thirds of the way to the summit, you would round a sharp turn—and see the falls up ahead, hear their splendid, endless roar. The air would turn misty and the sun would slip through the spaces between the trees and light up the falling water with a million pinpricks of shining light.

This trip, however, wasn't so much about the scenery. This was about getting safely to Collin's place and dealing with whatever obstacles the big storm might have left in its wake.

As they set out, you could cut the tension between them with a knife. He was pretty steamed at her. He seethed where he sat, strong hands viselike on the wheel, staring out the windshield with fierce concentration, never once glancing in her direction.

And frankly, well, she was annoyed with him, too. She only wanted to help. And he could have gotten rid of her just by honestly saying he didn't want her around.

But no. It had to be all about protecting her good name. Please. She wasn't buying that silliness and he should give her more credit than to imagine she would.

So she spent the first part of the ride until the pavement ran out keeping very quiet, not pushing her luck with him. Buster was in the back and they'd taken their bags of stuff up front with them. She had them both on her side, his on the floor, hers tucked in next to her with her pack against the console. She leaned on the door armrest and stared intently out at the trees and the occasional glimpses of blue Montana sky and told herself that when they got to his place, they would talk it out.

She was so busy staring out her side window she didn't see the first downed tree until he stopped the truck.

"This'll take a while," he said sourly. "Hope you brought a book or maybe a little knitting." He leaned on his door and got out.

Oh, for crying out loud. As if she hadn't helped her father and brother clear any number of fallen trees off the ranch in her lifetime. She'd come ready to work. She had on her old lace-up work boots from the box at her mother's. Her jeans were sturdy and her sleeves were long. She dug around in her plastic bag until she found the pair of work gloves she'd borrowed from Thelma.

Collin's chain saw roared out as she left the truck. Buster was already down from the bed and sniffing around on the side of the road. He would probably take off if she didn't put him on his leash, but he looked so happy and free, she didn't have the heart to tie him up.

So she decided to leave him free, but keep an eye on him. If he started ranging too far, she'd call him back.

She went to join Collin at the fallen tree.

Willa hauled and Collin expertly stripped the branches from the log, then cut the log into sections. When he was done with the saw, he helped her drag off the brush.

As they cleared the brush, he finally started speaking to her again.

"I hate to waste firewood," he said. "But I've got more than enough up at my place."

They left the stove-size logs and the cleanest parts of the branches stacked on the side of the road for anyone in need to collect. It wasn't that big of a tree. In an hour, they had the roadway clear.

She took off her gloves. With her sleeve, she wiped sweat from her brow. And then she remembered to check on the dog. Wouldn't you know? "Buster's run off again."

He put two fingers between his lips and let loose with a whistle so high and piercing, she put her hands over her ears. As soon as he stopped, Buster came bounding out of the trees. He ran straight to Collin and dropped to his haunches in front of him.

"Good dog," Collin said. "Stay."

Willa blinked in admiration. "Wow."

"I used to call Libby that way. Never failed."

She remembered his dog. A sweet-natured brown-spotted white mutt that followed him everywhere. "What happened to Libby?"

"Lost her last winter. She was pretty old."

"I'm sorry. She always seemed so devoted to you."

"Yeah. I guess she was." He made a low, thoughtful sound. "I still miss her. Now and then I think I see her out of the corner of my eye. I forget for a split second that she's gone and I turn to call her to me...."

Willa was nodding, thinking of Mr. Puffy, the barn kitten she'd claimed as her own when she was five. Puffs had become a house cat and lived to be seventeen. "Oh, I know the feeling. It's like they're still with you, somehow, even though you know that they're gone...."

"That's right." He regarded her for a moment that seemed to stretch out into forever. He didn't seem angry anymore and she realized that neither was she.

"Thirsty?" he asked at last.

At her nod, he turned and started walking, pausing only to signal her with a wave of his powerful arm.

"Come on, Buster." She fell in behind him.

A trail took off below the road. They followed it, pine needles crunching under their feet, Buster taking up the rear.

Maybe two hundred yards later, they came to a ditch full of rushing, clear water. They both got down on their bellies to drink. Buster tried to join them, but she shooed him downstream a ways.

It was so good, that water. Fresh and cold and perfect. When they'd both drunk their fill, they scrambled upright and returned to the pickup. They got in, Buster hopped in the back and off they went.

After that, it was stop and go. There were three more downed trees to clear and any number of rutted, rough places scattered with rock, where instant streams had formed during the storm, destroying the road surface, dragging debris. Often they would have to get out and clear away the biggest of the boulders. It was dusty, thirsty work. But there were plenty of ditches to drink from once the road was passable again.

At one of the outlook points, they found that the road had fallen away at the edge of the cliff. It was just wide enough for the pickup to proceed. Twice on that narrow spot, she felt the back wheel on her side slip over the edge.

But Collin had done a lot of driving on narrow, treacherous mountain roads. He knew when to change gears and when to hit the gas. Both times, there was only a split second of falling and then the truck gained purchase again and they went on.

They didn't reach the falls until a little after seven. More than two hours of daylight remained to them, so they stopped the truck. Buster following behind them, they walked close to admire the view.

"It was twice as wide when I came down on the Fourth," he told her, as they stared at the wall of shining water.

"So beautiful." She stood near the edge, looking over, entranced by the plumes of mist that rose from the rocks below. A prayerful kind of feeling came over her. It happened every time she visited the falls.

When they turned for the truck, he said, "It's not that far now." He put down the gate long enough for Buster to hop in the back again. Then he joined her in the cab.

Around the next sharp curve another tree lay, uprooted, across the road. They got out and got to work. By the time that one was out of the way and he was starting up the truck again, it was nine-thirty and the sky was steadily darkening.

He sent her a glance across the console. "We're there in five minutes, barring more crap in the road."

She grinned. "I will pray for an absence of crap."

"Good thinking." He started to shift into gear—and

then stopped. "I would be sleeping in this truck tonight, three fallen trees back, if not for you."

"If more crap happens, you could still end up sleeping in this truck."

He arched a brow. "That was a thank-you."

She felt hugely gratified. "Well, all right. You're welcome."

"And an apology."

"Which is accepted."

They did that thing, the eye-contact thing. The moment stretched out. Finally, he said, "I'm glad you're with me."

"That is so nice to hear." She said it softly, a little bit breathlessly. "Because I'm glad to be with you."

They shared another endless glance. The world seemed a fine place, exciting, a place where anything might happen. A place where a girl's lifelong forbidden fantasies might just come true.

Friends, she reminded herself. *We are friends and that's all.*

But the way he was looking at her, well, a girl could definitely get ideas.

"We should get going," he said.

"Yeah," she whispered, as though there was some kind of secret they were sharing.

He buckled his seat belt and put it in gear.

The headlights were on, the powerful twin beams cutting the thickening shadows. Everything looked clear up ahead. The road was very steep, though, there at the last. Gravel spun out from under the tires as they kept losing traction. But Collin held it in low, with an even pressure on the gas. They climbed steadily upward, almost there.

"One more switchback," he said. The sharp turn loomed ahead. Tires spinning, gravel flying, the truck slipping to one side and then the other, Collin guided them around it.

They'd made it without having to sleep in the cab. Through the tall, thick trees, she could see the shadowed form of his house up ahead. A light shone in the window, one he must have left on when he raced down the mountain four days ago, a light that still burned because he had a generator.

Lights that wouldn't be turned off promptly at 11:00 p.m. How wonderful. She had a couple of bestsellers she'd borrowed from Paige in the bottom of her bag. Why, she might read late into the night if she felt like it. She might blow-dry her hair—well, if only she'd thought to scare up a blow-dryer.

And not only would there be light that was hers to control, she would sleep on a real bed, in a real bedroom, without all those other people nearby snoring or mumbling in their sleep....

The truck slid, snapping her back to reality, and she felt a stomach-turning lurch as the rear wheels lost contact with the road. Collin swore under his breath.

The truck—and the world—hung suspended by two front wheels.

It was bad. She knew it. She tasted copper in her suddenly dry mouth. Her heart boomed, the sound a roar in her ears.

It took her a second or two to realize what had happened. As they came around the turn, the road had collapsed on the cliff side, just dropped off and fallen away under the back wheels.

"Oh, dear Lord," she whispered, and nothing more. Words were lost to her.

The truck was sliding backward, the bed dropping, dragging. They were going to go over the cliff, tail first....

But Collin hit the gas then. The front wheels grabbed

and held. Praise heaven for four-wheel drive. He eased the throttle even higher.

The truck lurched again, jumping forward this time, grabbing at the road. The front wheels had good purchase. Gravel flew every which way, grinding grooves in the dirt, but they did move forward. The truck leveled out as the rear wheels reached the road again.

He had done it. He had all four tires on solid ground again. She heard him suck in a long breath and realized that she was doing the same thing.

"We're okay," she whispered, as though to say it too loudly would somehow send them rolling backward over the cliff once more.

But then she glanced through the rear window. Buster wasn't there.

Chapter Nine

"Collin, Buster's gone!"

Collin hit the brake as Willa's door flew open. "Willa. Wait…" But she didn't wait. She was out the door before the truck came to a full stop. "Be careful at the cliff edge!" he shouted.

Not that she heard him. She was already out and running back to that last almost-deadly turn.

He slammed it in Park, turned off the engine, and shoved in the parking brake, grabbing a flashlight from the glove box before he jumped out and ran after her. "Stay back from the edge, damn it, Willa!"

She was already there, craning to see over, calling the dog. "Buster! Buster, here, boy!"

He went to her, grabbed her arm and hauled her back a few feet. She tried to shake him off, but he held on. "Don't," he warned. "It could be dangerous."

"But Buster…" Frantic tears clogged her voice.

He shone the light on the ground at the edge he'd dragged her back from. Hard to tell, but it looked pretty solid. "Careful, okay?" Reluctantly, he let her go. "Just take it easy... slow."

Together they moved toward the cliff again. He shone the flashlight down into the darkness, spotted the small ledge created by two joined sets of tree roots maybe thirty feet down. Buster was young and agile. All he would have needed was something to break his fall and chances were he would have been okay.

No sign of him on that ledge, though.

"Buster!" Willa called again, more frantic than before. "Buster!"

Not knowing what else to do, Collin put his fingers between his teeth and let out with the whistle that always brought the dogs running. He glanced over at Willa, at the tears already streaming down her soft cheeks.

He was just about to start blaming himself, when he heard the scrabbling sounds over the side, up the road a little, near where he'd stopped the truck.

Willa whipped around toward the noise. "Buster!" Collin turned the light on her, so she wouldn't trip on the uneven road surface as she took off again in the direction of the sounds.

About then, the white dog scrambled up over the bank, apparently unhurt. He got to the road and shook himself.

"Buster!" Willa dropped to a crouch and threw her arms around him. The dog whined and swiped his sloppy tongue all over her face and wagged his tail as though he'd just done something pretty spectacular.

And maybe he had.

Collin went to them. With another happy cry, Willa jumped up and threw her arms around *him*. "He's fine. He's okay. Oh, thank God." She buried her face against his neck.

He held her close and tried not to let himself think about how right she always felt in his arms.

Buster rode the last short stretch inside the cab, sandwiched between Willa's feet.

Collin didn't much care for dogs in the front. But he wasn't complaining. A couple of minutes after they'd piled in the truck again, Collin parked in the flat space not far from the front door to his house.

"We made it," Willa said softly. "I can hardly believe it."

He reached over and grabbed his bag out from under Buster's big feet. "I'm starving. Let's scare up something to eat."

Inside, he got Libby's bowl down from a cupboard and filled it with kibble leftover from last winter. Buster went right to work on the food.

Willa stood holding her black plastic bag, her pack slung on one shoulder, staring out the wall of windows that faced the valley. With the lamps on and the antler chandelier overhead casting its warm glow, there was nothing to see but her reflection in the glass. "This is so beautiful, Collin."

He left the open kitchen area and went to stand beside her. "Pretty dark down there tonight. Usually, even with the great room all lit up, you can see the lights of town."

She turned to him, her eyes so soft and bright. "You'll be seeing them again before you know it."

He took her arm and tried not to feel too happy to have her there, in his house, alone. "Come on. I'll show you the guest room and the spare bath."

Her face lit up. "A shower? You mean it?"

"Right this way."

Willa pushed her empty plate away. "Steak. A baked potato. Even a salad." She sent him a mock glare. "And to think, if I hadn't made you bring me along, it would have been macaroni and canned ham all over again."

He gave her one of those grins that always made her pulse speed up. "Is that what the church ladies are serving tonight?"

"I believe so, yes." She sat back and looked around her. The living area was all one room, with a comfy-looking sofa and chairs grouped around a rustic fireplace. He'd built a small fire that crackled cheerfully. Up on the mountain, even summer nights had a bite to them.

The galley-type kitchen had butcher-block counters, the cabinets painted a woodsy green.

She asked, "This place was your uncle's?"

"That's right." He polished off his beer. "Uncle Casper was an independent old coot—and he was always good to me."

She remembered Casper Traub. He had a handlebar mustache and he always wore a white Resistol hat. "A confirmed bachelor."

"Damn straight. Uncle Casper and I got along. We just seemed to understand each other—but I've made a lot of changes to the house since he passed. This area had a wall down the middle before, the kitchen separate from the living room. I like it open. And I had bigger windows put in to take advantage of the view."

"You did a great job." She stared up at all the lights strung on the antler chandelier. "It's comfortable and homey. Inviting, but not cluttered."

"That's good." He gestured with his empty beer bottle. "It's pretty much what I was going for."

"You got it right."

He was watching her. "But not what you expected." It wasn't a question.

She confessed, "Not really. I was thinking you would have more of a woodsy man-cave, to tell the truth."

Twin creases formed between his brows. "It's not a woodsy man-cave?"

"Collin. You can't have a man-cave with all those windows. With a man-cave, there would be stacks of girlie magazines. And the decor would focus on empty liquor bottles lining the walls."

He pretended to look wounded. "You're serious. You see me saving empty liquor bottles to use for decoration, surrounded by girlie magazines...."

"Oh, come on. You know I'm just kidding."

He shrugged and pointed the beer bottle at the big-screen TV. "Well, I've got the right TV anyway. And I get cable up here now, believe it or not—or I do when the cable service isn't down. Even my cell phone works most of the time." He grinned that wicked grin of his. "Admit it. You're impressed."

"Bowled over." She took a small sip of the beer he'd given her. "You miss your uncle?"

He gave her a slow nod. "Every day. He taught me all I know about the business and he left it to me with the house when we lost him. My shop's in the basement."

"*You* make the saddles now?"

He sent her a wounded glance. "Who would if I didn't? You think I keep a bunch of elves down there?"

"Of course not." But she *was* surprised. She'd known that Casper Traub had left everything to his favorite nephew, but somehow she hadn't really thought about what exactly that would mean—and that made her feel a little ashamed. The past few years, she'd been so busy judging him, she'd never stopped to think about who he was as a person, how he might have changed and grown from the wild, rude boy who used to spy on her out in the back pasture.

He got up, got a second beer from the fridge and twisted the top off. "You want one?"

She still had half of hers. "I'm good."

He came back to her and dropped into his chair again. "What? You're having trouble believing that I work for a living?" He took a drink, his Adam's apple sliding up and down in his strong brown throat. "You have one of my saddles in the tack room of your dad's barn."

Yet another surprise. "My dad's precious CT Saddle? *You* made it?"

"I did."

"But he got that saddle three years ago."

"I've been making saddles since before high school. Uncle Casper had me working with him as soon as I was tall enough to stand at a workbench."

"Oh. I...didn't know."

He grunted and shook his head. And she felt really bad. He seemed to sense her distress, and leaned across the table toward her. "What'd I do? Willa, come on. You look like you're about to cry."

She waved a hand. And then she sighed. "You didn't do anything. Honestly. It's only that I'm disappointed in myself, I guess."

"Why?" He asked it so quietly. Like he didn't want to push her, but he really did want an answer.

She gave him the truth. "We live in a very small town, where everyone knows everything about everyone else. Yet, I didn't know you made the most beautiful saddles in Montana. I didn't know much at all about you. In high school, I never wanted anyone to know that I was..." Her throat clutched. She gulped to loosen it. "Um, attracted to you. So I made real sure that I acted like I couldn't care less whenever anyone mentioned your name. That meant I never learned anything about you—about who you really are. Except that everyone said half the girls had been with you and the other half wished they might."

"Willa…" His voice was husky and his eyes were so soft.

She suddenly felt all warm and quivery inside and she had to force herself to say the rest. "And then, well, after that night at the Ace in the Hole, I was just so…bitter. So angry at you. And that meant I kept on not letting myself know anything about you, kept on judging you without even knowing you. It was all just so narrow-minded and, well, *small* of me, you know? And I like to think of myself as an open-minded and fair person. But maybe I'm not. Maybe I'm already just an old busybody, listening to rumors, believing the worst about people. Never stopping to find out what's really going on."

"You're too young to be an old busybody."

She wanted to smile—but he was letting her off too easy. "Don't be nice to me about this. I don't deserve it."

He set down his beer, got up and came around the table to her, dropping to a crouch beside her chair. "Hey." He took her hand. Heat flowed up her arm, into her heart. And lower down, too. "And I have to tell you, I kind of got a kick out of you avoiding me for four years."

She groaned. "You didn't."

"Oh, yeah. You were so determined. I'd walk in a room—and out you went through the other door."

"But still. Be honest. It did hurt your feelings a little, didn't it?"

"I survived."

She looked down at their joined hands and then back up into those beautiful deep-set eyes of his. "So you forgive me?"

"There's nothing to forgive." He seemed so earnest right then, his face tipped up to her, that lock of hair falling over his forehead the way it always seemed to do.

She couldn't stop herself—she didn't *want* to stop herself. She dared to smooth it back. It was just as she'd always imagined it might be—thick and warm and so very silky, a little bit damp from his recent shower. "I don't know what I would have done in these past few days without you."

"You would have been fine."

She grew bolder. She pressed her palm to his cheek. It was smooth, freshly shaved. "I would have drowned that first day. You know it as well as I do."

"Uh-uh. You're too ornery to drown."

"You think so?"

"Oh, yeah. You would have gotten that door open and made it to safety." His voice was rough and tender, both at once.

Her breath caught in her throat. *A kiss,* she thought.

What could a kiss hurt?

Just one. No harm in that.

His gaze seemed to burn her and his sensual mouth was slightly parted. He smelled so good, clean and fresh and manly.

"Oh, Collin…" She dared to bend closer—and then blinked in surprise when he caught her wrist and gently guided her hand away from his face.

He swept to his feet, grabbed up his empty plate and the salad bowl and carried them to the sink. Without turning back to look at her, he said, "You want to watch a movie or something? I've got a bookcase full of DVDs."

Her face was flaming. Talk about making a fool of herself.

What was her problem anyway? The poor guy couldn't be nice to her without her trying to jump his bones.

She reminded herself, as she'd reminded herself about a hundred times in the past few days, that he liked her and he was her friend. But he was not interested in her in *that* way and she needed get that in her head and keep it there.

His friendship mattered to her. She was not going to lose him because she couldn't stop throwing herself at him.

He still had his back to her as he rinsed out the salad bowl and then scraped off his plate in the garbage and stuck it in the dishwasher.

She picked up her plate and carried it over there.

He took it from her. "So. Movie?"

"As long as I get to choose which one."

He did let her choose. His taste ranged from horror to Western and action/adventure to raunchy guy comedies. Not a tender romance to be found.

She chose a Jason Statham shoot-'em-up. It was fast-paced and entertaining. When it was over, she let Buster out and waited on the step for him to take care of business. Back inside, she told Collin good-night and headed for the guest room, Buster at her heels.

The bed was big and comfortable and she'd worked hard all afternoon. She should have gone right to sleep.

But, no. She kept thinking about what an idiot she'd been at the dinner table, kept wondering if she should have done something other than pretend for the rest of the evening that nothing had happened.

Then again, if not that, what? Certainly they didn't have to discuss the fact that she regretted throwing herself at him and would try really, really hard not to do it again.

Sheesh. How pathetic. That was a conversation she just didn't need to have.

Willa plumped her pillow and turned over. Then she turned over again. Then she sat up and pushed back all the covers but the sheet.

Then she pulled the covers back over herself again.

It was hopeless. Sleep was not in the offing. She turned on the lamp and got her book from the bag and tried to read.

But she couldn't concentrate. The clock by the bed said ten after one.

Maybe she could find some cocoa in the kitchen. Or just some milk to heat up. Or *something*.

She threw back the covers. On the rug by the bed, Buster lifted his head—and then settled back to sleep with a soft doggy sigh. She yanked on a worn plaid shirt over the camisole and knit shorts she'd worn to sleep in and decided to just go barefoot. Flip-flops made too much noise anyway. She didn't want to take the chance of disturbing Collin. At least one of them should be allowed to get a decent night's sleep.

His bedroom was down at the far end of the hall. The door was open, but there was no light on in there.

Not that it mattered. She had no intention of bothering him. Willa went the other way, out to the great room and into the kitchen.

She flicked on the light and was heading for the fridge when Collin said, "Go back to bed, Willa. How many times do I have to tell you? I'm not having sex with you."

With a cry of surprise, she whirled toward the sound of his voice. He stood over in the living area, wearing his jeans and nothing else, his strong legs planted wide apart, hands linked behind him, staring out the wall of windows on the dark town below.

She didn't know whether to laugh or throw something at him…but wait.

On second thought, she did know. The latter. Definitely.

Okay, she'd tried to kiss him and she shouldn't have. But he didn't have to be mean about it. In fact, the more she thought about it, the more she realized how sick and tired she was of hearing him say he wouldn't have sex with her. It had been funny, for a while—but tonight, well, it was downright hurtful.

She zipped around the island counter that separated the living area from the kitchen and marched right for him. "Oh, please. Will you give that up? I couldn't sleep, that's all." She halted a few feet from him and glared at his broad back. "Nobody here is thinking about sex."

"Speak for yourself." Slowly, he turned and faced her. She gasped at the yearning she saw in his eyes.

Chapter Ten

Collin couldn't take it anymore.

The sight of her, in those little purple velour shorts and that skimpy, lacy top…well, it was too much. Even if she did have on an old plaid shirt over the top. That old shirt wasn't hiding anything. She hadn't even bothered to button it up.

He could see her nipples very clearly, poking at him through the thin fabric, could make out the tempting, ripe curves of her breasts. She was driving him crazy, that was what she was doing. He'd held out for years, done the right thing by her, even though she'd ended up hating him for it.

But tonight, well, it was too much.

And hadn't he known that it would be? She shouldn't have kept after him until he brought her up here with him. She shouldn't have tried to kiss him. Shouldn't have come out of her room dressed in those soft purple shorts and that skimpy silky top that didn't hide a damn thing.

He burned. He was on fire—to take her breasts in his two hands. To touch the skin of her thighs, to rub his rough palms along all that smooth softness, to inch his fingers upward, under the hem of those shorts, to touch her at last where he knew she would be hot and wet and waiting for him.

He wanted her, wanted sweet Willa Christensen, probably always had, from way back. From before he even realized what he was wanting. Oh, yeah. He wanted her.

And to hell with what was best for her. She wanted him, too. She'd made that more than clear on more than one occasion.

Tonight, he was going to give her exactly what she wanted.

Reaching out, he took her by the arms and hauled her up close to him, reveling in the feel of her body brushing along the front him, making him ache all the harder for her.

He brought his face good and close to hers, so close he could taste the heat of her breath. "You should have stayed in town tonight like I told you to, you know that, don't you?"

She licked her lips and gulped. "Um. I…" Her eyes were so wide. Wide and soft and wanting.

Those eyes of hers called to him. They always had. Those eyes said she knew him, was waiting for him to finally reach out and take her. Those eyes said she would do anything he wanted.

Truth to tell, those eyes had always scared the crap out of him. They seemed to hint of things a guy like him didn't deserve to know.

Things like forever. Things like a lifetime.

Things he wasn't planning for. He lived his life alone.

Which led back around to the basic issue: he shouldn't be doing this.

But too bad. He *was* doing this.

He was through making jokes about it, through trying to discourage her from wanting a little hot fun with the town troublemaker. If she wanted him so much, who was he to tell her no?

"Oh, Collin…" She said it so softly. So willingly. And then her eyes changed. All at once, they weren't so open and sweet anymore. They'd gone determined. They were sparking fire. "No. Uh-uh. I should *not* have stayed down in town. I'm here with you and I'm *glad* I'm here."

Some final scrap of that protectiveness he'd always felt for her prompted him to give her one last out. He met those eyes of hers. He didn't look away. "What I'm saying is, just tell me no, Willa. Just do it. Do it now."

She let out a strangled sound. It might have been a laugh. Or a sob. "Are you kidding? Don't try and pretend that you don't get it. All I've ever wanted was the chance to tell you yes."

It was the last straw.

"Tell me yes, then. You go ahead. You say it right out loud to me."

She didn't even hesitate. "Yes, oh, yes. Please, please make love to me."

So much for her last out. She'd refused to take it. So be it.

He closed that small distance between her mouth and his. He kissed her.

For the very first time.

He touched her mouth with his and it was…everything. A forbidden dream realized.

A promise so long denied, finally kept.

She kissed him back, sighing so sweetly. She melted into him, all that pride and orneriness and softness. Everything that was Willa.

Right there. In his arms.

Her breasts flattened against his bare chest, the way they'd only done in his dreams up till then. Through the flimsy material of that lacy top, he could feel her nipples, hot. Hard. She opened her mouth to him. He swept his hungry tongue inside and the kiss became something more than a dream. Deeper than a promise.

She moaned as he kissed her, and she ran her slim hands up over his shoulders, into his hair.

He needed…more of her. *All* of her. He had his arms good and tight around her, his aching hardness pressed into her belly. He let his hands roam freely, over the slim, smooth shape of her back, up under that cotton shirt, and then down to the cove at the base of her spine.

Her hair was loose. It brushed his forearms and the backs of his hands. Like feathers. Like a cloud of silk. He speared his fingers up into it, fisted them, pulling her head back so he could scrape his teeth along the slim, pure curve of her white throat.

She cried his name. He covered her mouth again and drank the sound.

He needed…more. More of her.

He had to have the feel of her bare skin under his hands. The plaid shirt was in the way. He fisted it by the sides and peeled it back over her slim shoulders. She moaned a little, as though in protest at having to let go of him, but she let him guide her arms down so he could push the shirt off. He whipped it away and tossed it in the general direction of a chair.

Then he clasped her bare shoulders. So smooth and tender, her skin. White, but with a pink flush on it. Beautiful.

He cupped her shoulders, pressed his palms against her upper chest—and lower, until he had her sweet breasts in his two hands with only the thin fabric of that clingy silky thing to protect her from his hungry touch.

She lifted up to him, sighing, offering him whatever he wanted from her.

And he knew what he wanted. To taste her.

He kissed his way down her slim throat again, scattered more kisses along the ridge of her collarbone, down the sweet-smelling skin of her upper chest and lower, over the tender swell of her breast.

He reached the goal at last and latched onto her nipple, sucking it through the silky fabric, flicking it with his tongue.

She clutched at him, holding him to her, whispering, "Yes. Oh, Collin, yes…"

He couldn't have agreed with her more. She smelled like flowers and lemons and a little bit musky, too. All woman, his Willa.

His? Well, fine, maybe not. Not forever. But at least for tonight.

The lacy thing—what did women call those things?—a cami. Yeah. The cami had to go. He grabbed the hem of it…and then got lost in the feel of her skin again. He eased his fingers up under it, stroking the tender flesh of her back, and then bringing both hands around to the front of her, caressing her flat, smooth belly.

She was breathing so frantically. He lifted his head and kissed her again. She moaned into his mouth.

And he moved his hands higher. He cupped her bare breasts under the cami. They were so perfect, so firm and round—not too big, not small, either. They fit just right in his hands.

He thought about seeing her naked.

He wanted to do that. Right away.

Now.

She made no objections, only moaned eagerly and whispered "yes," and "yes" again, as he pulled off the cami and took down the little shorts.

There.

At last.

He had everything off her. She was silk and fire and magic, all he'd ever wanted. Right there in his arms.

He bent enough to wrap his hands around the twin globes of her bottom. She moaned again and he went on kissing her as he lifted her up, dragging all that softness against him. He moaned, too.

It felt so good. *She* felt so good.

She wrapped those soft, smooth thighs around him and hooked her ankles behind his back.

Now he could feel her, feel the womanly heart of her, right there, pressed tight to his fly. He was so hard it hurt. Hurt in the best, most extreme, most perfect kind of way.

And then, still kissing her, her hair a froth of silk and shadows sliding across his skin, her mouth to his mouth, his breath to hers, he started walking.

Well, reeling was more like it.

He reeled across the great room and down the hall to his room at the end. She held on. She went on kissing him. She wrapped those soft, long arms and slim, strong legs around him like she would never, ever let him go.

In the doorway, he paused. Or more like staggered. He braced his back against the door frame and indulged in just kissing her. She didn't seem to mind that he'd stopped moving toward the bed. She just went on kissing him, went on rocking her hips against him, went on making him want to get out of his jeans and into her softness, pronto.

But then again...

No.

He didn't want to rush it. How many times in his life did

a man hold a dream in his arms? Once, if he was lucky. A man would be a fool to rush something like that.

Yeah, okay, he had a whole boatload of faults. And maybe he was a fool in some ways. But not when it came to holding Willa in his arms. He was taking his time about this.

He was making it last if it killed him.

And he was kind of afraid it just might.

She framed his face in her two slim hands. "Collin…"

He opened his eyes, stared into hers, which were shining so bright, even in the dim light from all the way back in the kitchen. "Willa."

She wrapped her legs tighter around him. He groaned at the perfect friction as all that willowy softness slid along the front of him. "You do have protection?"

He nodded on another groan.

"Oh, good." And she sighed and kissed him again.

Paradise. They went on kissing, there in the darkened doorway. Endlessly.

Until a terrible thought occurred to him. He broke the kiss so suddenly that his head bounced against the door frame.

She cried out, "Oh! I'll bet that hurt." And she clucked her tongue and fussed over him, rubbing the bumped spot in a gentle, soothing way. "Be careful…."

Gruffly, he reassured her. "I'll live—Willa, look at me."

She blinked at him owlishly, adorably. In the faint glow of light from up the hallway, her dark hair was a wild tangle all around her sweet, flushed face. A dream. No doubt. This had to be a dream. "What?" she demanded. "What's the matter now?"

"I need you to tell me. Is this your first time?" He did not have sex with virgins.

She pressed those amazing lips together, nervous. Unsure. And then she buried her face against his neck. "No." She said it softly.

"Good." Relief was coursing through him. That fatheaded idiot from high school, Derek Andrews, no doubt. And probably Mr. Wonderful, who wanted to marry her.

Mr. Wonderful, who was another reason Collin shouldn't be seducing Willa. She deserved a bright future with the right kind of guy.

But somehow, at that moment, he wasn't feeling all that guilty about Mr. Wonderful. What guy in his right mind proposed marriage and then went to Australia? Mr. Wonderful deserved a little competition for leaving her on her own at the mercy of a guy like him.

She pressed her plump lips to the side of his throat and he felt her tongue slide along his skin. He groaned and wrapped his arms tighter around her and was very, very glad that she wasn't a virgin.

He supposed he should have known she wasn't. She didn't act like a virgin. She acted like a woman who knew what she wanted.

"Willa," he whispered, and then again, "Willa..." He'd always loved the feel of her name in his mouth.

"I'm right here." She lifted her head from his shoulder and nuzzled his ear as he kissed his way across her cheek to take her mouth once more.

Then he gathered her tighter, closer, and launched them from the doorway, making it to the bed in four long strides. He laid her gently down and turned on the lamp, and then he just stood there above her, looking down at her, so slim and pretty, naked to his sight.

At last.

"So beautiful..." The words came out of him on a bare husk of sound.

She met his eyes—or at least she did at first. But then

she grew shy. She did that thing that women do—an arm across her pink-tipped breasts, a hand to cover the shining brown curls in the cove of her silky thighs.

"Don't..." His voice sounded desperate, ragged to his own ears.

And she reached out. She put a hand against his belly, palm flat. A groan escaped him when she did that. Her touch felt so good, so exactly right. Like the scent of her that seemed to call to him, to beckon him to her.

She said, gently, politely, "Take off your jeans, please."

He couldn't do what she wanted fast enough. Two of the buttons were undone anyway. He undid the rest and shucked them off and away.

"Oh, Collin, you're so...you're beautiful, you are."

"Men aren't beautiful," he argued gruffly.

"Oh, yes. They are." She held out her arms to him. "I'm so happy. After all this time, I never thought...never imagined..." She seemed to run out of words. It was all right. He understood, he knew exactly what she meant. "Come down here. With me...."

He pulled open the bedside drawer and got a condom from the box in there. And then he went down to her. He stretched out beside her, covered her mouth with his and let his hands wander.

Her body moved beneath his touch, so tempting, so soft. He kissed her as he stroked her hair, her throat, the smooth roundness of her shoulder.

So much to explore, all of her. Beautiful and willing and pliant and tender. The slim curve of her waist called to him. He stroked his hand from her rib cage to the swell of her hip and lower, down the long sweep of her thigh.

He palmed her knee and gently guided it open. Then he did what he'd dreamed of doing, sliding his palm up the inside of her thigh as she rolled her hips and tossed her head and moaned his name in hungry encouragement.

The dark curls were already wet with her excitement. He parted them. She cried his name out good and loud then.

He kissed her slow and deep. He whispered against her lips, "Like this, Willa?"

She gasped. "Yes, oh! Yes…"

He slipped a finger in. Two. Wet silk inside, warm and slick, welcoming him. Her hips moved rhythmically now, her thighs open, offering him everything. So much. All she had to give.

"Collin…" She said his name against his mouth. And then she gave him her tongue to suck. He kissed her endlessly as he stroked her.

And by then, touching her in that most intimate place wasn't enough. He had to taste her there.

He kissed his way down the center of her. She clutched his shoulders, murmured his name over and over, like she couldn't get enough of saying it. He just kept kissing her, all of her, as he lifted up and slid over and settled between her open thighs. She shifted, adjusting herself with a long, slow sigh, bracing her heels on his shoulders.

The scent of her was so sweet, lemons and musk. And the taste? Exactly as he'd dreamed it. Only better. Endlessly better…

He used his fingers and his mouth and she moved against him, sighing, her hands in his hair, her head tossing on the pillow. She was rising, reaching for the peak, and he stayed with her, all the way. Until at last she went over, crying his name as the soft explosion of her climax pulsed against his tongue.

The condom had been lost somewhere in the tangle of bedclothes. He felt around for it—and got lucky. His fingers closed around it as she sighed once more and went all loose and lazy.

He didn't stop kissing her. She tasted so good.

She moaned his name. And finally, she pleaded, "Oh, please. Oh, my. I can't...it's too much..."

With a low chuckle, he relented, backing off a little, resting his head on her thigh. She stroked his hair, traced the shape of his ear. He was aching to continue. He'd been hard and getting harder forever, it felt like right then.

But at the same time, he was satisfied just to lie with her that way, naked. Together. Unashamed.

A few minutes later, he sat back on his knees. She followed him, sitting up, brushing her wild hair out of her eyes, laughing. "Here. Let me..."

So he gave her the pouch. She tore the end off with her teeth. Hottest thing he ever saw. A guy didn't need those girlie magazines she'd teased him about having in his man-cave. Not with Willa Christensen naked in his bed.

She peeled away the wrapper and set it neatly on the bedside table. Then she bent close to him. She rolled it down over him.

He shut his eyes and tipped his head back and tried not to lose it just from the feel of her sliding it down over him.

"Collin?"

He let a low groan be his answer.

And then the bed shifted as she rose up on her knees and bent close to him, all tart and sweet and womanly. Her hair brushed his shoulder and her mouth touched his, lightly, teasing him.

It was too much. He rose up and took her shoulders and rolled her under him.

She let out a little cry and a soft laugh. And then he was on top of her, his elbows braced on either side of her, framing her sweet face in his hands, her hair all around them. He stared down at her and she looked up at him.

"Willa…"

"Collin."

"Willa, I…" There were no words. And it didn't matter. He was right where he'd never dared dream he would be.

"I'm so glad," she whispered.

He had her arms trapped at her sides. But she could move her legs.

And she did, lifting them, hooking them around the backs of his thighs. He was positioned just right, nudging her where she was so soft and wet and open.

She felt like heaven. Like some lost paradise, found at last, after he'd given up believing he would ever get there.

He entered her slowly, by aching degrees. And he held her gaze the whole time. He needed the sight of her face as he claimed her, so beautifully flushed. Lips softly parted.

Completely willing, with nothing held back from him.

She moaned as he went deeper. He made an answering sound and kept pressing, filling her.

Finally, he couldn't go slowly anymore. With a forceful thrust, he was all the way in.

She gasped. Her eyes widened. Her sweet lips invited.

He lowered his mouth to her and kissed her as he began to move.

After that, time folded in on itself. He lost control and rocked wildly against her. She held him closer, tighter than before.

She made soft, willing sounds that only drove him higher. Deeper. Harder.

His mind was gone, shattered. There was only her body and his body inside her, the feel of her soft, willing mouth pressed to his.

He hit the peak and sailed over, knowing a faint echo

of regret that he couldn't hold out for her—and then, all at once, learning he hadn't left her behind, after all. Her body pulsed around him, drawing him deeper. Pushing him higher.

Hurling him outward through a midnight-blue universe of fast-spinning stars.

Chapter Eleven

Faintly, far away, Willa heard music playing. It was that Joe Nichols song, "Tequila Makes Her Clothes Fall Off."

She smiled. She'd always thought that song was kind of cute.

The song stopped. And the bed shifted. She remembered.

It was Collin's bed....

"My cell," said a groggy, very masculine voice not far from her ear. He nuzzled her hair. "I left it charging in the kitchen...."

"Um." She cuddled closer to his big, hard, naked body. He wrapped a muscular arm around her and drew her closer, tucking her into him, spoon style, settling the covers more snugly around them.

She smiled some more and opened her eyes to morning light.

Amazing. It really had happened with Collin. Just like

in all her forbidden fantasies. It had been incredible and it had lasted all night long.

He smoothed her hair away from her neck and kissed her there. "You smell good...." Down the hallway, the phone beeped.

"Voice mail," she said on a lazy yawn.

His lips brushed her neck again. "It's after eight. I'd better go see if it's anything important."

She grabbed the arm he had wrapped around her and pretended to sulk. "Oh, no..."

But he only kissed her hair and pushed back the covers, pausing to tuck them around her again. "I'll be right back."

She rolled over and watched him get up. He looked so good without his clothes on. He had a cute little happy trail and a real, true six-pack.

And a beautiful tattoo on the hard bulge of his right shoulder, one of those tribal designs. She'd spent a while the night before studying it, tracing its curves and angles with her fingers. It looked a little like a mask, with horns and a pair of eyes that also seemed to resemble sharks, somehow. She'd asked him what it was supposed to represent and in typical Collin fashion, he'd answered, "Whatever you want it to represent."

He put on his jeans and buttoned them partway, which somehow only made him look manlier and more naked. "Keep the bed warm."

"Will do. Let the dog out?" Buster, who'd ended up on the rug by the bed, was already up and wagging his tail.

He nodded. "C'mon, Buster."

She watched him go, Buster close behind. The view of him walking away was every bit as inspiring as the one from the front.

She heard the outside door open and shut as he let Buster out. And then he came back.

He held out the phone to her. "Your brother."

She sat up, pulling the sheet with her to cover her breasts, and took the phone from him. "Um. Thanks." She hit the icon for voice mail.

Gage's voice said, "Collin, this is Gage. I'm in town. And looking for my sister. Could you have her call me?" He didn't sound especially cordial.

Collin was watching her. "Good old Gage. Finally made it into town and he's wondering where the hell his baby sister's gotten off to."

Willa hitched up her chin and put on a smile. "Oh, I doubt he's wondering. I'm sure someone in town has already told him exactly where I am."

His dark gaze ran over her. She thought of the night before and a hot shiver went through her. "Not feelin' quite so *unimpeachable* now, are you, Willa?"

She pursed up her mouth at him and narrowed her eyes. "Don't start. I do not regret a thing. Last night was beautiful. I mean that. Do you understand?"

He gave her a slow, insolent once-over. "Yes, ma'am."

She puffed out her cheeks with a frustrated breath. And then she whispered, "Come here. Please?"

His fine mouth curled. "You should call your brother back."

She reached out her hand.

He looked at it for a count of five. Her heart sank. She was certain he would turn and walk away.

But then he reached out, too. Their hands met, fingers lacing together. Relief, sweet and good as a long drink of cool water, washed through her.

He dropped down onto the bed at her side. "I feel bad, okay? I don't want to cause you problems with your family."

She dropped the phone onto the sheet and wrapped

her other hand around their joined ones. "You're not. You couldn't."

He leaned closer. She tipped her mouth up to him and their lips met. "Call him," he said against her lips. "I'll let Buster back inside and put the coffee on." He lifted their hands and kissed the back of hers.

Reluctantly, she let him go, picked up the phone again and called her brother back. He answered on the first ring.

"Gage, it's me."

"Willa. Where are you?"

She could tell by his tone that he already knew. "I'm up at Collin's. We drove up yesterday. The road's a mess. I helped him clear the way."

A silence on Gage's end, then, "I don't get it. You never even liked Collin Traub, and all of a sudden, you two are—what? What's going on, Willa? What about you and Dane?"

Dane. Oh, Lord. She'd really messed up with Dane. She never should have let him talk her into taking time to think things over. She'd put off the inevitable and now she felt like a two-timer.

"Willa, are you still there?"

"Yes. Right here." And no way was she getting into all this on the phone. "Listen. I'll call you as soon as we get back down into town. We can talk then—or, whenever you can get a minute."

"*When* will you be back in town?"

"I don't know for sure yet. Collin may have things he has to do up here. And we cleared the road as best we could, but there are some rough spots and some places where the cliff side collapsed. It could take a while to get down."

"Buster okay?"

"He's fine. Yes."

"And you?" He sounded worried. "You…okay?"

Love washed through her. Her brother was such a great guy. "I am just fine. I promise you. And I'm glad you're here. So glad." Rust Creek Falls really needed him now. But she didn't say that. She knew him, knew he had to be beating himself up that he hadn't been there when the levee broke. Telling him how much he was needed would only make him feel worse about everything.

"Call me," he said. "As soon as you're back in town."

When she entered the kitchen, Buster was in the corner, his nose buried in Libby's old food bowl. The coffee was brewing. And Collin stood at the stove, laying strips of bacon in a pan.

She leaned a hip against the counter and stuck her hands in the pockets of the flannel robe she'd found on the back of his bathroom door. "I hope you don't mind. I stole your robe." Her purple shorts, cami and plaid shirt were strewn around the living room.

He glanced over. "Looks better on you than on me anyway."

She wanted to go to him, brush his hair back off his forehead, tell him…

What?

She wasn't quite sure. "That bacon smells so good."

He tipped his head toward the open shelves with the dishes on them. "Put the plates on the table?"

She nodded and then got busy setting the table. He cooked the bacon and scrambled some eggs. She made the toast and poured the coffee.

They sat down to eat, the silence between them both sharp-edged and a little too deep.

She made herself break it. "Gage is fine. I said I would call him when we got back down into town."

"You need to get going right away, then?"

She sipped her coffee. "No. There's no hurry."

"You sure about that, Willa?"

The question seemed to hang heavy in the air between them.

Willa pushed back her chair. He watched her, dark eyes wary, as she went around the table to his side and did what she'd wanted to do since she entered the kitchen. She smoothed his hair back off his forehead. "I'm sure. No hurry."

He caught her hand. But he didn't push it away. Instead, he brought her fingers to his lips and kissed the tips of them. "Your food will get cold...."

"Um. Can't have that." She bent and he tipped his head up. They shared a quick kiss and she returned to her chair.

After that, the silence didn't seem so oppressive. But the romantic and sensual mood of the night before, of that morning before the phone rang, was definitely absent.

She wanted to talk—about everything. About how she was never going to marry Dane Everhart and she'd been wrong not to simply say no when Dane proposed, about how her brother would be fine with her and Collin being together, once she had a chance to talk with him. About how beautiful last night had been and how she was looking forward to more nights just like it.

But somehow, she didn't know where to begin. And that had her looking back wistfully at their recent nights on the front steps of the town hall, when talking with Collin had been as simple and easy as breathing.

And now, here they were. Lovers, at last. And it was suddenly neither easy nor simple. She had so much to say—and yet she feared she might mess things up if she started talking. She might end up blurting out something that would turn him off.

Was it true then, what they said about sex ruining a perfectly good friendship? She did hope not.

Collin knew he had to get her back to town as soon as possible. Her brother's call had been like a bucket of icy water in the face. It had snapped him back to reality hard and fast.

He shouldn't have taken her to bed. He knew that. Really, where was it going to go with them?

Nowhere. Things were crazy now, after the flood. Their whole world had been turned pretty much upside down. He knew that was all it was with the two of them: one of those things that happen when a man and a woman were thrown together by necessity in a crisis, with emotions running high.

It could never be anything permanent. She was a nice girl with a certain kind of life ahead of her. And his life suited him fine as it was. He liked his independence, always had. And she was going to marry a big shot from Colorado. She would remember that soon enough.

Probably already had. She'd been pretty damn quiet ever since she'd talked to Gage. Collin figured that just the sound of her brother's voice had gotten her to thinking twice. She'd realized it was a bad idea, what they'd done last night, that it never should have happened and it needed to stop now.

They loaded the contents of his freezer into coolers, strapped them into the pickup bed, and left for town.

The trip down went smoothly, all things considered. Collin knew the places to be extra careful—and they'd cleared away the worst of the storm debris on the way up.

He handed her his cell when they reached the base of the mountain. "Call Gage."

She made the call.

It was, "Hi, it's me...Yes...All right, I will...A few minutes...Okay." She handed him back his phone and asked him to let her off at the sheriff's office.

He pulled up to the curb.

She hooked Buster's leash to his collar and turned a dewy smile his way. "I...well, I can't tell you to call me, since I don't have a phone." She really did sound like she *wanted* him to call her.

But that had to be wishful thinking on his part. His chest was tight and his throat felt like it had a log stuck in it. "I'll see you." It came out way too gruff and low.

She searched his face. Whatever she was looking for, he didn't think she found it. He reminded himself how that was for the best. "Um. Okay, then. Have a good one."

"Yeah. Say hi to Gage."

"Will do." Another blinding, too-wide smile. And then she shouldered her pack, grabbed her big plastic bag of stuff and got out. Buster jumped down after her.

He didn't allow himself to watch her walk away. As soon as she shut the door, he put it in gear and got the hell out of there.

Gage was waiting for Willa in his office. He was on a cell phone arguing with someone about roadblocks or something, but he cut it short when he looked up and saw her in the doorway.

"Willa." He gave her a tired smile and ended the call. Then he got up and came around the desk to her. She ran to him and he hugged her close. He said in a voice rough with emotion, "I'm so glad you're all right." She let her bag and pack drop to the floor and hugged him back, hard. He'd always made her feel safe and protected. And right then, after the way Collin had seemed so eager to get rid of her, well, it felt good to have her big brother's arms around her.

When he let her go, she asked, "Have you been out to the ranch?"

His mouth formed a grim line. "Yeah. What a mess. I'll be staying down the street, in a FEMA trailer for a while."

"Why not stay at Mom and Dad's?"

"It's better if I'm right here in town, where I need to be." There was a tap on the door. He went over and opened it and said to the dispatcher, "I need a few minutes here. Won't be long." Then he shut the door again and turned to her. "Buster?"

"He's good. I tied him out in front."

He came back to her, clasped her shoulder and glanced down at the pile of belongings she'd dropped at her feet. "I heard you've been staying over at the town hall on a cot—until last night anyway."

She nodded, her gaze on his handsome face. He looked so weary, the faint lines around his eyes etched deeper than before. "It worked out."

He took charge, the way he always did. "So, then. You need a car, a phone and a place to stay."

She *had* a place to stay—with Collin. Or at least, she'd thought she did until a couple of hours ago. "A car and a phone would really help." She was going to have a long talk with Collin that evening, whether he liked it or not. And then, if that didn't go well, she'd find somewhere else to stay. "I need to get hold of the insurance people—for the house and for the Subaru."

"Have a seat." Gage gestured at one of the guest chairs and then went back to sit behind his desk, where he pulled open a drawer and took out another cell phone, a charger and the key to his pickup. "I've got cells I can use and the county provides me with a vehicle. For now, you take my cell and the pickup."

"Oh, Gage. I can't take your truck."

"Oh, yes, you can. And you will." He shoved it all across at her. "I programmed the number of the cell I'll be using into this phone. So you know where to reach me whenever you need me. Get a hold of your insurance agent. And call Mom. She's been asking about you."

"I will. Thanks."

"And with the truck, you can get around. Got money?"

She admitted, "I lost my wallet in the Forester."

He passed her some cash and a credit card. "You should get over to Kalispell and replace your license. And you need to call about your credit cards...."

She granted him a patient glance. "Yes, big brother."

He went right on. "There's gas available, too. The garage just got its tanks refilled. With the truck, you'll be able to stay at the ranch."

She wasn't committing to that. At least not until she'd had it out with Collin. "I'll be okay. Please don't worry."

He was looking way too bleak. She knew what was coming next. And she was right. "So...you spent the night at Collin Traub's." He practically winced when he said Collin's name.

She sat up straighter. "Yes, I did—and you can just stop giving me that pained look. Collin's not what I always thought, Gage. I'm ashamed of how completely I misjudged him. He's a great guy."

He had a one-word response to that. "Dane?"

"Dane is not the issue here."

"Willa." He used her name as a rebuke. "The man asked you to marry him. I thought you were considering it."

"I blew it, all right? I never should have told Dane I would think it over when he proposed. There's nothing to think over. Dane is not the man for me."

"You say that now...."

"Yes. And I should have said it from the first. As soon

as Dane's back in the country, I will apologize to him for keeping him hanging."

"Dane's a good man. Are you sure you want to just cut him loose?"

"I am absolutely certain."

"Well, even if that's so, it doesn't make the Traub wild man right for you. Willa, come on. You know about Collin Traub. He's not a man to hang your hopes on. The guy never met a heart he didn't break. And he's spent more than one night cooling his heels in the jail cell out there for being drunk and disorderly and picking a fight."

She refused to waver. "People mature. They change. Collin grew up without a lot of supervision. Yes, he went a little wild."

"A *little?*"

"He's just not like that anymore. I…I care for him and I respect him." Gage started to speak, but she didn't let him get a word in. "Listen. I know you only want to protect me and I love you for it. But I don't want or need protecting. I'm an adult and I know what I'm doing." *I hope.*

"Well, I don't like it."

"Gage…"

He surprised her and admitted, "All right. I know that he's made a go of his uncle's saddle-making business. I give him credit for that." Willa started to relax a little. At least Gage realized that Collin had created a productive life for himself. But then he went on, "However, when it comes to women, Collin Traub is bad news. I want you to stay away from him. Can you just do that, just stay away from him for my sake? Please."

"I'm sorry. No. You're the best brother any girl could have. But being the best doesn't give you the right to tell me how to run my life."

He started to rise. "Now, you listen here—"

"Sit down, Gage," she instructed in her best school-teacher tone. Surprisingly, he sank back to his chair. And she pressed her advantage. "I'm a grown woman. And I am fully capable of making my own decisions about my life—and the men in it. I want you to give Collin a chance."

"A chance to what?" he demanded. "To hurt you and mess you over?"

"No. A chance to make you see that there's more to him than your old ideas about him. All you have to do is ask around town and you'll learn a thing or two about everything he's done for Rust Creek Falls since the flood. He saved my life, Gage. He's been at the front line of the rescue efforts and the cleanup. He's a natural leader and he's right there when he's needed—and no, I can't say if what's happening with Collin and me is going to last forever. But I do know that, however it ends up with us, I will never regret being with him."

Gage gave her a long, dark look. And then he grabbed a pencil, pulled open his pencil drawer and tossed it in. He shut the drawer good and hard. "I'm not happy about this."

"That's your prerogative."

"But what can I say?"

She gazed at him coaxingly. "That you'll give Collin a chance."

He blew out a breath. "Fine. I'll stay out of it. For now. I'll just knock myself out being open-minded about Collin Traub."

She beamed him her fondest smile. "Thank you."

"But if that wild man breaks your heart, you can be damn sure I'll be first in line to break *his* face."

Willa spent the day taking care of personal business.

She used the cell Gage had loaned her to call her insurance agent and the FEMA flood insurance number.

The clerks she talked to took her number and promised she'd get calls back from adjusters within twenty-four hours—for the car and for the house and for her separate government-run flood insurance policy. Next, she made calls about her credit cards. That took a while, since she no longer had the cards, she was calling from someone else's phone and her records had been turned to mush in the flood. But in the end, she gave the ranch as a temporary address and was promised that new cards would arrive there within the week. After that, she decided to go ahead and drive to Kalispell to visit her bank and her cell phone provider, and to get a new driver's license.

As soon as she got her new phone in her hand, she called everyone back and told them she had her own phone now. Then she called her mom in Livingston.

"You got your phone back," her mother said when she answered. "Oh, honey. We miss you…."

"I miss you, too, Mom."

"I talked to Gage just today…"

"Yeah. He finally made it back. He loaned me his truck."

"Good. There are still a lot of problems with the roads, so we thought we'd just stay here in Livingston a little longer."

"That sounds wise, Mom."

"Gage says they're giving him a trailer so he can stay in town."

"Yes. You know him. He needs to be where the action is."

"Honey, I've been meaning to ask. You *are* staying at the ranch, aren't you?"

"Uh, no."

"But why not?"

Willa didn't want to go into her relationship with Collin. Not now. Not on the phone—and not after last night and the awkwardness of that morning. It was all too new and exciting and scary. Not to mention, up in the air. And evidently, Gage had stayed out of it and said nothing to their parents about where she'd slept last night.

Thank you, big brother.

"Willa? Are you there?"

"Right here. And I've been staying in the town hall." It was true. She had been. Until last night. "They have cots set up for people whose homes were flooded."

"But surely you should be out at the ranch. Even with the power out, it seems to me that you would be so much more comfortable there than sleeping on a hard, narrow cot in a public building...."

"Mom. I'm managing. It's working out fine."

"Just think about it, won't you? Consider it."

"I'll manage, Mom."

Her mother muttered something under her breath. "Always so independent."

"I love you, Mom. Give my love to Daddy. I have to go...."

"And we love you. You're eating right, aren't you? Taking care of yourself...?"

"I'm perfectly healthy and I'm getting plenty to eat. And I do have to go."

With a sigh, her mother said goodbye.

Willa and Buster got back to Rust Creek Falls at a little past three in the afternoon. She stopped in at Gage's office and returned his cell phone. Then she visited the town hall and the Community Church in hopes that Collin might be at one or the other.

He wasn't. She tried not to feel too disappointed. The

man could be back up on the mountain working in his shop, or out on flood cleanup—or just about anywhere.

She considered calling him, but decided to wait. Tonight, one way or another, she would track him down.

Summer school was out by then, so she went to Paige's house. Shelby was there with her little girl, Caitlin, who would be in Willa's class next year. Willa got a full report on the day's activities at the park. Shelby said the day had gone well and volunteered to fill in again for Willa whenever she needed a hand.

Willa thanked her. She really liked Shelby, who was a wonderful mother and a talented teacher. Shelby wasn't having an easy time of it raising her little girl alone. A blonde, blue-eyed beauty who had once been the most popular girl at Rust Creek Falls High, now Shelby made ends meet tending bar at the Ace in the Hole. Willa had been encouraging her to apply for a full-time teaching position with the district.

When Shelby and Caitlin left, Willa stayed to brainstorm with Paige on new projects for their summer school kids—projects that would lend themselves to an outdoor classroom setting.

At five-thirty, Willa put Buster on his leash and Paige walked with them to the church for dinner. The gas had never stopped working on the north side of town, but the power was still out. Paige had no generator, which meant she couldn't keep food refrigerated. The church, with the help of donations from a number of sources, would continue to provide meals for the community as long as people needed them. Refrigerated trucks brought in food daily.

Halfway there, Paige asked gingerly, "Are things okay with you and Collin?"

Willa sent her a sideways glance. "Ask me in a day or two."

"I'm here and ready to listen anytime you need me."

Willa hooked an arm around her friend's slim shoulders. "I know. It's just another reason why I'm so glad you're my friend."

At the church, Willa spotted Jerry Dobbs sitting at a table with three other members of Collin's cleanup team. Collin wasn't with them.

Willa told Paige she'd join her in a moment. She got a bowl of dog food from one of the church ladies and took it outside to Buster. As the dog wolfed down his dinner, she gave Collin a call.

He didn't answer.

She left a message. "Hey. It's Willa. Note this number. It's mine. I went to Kalispell and replaced my cell phone today, along with my driver's license. I also dealt with replacing my credit cards, insurance adjusters and with my bank..." And really, did he need a blow-by-blow? She realized she was nervous because he hadn't picked up when she called. She tried again. "Right now, I'm down at the church for dinner. No sign of you. Give me a call...." She couldn't think of anything else to say, so she left it at that.

Back inside, she went through the serving line and sat down with Paige. Throughout the meal, she kept waiting for the phone to ring.

Didn't happen.

She couldn't help but feel a little bit dumped. Which was ridiculous, and she knew it. How could she be dumped? To be dumped implied that you'd shared some sort of at least semi-committed relationship with a guy. She and Collin? They were friends who'd slept together. One time.

So then, did that make her just another of Collin Traub's one-night stands?

Oh, dear Lord. She did hope not. Collin couldn't be that disappointing and hurtful. Could he?

She wished she could stop remembering her argument with Gage that morning.

Was Collin going to go and prove her big brother right? *No.*

She needed to stop this. She was not going to think like this. If she kept on in this vein, she'd be right back where she started before the flood: racing out of rooms just because Collin Traub entered them.

That morning, she'd argued fervently with Gage on Collin's behalf. She'd said how Collin had grown and changed from the no-strings wild boy he used to be. And she had absolutely believed what she'd said.

Collin *had* changed. And if he could do it, so could she.

The friendship they'd found since the flood meant a lot to her. And last night had been beautiful—no matter what happened next. One way or another, she was working this out with him. If he didn't want to be with her in a man-woman way, well, that would hurt.

A lot.

But she would get over it.

Right now, what she needed to do was talk this out with him. And to do that, she had to *find* him.

Jerry Dobbs had finished his meal. He was busy putting his tray away, tossing his trash and separating his dishes from his flatware.

Willa told Paige she'd see her tomorrow, picked up her tray and went to ask Jerry if he might know where Collin had gone.

Collin tried to concentrate on the intricate pattern of leaves and vines, on the good, clean smell of veg tan top-grain leather, on the slow, exacting process of stamping the custom design with his stylus and mallet.

But his mind was not cooperating. His mind was on a

certain brown-eyed woman. On the scent of lemons, on the way it had felt to have her tucked up against him naked all night long.

She had called over an hour ago. He hadn't answered and he hadn't called her back, though he *had* played her message. Three times. So far.

Yeah, he was being a real jerk and he knew it.

Still, he kept thinking it was better this way. Let her be completely disappointed in him, start avoiding him again.

Better for everyone.

Being her friend was one thing. But taking it further…

Bad idea. He'd blown it and he knew it. He shouldn't have given in to that thing he'd always had for her. He'd seriously stepped over the line and he wasn't going to let it happen again.

The sound from upstairs stopped his thoughts in midramble and his mallet in midair.

Someone was knocking on his front door.

He dropped the mallet and stylus and headed for the stairs as fast as his boots would carry him.

"Why do I get the feeling you're avoiding me?" she asked when he pulled open the door. She stood there in old jeans and a frayed T-shirt, her hair loose on her shoulders, Buster at her feet. He'd never in his life seen a sight quite so beautiful. She tapped her booted foot. "Do I get to come in or not?"

Chapter Twelve

Collin glanced past her shoulder, saw her brother's pickup parked next to his. Of course, Gage would have seen to it that she had transportation.

He accused, "The road up here is still dangerous."

"You'll be happy to know that Buster and I made it just fine." She stuck out her chin at him. "Ahem. May I come in?"

It was a bad idea. And he was way too crazy happy to see her.

"Collin. *Hello?*"

He stepped back automatically. She moved forward, the dog right behind her. He edged around her, shut the door and turned to her. "What?"

She squared her shoulders, kind of bracing herself. "Look. If you regret last night, that's fine. I can deal with that. I would rather you *didn't* regret it. I would rather be, um…" She paused, swallowed. He watched the warm color flood upward over her sweet, soft cheeks. "I would rather be your lover. But if you don't want that, well, okay. If you think it was a big mistake, what we did last night, okay. I won't like it and it…hurts me. But I *will* get over it. Because what I really want, most of all, Collin Traub, is to still be your friend."

He drank in the sight of her. It occurred to him that he would never get tired of seeing her pretty, clean-scrubbed, earnest face. "My friend." It came out low and kind of threatening, though he didn't really mean it that way. "You want to be my friend."

She hitched her chin higher. "Yes. I do. I want to *remain* your friend, above all."

"What about that guy you're going to marry?"

"Collin. I'm not marrying Dane. And I will tell him that as soon as I get a chance to talk to him."

He wasn't sure he believed her. "Why keep the guy hanging if you're only going to say no?"

"I'm not keeping him hanging. He asked me to think it over. I said I would. I *have* thought it over and I'm not going to marry him."

Collin still wasn't really buying it, still had that feeling that this thing between them was only temporary, something born out of the chaos caused by the flood. Not the kind of thing that lasted.

Which should have been fine with him. He'd never been a guy who worried about whether or not what he had with a woman was going to last.

Because for him, it never did.

Three steps separated them. He took the first one. Couldn't help himself. Looking at her was like drowning in a whirlpool, the spinning current dizzying, sucking him down.

And then, when he was only two steps away, well, he had to get even closer. He took the second step.

And the scent of her came to him: sweet and tart and way too womanly.

That did it.

To hell with trying to do the right thing here. She wanted him and he wanted her and why shouldn't they both have what they wanted?

He snaked out a hand and caught her wrist.

She gasped. "Collin! What…?"

He pulled her to him, wrapped an arm around her. How could she be so perfect, so slim and soft and way too exciting, bringing the scent of lemons and Ivory soap to drive him wild? She stared up at him, her eyes so wide. Heat flared in his groin. "Right now, Willa, I'm not really thinking about being your friend."

That full mouth formed a round O. "Well." Breathless. Hopeful. "It's all…workable. Don't you think?"

"Thinking," he said roughly. "Who's thinking?"

And then she lifted a hand and cradled the side of his face. "Don't be afraid…."

Another wave of heat blasted through him. He put on a scowl. "I'm not afraid."

"Right." Soft. Indulgent. Way too knowing. Her eyes had that gleam in them now.

He still couldn't really believe she was here, in his house. In his arms. "You shouldn't have come up here."

"Yes. Yes, I should have."

"Your brother warned you about me, right?"

"Gage is willing to be open-minded."

"You mean he warned you and you argued with him."

"And now he's willing to be open-minded."

"I know how you are, Willa. So damn determined."

She smiled then, dimples flashing. "I am, yes. It's one of my most sterling qualities."

He bent his head closer, nuzzled her hair, breathed her in. Nothing. No one. Ever. Not like her. "Willa…" It came out harsh, low. Hungry.

She clung to him. She felt like heaven. She closed her eyes and pressed her lips to his throat. "Yes." She kissed the word into his skin, once. And then again. "Yes."

He put a finger under that stubborn chin of hers. With a sigh, she opened her eyes. He advised, "I should send you back down the mountain right now."

"Oh, but you won't." She clucked her tongue. Softly. "It's much too dangerous, remember?"

He pulled her even closer. "*This* is what's dangerous." There were a thousand reasons they should stop right now. He tried to remember at least a few of them, but it wasn't happening. "I'm not the right guy for you."

"That's for me to decide. All you have to figure out is whether *I'm* the right girl for *you*."

"I don't—"

"Shh." She put two fingers against his mouth. It took all his will not to close his teeth around them and suck them inside. "We don't have to decide anything now," she whispered. "We can just…be together, you and me. Just enjoy every minute we have, for now. Just kind of wing it and see where it takes us."

"It's not a good idea, Willa." He formed the words against the soft pads of her fingers.

"Your mouth says one thing, but the rest of you is sending another message altogether." She pressed herself against him, snugger. Tighter.

He caught her fingers, touched his lips to them. Somehow, he couldn't help it—couldn't help holding her, touching her. Wanting her. "You're getting pretty bold lately…."

She lifted her mouth higher, offering it to him. "Must be the company I'm keeping."

That did it. He dipped his head and settled his lips on hers.

She sighed in welcome.

He wrapped his arms tighter around her and kissed her slowly. With care and attention and longing and heat.

She responded by sliding her hands up his chest to his shoulders, by sifting those soft fingers up into his hair. By sighing her willingness against his parted lips.

And by then, he'd pretty much forgotten all the reasons they shouldn't be doing this.

If she wanted to be with him, he could only put up so much resistance. After all, *he* wanted to be with her.

He burned to be with her.

And now, tonight, again, at last, he *would* be with her.

He started undressing her, right there in the entryway.

She didn't object—on the contrary, she started undressing *him*. He got rid of her T-shirt and she returned the favor. He unhooked her bra. She undid his jeans.

And then he lifted her high and carried her down the hall to his bedroom. He set her on the bed and knelt to unlace her boots. He got one off, and the sock beneath it, and he was starting on the other one when she reached out and laid her palm on his hair.

He looked up.

She gazed down at him, her eyes and her mouth so soft. So tender. "Collin...."

He kind of lost it then. He got her other boot off, ripped away the sock. And then she was clasping his shoulder, pulling him up to her.

It all happened so fast. He got the condom from the drawer as she pulled down her jeans and panties and kicked them away.

Her hands were on him again, pushing his jeans down. He still had his boots on. Neither of them cared.

He rolled the condom on and then went down to her. He tried to take it slow, to make sure she was ready.

But she tugged at him. She was so insistent, making tender sounds of need and encouragement, wrapping her arms and her long legs around him and pressing herself up to him, inviting him.

What could he do, given an invitation like that?

Accept. With enthusiasm.

And he did. He kissed her deeply as she slid her arm down between their bodies. She closed her soft fingers around him and guided him home.

After that, he was lost. Lost in the best, sweetest, hottest way.

She was all around him, all woman and softness and heat.

He surrendered. She moved against him, calling him down.

He was lost in her. As his climax rolled through him, he couldn't help hoping he might never be found.

When he could move again, he took off the rest of his clothes and pulled the covers up over them.

They made love again, more slowly that time.

And then, for a while, they just lay there, arms around each other, watching the shadows lengthen out the window across from his bed. He started talking about his Thunder Canyon relatives, about the wedding of his long-lost cousin that had taken place over the Fourth of July.

She asked, "Why didn't you go to the wedding with the rest of your family?"

He stroked her hair. "I had work that needed doing. And anyway, weddings have never been my kind of good time. They're like family reunions—there was one of those going on down in Thunder Canyon, too, over the Fourth—both are just excuses for the old folks to ask me when I'm getting married and how come I'm such a troublemaker."

She laughed. "Well, when *are* you getting married? And why are you such a troublemaker?"

"I'm not getting married. And troublemaking's fun."

She wrapped her leg across him, ran a soft finger down his arm in a slow, teasing caress and whispered, "I think you've put a big dent in your troublemaker reputation lately."

"Naw."

"Yeah. Jerry Dobbs told me you talked old Mrs. Lathrop into putting her shotgun away and relocating to a FEMA trailer today."

He traced the wings of her eyebrows, one and then the other. "You know Mrs. Lathrop. She's so, so proud. She moved back into her house, even though it's not safe in there since the flood. We had to talk her into leaving."

"Jerry said *you* talked her into leaving—and that she had her shotgun on you while you did it."

"Jerry exaggerates. And is he the one who told you I'd gone on up the mountain?"

"Mmm-hmm."

"Jerry's also got a big mouth."

"Oh, now. You like Jerry. You and Jerry get along."

He pressed his nose against her throat. He loved the texture of her skin almost as much as the way she smelled. He also cupped her breast. Because he could. Because it felt so good. Because it fit his hand just right. "Stop trying to make a hero out of me."

She laughed again, husky and low. "Oh, I'm not trying anything. You're being a hero all by yourself."

* * *

Willa had decided to take the advice she'd given Collin that Tuesday evening.

She was going to take it day by day. Enjoy being with him.

And she wasn't expecting anything. She was letting this beautiful, exciting thing between them unfold in its own way.

She taught summer school both Wednesday and Thursday. In the afternoons, she met with insurance adjusters.

She and Gage, as it turned out, were two of the "lucky" ones. Their houses would have to be taken down to the studs and rebuilt—but at least they had flood insurance. Too many didn't.

In the evenings, Willa and Buster went up the mountain, where Collin was waiting. Those two nights were glorious, perfect. Just Willa and Collin all wrapped up tight in each other's arms.

Friday, Willa got a call from her insurance company. They would provide her a rental car until the replacement check came through. After summer school was done for the day, she gave Gage back his truck and Collin drove her to Kalispell, where she got the keys to a green Forester.

By then it was after six, so they stopped in at a little Italian place Collin liked. It was wonderful, to sit in a restaurant lit by actual electricity and be served crisp salads, fragrant garlic bread and piping-hot lasagna. She was feeling so festive she even had a glass of red wine while Collin enjoyed a cold beer.

"I could sit here forever," she confided when her plate was empty and the waitress had whisked it away. "It's funny how easy it is to take simple things like restaurants and electricity for granted. I keep telling myself that I'll never consider basic services as a given again."

He was looking at her so…intimately. A look that curled her toes and made her think of the night to come. "How 'bout dessert?"

They ordered gelato with yummy waffle biscuits. Willa took her time savoring the cool, creamy treat.

It was almost nine when they started back to Rust Creek Falls. The plan was to skip stopping in town and caravan up the mountain, but when Willa saw that the Sawmill Street Bridge lights were on, she honked at Collin, who was in the lead.

He pulled over and she swung in behind him, jumping out to run to his side window. He rolled it down. "Looks like the power's back on."

She felt like a little kid at Christmas. "I can't believe it. I sat in that restaurant fantasizing about all the lights coming on. And what do you know?"

"Let's go into town. See what's going on." His eyes had a gleam to them, one she completely understood. He had that troublemaker image he sometimes hid behind, but she wasn't fooled, not anymore, not since the flood. He loved Rust Creek Falls as much as she did. Every step toward recovery from the disaster that had wiped out half the town mattered. To both of them.

She glanced across the bridge. It wasn't fully dark yet, but the streetlights were on. "Yes!" She ran back to her rental car and followed him across the bridge.

Main was blocked off between Sawmill and Cedar. They parked in the Masonic Hall parking lot. Willa left the windows down partway for Buster and they went to investigate.

It was a street dance.

They ran into Thelma on the corner. She told them that not only was the power back on, the landline phones were operational again, too. People had decided to celebrate by throwing a party.

At least half the town was there. Several local musicians had grabbed their instruments and formed an impromptu band. They were set up on the sidewalk midway between the two roadblocks. Folks stood around, clapping and laughing. And the street was full of dancers, everyone spinning and whirling under the streetlights. Willa spotted Paige dancing with her dad and Shelby and little Caitlin dancing together. Gage stood over by Nathan Crawford across the street from the musicians. He spotted Willa and gave her a wave.

Collin grabbed her hand. "Come on." He led her out into the crowd and they danced a couple of fast ones. And then came a slow one. He pulled her against him. She went into his arms and closed her eyes and swayed with him beneath the streetlights, thinking how the moment was about the most perfect that ever could be: dancing with Collin in the middle of Main Street on the night the lights came back on.

The next day, Saturday, Collin's parents and brothers returned at last from Thunder Canyon. They all rolled in to the Triple T in the early afternoon.

Collin was in his workshop up on the mountain when his mother called.

Ellie had a lot to tell him. She and his dad and his brothers and Dallas's three kids hadn't come home alone. They'd brought friends from Thunder Canyon, people who wanted to help and who had the kinds of skills that would be needed to begin to rebuild the south side of town. There were several members of the Pritchett family, who owned a carpentry business. And there were also Matt Cates and his dad, Frank, of Cates Construction, among others. Lots of others.

"You come on down to the ranch for dinner tonight," his mom commanded.

He thought of Willa. He'd been indulging himself in a big way with her, spending every spare moment at her side. She'd gone down the mountain to help with a food drive at the church that morning, but she would be back around five. He'd been looking forward to that—to a quiet dinner, just the two of them.

To another whole night with her in his bed.

On the floor by his feet, Buster raised his head from his paws and twitched an ear at him. Collin bent and gave the dog a pat. It had just seemed a natural thing that Buster would stay on the mountain with him while Willa went to help out down in town.

They were getting real…settled in together, him and Willa. He probably needed to dial it back a notch with her.

But somehow, every time he thought about that, about putting a little space between the two of them, he got this ache in the center of his chest. It was the kind of ache a man gets when he's making himself do something he doesn't want to do.

Because he didn't want to dial it back with Willa. He only thought it would be better for her if he did.

But not for him. Uh-uh. He liked it with her.

He liked everything about being with her.

He liked it too much.

"Collin?" His mother's voice sent his dark thoughts scattering. "You're too quiet. What's going on?"

"Not a thing. I'm right here."

"You come home for dinner."

"Tomorrow, okay? Tonight, I have plans."

"I said, tonight. Your family's home and we want to see you. Bring that sweet Willa Christensen. I'm so glad you're seeing her. I always did like that girl."

Swear words scrolled through his mind. His mom already knew about Willa.

Was he surprised?

Not particularly. His mom knew everyone and he had no illusions that he was the only one in town she'd been talking to while she was away.

"Who told you about me and Willa?" He knew he shouldn't ask. But he was kind of curious.

"Are you kidding me? Who didn't? She's a prize, that girl. I never dared to hope. My own Last Straw and the dear little Christensen girl." *The Last Straw.* It was his mom's pet name for him. She always claimed it was only because he was the last of her children. He knew better and so did everyone else. She called him the Last Straw because he'd given her so much grief with his bad behavior and untamed ways. "I'm very pleased," she added. "Very. Don't you blow it with her, now. Hear me?"

"S'cuse me, Mom. But what's going on between Willa and me has got nothing to do with you."

Ellie sighed. Deeply. "Dear Lord in heaven, you are a trial to me. I only asked you to come to dinner tonight and bring Willa. Please. Six o'clock. Don't be late."

"Mom, I..." He let the objection die unfinished. He was talking to dead air anyway.

Willa's cell rang as she carried a case of baked beans into the church's multiuse room.

She passed the beans to Mindy Krebs and took the phone from her pocket. The display read "Collin." Her heart did a happy dance and she was grinning like a lovestruck fool as she answered. "What?"

"My mom, my brothers and about half of Thunder Canyon just arrived in town. Mom knows about you and me. And she wants us both to come to the ranch for dinner."

Willa couldn't help laughing. "Collin. You should hear yourself. You sound like a covert operative passing state secrets."

"She drives me nuts."

Willa had a hard time believing that. "But your mom's so thoughtful and generous and smart and perceptive. I just love her."

He made a low, growling sound. "So does everyone else in town. And she's a good mom, don't get me wrong. She's just way too damn pushy sometimes, that's all. At least when she's dealing with me."

"Because you never did do what she told you to do."

"That's right. It's kind of a point of pride with me never to do what my mother says."

"You know that's childish, right?"

A silence on his end, then, in a surly tone, "Will you come to dinner at the Triple T with me tonight?"

She smiled widely. "Of course. Dinner at the Triple T would be lovely."

Ellie and Bob Traub knew how to throw a barbecue.

Their house was packed with people. Neighbors, friends, ranch hands, Thunder Canyon visitors and a whole lot of family spilled out onto the wide front porch and into the yard, where Bob had two smokers going along with a grill.

Gage was there. Willa spotted him on the front porch when she and Collin arrived. She worked her way through the groups of people to give him a hug.

He offered his hand to Collin. The two men shook.

And Gage said, "Been hearing good things about you lately."

Willa felt a wash of love and appreciation for her brother. He'd done what he'd promised, kept an open mind about Collin and been willing to listen when people told him all Collin had done for their town since the flood.

Collin grunted. "But you know not to believe everything you hear, right?"

Gage chuckled. "Word is you have good ideas, you don't lose your head and you're willing to pitch in." He grew serious. "So I'm asking you for what Rust Creek Falls needs from you. I'm asking for your help with the big job ahead of us."

Willa hid her smile at Collin's wary expression. "Sure," he said at last. "What can I do?"

"Come to the town hall Monday morning at ten? We're putting a group together. We'll start figuring out ways to get funding and volunteers to rebuild south-side homes for folks who had no flood insurance. Also, there's the clinic. We want to get it operational again. And most important, the elementary school. The high school isn't big enough to hold the younger kids, too. We have to do something so the K through eighth graders have a place to go in the fall."

Willa was nodding. "Good. September is just around the corner."

Gage asked, "So what do you say, Collin?"

He didn't hesitate. "I'll be there."

"Willa, dear." Ellie Traub descended on them, all smiles. "I'm so glad to see you!" She grabbed Willa in a bear hug.

Willa laughed in surprise at being clutched so close by Collin's mom. "Good to see you, too, Ellie."

Ellie took her by the shoulders. "I heard you were flooded out—and Gage, too." She sent Willa's brother a sympathetic frown. "It's horrible. Awful...."

"We'll survive," Willa said. "And we'll rebuild."

"Lavinia and Wayne...?" Ellie asked about Willa and Gage's parents.

"They're fine," Gage assured her. "I talked to them just

an hour or so ago. They should be back at the ranch some-time tomorrow."

Collin said, "They were in Livingston, at the big rodeo, when the storm hit."

"So was I," Gage told Ellie, regret in his voice. "Mom wouldn't leave me alone until I agreed to go with them. She had some idea I was working too hard and needed to take a break and forget everything for the holiday."

"She knows what you need better than you do, huh?" Collin sent his mother a meaningful glance.

"Yes, she does," Gage confirmed, sounding weary. "Just ask her."

Ellie grabbed Collin. "We only do it because we love you. Now, give me a hug," she demanded fondly.

"Aw, Mom..." Collin embraced her with obvious af-fection.

Then Ellie hooked one arm with Collin's and the other with Willa's. "Gage, there's beer in the cooler out on the lawn."

"Thanks, Ellie."

Eyes shining, Ellie commanded, "You two come with me. I want everyone to know how pleased and happy I am that you're both here—together."

"It was embarrassing," Collin grumbled much later that night, when they were alone in his bed. "Dragging us all over the yard, announcing over and over again that you were with *me*."

Willa lay with her head on his broad chest. She could hear his heartbeat, so strong and steady. There was no place in the world she would rather be than right there, held close in Collin's strong arms. "She loves you. She's proud of you."

He made one of those low, growly sounds. "She can't

believe that someone as amazing as you would be hanging around with me."

"That's not so."

"Yeah, it is." He pressed his lips to her hair.

"No."

"Yeah—and what do you want to bet that Nathan Crawford will be at that meeting your brother talked me into going to Monday morning?"

She tipped her head back and kissed his beard-scratchy chin. "Probably. But you can handle him."

He looked down into her eyes and said gruffly, "You realize my mom is right, don't you? You're much too fine a woman to be wasting your time with me."

"I am not wasting my time. And I really get annoyed with you when you put yourself down."

"It's only the truth."

"No, it isn't." She tried to look stern. "Will you stop it? Please?"

He smoothed her hair and answered grudgingly, "Yes, ma'am."

She gave him a slow smile. "Actually, I'm a lot like your mother."

He widened his eyes in a comical way and faked a gasp of shock. "Don't say that. Anything but that."

"Oh, but I *am* like Ellie. I'm pushy. And determined. And very sure of what's good for the people I love…."

Love. She'd said the word so casually.

But then, as soon as it was out, she didn't feel casual at all.

Love. Once the word had escaped her lips, it seemed to hang by a thread inside her mind, slowly swinging. Tempting her to grab it and run with it.

Love.

The big word, the one that mattered. The word that changed everything.

She dared for the first time to admit to herself what was happening to her, how her life had become something new and fresh and beautiful. The world had a glow to it now.

Because of him.

I love you, Collin Traub.

Buoyant light seemed to fill her. All at once, she was weightless, defying gravity through pure joy.

I love you, Collin Traub.

She opened her mouth to say it—and then she shut it without making a sound.

Saying it out loud would be dangerous. Risky.

He was frowning down at her. "Hey."

She kissed his chin again. "Umm?"

"You okay?" Cautious. A little worried. "You seemed a thousand miles away just now."

"I'm right here." She took his arm, wrapped it snugly around her and settled herself more comfortably against his warm, broad chest. "And I'm fine. Better than fine."

He chuckled then. "You certainly are—and never admit you're like my mother, unless you're purposely trying to creep me out."

She laughed and promised, "Never again," as her heart cried, *I love you, Collin. I love you, I do.* The simple phrases seemed to tickle the back of her throat, working themselves closer to being said.

But she didn't say them.

Not yet. It had only been nine days since the flood, and only five since that first night she'd spent in his arms.

Yes, to her, what they had together now wasn't all that surprising. It felt like a simple progression, a natural unfolding of something that had been there all along. She'd known him all her life, wanted him for so long, been waiting, even when she thought that she hated him, for a chance with him.

She was more than ready to talk about that. About their lives, about their future.

About love.

But she was no fool. She knew that *he* wasn't ready.

So, then, she could wait.

She had a feeling it wouldn't be long.

The time wasn't right yet.

But it would be.

Soon....

Chapter Thirteen

Collin had an ever-growing backlog of work he needed to get going on down in his shop. The next morning, as they were finishing breakfast, he told Willa he would have to spend the whole day at it.

She pushed her empty plate away and rose slowly from her chair.

He stared at her, feeling suddenly wary. "I'm not sure I trust that look in your eye."

She gave him one of those sweet, innocent school-teacher smiles of hers as she came around to his side of the table. He gazed up at her, narrow eyed. He knew she was up to something. She sat on his lap.

He growled her name in warning.

She only brushed his hair back from his forehead with her soft, cool fingers and then kissed his cheek. "Come to church with me."

"Willa..."

"Please. It'll only take a couple of hours, total, including the drive up and down the mountain. After church, I promise I'll leave you alone to work in peace for the rest of the day."

The problem with her sitting on him was that the feel of her only made him want to touch her. To kiss her. And then to kiss her some more.

He caught her earlobe between his teeth and worried it lightly, because he couldn't quite stop himself. She trembled and let out one of those reluctant little moans that always drove him crazy.

"Shame on you, Willa Christensen," he scolded. "Talking about church while you're sitting on my lap. You know very well what happens when you sit on my lap...."

She wiggled her bottom against him and then he was the one trying not to moan. "Church," she whispered way too damn seductively. "It'll be over before you know it and then you can come right back up here and work all day and half the night if you want to...."

"Wiggle like that again and I won't be getting any work done. We won't be going to church, either. We won't be going anywhere but back down the hall to bed."

"Church. You take your truck and I'll take the Forester. That way, as soon as the service is over, you can head right back up the mountain." She kissed him. And then she slid to the floor and stood above him.

He grabbed her hand. "Get back down here...."

She bent close and kissed him again. "I'll be ready in twenty minutes."

They went to church.

It was kind of nice, really, Collin thought. His family was there, his mom all smiles at the sight of him and Willa together. Pastor Alderson gave a sermon about finding joy in simple things.

Collin could relate to that, especially lately. Just being around Willa all the time, that was a pretty damn joyful thing for him.

Yeah, it was partly the sex, which was amazing…and which he probably shouldn't be thinking about in church.

But the thing was, the sex wasn't everything.

It wasn't even the most important thing.

Willa herself. *She* was the important thing. The way she would laugh, kind of husky and happy both at once. The way she cuddled up close to him, her ear against his chest like she only wanted to listen to the sound of his heart beating. The way she listened so close when he talked, but then had no problem speaking up if she didn't like something he'd said.

The way she could be so kind and gentle—and then turn right around and be tough as nails when something mattered to her. The way she could pull on a pair of work gloves and keep up with him clearing storm debris all the way up the mountain. The way she wasn't ashamed to be with him in front of everyone. Even if she *was* a schoolteacher with a certain reputation she really ought to be looking out for.

He'd thought he was happy before Willa.

But the past few days, he'd started thinking that before Willa, he hadn't even known what happiness was.

He was living in a dream, and he knew it. This thing with her, well, it couldn't last. He was who he was and he'd always seen himself in an honest light. He'd grown up wild and he hadn't been to college. He could change some, but not completely.

Not enough to be with a woman like Willa in a forever kind of way.

The pastor told them all to rise. They sang an old hymn that Collin had known since childhood.

Out of the corner of his eye, in the pew across the center aisle, he caught sight of Nathan Crawford, standing so tall and proud, singing good and loud. Nathan saw him looking and shot back a narrow-eyed glare. Nathan would probably be ticked off that Gage had asked him to the meeting about flood relief tomorrow.

Well, too bad. Collin was going. He had a few ideas for raising money and getting folks together to rebuild what they'd lost. And he wanted to help in any way he could.

There were other Crawfords in church that day. He got a few scowls from more than one of them. They'd always looked down on him. Not only was he a Traub, he was the no-good, skirt-chasing, *troublemaking* Traub.

Since he and Willa started in together, he'd worried that the Crawfords might come after her for being with him, might smear her good name. So far, that hadn't happened. But it still nagged at him. In a little town like Rust Creek Falls, people had certain standards. They didn't like to think of their schoolteachers living in sin. Especially not with the local bad boy.

Willa nudged him with her elbow. He sent her a glance. She sang even louder, brown eyes full of teasing laughter.

He forgot his worries and let himself enjoy just being with her. It couldn't last forever, but as long as it did, he intended to enjoy himself.

After church, Willa longed to ask Collin to take her to the doughnut shop for a Sunday snack. The shop had reopened the day before and it was a Sunday tradition in town. Folks went to church and then to the Wings to Go or Daisy's Donuts over on North Broomtail Road.

But he did need to work and she'd already made her

deal with him. So she kept her word and sent him back up the mountain.

When he got in his pickup, Buster whined to go with him. Collin shot her a questioning look.

"Go ahead," she said indulgently. "Take him." So Collin got out and let the dog in—ever since the day Buster fell from the pickup bed on the way up the mountain, they'd been letting him ride in front. "I'll be back by five or six," she promised. Thelma was expecting her to help sort donated clothing for flooded-out families.

Collin kissed her, a warm brush of his lips against her cheek—and then he climbed back up behind the wheel and headed for Sawmill Street.

Willa's mother called her from the ranch at a little past two. "We're home," she announced, then, "Where are you? We've missed you."

"I'm at Thelma McGee's, helping out."

"Honey, we would love to see you. Can you come on over?"

"I'll check with Thelma…"

The older woman made a shooing gesture. "Go on, now. Go see your mother. Give her my best."

When Willa arrived, her dad was out in the northeast pasture somewhere, repairing a fence.

Her mom had the coffee ready and a box of bakery sweet rolls she'd picked up in Kalispell. After hugs and greetings, they sat at the table together, each with a steaming mug and a treat from the bakery box.

Willa knew her mother. She could tell by the way her mom sipped her coffee thoughtfully and then said nothing for a moment, her head tipped to the side, that she was working up to broaching an uncomfortable subject.

"Ellie Traub came by," Lavinia said at last.

Willa got the message then. Ellie must have mentioned her and Collin. Willa picked up her fork and ate a bite of cheese Danish. "I'm sure she's happy to have you home safe and sound."

Lavinia took a big sip of coffee and set the mug down a little too firmly. "Ellie's *happy* because she's always liked you so much. She's always hoped that you might end up with one of her boys."

"I like Ellie, too, Mom. But then, you know that."

Her mom gave up on subtlety. She leaned across the table. "Oh, honey. *Collin?*"

Willa drew in a slow, calming breath and reminded herself that she'd gotten through to Gage about Collin and she could get through to her mom, too. "I care for Collin. I care for him a lot. Since the flood, I've gotten to know him—really know him. He's strong and good and brave. And he doesn't give himself enough credit, but I'm working on getting him to see that he's a much better man than he's willing to admit. And I've been staying with him, up at his house, since last Monday night."

Her mother winced and sipped more coffee. "Staying."

"Yes."

"But is that wise?"

"I'm proud to be with him, Mom. He's a wonderful man. He's done a lot to help people, to keep people's spirits up, since the flood. Ask around town. Please. Ask Gage. *He'll* tell you."

Her mother frowned. "Gage hasn't said a word to me about you and Collin Traub."

"I'm sure Gage was waiting for me to talk to you first. I appreciate his staying out of it."

"But you never even seemed to *like* Collin. And what about Dane Everhart?"

"I *always* liked Collin. A lot more than I ever wanted to admit."

"But—"

"And as for Dane, it was never going to work with him and me." Lord, she was tired of explaining about Dane. It was her own fault, though, and she had to remember that. She should have had the courage to say no when she meant no. "Dane's a great guy. He's just not the guy for me."

"But Collin is?"

Willa sat back in her chair and folded her arms across her chest. "I love you, Mom. A lot. I will always be there if you need me. But I'm twenty-five years old and perfectly capable of managing my own life. I can't say what the future will bring, but I am with Collin now and I am proud to be with him."

Her mother tipped her head to the side again. Willa braced herself for another onslaught. But her mom surprised her and slowly smiled. "I always did kind of wonder about you and Collin. I had a feeling there might be a spark or two between you…"

A burst of relieved laughter escaped Willa. Her mom was going to be all right with Collin, after all. She teased, "No way."

Lavinia nodded, looking smug. "Yes." And then she scolded, "But you really must clear things up with Dane as soon as possible."

"You're right. And I plan to. I'll be going to see him as soon as he gets back from Australia."

Her mom got up, brought the coffeepot over and refilled their mugs. "Collin has done well with the saddle-making business. He made your dad's CT Saddle, did you know?"

"I didn't know. Until Collin told me."

"And I hear that he's turned that old cabin of Casper's into something quite beautiful."

"Yes, he has. You and Daddy will have to come up for dinner. Maybe next weekend."

"We would enjoy that, honey. Very much."

* * *

Willa got back to Collin's at five. The main floor was deserted.

She called down the stairs. "I'm here!"

Buster came bounding up. As she scratched his ears in greeting, Collin called from below, "Half an hour?"

"Take your time!"

She fed Buster. There was leftover meat loaf and several servings of browned potatoes in the fridge. She put them in the oven to reheat and cut up a salad. Then she set the table.

By then, fifteen minutes had passed. The oven was on a timer, so she felt safe grabbing a quick shower.

She was rinsing off when the shower door opened and Collin stepped in.

"S'cuse me," he said with that slow smile that seemed to fire all her circuits at once. "Just need to freshen up a little...."

She laughed as he grabbed her close. "Don't get my hair wet!"

Of course, he took that as a challenge, turning her beneath the spray so the water poured down directly over her head. "Oops."

"Collin!" she sputtered, trying to wiggle free.

But she didn't try too hard.

And then he kissed her again. She realized it didn't matter that her hair was soaking wet.

All that mattered was that his mouth was pressed to hers and his arms were nice and tight around her.

The meat loaf was a little dry when they finally sat down to eat.

"Delicious," he said, and poured on the ketchup.

She asked him how the work was going. He said he'd

made progress, but there was still a lot to catch up on. Tomorrow he had that morning meeting in the town hall, but after that, he would come right back up the mountain and work for the rest of the day.

"I've been thinking I'm going to need to hire someone to work with me," he said. "Not right now. But it's coming. I know a couple talented saddle makers in Kalispell. I'm going to contact them, see if they have any interest in joining forces with CT Saddles. They could work in their own shops, but put in some of their time on projects I bring them."

"Growing the business. Excellent. And you can't do everything yourself—especially when you also want to help out with the rebuilding effort."

"There should be more hours in a day."

"No argument there." She ate a bite of potato. "Thelma told me today that she thinks you should run for mayor. She thinks you're the one to carry on, to build on what Hunter started."

He sent her a look from under his thick eyelashes. "Don't."

"Don't what?" She widened her eyes at him.

"Don't start in about me running for mayor. It's not going to happen."

She cut off a bite of meat loaf neatly. "I think it is."

"You don't know what you're talking about."

She set down her fork and put up a hand. "All right. Subject closed." She pressed her lips together to keep from smiling. "For now."

He made a low, grumbling sound, but let it go at that.

She ate the bite of meat loaf. And then she said, "My parents got back today. I went out to the ranch and had a nice visit with my mom."

He studied her for a moment, his grumpy expression

softening. "Sometimes I don't believe you're actually here, in my place, heating up the meat loaf, naked in my shower, harassing me over dinner...."

Tenderness filled her. "I like it, being here with you. I like it a lot." For a moment or two, they simply gazed at each other. They were both smiling by then. She remembered what she'd been about to tell him. "*Your* mother got to *my* mom before I did."

He forked up more meat loaf. "That doesn't sound good."

"Well, it was kind of scary when Mom started in on me, I'll admit."

"Started in on you about being with me?"

"She was surprised, that's all."

"Your mother knows you're too good for me," he said in that voice that seemed to be joking—but really wasn't.

She set down her fork. "No. She doesn't think that. She doesn't think that at all."

"Yeah, right."

"And neither do I, which you really ought to know by now."

He grabbed the big glass of milk he'd poured himself and guzzled about half of it. "This is a dumb thing to argue about."

"I agree. As soon as you admit what a great guy you are, we can *stop* arguing about this."

He actually rolled his eyes. "Okay, okay. I'm great. I'm terrific."

She raised her own glass of milk in a toast. "Yes, you are." She drank. When she set the glass down, she asked, "Would you mind if we had my parents up here for dinner? Maybe Friday or Saturday night? I was thinking we could have your folks, too. And maybe Gage and any of your brothers who wanted to come."

He was silent. A definite hesitation. "I have a lot of work I need to be doing, Willa."

"I understand. But I would do the dinner. You only have to come upstairs when everyone gets here."

"The road is still iffy."

"I go up and down it every day. As long as you know the spots to watch for, it's fine. I'll just tell them all where to be extra careful." She waited. He said nothing. Finally, she said, "If you don't want to have the family here, I think you ought to just say so."

He looked away. "It's not that."

"Then what is it?"

He pushed his plate away. "Come on, Willa. People get...expectations. Especially in this town. You saw how my mom was last night, dragging us all over the yard, making sure everyone got that you and me are together."

She had a sad, sinking feeling—at the same time as she told herself not to be in such a hurry about everything. She needed to let him adjust to what they shared in his own way, in his own time. She reminded herself that it had only been six days since they became more than friends, and that only a few minutes ago, he'd told her how happy he was just to be with her.

"So." She made an effort to keep her voice calm and reasonable. "You don't want to have the family up here for dinner this weekend. Am I right?"

He gave it to her straight, at least. "That's right."

Something shifted within her. Something died just a little. For the first time since they became lovers, she found herself thinking that it was simply not going to work out with them.

And then she told herself to stop. Just stop.

Maybe it was pushing it a little, to have the whole family over for dinner so soon. He did have a lot of work to do. And he was also unaccustomed to being half of a couple.

In fact, from things he'd said in the past, she had a sense that he'd never planned to be part of a couple. She needed to let him deal, give him the time and the space to start to see himself in a new light.

"You're mad," he said softly. Sadly.

She swallowed and shook her head. "No. It's okay. Really. It's fine."

The rest of the evening was lovely, Willa thought.

Collin was tender and attentive. He was passionate in bed. They talked for over an hour before they fell asleep. There was laughter. He held her close.

He honestly did seem happy just to be with her. More than happy.

Still, Willa couldn't shake the feeling that he'd drawn a line between them when he told her he didn't want the family over. An invisible but uncrossable line, a line that cut them off from a future together.

For him, they were lovers. The best of friends.

But no more than that.

Never more than that.

On Monday, Willa told her mother that she would have to put the family dinner on hold for a bit. Her mom didn't push. She said she understood. Everyone was scrambling since the flood, trying to catch up with their lives, to get things back to normal. Of course, Collin needed to focus on his work. They would all get together for an evening soon enough.

Willa smiled and nodded. But she was thinking, *I love him. I love him so much.*

And she was starting to get the feeling that loving him

wasn't enough, that he would never want to hear her say what was in her heart for him.

That she would never wear his ring.

Collin knew that he'd hurt Willa when he'd dug in his heels about having the family over.

He was trying not to think about that, about how he'd hurt her. He was trying to keep her with him, even though he knew that in the end, what she wanted and what he wanted were two different things.

Tuesday afternoon he sat through a second endless meeting with Gage, Nathan, Thelma and the rest of the group of community leaders they'd put together to come up with ways to speed flood recovery. When he finally left the town hall, he spotted Dallas, his oldest brother, coming toward him on the sidewalk, looking bleak.

But then, who wouldn't be bleak in Dallas's position? His wife, Laurel, had left him and their children last year. He was a single dad raising three boys on his own.

The brothers shook hands and clapped each other on the back. Dallas said he'd driven into town to pick the boys up from summer school.

"You got a little time to kill?" Collin asked him. "We could grab a beer at the Ace...." It was one of those invitations made only for form's sake. Collin had work waiting on the mountain and didn't really expect Dallas to say yes.

But his glum-faced brother surprised him. "Sure. I got about a half an hour until they turn the boys loose. Let's go."

They sat at the bar and ordered a couple of longnecks.

Collin asked how things were going and his brother said, "I'm proud of my boys and I'm getting by—and what's going on with you and Willa Christensen?"

Great. Getting grilled about Willa by his gloomy big

brother. That hadn't really been in the plan. Collin sipped his beer and tried to decide how to answer.

Dallas kept after him. "You've made Mom happy for once. I'll say that. But come on. Everyone knows Willa's living up at your place. Yeah, you're the hero of the day and all. You definitely manned up when the flood hit. But do you really think moving Willa in with you was such a great idea?"

By then, Collin just wanted to cut through the crap. "Dallas. What are you getting at?"

"Willa's a great person. And you're not so bad yourself. But she's the marrying kind and we both know it. The big question is, are you?"

Collin wanted to tell his brother to mind his own business. Unfortunately, Dallas had a point. "I'm nuts over her," he said low, so only his brother would hear him. "I've got it bad."

"I kind of noticed that. But let me point out the obvious. You don't move a nice girl like Willa into your place unless you're putting a ring on her finger real soon. Especially not when she's the kindergarten teacher. That's not a thing a man should do—well, maybe in New York City. But not in Rust Creek Falls."

Collin thought about what his brother had said. He thought about it a lot—constantly, as a matter of fact.

He felt bad. Rotten. Low.

He never should have let Willa move in with him. It wasn't good for her. He should have thought of her first, instead of how much he wanted to be with her, instead of indulging himself just because he couldn't shake the hold of needing her so bad.

Wednesday night, she asked him if something was bothering him.

He didn't know how to answer. If he told her that he was feeling like a low-down loser for living with her when he never intended to marry her, well, where would that lead?

To her moving out.

He knew her. There was no way she was going to hang around if he told her to her face that it was going nowhere between them.

And he couldn't let her move out. Everyone would say that he'd dumped her. She would be shamed in front of the whole town. He couldn't ever let that happen to her.

Plus, he didn't *want* her to move out. He just wanted to be with her. And not to have to think about what was going to happen next.

But then, he *did* think. He thought way too much. His mind was like a hamster on a wheel. A hamster on speed, thoughts going nowhere fast, endlessly chasing themselves in a circle.

He thought about that other guy, that guy from Colorado, the one who'd asked her to marry him. The other guy was a stand-up guy, she'd said.

She'd also said she was telling him no.

But *should* she be telling him no?

It made Collin feel sick in the pit of his stomach to think of her with that other guy. But what if the other guy was the *better* guy?

Collin wanted her. A lot. But he also wanted the best for her. And if the best for her was that other guy, well, Collin ought to step aside and give her some space to make the right decision.

He could do that much for her, at least.

But he did nothing.

Every day, every hour, his thoughts got more and more tangled up and confused. He didn't know how to talk to her about all of it. So he didn't talk to her.

He lied and acted oblivious and said there was nothing wrong—and that only made him more disgusted with himself. He started thinking how he really had a problem with seeing ahead to the consequences of his own actions. He had a part missing, emotionwise. He'd always been that way, chasing the thrill, hungry for excitement. Not thinking who would be hurt or damaged by his doing exactly what he wanted to do when he wanted to do it.

All day Thursday and half of Friday, as he worked in his shop to catch up on his orders, he tried to figure out what he was going to do to make things right with Willa. By three in the afternoon on Friday, he finally came to an actual decision. He realized there was only one choice for him now, only one thing to do.

He took a quick shower, put Buster in the pickup and headed for Kalispell.

It was no good lately with Collin, and Willa knew it.

Things had only gotten worse with every day that passed since Sunday, the day he'd told her he didn't want the family over. Every day since then, he'd become more distant, more uncommunicative. And she wasn't sleeping well at night now. She kept waking up and staring at the ceiling and trying to lie very still so that Collin wouldn't notice she wasn't asleep.

Wednesday, she'd asked him about it, about what might be on his mind. He'd looked right in her face and told her there was nothing.

She'd wanted to believe him. But she didn't believe him.

There was a falseness now between them. And it was growing. She needed to break through it.

But how?

It was starting to seem to her that there was only one

way to get through to him. She needed to put herself out there, tell him the hardest thing.

She'd wanted to wait a while, to simply be with him and let the closeness between them grow. But the only way they were growing since Sunday was further apart.

Yes, opening her heart to him was a big risk. She could end up without him. From the way he'd been behaving lately, she probably *would* end up without him as soon as she uttered those three oh-so-dangerous words.

But who was she kidding? In the deep ways, the ways that mattered, she was already without him.

So why keep lying to herself? She might as well go for it, might as well pull out the stops, put her heart on the line and accept the consequences. At least then she would know she'd given it her best shot.

On the way up the mountain Friday afternoon, she decided she would tell him as soon as he came upstairs from his workshop.

But when she got there, the house was empty. He'd left a note on the table: *Quick trip to Kalispell. Took Buster. Back by six.*

All right, she thought. She would tell him when he got back.

She could start dinner....

But no. Dinner could wait. She was much too on edge to think about food right then. She had lesson planning she could do, so she went to the spare room, where she'd set up a desk and computer, and she got to work firming up her choices for activities for the following week, making lists of materials she hadn't pulled together yet.

An hour dragged by. She finished at the computer and went back out to the kitchen to face the prospect of cooking something.

Anything to keep busy until he returned.

She was standing at the refrigerator with the door wide-open, staring blankly inside, when she heard the crunch of tries on gravel outside.

Her heart gave a sick lurch inside her chest and then started beating so fast she felt dizzy. She shut the refrigerator door and turned toward the hall and the short entry area.

The door opened. She heard his boots on the wide planks of the hardwood floor, heard the door close, knew he would be pausing at the coatrack to hang up his hat.

Buster came bounding in ahead of him. She knelt and pressed her face to the warm, sweet scruff of his neck. He wiggled and made happy whining sounds—and then left her to lap water from his bowl.

Slowly, her knees feeling absurdly shaky, she rose.

And there he was. "Willa." He wore clean jeans and a blue chambray shirt rolled to the elbows and her heart just ached at the sight of him. "Come here…." He held out his hands.

She hesitated. She couldn't…read him, had no idea what was going on with him. He seemed to be looking at her so seriously, with such determined intention. "I…" Words simply failed her.

And then he was right there, so close. In front of her. He smelled of mountain air, of pine trees. He took her hand. "Come on…" And he pulled her with him, around the jut of the counter, into the main living area, over to a fat brown chair by the window. "Sit down."

She did what he told her to do.

And then he was kneeling at her feet, looking up at her, his jaw set, his full mouth a determined line. He had something in his hand.

And then he was sliding it on her finger.

A ring. A beautiful diamond solitaire on a platinum

band. Exactly the kind of ring she would have chosen for herself. She stared at it, gaping. "Collin, what...?"

And then he said, "Marry me, Willa. Be my wife."

It was just what she'd hoped to hear him say someday. And for a moment, she knew the purest, most wonderful spiking of absolute joy.

It was all going to work out, after all. She would have her life with him. They would be married, have children. Be happy forever, just as she'd almost stopped dreaming they might be....

She opened her mouth to tell him how glad she was, to say how much she loved him and how scared she had been that it was all unraveling, all going wrong.

But then, before a single sound got out, she saw that it wasn't right, after all. She realized what he *hadn't* said. It was the part about how he loved her. He'd left that out.

And instead of saying *Yes,* or *Oh, Collin, I do love you,* what came out of her mouth was, "Why?"

He blinked.

He actually blinked.

And that was when she knew that it wasn't going to work.

To his credit, he managed to pull it together. Sort of. "It's the right thing. And I'm nuts for you. That's not going away anytime soon. It's the right thing and..."

She stopped him by reaching out and pressing a finger to his lips. "The right thing, why?"

He swallowed. "Well, we *are* living together. And I want to keep on living with you and I..." He paused, tried again. "Okay. I love you, all right? I love you and I want to marry you and all you have to do is say yes."

She laughed. It wasn't a happy sound. The laugh caught in her throat and ended on something very much like a sob. "Oh, Collin. You're not telling me the truth. I know it. *You* know it. Can't you just say it? Just tell me what's going on with you, whatever it is."

He gazed up at her. He looked absolutely miserable. "You're not going to say yes to me, are you?"

She took off the beautiful ring. "I can't say yes to you. Not like this. I just can't." She reached for his hand. Reluctantly, he gave it to her. She put the ring in his palm and folded his warm, strong fingers over it. "You don't really want to get married, do you?"

He rose then. He gazed down at her, dark eyes so deep, full of turmoil and frustration.

She stared up at him and asked him again, "Do you?"

His mouth curved downward; his big body stiffened. And then he turned from her to the wide windows that overlooked their town. He stared out, showing her his broad, proud back. "What I want is you. What I want is for you to be happy, for you to have what *you* want. I don't want folks in town saying crappy things about you. I want you to have the best of everything. I don't really think I'm it, but you've told me over and over you won't marry that other guy, so it kind of seems to me that you'd better marry me."

"You *want* me to marry Dane?"

"No." On that, he didn't hesitate. "But you deserve the best. Is he the best? The way you talked about him the night of the flood, I guess so."

"I was stupid and small and petty the night of the flood. I wanted to get to you, to hurt you. I'm sorry I did that. It was wrong. Now, how many times do I have to tell you, Dane is not the guy for me?"

He didn't say anything. He only shook his head.

She tried again. "Who said crappy things about me?"

He still wouldn't look at her. "No one. I don't know. I just... I don't want them to, okay? And as long as you're living up here with me without my ring on your finger, well, they could, all right? In a small town like ours, they might. Especially the damn Crawfords. They'd do it just because I'm a Traub—the troublemaking, skirt-chasing Traub—and you're with me."

She got up then. And she went to him. When she stood at his shoulder, she said, "But they haven't."

He faced her at last. "Not that I know of." It was a grudging admission.

She wanted to touch him, to clasp his muscled shoulder, to lay her palm against his cheek. To lift up and press her lips to his, to kiss him until he pulled her close and kissed her back, until she forgot everything but the taste of him, the heat and wonder of him in her arms.

But no. Better not.

She said, "You keep evading the basic question. So I'll tell you what I think. I think you are a wonderful man—a much *better* man than you're willing to give yourself credit for. But I don't think that you want to get married. And you know what? I want *you* to have what *you* want. What you need."

He scowled down at her. "I don't like the sound of this, Willa."

Her throat clutched. The hot tears were pushing at the back of it. She refused to let them fall. "I love you," she got out on a bare husk of sound. "With all of my heart. And that's why I'm going to pack up my things and go."

Chapter Fourteen

It was five minutes to eight when Willa arrived at the ranch that night. Buster leading the way, she came in the door carrying two big boxes full of her things. Her parents, settled into their recliners for a quiet evening at home, glanced over at her with matching expressions of surprise.

Her mom jumped up. "Willa. What in the world...?"

The tears broke free then. They streamed down her cheeks. "Collin asked me to marry him. He bought me the most beautiful ring. The perfect ring. And I said no."

Her dad got up, too, then. He came and put his big, rough, rancher's hand on her hair, pressed a kiss to her forehead. And then he took the boxes from her and carried them down the hall to her old room.

"Oh, honey..." Her mom held out her arms.

Willa went into them, into the kind of a comfort only a mom can give. "Oh, Mom. I love him."

"I know, I know...."

"But it's not... Oh, Mom. It's just...not..."

"Shh. Shh, now. It's okay. It's all right."

She was openly sobbing by then. She couldn't seem to stop herself. "It's not. No, it's just not..."

And her mom held her and stroked her hair and patted her back and kept saying how everything was going to work out. Her dad came back up the hall. Buster followed him out as he went to get the rest of her things.

After Willa left him, Collin went down to his shop and he went to work. He worked straight through Friday night. When the sun came up Saturday morning, he climbed the stairs, plodded down the hall and fell into bed.

He slept for a couple of hours, his dreams full of Willa. It was still morning when he woke up, by himself, in the bed that he'd gotten way too damn used to sharing with her.

In those first few seconds when consciousness found him, he forgot she wasn't there. He reached for her, but there was only emptiness on the other side of the bed.

That was when it all came flooding back. She was gone. He got up and went back down to work.

Willa woke up early that Saturday. There was no summer school, but she went to town anyway. She wanted to talk to her brother before somebody else told him that she and Collin were through.

Gage was in his office.

She went in, closed the door and said, "I broke up with Collin. It's not what you think, so please don't try any big-brother heroics."

He was already looking thunderous. "What do you mean, it's not what I think?"

"He asked me to marry him. I turned him down. I made the decision to move out, not him. He wanted me to stay—

and do not ask me why I left, because I'm not explaining myself. All I'm saying is that he only wanted to do the right thing."

Gage got up from behind his desk then. He came around and he took her by the shoulders. For several seconds, he simply held her gaze. And then he pulled her close and gave her a hug. When he stepped back, he said, "So what you're saying is, you want me to stay out of it. You don't want me to bust his face in. And you want me to keep him on the Recovery Committee, to treat him like nothing has changed."

"Yes," she answered softly. "That is exactly what I'm saying."

Around five in the afternoon that day, Collin trudged back upstairs. He drank a quart of milk and ate a tuna sandwich standing up at the counter. Then he went down the hall and fell across the bed. When he woke up a few hours later, he returned to the lower floor and worked some more.

That was kind of the tone for the whole weekend. He didn't bother to shower or shave or even use a toothbrush. He worked. When he started to feel like he might fall over or hurt himself with his own tools, he went upstairs, grabbed something to eat, fell across his bed for an hour or two—and then woke up, remembered all over again that Willa was gone and staggered back down to his shop.

On Sunday, his mother called twice. He let the calls go to voice mail.

He might have stayed on the mountain indefinitely, but on Monday morning as he stood at the counter, staring blankly into space, downing a mug of coffee, he heard a scratching noise. And then a whine.

He went to the front door and opened it.

Buster.

The dog whined again and wagged his tail. When Collin only stared down at him, he plunked his butt on the porch boards and whined some more.

"You're not supposed to be here."

Tongue lolling, the dog stared up at him hopefully.

"Fine." Collin stepped back and Buster came in. He went right to his water bowl and lapped up what was left in it. Then he sniffed the food bowl. "Oh, pardon me. I had no clue you were coming." Collin laid on the sarcasm. Unfortunately, it was wasted on Buster. "Okay, okay." He went and got the bag of kibble. Buster sat and waited as he filled the bowl. "Go for it." And Buster did exactly that.

Willa was probably worried about the mutt. He would have to call her....

His heart lurched into overdrive and his throat felt tight, his tongue thick and heavy in his mouth as he autodialed her cell.

She answered on the second ring. "Collin." A small voice, so soft. And then she must have realized why he'd called. "You have Buster?"

"Yeah. He just now showed up at the door."

"Oh. I'm glad. We were worried...."

"I'll bring him down today."

"You don't have to. I can drive up after—"

"I said I'll bring him. I have a meeting anyway." A meeting he hadn't planned to go to, but hey. He couldn't hide in his shop forever. Life went on. Such as it was.

"I have summer school."

"Yeah, I know." He was aching for the smell of lemons, for that soft place in the curve of her throat. He loved to kiss her there.

"I'll call Thelma. She never minds watching him."

"But she's going to the meeting."

"It's okay. I'll ask her to wait for you. He's fine in the house without her. I'll pick him up there after school."

So, then. He wouldn't see her. That was good. Or so he tried to make himself believe. "All right, then."

"Thank you for bringing him...."

He tried to think of what to say next.

But then it didn't matter. She was gone.

Off the phone. Not in his house. Out of his life.

I love you, she'd told him. *With all of my heart.*

The bleak numbness of the weekend was fading. He'd started getting the feeling that he'd messed up bad, that he'd gotten stuck somewhere in his mind, stuck being some guy he really wasn't anymore. He'd thrown away what he wanted most because he didn't have the sense to say the things Willa needed to hear. It was all doubly discouraging because the things she needed to hear really were there, inside him, even though he'd gone and pretended they weren't.

He'd pretty much told her to go marry that other guy. The more he thought about that, the more disgusted he got with himself. It would serve him right if she took his advice.

Thinking about it all made his head spin. A spinning head and a broken heart were a real unpleasant combination.

He told himself that now, to be fair, he had to wait. He had to let her work it out with Dane Everhart one way or another. If she turned down the guy from Colorado, then maybe...

Maybe what? Seriously, what was the matter with him? What he needed to do was leave her alone. If there'd ever been any hope for him with her, he'd pretty much blown that by the way he'd treated her.

He scrambled some eggs and ate them, took a shower,

loaded Buster into his pickup and drove down the mountain. He dropped off the dog and went to the meeting.

Gage was there. Once or twice, Collin caught the other man watching him. But Gage didn't say a word about Willa. They discussed the donations that were coming in—and how to get more. They talked about the volunteers who'd come in from Thunder Canyon and elsewhere and how best to put them all to work rebuilding Rust Creek Falls. The meeting lasted three hours and they were still only two-thirds down the agenda. They agreed to meet Wednesday, same time, and finish up.

Collin drove to Kalispell and stocked up on groceries. He went home and went back to work—and deleted, unheard, all the messages his mom had left him over the weekend and that day.

The next morning, there was Buster, big as life, waiting at his front door. That time he texted Willa instead of calling. It just seemed wiser not to talk to her. Not to put his overworked heart under that kind of pressure, not to give himself any opportunity to make an idiot of himself all over again by begging for another chance. He took the dog to Thelma's and went back up the mountain.

On Wednesday morning, he couldn't help expecting Buster to show up again. But he didn't. They must be keeping a closer eye on him.

Which was good. For the best.

He was standing at the counter drinking his coffee, staring into the middle distance, wondering what Willa might be doing at that moment, when someone knocked at the door.

Willa?

He choked in midsip and his pulse started racing. Hot coffee sloshed across his knuckles as he set the mug down too hard. He wiped the coffee off on his Wranglers and made for the door.

It couldn't be her....

And it wasn't.

It was his mom, wearing tan pants, riding boots and an old plaid shirt, her straw Resistol in her gloved hands. She'd come on horseback, ridden her favorite mare, Sweetie, who was hobbled at the foot of the steps, nipping at the sparse grass.

"You deleted my phone messages, didn't you?" She asked the question softly. Kind of sadly. And that, somehow, was a thousand times worse than if she'd just started lecturing him as usual, if she'd called him her Last Straw and threatened to hit him upside the head to knock some sense into him.

He shrugged. "Yeah. I deleted them."

"Are you all right?"

"No."

"Sometimes you can be your own worst enemy."

"That's a fact."

"Not so much now as when you were younger, though." She almost smiled, but not quite. "I'll call that progress."

"You want to come in?"

She shook her head. "I'm just checkin' on you. I didn't check on you enough when you were little. Too late to make up for all that now, I guess."

"You're doing all right."

She put her hat back on. "You keeping fed?"

"Mostly."

"There's no law says you can't try again, and do a better job than you did before. Messing up is just practice for the next time, when you get it right." She turned and started down the steps.

"I love you, Mom," he said softly to her retreating back.

The words felt strange in his mouth. He knew he hadn't said them to her enough. And this time she probably hadn't even heard him.

Gathering the reins, she mounted. "Love you, too." She clicked her tongue and the horse turned and started back down the road. He stayed in front of the open door, watching her, until she disappeared from sight.

About then, he heard a whine. He glanced over and saw Buster sitting in the scrub grass beside the porch.

For the first time in days, Collin smiled. He slapped his thigh.

The dog barked, jumped to his feet and came running.

That morning, Willa got the call she'd been dreading.

The one from Dane. "Willa. My God. I just came from the airport, just heard how bad the flooding was in Rust Creek Falls. Are you all right?"

"I'm fine. Really." *Except for the little matter of my shattered heart.* "I lost my house and my car, though."

"Oh, sweetheart. I'm so sorry."

"Dane. Listen. I need to see you. I'm coming to Boulder, right away." Shelby could fill in for her. And Buster had taken off again, but it was no mystery where he'd gone. Maybe she would just call Collin and ask him if he could look after the dog until she got back.

"Coming to Boulder?" Dane boomed. "Not on your life."

"But, Dane, I—"

"I'm coming to you."

"No. Really, I'll find a flight and—"

He interrupted her. Again. "Sit tight, honey. I've got a plan."

Lord. She blew out a long breath. "Don't you always?"

He laughed, a bold, booming sound. "I'll be there before noon, you watch me."

"We'll have to arrange to meet somewhere. As I said, my house is a total loss." And she didn't want to meet him at the ranch. Too awkward, with her parents there....

"How about the middle of Main Street? You'll see me coming. I'll be the one in the CU helicopter."

"A helicopter?" How very, very Dane.

"Yeah. I'm getting the use of it courtesy of a generous alumnus. I'm coming, honey. I am as good as on my way...."

Collin, Gage and the rest of the committee were finishing up their endless meeting in one of the town hall conference rooms when they heard a helicopter overhead.

Nathan frowned. "We're not expecting a visit from the governor."

But then the helo loomed outside the window, coming in. Apparently, it was going to land in the street out in front. It was black and silver, with a giant gold CU painted on the belly.

Gage leveled that steady gaze of his on Collin. "Looks like Coach Everhart is dropping in to see how Willa's doing."

Collin reminded himself that he had to stay out of it. He needed to let Willa figure out what she wanted for herself.

But then, he couldn't do it. He could not just sit there.

He shot to his feet and headed for the door. Behind him, he thought he heard a low chuckle from Gage.

Willa was waiting on the sidewalk as the helicopter touched down. There were people all around her, folks she'd known all her life. They'd come running out of the library, the church and the town hall. Others had halted on the street. Everyone stared upward. It wasn't every day that a helicopter flew down and landed in the middle of town.

Leave it to Dane to make his arrival an event.

The chopper touched down. Dane jumped out before the blades stopped whirling, bending low to keep his handsome blond head out of danger. "Willa!" He ran toward her, rising to his full six feet six inches as he cleared the slowing blades.

Dread and misery and a healthy dose of embarrassment formed a leadlike ball in the pit of her stomach. She wrapped her arms around herself and waited grimly for him to reach her. Paige had given her the use of her house so she and Dane could be alone when she said the things she had to say.

"Willa!" The wonderful, rough deep voice came from behind her.

She stiffened, gasped, certain she couldn't have heard right. And then she whirled toward that voice, her heart in her throat.

Collin.

He was real. He was there. He reached out and put his warm, strong hands on her shoulders and she trembled with happiness just at his touch.

"Willa..." He stared at her with such frank longing in those beautiful dark eyes. She blinked at him, hardly daring to believe, and a ragged, hopeful sound escaped her. And he said, "Willa, damn it. I want you and I love you. Maybe I've always loved you, since way back when we were kids and I used spy on you playing with your Barbie dolls out in your dad's back pasture. Yeah, I know..." He tipped his head in the direction of the tall man behind her. "That other guy may be a better man. But there's no way he loves you like I do. And there's also no way I'm not trying again, no way I'm letting you go without pulling out all the stops." And then he dropped to his knees in front of her, the way he had last Friday. Only, somehow, nothing at all like last Friday. Because that had been all wrong.

And this, now, this moment? It was so very right.

He grabbed her hand and said fervently, "Stay, Willa. I'm asking. I'm begging. Stay here in Rust Creek Falls and be my wife."

People started clapping. Some shouted encouragements.

"You tell her, Collin!"

"Say it like you feel it!"

"Don't let her get away!"

There were whistles and catcalls.

Willa hardly heard them. For her, at that moment, there was only Collin, though he was looking kind of hazy through her happy tears. She confessed, "You really had me worried there."

"I know. I messed up. But I swear to you, right here on Main Street, in front of God, the library, that other guy— and way too many of our friends and neighbors—that when it comes to you and me, I won't mess up again."

She tugged on his hand. "Come here. Up here to me." And he swept to his feet once more. "I love you, Collin Traub," she told him. "I will always love you. And yes. Absolutely. You and me. From this day forward."

"Willa…" He grabbed her close and kissed her, a real kiss, deep and long and sweet. Everybody clapped all the harder.

When he lifted his head, she blinked up at him, dazed with joy. "Buster?"

"At Thelma's." He bent to kiss her again.

"Ahem," said the man behind her.

Willa pressed her hands to Collin's warm, hard chest. They shared a long, steady look, one of perfect understanding. And then, together, they turned to face Dane.

As it happened, Dane Everhart was not only a great guy, he was also a good sport. He said wryly, "Looks to me like I don't have a chance here."

Willa answered gently, "You're a good man, Dane. And I was wrong not to be straight with you from the first."

Dane gave a low chuckle. "Sometimes I'm a little pushy when it comes to going after what I want." He nodded at Collin. "You're a lucky man."

Collin pulled Willa closer to his side. "You're right. And I know it. I'm the luckiest man alive."

Dane held out his hand to Willa. She took it and they shook. "Be happy," he said.

"I will."

And then he turned and ran to the helicopter. The blades started whirling again.

Willa threw herself into Collin's waiting arms. They didn't see Dane go. They were too busy sharing another long, hot, perfect kiss, one that sealed their mutual commitment to their town, to each other and to the future they would build together with their own loving hands.

They were married three days later, on Saturday, July 27 with Pastor Alderson presiding.

It was a simple afternoon ceremony in the Community Church. The whole town attended and there was a big potluck afterward. Willa wore her mother's wedding dress. Paige stood up as her maid of honor and Collin asked his brother Sutter to come out from Seattle to be his best man.

If people whispered about how the maid of honor and the best man used to be together, they didn't whisper for long. Paige and Sutter conducted themselves with quiet dignity and the talk quickly died down.

It was one of those weddings where all the guests were smiling, a feel-good kind of day. Rust Creek Falls may have suffered through the flood of the century. But now the sun was shining and love ruled the day. Everyone could see that the bride and groom were meant for each other. Willa glowed with pure happiness.

And the former Traub bad boy had eyes only for his bride.

* * * * *

A SUMMER WEDDING
AT WILLOWMERE

BY
ABIGAIL GORDON

Abigail Gordon loves to write about the fascinating combination of medicine and romance from her home in a Cheshire village. She is active in local affairs, and is even called upon to write the script for the annual village pantomime! Her eldest son is a hospital manager, and helps with all her medical research. As part of a close-knit family, she treasures having two of her sons living close by, and the third one not too far away. This also gives her the added pleasure of being able to watch her delightful grandchildren growing up.

For David, with all good wishes

CHAPTER ONE

LAUREL MADDOX groaned as the train pulled into the small country station that was her destination. She had two heavy cases to unload and there wasn't a porter in sight. Just two deserted platforms and an unattended ticket office were all that were visible as the doors began to open.

For someone used to the big city where platforms and staff were many and varied it was a depressing introduction to the place that was going to be her home for some time to come. Yet all was not lost as she prepared to heave the cases out onto the platform.

A voice said from behind, 'Can I help?' and when she turned the man it belonged to didn't wait for an answer. He moved past and swung the offending luggage out onto the platform, then turned and offered a firm clasp from a hand that was protruding from the cuff of a crisp white shirt.

As she thanked him Laurel was thinking that he was the only part of the scenery that she could relate to. Tall, tanned, trimly built, wearing a dark suit, he seemed more in keeping with the place she'd come from than the countryside that her aunt had described in such glowing terms.

'I need a porter,' she said. 'Is there such a person in this place?'

'Just one,' he replied. 'Walter does the job of porter, mans the ticket office, collects them when necessary.' He gave a wave of the arm that took in the spotless platforms and the tubs of summer flowers gracing them. 'And also keeps the place clean and attractive. Willowmere won the prize for best country station last year. But he does stop for lunch at this time of day.'

'So what about a taxi?' she asked wearily, obviously unimpressed by his description of the absent Walter's devotion to duty.

'There is one, but…'

'Don't tell me. Amongst all of that he drives the local taxi.'

'No. His brother does that,' he said with a smile of the kind not soon forgotten, 'but it doesn't look as if he's around at the moment. I have a car and it's parked just here. Can I give you a lift to wherever you're going? I know we're strangers, but I'm a doctor in the village surgery, if it helps.' He showed her his ID, which proclaimed him to be Dr David Trelawney.

'Well, OK. Thank you,' she said, trying to smile despite feeling weary and irritable and wishing she hadn't allowed herself to be persuaded to move to the Cheshire village of Willowmere. 'So you must know my Aunt Elaine. I'm going to stay with her for a while.'

'Elaine Ferguson, our practice manager? Yes, of course,' he said in surprise, and bent to pick up her cases. 'So you'll be wanting Glenside Lodge, then. If you'll follow me.'

As she tottered after him across the cobbled forecourt of the station on high-heeled shoes Laurel was feeling nauseous from lack of food and the journey. It had been a month since she'd been discharged from hospital and she was gradually getting stronger, but at that moment she felt as weak as a kitten and was wishing she'd stayed put in her own habitat.

'There's a vacancy coming up at the surgery for a practice nurse,' Elaine had phoned to say. 'Why don't you give James Bartlett, the senior partner, a ring?'

'You mean live in the country,' Laurel had said doubtfully. 'I'm not so sure about that. It just isn't my scene, and I'm not sure I want to go back to nursing after what happened.'

Elaine was not to be put off. 'The air here is like wine compared to the fumes in the city, and with some good food inside you it will help to complete your recovery. You've done so well, Laurel, and I'm so proud of you. Come to Willowmere and carry on with your nursing here. You are too good at it to give it up. A country practice is a much less stressful place than a large hospital...and I want to pamper you a little.'

Elaine was clearly looking forward to her coming to live in her beloved village and the thought of her waiting to welcome her with open arms had been too comforting to refuse. As well as that, her aunt made the best omelette she'd ever tasted and if there was one thing her appetite needed, it was to be tempted.

There was also the matter of the job at the practice. Laurel had eventually phoned the senior partner, and having explained that she was coming to live in

Willowmere and was a hospital-trained nurse, he'd said that once she arrived he would be only too pleased to have a chat.

Returning to the present, Laurel thought that Elaine was going to be mad when she knew she'd come on an earlier train. She would have been there to meet her if she'd kept to the arrangements, but the opportunity had presented itself and she'd thought it better to get on a train that was there than wait for one that might not arrive.

'Is she expecting you?' David asked as he drove along a country lane where hedgerows bright with summer flowers allowed an occasional glimpse of fertile fields and their crops.

'Yes and no,' she told him. 'Elaine knows I'm coming but not on the train I arrived on. I caught an earlier one.'

'That explains it.'

'Explains what?'

'She won't be at Glenside Lodge at this time. Elaine will be at the surgery. So shall I take you there instead?'

'No!' she said hurriedly. 'She's told me where to find the key. I'd like to go straight to her place if you don't mind.'

'Sure,' he said easily. 'Whatever you say.'

At that moment she slumped against him in the passenger seat and when David turned his head he saw that she'd fainted. Now it was his turn to groan. What had he let himself in for with this too thin, overly made-up girl in sheer tights and heels like stilts, wearing cotton gloves on a warm summer day...and with the appeal of a cardboard box.

He stopped the car and hurried round to where she was

crumpled pale and still in the passenger seat. When he felt her pulse Laurel opened her eyes and sighed. 'I'm sorry,' she said listlessly. 'It's just that I'm hungry and tired.'

'And it made you faint?' he questioned, but the main thing was she'd come out of it quickly and in a very short time they would be at Glenside Lodge.

'So where is the key?' he asked when they arrived at the end of a long drive that in the past the carriages of the gentry had trundled along.

'Under the water butt at the back,' she told him weakly, and he observed her anxiously.

The moment they were inside he was going to phone Elaine and get her over here as quickly as possible, he decided, and in the meantime he would keep a keen eye on this strange young woman who looked as if she'd stepped out of a back issue of one of the glossies.

When she got out of the car Laurel's legs wobbled beneath her, and afraid that she might collapse onto the hard surface of the drive he put his arm around her shoulders to support her while they went to find the key and then opened the door with his free hand and almost carried her inside.

There was a sofa by the window and after placing her carefully onto its soft cushions he went into the kitchen to see what he could give her to eat and drink before he did anything else.

A glass of milk and a couple of biscuits had to suffice and while she was nibbling on them and drinking thirstily he phoned the surgery.

'What?' the practice manager exclaimed when he told her that her visitor had arrived and wasn't feeling very well. 'Laurel wasn't due until later in the afternoon. I'll be right there, David.'

With that she'd put the phone down and now he was waiting to be relieved of the responsibility that he'd brought upon himself by offering to help Elaine's niece.

'I'm not always like this, you know,' she told him languidly as she drained the glass. 'I'm known to be friendly and no trouble to anyone.'

'You don't have to explain,' he told her dryly as the minutes ticked by. 'I suggest that you see a doctor in case you're sickening for something.'

She managed a grimace of a smile. 'I've seen a doctor, quite a few of them over recent months, and lo and behold, now I've met another.'

Elaine's car had just pulled up outside and she became silent, leaving him to wonder what she'd meant by that. Maybe she was already suffering from some health problem as she didn't look very robust.

During the short time that he'd been part of the village practice David hadn't known anything to disrupt the calm efficiency of its manager. A petite blue-eyed blonde in her late thirties, Elaine Ferguson had accountancy qualifications and controlled the administration side of it in a way that kept all functions working smoothly. But when she came dashing into the small stone lodge that had once been part of an estate high on the moors, Elaine was definitely flustered and the young woman he'd picked up at the station wasn't helping things as on seeing her aunt she burst into tears.

'Laurel, my dear,' she cried. 'Why didn't you stick to the arrangements we'd made?'

'I know I should have done,' she wailed, 'but it was so quiet in the apartment and I felt so awful. I just couldn't wait any longer to be with you.'

David cleared his throat. Now that Elaine had arrived he wanted to be gone, but first he had to explain that her niece had fainted due to what she'd described as hunger and exhaustion and he was going to advise that she see a doctor *at the surgery* to be checked over.

'I hope you will soon feel better,' he said to the woebegone figure on the sofa who was sniffling into a handkerchief, unaware that her mascara had become black smudges around green eyes that looked so striking against her creamy skin and red-gold hair. The hair in question was quite short and shaggy looking and he presumed it must be the fashion back in London.

Elaine came to the door with him, still tense and troubled, but she didn't forget to thank him for looking after her niece and it gave him the opportunity to say his piece.

She nodded when he'd finished. 'I have quite a few concerns about Laurel and the first one is to get her settled here in Willowmere where I can give her some loving care. I've persuaded her to leave the big city for a while and come to where there is fresh air and good food.'

'Your niece isn't impressed with what she's seen so far,' he warned her whimsically. 'A station with just two platforms and no porter to hand.'

'So she didn't notice the shrubs and the flowers that Walter tends so lovingly, but she will,' she said with quiet confidence. 'Laurel just needs time to get a fresh hold on life. I'm taking what's left of today off and the rest of the week. I'd already arranged it with James so everything is in order back at the surgery.'

'I can't imagine it ever not being in order,' he said as he stepped out onto the porch.

'That could change,' she said wryly, casting a glance over her shoulder at the slender figure on the sofa, and as he drove to the practice on the main street of the village David was wondering what Elaine had meant by that.

'So you've met Elaine's niece already!' James Bartlett, the senior partner, exclaimed when he arrived at the practice. 'How did that come about?'

'I went by rail to collect the last of my things from St Gabriel's,' David explained. 'I thought it would be quicker than driving there, and when the train pulled in at Willowmere on the return journey I saw this girl about to get off and she had two heavy cases. So I stepped in and lifted them down onto the platform for her.

'She asked about a taxi but the one and only was nowhere in sight so I drove her to Glenside Lodge then rang Elaine and by that time she wasn't looking very well.'

James nodded. 'I know there is or was a medical problem of some kind. There was a period when Elaine was dashing off to London to see her whenever possible and it is why she has persuaded her niece to come and stay with her as they're very close.'

'I'm sorry for the delay on my part,' David said. 'I'd expected to be away only a short time.'

'Don't be concerned,' James told him. 'You couldn't leave a damsel in distress and Ben was here until midday. He's been on cloud nine ever since little Arran

was born. It's a delight to see him and Georgina so blissfully happy.

'But getting back to practice matters, would you take
over the house calls now that you're back, while I have
a chat with Beth Jackson? Our longest-serving practice
nurse is champing at the bit to hang up her uniform.'

'Sure,' David agreed. 'It's a delightful day out there
and a delightful place to be driving around in. I'll get
the list from Reception and be off.'

His first call was at the home of eighty-six-year-old
Sarah Wilkinson, who had recently been hospitalised
because of high potassium levels in her blood due to
drinking blackcurrant cordial insufficiently diluted.

She was home now and due to have another blood
test. Sarah had been quite prepared to go to the surgery
for it, but they'd told her that the district nurse would
call to take the blood sample.

Today his visit was a routine one. All the over-
eighties registered with the practice were visited from
time to time, and when it was Sarah's turn there was
always an element of pleasure in calling on her because
outwardly frail though she was, underneath was an un-
complaining, good-natured stoicism that had seen her
through many health problems of recent years.

One of them had been a sore on her arm that had
refused to heal. It had resulted in visits to the surgery
for dressings over a long period of time, but the old lady
had never complained and of recent months a skin graft
had finally solved the problem.

When she opened the door to him she said with a

twinkle in her eye, 'Can I offer you a drink of blackcurrant cordial, Doctor?'

David was smiling as he followed her into a cosy
sitting room. 'Do you intend to put plenty of water with
it, Sarah?'

'One can't do right for doing wrong in this life,' she
said laughingly. 'I thought by taking the cordial almost
neat I was building myself up, but no such thing.'

'I know,' he soothed. 'But we've sorted you out,
haven't we?'

'Yes, you have and I'm grateful. So to what do I owe
this visit?'

'It's a courtesy call. Just to make sure you are all right.'

'I'm fine. I'm not ready for pushing up the daisies
yet. I'm going to enter my home-made jam and Madeira
cake at the Summer Fayre at the end of July just to
prove it. Are you going to be there?'

'Yes, now that you've told me about it. Although it's
a while off yet, isn't it, as June is still bursting out all
over. What time does it start?'

'Eleven in the morning until four in the afternoon.
The café and the judging take place in a big marquee
that Lord Derringham lends us. He's the rich man who
owns the estate on the tops. One of your practice nurses
is married to his manager and Christine Quarmby, who
has that ailment with the funny name, is his game-
keeper's wife.'

'I can see that if I want to get to know what is going
on in the village this is the place to come,' he commented. 'Do the people in Willowmere see much of
His Lordship?'

Sarah shook her head. 'No, keeps himself to himself, but on the odd occasion that he does appear he's very pleasant and, like I said, he lets us use the marquee.

'On the night before the Fayre we have a party in the park that runs alongside the river. There's food and drink, and a band on a stage to play for dancing, with us women in long dresses and the men in dinner jackets. You must come.'

'Why? Will *you* be there?'

'Of course.' She had a twinkle back in her eye. 'Though I'm not into rock and roll. A sedate waltz is more in my line.'

'So can I book the first one?'

'Yes, you can.'

'I'm impressed.'

'Get away with you.' She chuckled. 'When the young females of Willowmere see you all dressed up, the likes of me won't be able to get near you.'

David laughed. 'Talking about young females, I gave one a lift from the station today.'

'Oh, yes? And who would that be?'

'She's called Laurel and is the niece of Elaine the practice manager.'

Sarah smiled. 'So that's another one that'll be in the queue.'

I don't think so, he thought, and returned to more serious matters by changing the subject. 'Right, Sarah. So shall I do what I've come for?'

He checked her heart and blood pressure, felt her pulse and the glands in her neck, and when he'd finished told her, 'No problems there at the moment, but before

I go is there anything troubling you healthwise that you haven't told me about?'

She shook her silver locks. 'No, Doctor. Not at the moment.'

He was picking up his bag. 'That's good, then, and if I don't see you before I'll see you at the party in the park.'

'So tell me more about Dr Trelawney,' Laurel said after David had gone. 'He told me that he's one of the GPs here.'

'He joined us just a short time ago from St Gabriel's Hospital where he was a registrar seeking a change of direction,' Elaine explained. 'David has replaced Georgina Allardyce, who has just given birth and tied the knot for a second time with the husband she was divorced from almost four years ago.

'Georgina is on maternity leave at the moment and may come back part time in the future. In the meantime, we are fortunate to have David, who is clever, capable, and has slotted in as if he was meant to be part of the village's health care.'

'He was kind and I don't think I behaved very well,' Laurel said regretfully. 'In fact, I was a pain. I'll apologise the next time we meet, but I felt so awful. I'm a freak, Elaine.'

'Nonsense, Laurel. You are brave *and* beautiful,' her aunt protested. 'The scars, mental and physical, will fade. Just give them time, dear.'

'Everything is such an effort,' she said despondently. 'I'd put on my war paint and nice clothes to make a statement, but didn't fool anyone, certainly not the Trelawney guy. He suggested that I see a doctor.'

'And what did you say to that?'

'That I'd seen plenty over the last few months and was about to tell him that I'm no ignoramus myself when it comes to health care, but you arrived at that moment.'

'Right,' Elaine said briskly, having no comment to make regarding that. 'Let's get you settled in. David said you fainted, so how do you feel now?'

'Better. He gave me some milk and biscuits.'

'Good. So let's show you where you'll be sleeping. Take your time up the stairs, watch your leg. I've put you in the room with the best view. It overlooks Willow Lake, which is one of the most beautiful places in the area.'

'Really,' was the lacklustre response, and Elaine hid a smile. Laurel was a city dweller through and through and might be bored out here in the countryside, but she needed the change of scene and the slower pace of life. Elaine wasn't going to let her go back to London until she was satisfied that her niece was fully recovered from an experience that she was not ever likely to forget.

'Is your fiancé going to visit while you're here?' Elaine asked after she'd helped bring up Laurel's cases. 'He will be most welcome.'

'It's off,' Laurel told her as she peered through the window at the view that she'd been promised. 'I'm too thin and pale for him these days…and then there are the scars, of course.'

'Then he doesn't love you enough,' Elaine announced, and without further comment went down to make them a late lunch.

She was right, Laurel thought dolefully when she'd gone, but it hurt to hear it said out loud. Darius was in the process of making his name in one of the television soaps and had rarely been to see her while she'd been hospitalised, and less still since she'd been discharged. When she'd said she was going to the countryside to assist her recovery he'd thought she was out of her mind.

'You're crazy, babe,' he'd said. 'Why would you want to leave London for fields full of cow pats?'

If his visits had been sparse, not so Elaine's. Her aunt had been to see her in hospital whenever she could and Laurel loved her for it. Other friends had been kind and loyal too. But Darius, the one she'd wanted to see the most, had been easing her out of his life all the time. In the end, dry eyed and disenchanted, she'd given him his ring back.

After they'd eaten Elaine said, 'Why don't you sit out in the garden for a while and let the sun bring some colour to your pale cheeks while I clear away?'

'If you say so,' Laurel agreed without much enthusiasm and, picking up a magazine that she'd bought before leaving London, went to sit on the small terrace at the back of the lodge. But it wasn't long before she put it down. It was too quiet, she thought, spooky almost. How was she going to exist without the hustle and bustle of London in her ears?

For the first time since she'd arrived, she found herself smiling. What was she like! Most people would jump at the chance to get away from that sort of sound, yet here she was, already pining for the throb of traffic.

The silence was broken suddenly by the noise of a car pulling up on the lane at the side of the garden and when she looked up Laurel saw that the window on the driver's side was being lowered and the village doctor that she'd met earlier was observing her over the hedge.

'So how's it going?' David asked. 'Are you feeling better?'

'Er, yes, a bit,' she said, taken aback at seeing him again in so short a time. 'You didn't have to come to check on me, you know.'

'I'm not,' he told her dryly. 'There are plenty of others who will actually be glad to see me. I'm in the middle of my house calls so I won't disturb you further.'

She'd given him the impression that she thought him interfering, Laurel thought glumly as he drove off. What a pain in the neck he must think she was.

Elaine appeared at that moment with coffee and biscuits on a tray and as they sat together companionably, she asked, 'Did I hear a car?'

'Yes. It was your Dr Trelawney.'

'David?'

'Yes, on his home visits. He saw me out here and stopped for a word. He doesn't look like a country type. How does *he* cope with it, I wonder?'

'The job?'

'No, the silence.'

'You ungrateful young minx,' Elaine declared laughingly. 'Lots of people would give their right arm to live in a place like this.'

'Yes, but what do you do for fun?'

Still amused, she replied, 'Oh, we fall in love, get married, have babies, take delight in the seasons as they come and go, count the cabbages in the fields…'

'*You* haven't done that, though, have you?'

'Counted the cabbages? No, but I've been in love. Sadly I was never a bride. I lost the love of my life before our relationship had progressed that far.'

'Yes, and it's such a shame,' Laurel told her. 'You would have been a lovely mum. That's what you've been like to me, Elaine.'

'You are my sister's child,' she said gently. 'I've tried to make up for what she and your father lacked in parenting skills, but they did turn up at the hospital to see you, didn't they?'

'For a couple of hours, yes, because they'd read about me in the papers, but they were soon off on their travels again.'

'That's the way they are,' Elaine said soothingly. 'Free spirits. We'll never change them and they do love you in their own way.'

'I've lost *my* way, Elaine,' she said forlornly. 'I used to be so positive, but since it happened I feel as if I don't know who I am. My face isn't marked, for which I'm eternally grateful, but there are parts of the rest of me that aren't a pretty sight.'

'That won't matter to anyone who really loves you,' she was told. 'Like I said before, you're brave *and* beautiful.'

'I wish,' was the doleful reply.

David Trelawney was house hunting. Since moving to Willowmere he'd been living in a rented cottage not too far from the surgery and Bracken House, where James Bartlett lived with his two children.

So far it was proving to be an ideal arrangement. It wouldn't have been if his high-flying American fiancée had wanted to join him, but that was not a problem any more.

They'd called off the engagement just before he'd accepted the position at St Gabriel's, and though it had left him with a rather jaundiced attitude to the opposite sex, his only regret was that he'd made an error of judgement and would be wary of repeating it.

Yet it wasn't stopping him from house hunting. He didn't want to rent for long, but so far he hadn't made any definite decision about where he was going to put down his roots in the village that had taken him to its heart. He told himself wryly that he'd made a mistake in his choice of a wife and wasn't going to do the same thing when it came to choosing a house.

He'd spent his growing years in a Cornish fishing village where his father had brought him up single-handed after losing his wife to cancer when David had been quite small, and once when Caroline had flown over to see him he'd taken her to meet him.

'Are you sure that she is the right one for you, David?' Jonas Trelawney had said afterwards. 'She's smart and attractive, seems like the kind of woman who knows what she wants and goes out to get it, but I know how you love kids and somehow I can't see her breast feeding or changing nappies. Have you discussed it at all?'

'Yes,' he'd said easily, putting from his mind the number of times the word 'nanny' had cropped up in the conversation.

He'd met her on a visit to London. She'd been staying in the same hotel with a group of friendly Texans who, on discovering that he had been on his own, had invited him to join them as they saw the sights.

She'd made a play for him, he'd responded to her advances, and the attraction between them had escalated into marriage plans, though he'd had his doubts about how she would react to the prospect of living in a town in Cheshire, as at that time he'd been based at St Gabriel's Hospital.

It was going to be so different to the glitzy life that he'd discovered she led when he'd visited her in Texas. Yet she hadn't raised any objections when he'd said that he had no plans to leave the UK while his father was alive. But he was to discover that the novelty of the idea was to be short-lived as far as Caroline was concerned.

His uneasiness had become a definite thing when he'd been expecting to go over there to sort out wedding arrangements and she'd put him off, saying that she had the chance to purchase a boutique that she'd had her eye on for some time and didn't want any diversions until the deal was settled.

'I would hardly have thought our wedding would be described as a diversion,' he'd said coolly, and she'd told him that she was a businesswoman first and foremost and he would have to get used to that.

'I see, and how are you going to run a boutique in Texas if you are living over here?' he'd asked, his anger rising.

There was silence at the other end of the line and then the dialling tone.

She phoned him again that same day at midnight Texas time. It sounded as if she was at some sort of social gathering if the noise in the background was anything to go by, and as if wine had loosened her tongue Caroline told him the truth, that she didn't want to be a doctor's wife any more in some crummy place in Britain and wanted to call off the engagement.

As anger came surging back he told her that it was fine by him and coldly wished her every success in her business dealings.

He discovered afterwards that there'd been more to it than she'd admitted that night on the phone. A certain senator had appeared on her horizon and she'd used the boutique story as a get-out.

In his disillusionment David decided to make a fresh start. His father had once told him that his mother had come from a village in Cheshire called Willowmere, and shortly after his engagement to Caroline had ended he met James Bartlett's sister Anna in the company of a doctor from the village practice. They'd been involved in a near drowning incident in a village called Willowmere and the way they described the place made him keen to find where the other part of his roots belonged.

When he'd found his mother's childhood home the discovery of it pulled at his heartstrings so much that he decided he wanted to live in Willowmere, and as if it was meant he was offered a position in the village practice.

What was left of the house stood in the centre of a field on the way to Willow Lake, a local beauty spot, and as he'd stood beside it he'd felt that this was where he wanted to be, where he wanted to bring up his children if he ever married, and at the same time contribute to the health care of those who lived there.

All that remained of it was four stone walls, the roof

having long since fallen in, and he remembered his father telling him how his mother had left it as a bride and gone to live with him in Cornwall where *his* home had been.

David found no reason to regret his decision to move to the Cheshire countryside. He was totally happy there, but supposed it might not be everyone's choice. For instance, there was the girl he'd met at the station, he thought as the day took its course. She'd taken a dim view of the place.

So far he hadn't found a property that appealed to him and knew it was because every time he went back to the ruins of his mother's home the idea of restoring it was there.

Laurel and Elaine had had an omelette for their evening meal with chips and fresh green runner beans out of the garden, and when she'd placed the food in front of her niece she'd said, 'I know it's not exactly the fatted calf but it's something that I know you like.'

'I love your omelettes,' Laurel told her. 'I used to dream about them when I was in hospital.'

'Yes, I'm sure you did,' Elaine said laughingly. 'You must have had better things to think about than my cooking.'

'It was the only thing that cheered me up,' Laurel insisted. 'Darius was in the process of ditching me slowly, the skin grafts weren't a bundle of joy, and neither was my leg that they'd had to pin all over the place.'

'I know, my dear,' Elaine said soothingly. 'It isn't surprising that you're feeling low with all that has happened to you but, Laurel, it could have been so much worse.'

'Yes, I know,' she said flatly, 'and I really do want to like it here and get fit again. I look such a sight.'

'Not to me you don't.'

'Maybe, but your Dr Trelawney kept looking at me as if I was some peculiar specimen under the microscope. I wish my hair would grow more quickly.'

'Have patience, Laurel,' she was told. 'What has grown so far is still the same beautiful colour.'

'Yes, the colour of fire,' she said with a shudder as she ate the food beneath the watchful gaze of her hostess.

'I think an early night would be a good idea,' Elaine suggested when they'd tidied up after the meal, 'but how about a breath of good country air first? Perhaps a short walk through the village, past the surgery where David and I spend our working lives, and where you might be joining us when you feel like going to see James.'

'Yes, sure,' she agreed, 'and if that is where he works, where does he live?'

'David lives in a small cottage nearby. He's staying there until he finds a property to buy. I know that he's house hunting quite seriously but hasn't mentioned finding anything suitable so far.'

'And will he be living alone when he does?' Laurel asked.

'Yes, as far as I know, unless he has a wife tucked away somewhere, and I doubt that.'

David was returning from his usual nightly stroll to gaze upon his mother's old home when he saw them coming towards him. Elaine, trim as always in slacks and a smart top, and the strange young woman he'd met at lunchtime still in the same outlandish garb as before that looked totally out of place in the setting.

'Hello, there,' he said when they drew level. 'Have you been showing your niece the sights of Willowmere, Elaine?'

'Yes, some of them,' she replied, 'such as the surgery and your spacious accommodation.'

He smiled. 'It's all right for one, two at the most.'

'And are you still house hunting?'

'Er, yes, sort of. I've got something in mind but it won't be a fast solution.'

He was aware that Elaine's companion hadn't spoken at yet another unexpected meeting and thought that maybe now she was established in the village she was keeping a low profile, but he was to discover there was nothing wrong with her vocal cords.

'I don't remember thanking you for coming to my rescue when I was getting off the train,' she said in a less abrupt manner than the one she'd used then.

'Think nothing of it,' he said easily, as if the whole episode had been a pleasant break in the day. 'The main thing is how are you feeling now?'

She smiled and David was struck at the transformation.

'Improving,' was the reply, 'and once Elaine has shown me the lake it's off to bed for me. It's been a long day, but not as long as some have been recently.'

As they moved off in opposite directions David was thinking how pale she was. James had said there was a health problem of some kind regarding Elaine's niece, and he wondered what it was.

CHAPTER TWO

WHEN Laurel awoke the next morning she found herself looking up at an unfamiliar ceiling dappled by a summer sun and for the first few seconds couldn't think where she was, but not for long.

She was in Elaine's quiet backwater, she thought, with birdsong the only sound breaking the silence. Recalling how she'd asked her aunt what they did for fun in Willowmere, she wondered why she'd brought up the subject. *That* kind of thing wasn't going to be on her agenda with a broken engagement behind her and some unappealing scarring.

But now here she was and glad of it in spite of her lack of enthusiasm for country life. As sleep had stolen over her the night before she'd vowed she was going to make an effort to fit in and if she got the job at the surgery at least she wouldn't be moping around all day.

'Does anyone in Willowmere know what happened to me?' Laurel asked of Elaine as they ate a leisurely breakfast out on the sunny patio.

Her aunt shook her head. 'No. At the time I was too

distressed to talk about it, my beautiful niece caught up in the stupidity of others, and if anyone around here saw it in the papers they wouldn't see any connection.

'Right from the start I've felt it would be an invasion of your privacy to discuss you with others even though I've been bursting with pride every time I thought of what you did. But as far as I'm concerned, that is how it will stay, Laurel. If you should want to tell anyone, that is a different matter.

'And now what would you like to do today? If you're not over the moon with our lovely village we can go into the town and shop if you like, but I would rather we saved that sort of thing for when you've had some rest and relaxation, which could be in short supply when you're working at the surgery.'

'You mean *if* I'm working there. I'm not exactly spectacular at the moment with a gammy knee that sometimes lets me down and hair that looks as if it's been cut with a knife and fork.'

'Nonsense,' Elaine soothed gently. 'Your hair is growing back nicely and you're beautiful with your green eyes and lovely, curvy mouth.'

'And my rough red hands,' Laurel reminded her with dry humour. 'I wear the gloves all the time so that I won't be mistaken for a domestic drudge.'

'Get away with you,' was the response. 'People around here are very kind and if they knew how you'd got the scarring they would acclaim your courage and dedication to the job. But, as I've just said, that is entirely your affair, and as to how we are going to spend your first day away from London, what is it to be, the town or the village?'

'The village, I think,' Laurel replied. She would have preferred to go shopping but she knew how much Elaine wanted to show her Willowmere and they could always shop another day.

'So how about a leisurely stroll and then we'll have lunch at the Hollyhocks Tea Rooms? It may not be as upmarket as the places where you usually eat, but they won't be able to beat the food that Emma and her husband serve to their customers.

'Then if you like I'll take you to the surgery and introduce you to James. He will want to arrange a time to interview you. Beth Jackson, who is leaving, wants to go as soon as possible. She and her husband are opening a business next to the post office and if you feel the need, by all means wear the gloves, though I do think that you have no call to be so self-conscious about your hands.'

Laurel wasn't sure about visiting the surgery. 'Don't you think that David Trelawney might feel that since arriving here I've been continually in his line of vision?' she said dubiously. 'At the station, in the garden, when he was driving past on his way to house calls, and at sunset last night.'

'He'll be seeing much more of you than that if you're working at the same place,' Elaine said laughingly. 'And how do you know he won't feel that he can't get too much of a good thing?'

Laurel couldn't bring herself to share in Elaine's amusement. How long, if ever, was it going to be before she felt desirable once more? Each time Darius had visited her in hospital it had been clear that he wasn't keen on the damaged version, and as she'd fought her way through the pain it had been with her confidence at a very low ebb.

As they walked along the main street Elaine was greeted by everyone they met and Laurel was aware that some curious glances were coming her way, which was not surprising as she was wearing a high-necked sweater, a hat and gloves on a hot summer day.

This is so different from city life, she was thinking as she took in the friendliness of the people. She and her fellow nurses had often commented that in London people were always rushing about, and getting to know one's next-door neighbour was a rare event, but in Willowmere life seemed to be lived at a slower pace, as if each moment was to be cherished rather than passed quickly by.

It had always been Elaine who had been *her* visitor before this, staying at the apartment and enjoying every moment with the niece that she loved like a daughter, but now it was Laurel's turn to leave her natural habitat for a while.

And now here she was, happy to be with the one person who loved her unconditionally, yet feeling totally out of her depth amongst quaint limestone cottages and shops that had an individuality all their own.

'We passed the surgery last night if you remember,' Elaine said, indicating a large stone building across the way from where they'd just had an excellent lunch. Noting Laurel's lack of enthusiasm, she added, 'Are you sure you want to meet the people who work there?'

'Yes, of course,' she said with assumed heartiness, deciding that she may as well get it over with. At least it was only a place for local people with their ailments. There would be no rows of beds or doctors with sombre expressions looking down at her, and nurses treating one of their own with sympathy and efficiency.

She'd been introduced to the two receptionists, both of them middle-aged, pleasant and organised, met the two practice nurses and discovered that it was a delicatessen that Beth Jackson and her husband were going to open very soon at the other end of the main street.

At that moment the door of the nearest consulting room opened and an attractive, dark-haired woman was framed there, holding a baby in her arms. The doctor she'd been consulting was close behind and as she was about to leave he bent and kissed her tenderly.

Laurel's eyes widened and as Elaine steered her in the opposite direction she explained, 'That is baby Arran Allardyce come to see his daddy. Ben is helping out while Georgina, his wife, who is one of our regular doctors, is on maternity leave.'

'I see,' Laurel said, and wished that she had a man in her life to kiss her like that and a beautiful baby to go with it. Day would turn into night before that ever happened in the light of recent events.

James Bartlett, the senior partner, was all that Elaine had described him to be, pleasant, handsome, a very likeable man with two lovely children if the photograph on his desk was anything to go by, and when they'd been introduced her aunt left them to get acquainted.

She'd removed the hat by then, deciding that if she was going to be employed there it was only fair that the man sitting opposite should see what she really looked like, yet she needn't have worried. James didn't seem to see anything too odd about the young woman that Elaine had brought to the surgery. 'When could you come for an interview, Laurel?'

'Whenever,' she replied. 'My time is my own at present.'

'Then how about on the afternoon of the day that Elaine returns from the leave that she arranged in honour of your arrival? Say two o'clock?' As she got up to go he shook her hand and said, 'We'll look forward to seeing you then.'

She was missing nursing, but until Elaine had suggested she work at the practice had felt it would be too painful to go back to it. But there was something about this pleasant village health care centre that was reaching out to her…and of course there was David Trelawney. Where was he today?

Yesterday she'd been too frazzled to really register the man who'd come to her rescue when she'd been getting off the train, but now she was curious to see if he was as presentable as she'd thought. It would be nice to see him again now that she was in residence, so to speak, and it would give her the opportunity to express further gratitude for his assistance, but it seemed that it was not to be on this bright summer day, and it did rather take the edge off it.

If she and Elaine had walked a little further she would have had the answer to her question. David's car was parked outside the village hall. He'd been about to start his home visits when a call had come through and he'd gone straight there to find the chairlady of the Women's Institute, who were holding their usual monthly meeting on the premises, looking far from well.

She was experiencing severe chest pains, perspiring heavily, and her lips were blue. Before he'd even sounded her heart David was phoning for an ambulance and telling her gently, 'I'm sending you to hospital, Mrs Tate.'

She nodded. Maisie Tate was no fool. She wouldn't be chairlady of Willowmere's branch of the Women's Institute if she was. She could tell that the new doctor at the practice had her down for a heart attack and she didn't think he was wrong.

But if that was the case, who was going to look after her husband? Barry always had kippers for tea on a Thursday and she wasn't going to be able to call at the fishmonger's on her way home today.

David had finished examining her and as another stab of pain ripped across her chest he said reassuringly, 'The ambulance will be here any moment, Mrs Tate, and they'll take you straight to hospital when I've had a word with the paramedics.'

The rest of the Women's Institute was hovering around her anxiously and one of them, who must have known her routine, said, 'Don't worry, Maisie. I'll get your Barry his kippers.'

She nodded and David thought incredulously that this was the age group who'd been brought up to have a meal ready for the man of the house when he came in from work. But surely when he knew what was happening to his wife the absent Barry wouldn't have any appetite.

As he drove along the main street of the village on his way to the delayed calls he was surprised to see Elaine and Laurel walking slowly along the pavement ahead of him, and as he pulled up alongside them he saw that the short skirt, high heels and sheer tights had been replaced by jeans and sandals.

But the rest of her attire was still strange and he didn't think it was what the fashion-conscious were wearing for the summer in London. A soft felt hat was completely covering the short red-gold hair and she was still wearing the white cotton gloves.

'Hello, there, and what are you folks up to on this glorious day?' he asked with a smile that embraced them both.

'I'm showing Laurel around the village,' Elaine replied. 'We've just been to the surgery and she's been introduced to everyone there. Where were you, though? You were the only one missing, David, although you've already met my niece, haven't you?'

I have indeed, he thought, three times to be exact.

'Yes,' he replied with the smile still in place, and went on to explain with his glance on her so-far silent companion, 'I was out on an emergency call.

'And how are *you* this morning, Laurel?' he said easily, wondering if she was anaemic or something of the kind to be wearing that sort of jumper in the heat of summer.

'Much better, thank you,' she said flatly, and he sighed inwardly.

He turned to Elaine. 'I was called to the village hall where the Women's Institute are having a meeting and found their chairlady with a suspected heart attack.'

'Oh! No!' Elaine exclaimed. 'That would be Maisie Tate. Poor Maisie!'

'Yes, it was,' he replied, and thought he couldn't imagine her companion having much interest in the ills and ailments of the Willowmere villagers. There was an aloofness about her today and he was curious to know what lay beneath it as he never could resist a challenge.

'And so what do you think of our beautiful village?' he asked Laurel.

'I thought that you were a newcomer too,' she commented dryly, while comparing his clear-cut attractiveness to the wavy dark hair and fashionable stubble of Darius, who'd not wanted her any more because he'd seen the scarring and been revolted...

It wasn't a situation that would ever occur with this man, she thought with a rush of blood. There would never be an occasion when *he* saw her minus clothing and...where had such an idea come from anyway?

He was smiling at the comment and she thought how likeable he was as he said, 'I am a newcomer in one way, yet I feel as if Willowmere has always been part of me. Sometimes we find the place of our dreams and are given the opportunity to live there and that is what I intend to do when I've found a house.'

There was no mention of a woman in his life, Laurel noticed, which was incredible, but the odds were that there would be one tucked away somewhere, or relegated to the past for some reason.

'I must go,' he said, unaware that she was surmising about his love life. 'I have a few visits to make and am already late after the callout to Mrs Tate.'

'Yes, of course,' Elaine said, and to Laurel's horror she went on, 'Would you like to come over for dinner one evening so that I may show my appreciation for the way you looked after my niece yesterday?'

Ugh! Laurel thought, taken aback at the suggestion and its implications. It made her appear to be some sort of helpless, clinging vine, just as she'd been when they'd met at the station and afterwards. But she wasn't usually like that. It was just unfortunate that David Trelawney had been an observer of her moments of weakness.

If she was taken aback, so was he, she thought, seeing his surprise, but he soon recovered his poise and said politely, 'Er…yes…I'd love to.' He glanced warily in her direction. 'But please don't feel that you owe me anything for yesterday. It was just a matter of common politeness.'

As Elaine nodded understandingly Laurel thought wistfully that it would be, wouldn't it? The time was gone when she attracted admiring looks, or handsome men asked her out to dinner.

'When would you like to come?' Elaine was asking.

He gave a wry grimace. 'I'm free most nights. I spend most of my time house hunting or dreaming of renovating an old house I've seen.'

'And where would that be?' she questioned curiously, while Laurel stood by silently once more.

'It's a derelict building in one of the fields beside Willow Lake.'

'Ah! I know the one. It's called Water Meetings House. Why that one, though, when there are lots of nice properties in the area? It would need huge restoration work to make it habitable again. It's been like that for years.'

'Mmm, I know, but I do have my reasons,' he said, and without questioning him further Elaine returned to the subject of dinner.

'So how about one night next week?' she suggested. 'Say Friday when there is no surgery the following day?'

'Yes, fine,' he replied. 'What time?'

'Sevenish, if that's all right.'

He nodded and with a wave of the hand drove off.

As his car disappeared from view Laurel groaned openly and Elaine said, 'I know what you're thinking. That it is unkind of me to invite David to dinner when you want to keep a low profile, but Laurel, I'm not matchmaking. He is a stranger in the village, just as you are, and we in Willowmere are renowned for our hospitality.'

'I'm sorry,' she said contritely as the moment of gloom disappeared. 'The last thing I want is to become a me, me, me sort of person. Self-pity is a form of selfishness.'

'It can be,' Elaine agreed gently, 'but not in your case. And now let's take you home and put you to bed for a couple of hours and I guarantee that as each day passes you are going to feel more ready to face the world, and whatever you think of Willowmere you couldn't be recuperating in a better place.'

'You might be right,' Laurel said with spirits still lifting as she thought that it was more likely to be the village's inhabitants than its peace and fresh air that were going to help her take a hold on life again.

Yet as she looked out of her bedroom window before going to bed that night and saw a golden sun setting on the skyline, with the lake glinting in the distance amongst the drooping willows that had given it its name, it didn't all feel quite so strange as it had the night before.

Within minutes of placing her head on the pillows she slept and for once there were no smoke and flames turning her dreams into nightmares.

Beth called at Glenside Lodge for a chat in her lunch hour the following day and as the three of them relaxed over coffee she said, 'James must be feeling that it is one departure after another at the surgery. First it was Anna and Glenn going to work in Africa. Then Georgina and Ben had a blissful reunion, which resulted in them re-marrying and her giving birth to Arran in the spring, so *she* is going to be missing for quite some time too, hence David's most welcome appearance, and now I'm about to try a new slant on village shopping. You will be most welcome in the practice, Laurel, if you can sort something out with James, but are you happy that it might only be temporary?'

'Yes, it would suit me fine,' she replied. 'I'm rather at a crossroads in my life at the moment, so it would give me a short breathing space before I make up my mind what I want to do and where I'm heading.'

Elaine was nodding in silent agreement. Laurel was improving physically, but it was the mental scars that worried her. Her niece had been a bright and trendy twenty-five-year-old when it had happened, totally dedi-cated to the career she'd chosen and enjoying life in the big city when she hadn't been working, but now all of that had gone.

Her interest in the village surgery had been lukewarm

when she'd taken Laurel there, as had been her interest in life in general, but she wasn't going to sit by and let her stay in the doldrums. Her beautiful girl still had a lot to offer to those needing health care *and* to the man who would one day love her for who she was.

Willowmere in summer was a bright haven of colour. The new life that had come bursting through in fields and gardens in the spring was now established in abundant growth. Trees along the riverside, some of them hundreds of years old, were in full leaf, providing a background of fresh greenery against the flimsy craft of the canoe club as they sailed along on practice days, and bird life of every kind imaginable was to be found in cottage gardens and in the park that ran parallel with the river.

The charm of the village attracted walkers and visitors from miles around and as the days passed Laurel was aware that the Hollyhocks Tea Rooms were busy all the time with those seeking appetising meals to complement a summer day, and The Pheasant, its only pub, did much trade with others who had less discerning tastes but could guarantee a thirst.

Often it wasn't until late in the evening that the quiet that she'd been so dubious about descended. It was on one of those occasions that she went for a stroll in the gathering dusk beside the lake that was visible when she looked through her bedroom window.

Elaine had gone to bed and she'd been about to do the same when the urge to go out into the gloaming had overtaken her. The sunset had been magnificent and now it was still and sultry with a yellow moon above.

She'd been wearing a sundress in the house and instead of changing into something less revealing threw a light cardigan across her bare shoulders and sallied forth, minus the gloves.

There were still a few people about loath to be inside on such a night, but they thinned out as she drew nearer to the lake, and by the time she was only a field away she was alone, and looming up in front of her in the moonlight were the ruins of a big stone house. Could this be the place that David Trelawney had mentioned? she wondered. If so, what a mess it was in, yet what a position, just a hundred feet or so from Willow Lake, and on the other side of the house, not far away, the place where the two rivers that flowed through the village met. There was a tattered sign on the fencing that separated the field from the road and as she peered at it she saw that it said appropriately 'Water Meetings House.' She shook her head in disbelief. Was the man insane? It would take forever to restore this place.

'Hello, there,' a voice said from behind her.

She turned slowly and he was there, the village doctor who was considering rebuilding the shell of what must have once been a gracious home.

'Hi,' she said lightly, pulling the cardigan tightly around her shoulders. 'I came out for a stroll and stumbled upon this derelict house. It's the one that you mentioned the other day, isn't it?'

He was smiling. She could see his teeth gleaming whitely in the moon's light. 'Yes, it is. I expect you think I'm crazy to be considering restoring it.'

'Yes, I do as a matter of fact,' was the reply. 'Yet I can see why. It's in a fantastic position and so aptly named.'

She was a dedicated city dweller, but there was something about the moment with the two of them wrapped around by the silent night and the remains of the limestone house shining palely in the moonlight that was firing her imagination, and she thought whimsically that it was as if there were forces abroad that were out to entrance her, when she didn't want to be entranced.

As he observed her bemused expression David was thinking along similar lines. It was weird that Laurel of all people should be so much on his wavelength about this place and the ruins of his mother's old home. Meeting up with her out there in the moonlight was just as odd as on the other times they'd met.

It had come at the end of a very strange day. In the early afternoon he'd had a phone call from one of the Texan wives who'd been in Caroline's group when he'd first met her in London.

He'd been surprised to hear from her and even more so when he'd heard what she had to say. She'd rung to tell him that Caroline had married the senator that she'd been seeing at the time they'd ended their relationship.

'My Jerome said we should let you know,' she'd said gently in a soft Texan drawl, 'so that if you hear it from someone else it won't be such a shock.'

He'd thanked her and after chatting briefly had finished the call with no feelings of regret. There'd been just the relief of knowing that the big mistake he'd almost made had reached its final conclusion, and it would be a long time before he made such an error of judgement again.

He'd picked up the phone again and rung his father, and when he'd told him about the call from America and that it was definitely over with his ex-fiancée Jonas had exclaimed, 'Praise be! But I thought it already was?'

'Yes, it was, but now there is closure, Dad,' he said calmly.

'And are you sure you're all right with that?'

'Spot on,' he replied. 'It would never have worked. We had a different set of values.'

'One day you'll meet the right woman and when it happens you will know beyond any doubt,' Jonas said. 'When I met your mother I knew she was the only one for me, and it will be the same for you.'

'If you say so,' he agreed dubiously, with the old proverb about once bitten, twice shy in mind.

With the feeling of contentment still there he went to the local estate agent's while out on his calls and ended his uncertainties about the house by the lake by making an offer for it and the land it stood on.

In the summer twilight he'd gone to gaze upon what he hoped would soon be his and found that the strange day was not yet over. He'd found Laurel Maddox there, standing silent and alone in front of what had been his mother's childhood home.

CHAPTER THREE

HER eyes looked huge in the light of the moon. She was still clutching her cardigan tightly around her, and once again he wondered what it was with this strange newcomer to the village.

She was different from any woman he'd ever met. There was a sort of touch-me-not aura about her and yet he sensed hurt and vulnerability there too.

'I'll walk you home,' he suggested. 'We don't get much crime around here, but even so it isn't a good idea to be out on your own in the dark.' She didn't reply, but as he began to move in that direction she fell into step beside him.

As they walked along the road that separated the house from the lake she tripped over a loose stone and his arm came out to steady her. He felt her flinch at his touch and let his hold fall away as soon as she'd regained her balance.

She was happy enough when she was with Elaine, he thought, and no one at the surgery had had any adverse comments to make about her after she'd been introduced to them, so maybe it was him that she didn't care for.

Two in one day, he thought wryly. Caroline marrying her rich lover and Laurel behaving as if he'd got the plague, yet it didn't prevent his concern about her increasing.

When they reached Glenside Lodge and stopped at the gate he said, 'Take care, Laurel. If we don't meet before, I will see you on Friday.' Leaving her to go quietly up the stairs without disturbing Elaine, he strode off towards the village green and the cottage he was renting.

As she settled herself beneath the covers Laurel was wishing that she could act naturally when she was with David instead of being such a pain. She wasn't like that with anyone else, *but he wasn't like anyone else*. He was attractive and so likeable that he took her breath away, and the last thing she needed at the moment were those sorts of feelings.

It was Friday night. David had arrived with flowers and chocolates for his two hostesses and the three of them were having a drink before dinner in the sitting room of Glenside Lodge.

From the moment of his arrival his gaze had been on Laurel. She wasn't looking so drained, he decided, and though she wasn't saying much she looked happier. He wasn't to know that the moment he'd appeared again all her resolutions to keep her distance had disappeared.

He noticed that she wasn't quite so covered up tonight in the cream cotton dress she was wearing. It was full skirted and calf length, and revealed a slender neck decorated by just a fine gold chain. But the gloves were still on view, cream this time, and he decided that they had to be some sort of fad.

They'd taken their coffee out into the garden at the end of the meal and were chatting about minor matters when Elaine said, 'I'm told that Maisie Tate is still in the coronary unit.'

'Yes,' he agreed. 'However, she is making good progress and could be home by the end of the week.'

'That's good, then,' she replied.

'Indeed. Plus Barry might soon be getting his kippers once more,' he said, and both women laughed.

As the night fell around them David asked, 'How long have you lived in Willowmere, Elaine?'

'Four years,' she told him. 'I was in business management in London and felt ready for a change. I'd always wanted to live in the countryside so applied for the post of practice manager at the surgery. Laurel was twenty-one at the time and didn't want to move out of her job, so she stayed behind.'

'And what job would that be, Laurel?' he asked, his curiosity about her unabated.

There was silence for a moment and then she said flatly, 'I was a nurse in a London hospital before I came here.'

David was taken aback. That was one for the book, he was thinking. 'So you were hospital based the same as I was,' he said, 'but aren't any longer?'

'Yes, that is so,' she informed him, and without giving him the chance to ask any more questions went into the kitchen to make more coffee. As she waited for the kettle to boil she thought wryly that he had done his best to hide his surprise but he couldn't see her in the role, and if the senior partner decided she was what he wanted at the surgery, David was in for an even bigger surprise.

He'd got her labelled as something and it wasn't a nurse. But, then, he hadn't known her before it had happened.

When she went back into the garden he and Elaine were chatting about the Summer Fayre that would soon be taking place in the village, and Laurel thought with sudden recklessness if he was going to be there, then so would she.

David had them smiling as he recounted his visit to the indefatigable Sarah Wilkinson, who was going to enter her home-made jam and cakes in the competitions and had promised him the first waltz at the party the night before.

'I hope you'll both be there,' he said.

Her moment of bravado had disappeared into thin air so Laurel steered the discussion away from the party and asked, 'Have you decided what to do about Water Meetings House yet?'

He smiled. 'Yes. I've made an offer and it's been accepted. The land and what is left of the house will soon be mine and then it will be action stations. I was brought up in Cornwall. My father still lives there, and will be coming shortly to see what I've bought. He is the only one who won't think I'm crazy because he knows why I'm interested in the place.

'I'd never seen it before until I came to this part of the world, though I knew about it. My mother lived in Water Meetings House until she married my father and they moved to Cornwall where he came from. She died when I was very young, so you see the desire to restore it and make it my home comes from that.'

'And is he coming to live with you when it's finished, or have you someone else in mind?' Elaine asked, and Laurel found that she was holding her breath.

'Not now,' he told her. 'I was engaged but it didn't last and the way of it ending has left a nasty taste in my mouth.' He was aware of Laurel's clear gaze upon him and now it was his turn to want to steer the conversation into other channels. The last thing he wanted to talk about was his love life, or the lack of it.

'With regards to my dad I can't see him wanting to leave Cornwall. He's a Cornishman through and through, but the offer will be there if he wants to join me. Otherwise I shall live there alone, but that is way in the future. I've got to rebuild the house before I can live in it.'

He rose to his feet as if talking about what lay ahead had made him restive and Laurel asked, 'Am I right in thinking that is where you intend going now? For a last look before you call it a day?'

He nodded. 'It would seem that you haven't forgotten our meeting there the other night. Yes, it might be. Do you want to come?'

If Elaine was surprised at the invitation she didn't show it. 'Yes, why don't you?' she suggested, and telling herself that it would seem ungracious if she refused after what her aunt had just said Laurel rose to stand beside him.

'Yes, all right,' she agreed. 'I've been inside all day and could do with some exercise.'

It sounded trite and she knew it, but maybe this time she might get the chance to show David something of the real her, the blithe spirit that until recently hadn't a care in the world.

As they walked towards the lake and the house nearby Laurel surprised him by saying, 'I think it's lovely that you want to rebuild your mother's home. Did you miss her very much?'

'I suppose I did,' he replied thoughtfully, 'but when she died I was too young to realise what was happening and my dad was wonderful. He brought me up on his own, but always kept her memory fresh in our lives. Where are your parents, Laurel? I haven't heard you mention them.'

'They're travelling around somewhere. Mum and Dad are free spirits, always wanting to be on the move. I see them from time to time but it is Elaine who has always cared for me. She is always there for me when they aren't.'

There was no condemnation in her voice, just a description of what *her* life had been like, and he asked, 'Has Elaine never married?'

'No. She was engaged once a long time ago but it didn't work out.'

Tell me about it, he thought, with the memory of Caroline's disparaging description of the future they'd been planning coming to mind.

The moon was on the wane but there was still enough light for him to see Laurel walking beside him in the cream cotton dress as they skirted the lake, and he felt instinctively that *she* wouldn't be deceitful. There was nothing devious about Laurel Maddox. What you saw was what you got and the more he saw the more he wanted to see, though it *was* just curiosity.

Aware that he was observing her, she asked, 'What?'

'You know that you puzzle me, don't you?'

'Do I? I puzzle myself sometimes.'

'You're a strange creature.'

'I'm what life has made me.'

'You mean your home life?'

'No, my working life.'

'I see.'

He didn't. Didn't see at all, but short of being intrusive there didn't seem much else to say, so he carried on moving towards the house, and when they were standing in front of the remains of it once more surprised her by saying, 'I have to rebuild it as it was before. It's a listed building, but when it's finished I'll be looking for some suggestions regarding the interior. Is that sort of thing in your line?'

'It might be if it was a smart apartment in the city,' she said slowly, 'but I don't think I would be much good at fixtures and fittings in a place like this.'

'Not to worry,' he told her easily, surprising himself that he was still persisting. 'I'll ask you again when I'm ready. I feel that you might have some original ideas, but it will be a while before I get to that stage. I've been shopping around for limestone to match the original structure and getting in touch with the kind of builders who could take on this sort of work, and have to admit that I'm finding it quite exciting.'

'I wish something as exciting would happen in my life,' she said with a twisted smile, and once again he found himself wanting to know more about her.

'Shall we make tracks?' he suggested before he started asking questions that she might not want to answer.

Laurel nodded and once again they walked side by side along the road that led back to the village, and said goodbye again at the gate of Glenside Lodge, but this time it wasn't so stilted.

'You are a good listener, Laurel,' he told her whimsically. 'I would never have thought so that day at the station when I offered you a lift, which only goes to show one shouldn't judge by first impressions.'

'Maybe so,' she agreed with the recklessness surfacing again, 'but my first impression of you hasn't changed.'

He faked a groan. 'That could be ominous.'

'It could be, yes, but it could also be the opposite.' And leaving him to make what he would of that she began to walk up the path, and on reaching the porch waved a casual goodbye.

Elaine's first hour at the surgery on Monday morning was spent with James, bringing herself up to date with surgery matters that had occurred while she'd been off, and at one point she asked, 'What did you think of Laurel?'

'Cool, composed—could be just what we want,' he replied, 'and the place where she was before doesn't take on inferior staff. We'll see how the interview goes this afternoon. By the way, I heard from Anna and Glenn over the weekend. They're coming back before Christmas and are going to settle permanently in Willowmere when they return, which I am delighted to hear.

'They were asking if there would be any vacant slots in the practice when they come back, which is why I only want someone temporary as practice nurse, so

Laurel would be perfect as she said that she would prefer that sort of arrangement.

'I've really missed Anna, and the children will be so happy to see her again, but Jess will still be their nanny.'

When David arrived back from his house calls James was returning from his at the same time and as the two men stood on the practice forecourt the senior partner said, 'Did you know that Elaine's niece is a trained nurse, David, previously hospital based like yourself?'

'Yes,' he replied, wondering what was coming next but having a good idea, 'though I only found out on Friday night when I went to have a meal with them.'

'I've asked her to come to the surgery this afternoon regarding taking her on as a temporary replacement for Beth and would like you to be present as I would welcome your input. Employing her would not be a major admin matter as it will only be for four months at the most, but you've seen more of her than I have, so do you think she would be right for us?'

'I can't say,' he said slowly. 'Laurel isn't the easiest person to get to know, yet I feel she could make a worthwhile contribution to the work here and although Elaine is her aunt she is also practice manager, and from what I've seen of her so far the efficient running of the practice is one of her top priorities.'

'You are quite right about that,' James agreed, 'so we'll play it as it comes.'

What next? David thought as he ate a solitary lunch in his consulting room. It seemed as if his curiosity regarding Laurel was going to be satisfied if she came to work at the surgery.

He was only just getting over the surprise of discovering she was a qualified nurse then she was being considered as a possible replacement for Beth.

When he went to the derelict house by the lake each night before turning in he kept expecting to see her there, but since Friday when they'd gone together there had been no sign of her, and each time he'd gone back to the cottage unaccountably disappointed.

He was standing by Reception when Laurel came through the main door of the surgery and her heart skipped a beat. She hadn't realised how much she'd wanted to see David again until that moment and here he was, smiling the smile that soothed her fractured nerve ends and making a pretence of being glad to see her, when all the time she felt he must be groaning inwardly at the thought of having her around the place all the time.

For his part David was noting that the high heels and the tights were back, but today they were matched by a black mini-skirted suit relieved by a white silk shirt.

All in all the outfit looked more fitting for an executive position than that of a practice nurse, but he wasn't to know that she'd dressed up more for him than the interview.

'So will I do?' she asked as she drew near.

His smile deepened and she felt her knees go weak. 'Yes, indeed,' he informed her, and ushered her into where James was waiting.

They were both attractive men, Laurel thought as she seated herself opposite the two doctors, but it was David who had her attention. She thought about him a lot, too much for her own good, but today it was business, not pleasure that she was there for.

This was her first move towards normality if there would ever be such a thing in her life again, and it had come from the unexpected source of a country practice in Cheshire. The last place she could ever have imagined herself working in at one time, but something like this was what she needed, small and friendly while doing nursing, the thing she loved best.

First, though, she had to convince those about to evaluate what she had to offer that she was up to it, and as calm descended upon her Laurel answered James's questions with a quiet confidence that David had to admire.

He would have admired it even more if he'd known the heartache that lay behind it. Laurel had thought she would never be able to face going back to nursing after what had happened, yet here she was, and it could only be the peace and tranquillity of Willowmere that was giving her the strength to be there.

David's first thought as she settled herself in front of them was that her gloves were missing, but for the moment Laurel's hands were tucked away behind a large handbag and he couldn't see much of them.

She was in control, he thought, calm and lucid. Yet she wasn't always like this. But James hadn't seen her when she'd first arrived and he was visibly impressed today. It was going to happen. Laurel was going to be working at the practice, temporarily maybe but there nevertheless.

'You can start immediately if you wish,' James told her after he'd offered her the position. 'Beth is keen to get away as soon as possible as they have much still to do before the delicatessen opens.'

'Yes,' she agreed and with a smile in David's direction, 'Elaine is going to have to get used to me cluttering up her working life as well as her home.'

'I don't think she'll mind too much,' he told her. 'After all, it was she who recommended you.'

'Which reminds me,' James said, 'if you ask her she she'll sort out your uniform for you. Unless you've still got the one from your previous position and would rather wear that.'

'No,' she said flatly. 'I haven't still got it.' With the comment came the terrible memory of being told how they'd had to cut it off her.

When she was ready to leave Elaine was closeted with a medical rep so she wasn't able to tell her the result of the interview and David walked to the door with her.

'So what have you been up to since Friday?' he asked.

'Not a lot. Why do you ask?'

'I thought I might have seen you up by the lake over the weekend.'

'And I thought you might think I was getting in the way,' she flipped back breezily. There was no way she was going to tell him that she'd forced herself to stay away from the place that had caught her imagination because if she wasn't careful, the lake, the house and the man standing next to her were going to take over her life...

'That sounds like an excuse.'

'Maybe it is, but does it matter?'

'Yes, it does. Why can't we be friends?'

She didn't want to be his friend, Laurel thought. She wanted to be more than that, but there was no way it was going to happen. Darius had shattered her confidence in her desirability just when she'd needed to find it again and as she met David's steady blue gaze she said, 'I already count you as a friend. How do you see me? As some sort of lame duck maybe who needs helping to the water?'

'Is that what you think?' he said in a low voice for her ears alone. 'I'm concerned about you, yes, but that's all. OK, you had a fall and injured your knee quite badly from what you say, but does that stop us from getting to know each other?'

He'd opened the door and now they were out on the forecourt of the surgery and she said, 'Yes, I had a fall and sustained a tricky fracture. I just wish that was all.'

'So what else is there?'

'Again, does it matter?'

'Yes, it does,' he told her for a second time, and thought it mattered a lot but he wasn't sure why.

'I'll see you tomorrow,' she said, clutching her bag to her, and he saw her hands. They looked red and rough, standing out against the rest of her pale, smooth skin.

Laurel had seen where his glance was and said abruptly, 'I haven't got anything catching.'

'I'm sure you haven't,' he said patiently, and thought, *You might not have, but I think I have and it isn't because I'm on the rebound.*

'I'm going,' she announced, breaking into his

thoughts. 'I'll see you in the morning, David. It's like a dream. I can't believe it, me Laurel Maddox, working in a country practice.'

He was smiling, his annoyance gone, 'Yes, indeed. I'm not sure which of us is the more surprised.'

She was good, David thought the next morning as he watched Laurel change the dressing on the leg of a tearful small boy. Her touch was deft and gentle, her manner reassuring, and by the time she'd finished smiles had replaced the tears.

It was the same later when he took a worried fifty-year-old farmer to the nurses' room for blood tests, having found changes in his prostate gland.

The other two nurses had gone for a break and it was Laurel who greeted John Price. He was a nervy type and almost before he'd closed the door behind him was voicing his fears. As David was about to return to his consulting room he stopped in mid-stride when he heard her say, 'I've worked on a men's surgical ward, Mr Price, and there are other problems besides cancer that can affect the prostate gland. So let's just take some blood, shall we, and see what our friends in the path lab come up with, and while we're waiting for the results put your fears to one side. Time enough to worry when there is something to worry about.'

David was smiling as he went to greet his next patient. Laurel had seemed alien in the dark blue nurse's uniform when she'd first presented herself, but she was settling in like a natural.

He was used to seeing her in high-necked jumpers

and buttoned-up cardigans, but as the morning progressed he was adjusting to the new image and liking what he saw, while Elaine was looking less anxious by the moment as Laurel slotted herself into the routine of the surgery.

It was Beth's last day. She was taking advantage of the chance to finish sooner than she'd expected and was only too pleased to welcome Laurel into the slot that she was leaving.

Gillian Jarvis, the other practice nurse, was also happy to have her there as it meant that she wasn't going to be coping alone when Beth had gone, and as Laurel looked, listened and learned, the new nurse felt the adrenaline start to flow.

She was acutely aware of David every time he appeared in her line of vision. When on one occasion he handed her the notes of a patient requiring a spirometry test with a hand that was protruding from the cuff of a smart white shirt, she was reminded of that day at the station when he'd lifted her luggage out onto the platform and then helped her off the train.

She'd thought then that he seemed out of place in the rural backwater where Elaine lived, but that impression was long gone. He fitted in perfectly, which was more than she was expecting for herself.

That occasion was a memory that kept coming back and when it did she cringed at the thought of what she'd been like. Did he still see her as the sort of useless creature she'd appeared then? If he did, this was her chance to show him that she wasn't.

'So how's it going?' he asked in the lull between surgeries and house calls. 'It must seem very different to hospital work. Did you not have any yearnings to go back on the wards? If you had wanted to, we have a big hospital not far from here called St Gabriel's.'

'I miss the bustle and thrust of hospital life,' she told him, 'but I'm really enjoying the change. The job satisfaction is great because it is so friendly and rewarding to be providing health care to people who say hello to you on the street and in the pub. It bridges the gap between doctor and patient.'

I wish I could be my natural self and bridge the gap between us, Laurel thought, but the chances of that were remote. David had just asked her if she wanted to go back to hospital nursing and could not be expected to know that the question had touched a very raw nerve.

'Working here is fine for now,' she told him, 'and by the time Dr Bartlett's sister comes back, I might have some clear idea of where I'm heading.'

'So why not join me for a drink in The Pheasant this evening to celebrate your first day in the village practice?'

There was silence for a moment as common sense battled with the longing to be with someone who actually wanted her company. David had already said he'd missed her at the ruins by the lake and now he wanted to take her for a drink. Could it be that he really wanted to be with her, or was he trying to be nice because for some reason he sensed her inner misery?

With colour rising, she said, 'Er, yes, all right. What time shall I be there?'

'I'll come for you in the car,' he said. 'You could be feeling the effects of your first day here by then.'

His consideration for her well-being brought a lump to her throat. Could it be that David guessed that as well as frailty of mind she also had frailty of body?

At that moment one of the receptionists called to him from the doorway. 'There's a firm of builders on the line wanting to speak to you, Dr Trelawney.'

As he took the phone from her, he said, 'I'll come for you about eightish, Laurel, if that's all right.'

She nodded and left him to take the call and for the rest of the day the evening ahead beckoned like a bright star on the horizon.

CHAPTER FOUR

WHEN DAVID RANG THE bell at Glenside Lodge that evening there was no answer, and his first thought was that Laurel had changed her mind. But if that was the case he would have expected her to let him know beforehand. Where was Elaine? Had they gone somewhere together maybe?

The door was unlatched and he pushed it open a few inches and called, 'Hello, anyone at home?' But there was still no sign of life and with sudden anxiety on their behalf he stepped inside and walked slowly towards the sitting room where he had laid Laurel on the sofa on the day of their first meeting.

It was as if the clock had been turned back. There she was again, curled up asleep with one hand pressed against her cheek and the other lying limply by her side, but this time there was nothing outlandish about her attire. She was wearing a long fluffy robe that covered everything except her feet.

Of Elaine there was no sign and remembering that he'd seen cars outside the village hall as he'd driven past he recalled her mentioning during the day that there was a meeting of the Summer Fayre committee planned for that evening.

As he stood looking down at Laurel he thought how defenceless she looked curled up on the sofa. It seemed as if her first day at the practice *had* taken it out of her and he wondered once again what it was with her.

The rough hands and short red-gold hair had a message for anyone involved in health care and yet she wasn't divulging anything regarding them and why should she? he thought. They were her affair and hers only, but he did wish she would let him share whatever the burden she carried might be. She was a mixture of many things, amongst them strong and positive one moment and the next frail and vulnerable.

She'd been adamant that the fractured knee was in the past and she seemed to walk normally, but was there something else, a more serious cause for concern right here in the present? He supposed he could ask Elaine what ailed her niece and could imagine the practice manager's expression chilling at what she would see as an intrusion into Laurel's life.

He pulled up a chair, settled himself beside her, and waited for her to wake up, but she slept on and the sun was setting on the horizon in the summer night when she sobbed in her sleep and lifted the arm that was lying beside her in a defensive movement.

In the same moment her eyes opened wide. 'Oh, no!' she groaned. 'How long have you been here, David? I am so sorry. I'd just had a shower, lay against the cushions for a moment and...'

He was smiling down at her, concealing his dismay

at her distress before she'd woken up. 'Don't apologise. You are so much less complicated when you're asleep.'

'And also less reliable, it would seem.' She was raising herself to a sitting position and was pulling the robe around her more tightly as she asked drowsily, 'Is it too late to go to the pub?'

'Not if you want to. Or we can stay here if you don't feel up to it. Where is Elaine, by the way?'

'She's at a meeting. If she'd been here she wouldn't have let me fall asleep so soundly,' she informed him, with the memory of her aunt's delight when she'd told her that she was going to The Pheasant with David.

'We are only having a drink together,' she'd protested, and had thought that after Darius she'd intended steering clear of relationships until she'd got her confidence back regarding her appearance. But out of the blue had come David and she could not stop thinking about him.

'Yes, well, enjoy your evening,' Elaine had said gently.

She was sliding her feet off the edge of the sofa and once she was in a standing position said, 'If you don't mind waiting a few moments while I get dressed, we'll stick to plan A—a drink at The Pheasant.'

It would be easy to suggest they stay where they were and to let the robe fall off her shoulders so that the damage to the smooth pale skin was visible. It would be one way of telling David why she wasn't always as happy as she would like to be.

He was a doctor and would have seen things a lot worse than the state of her back and shoulders, but not in this sort of situation would he have seen them. Once she'd done something like that it wouldn't be the same afterwards, no matter how he reacted. It could destroy the fine shoots of their blossoming relationship, so a drink at the pub was the safest option.

'Fine,' he was saying easily. 'I'll pick the car up in the morning before surgery. I don't mind what we do and once we've had a drink, if you feel rested enough we could go for my usual walk to the house of my dreams— or nightmares as the case may be. What do you say?'

'I say yes,' she agreed, and climbed the stairs quickly before the voice of reason said its piece.

She came down dressed in smart jeans, long boots, a pretty top and the inevitable cardigan and said, 'Let's go and forget about everything except that it's a mellow summer night and we are alive to see it!'

'You're on.' He smiled at her enthusiasm. 'I'll drink to that when we get to The Pheasant, but a couple of questions first.'

'Yes?'

'What are these things that we are going to forget? And obviously, we're glad to be alive—why wouldn't we be?'

'I was meaning such things as sick people and builder's quotes,' she said airily, 'and shouldn't we always be glad to be alive? I know that I am.'

Some of us are more grateful for it than others, she thought with the nightmare grimly remembered of the days and weeks after it happened when pain had been the enemy, and even as it had lessened she'd dreaded what lay ahead, feeling that there would never be any brightness in her life again.

But that was past, she was rebuilding her life in a new

place, with a new job to look forward to, *and* she'd met a new man. What would he say if she told him that being alive was something to be everlastingly grateful for when one had been so close to eternity?

By the time they arrived at the pub the moment of looking back had passed and as locals in The Pheasant smiled across at the two most recent newcomers to the village and others eyed them with mild curiosity, Laurel began to relax.

Maybe it was the friendliness in the atmosphere, she thought as farmers chatted to each other about their crops and parents about their children. When the landlord called time it wouldn't be a case of trying to flag down a taxi or going for the tube.

For most of them it would be a leisurely walk home, with the nearest of the two rivers that met beside Water Meetings House bustling along beside them, or taking a path alongside fields of ripening corn. For those in the limestone cottages scattered around the main street and on the lanes leading from it, there would be just a short stroll to the homes they held dear.

David was observing her thoughtfully and she wondered what was going on behind his steady gaze. She hoped he wasn't going to start asking questions that she didn't want to answer.

He did have a question, but thankfully it was one that she could cope with.

'So how did you enjoy your first day in the village practice, Nurse Maddox?' he asked. 'Was it up to expectations?'

'Yes, it was, Dr Trelawney,' she said with a smile. 'It wasn't until today that I realised just how much I was missing nursing.'

His next question was not so easily answered. 'So why did you leave it?'

'Circumstances,' she said in a low voice as clouds appeared on her horizon. He was unwittingly taking away the tranquillity that had wrapped itself around her while they'd been together, and before he said anything else she told him flatly, 'They are on the list of things that I want to forget about, so if you don't mind...'

'Sure,' he said levelly. 'Message received and understood. Shall we move on to plan B and take the walk to you-know-where?'

Laurel hesitated. She wanted to be out there with him, just the two of them in the warm darkness, but then what? If David came near her she would melt and another nightmare would have been born. This time of the senses, rather than the body that she sometimes felt was no longer hers.

She'd agreed when he first suggested it because she'd felt as if she'd needed to be near him as she needed to breathe, but she was aware that he saw her as an oddity and it was the last thing she wanted to be to him.

They'd known each other for only a short time, yet it was as if she'd always been waiting for him to come into her life. But why couldn't it have been before her world had come crashing down?

'I think I'll give it a miss if you don't mind,' she told him. 'I *am* rather tired still and I want to be at my brightest and best for my second day at the surgery.'

'Fine,' he agreed equably. 'In fact, I might do the same this once. Sometimes it can be frustrating only being able to stand and stare. The solicitor is pushing ahead with the sale and the builder I've appointed is raring to get started, but until the land and the house are legally mine there is nothing he can do. So I'll see you safely home and we'll call it a day, shall we?'

Laurel didn't want to be alone with him, he thought as they walked back in silence to Glenside Lodge. She'd been keen enough before, but the moment he'd asked why she'd left nursing she'd clammed up. If it was always going to be like this, what was the point of trying to get to know her?

He saw that Elaine wasn't back as they walked the last few yards to the gate and loath to let the evening finish on such a flat note he broke the silence by asking casually, 'Have *you* ever been in a serious relationship like I was, Laurel?'

He knew he was probably going to make matters worse by asking, but they couldn't deteriorate much further.

'Yes, I have,' she replied, 'but it is well and truly in the past, and before you ask yet another question, it ended because the man involved had lost interest. I didn't come up to scratch.'

He could see her face in the light of the lamp by the gate and was aghast to see her eyes bright with tears.

He took a step towards her and with arms outstretched said softly, 'Come here. The last thing I intended was to make you cry. Let me hold you for a moment.'

'No!' she cried, pushing him away.

'Why ever not?' he asked as his arms fell to his sides.

'I might get to like it and I don't want that to happen. I changed my mind about going to your house with you for the same reason.' As he stared at her in amazed dismay she ran up the path and into the house, closing the door behind her with a dismissive click.

Why couldn't he have let well alone? David thought sombrely as he crossed the village green to where the rented cottage stood small and compact. No wonder Laurel had wept if she'd been dumped by some moron who couldn't see any further than the end of his nose.

Yet it wasn't so long ago that he'd decided that she was the last woman *he* would ever be attracted to and it hadn't changed...or had it? If the number of times he thought about her was anything to go by, it had.

He was captivated by her mood swings, and by the frailty that was sometimes there, while at other times, as in her nurse's role, she was capable and energetic...

Cool it, he told himself as he stripped off and went to switch on the shower. *If you hadn't become involved with Laurel that day at the station you wouldn't have given her a second glance.*

So she's had an engagement that turned sour too. You can identify with that, but now leave it, get her out of your mind. Laurel has Elaine to look after her. It isn't as if she's on her own, and what you are doing borders on interference.

You have your answer now. She's been hurt by some guy and is wary of it happening again, and an accident where she fractured her knee badly at some time or other won't have helped.

* * *

When she'd closed the door behind her Laurel had stood without moving. There was perspiration on her brow and it wasn't due to the warm night or the sprint she'd done up the path.

To have stepped into David's arms would have been so easy, but the reasons for not doing so had been so clear in her mind that she'd made a scene instead of tactfully sidestepping the moment, which would then have passed off smoothly enough.

But there'd been the knowledge that they were on two different wavelengths to keep in mind. David saw her as some sort of mixed-up nurse-cum-city type who was as prickly as a hedgehog. To her he was like all her dreams come true and she'd nearly let him see how she was beginning to feel about him.

He'd probably gone home feeling totally embarrassed about the way she'd responded to what had been just a comforting gesture, but if he ever got the full picture of how she was beginning to feel about him it would take away what little confidence she had left since being disfigured, and she couldn't afford to go back to how she'd been then.

She'd ignored the voice of common sense by allowing herself to be committed to being with him every day at the surgery and if that wasn't a prescription for heartache she didn't know what was.

When she heard Elaine come in she pretended to be asleep because the first thing she'd want to know would be how she'd enjoyed her evening with David. She would feel better equipped to answer the question over breakfast when she was feeling less fraught.

* * *

As it turned out, it was a comment about David's car still being on the drive that was the first thing Elaine said the next morning. It had been there when she'd returned from the meeting and she'd expected to find him inside, but he hadn't been and Laurel had been fast asleep when she'd had a peep into her room. So he was going to have to come and pick it up before the day got under way.

'When did David say he was coming to get the car?' she asked.

'Some time before surgery,' Laurel said disinterestedly, and waited for what was going to come next, but Elaine felt she didn't need to ask. There was a glumness about her that told its own tale and maybe later in the day Laurel would feel like talking about it, but clearly not now.

As Laurel buttoned up her uniform in preparation for the day ahead, she heard his voice downstairs, mingling with Elaine's lighter tones, and she cringed at the thought of coming face-to-face with him at the surgery after her exhibition of the night before.

The morning was well under way before she saw him. He was dealing with both lots of patients because James had taken time off to go to the end-of-year concert at the village school.

Soon the twins would be on the long summer break and Helen, his housekeeper, and Jess, their nanny, would be kept busy keeping them fed and occupied.

The children both had speaking parts in the play that their class was presenting to mothers, fathers and other relatives, and while James had no qualms about

Pollyanna's performance, he knew that Jolyon's was another matter.

A more serious child than his sister, he didn't have much to say, but when he did the words issuing forth weren't the usual childish chatter and his father wasn't sure how he was going to perform on stage.

It was at times like these that he felt inadequate. The twins missed having their mother around, but the years came and went and he always managed to cope somehow. He didn't think he would ever find anyone to replace Julie but, then, he'd never tried to.

With James absent, Laurel saw David just twice during the morning when he came to the nurses' room to discuss the requirements of patients.

The first one was elderly Sarah Wilkinson and instead of asking her to wait on the chairs in the corridor he ushered her in personally and told the two nurses, 'Mrs Wilkinson needs some blood tests and I think we'd better have the full monty. I told her we would send someone to her home to take the bloods, but she is determined to save us time and has come to the surgery.'

The sprightly octogenarian was smiling as she told them, 'The doctor here is going to have the first waltz with me at the party on the night before the Summer Fayre, so I want to make sure I'm fit. I've told him that there'll be a queue wanting to dance with him when it gets around that he's going to be there.'

'I doubt it,' he told her with a wry smile. 'I'm not the flavour of the month in some quarters.'

That was one for her, Laurel thought, *and how wrong he was.*

An hour later he appeared again and this time she was alone, but as if the formal approach was still the order of the day he said briskly, 'There's a patient waiting outside, Laurel. He's come from a building site where they're doing demolition work and has an abscess on his forearm. It isn't bad enough to require hospital treatment, but it needs to be lanced. I'll leave him with you.'

'Yes, David,' she said with a similar lack of warmth, and then, in the pleasure of being in his company again, put to one side her decision to stay aloof and said teasingly, 'Not *your* demolition site by any chance, is it?'

'Are you referring to the one that you turned me into last night? Or the ruins by the lake?' he asked dryly. 'If it's Water Meetings House that you are speaking of, I wish it was, but as you well know I'm still waiting for the sale to go through.'

Leaving her feeling as if she'd been well and truly put in her place, he opened the door and called to the man seated outside, 'You can come through, Mr Peterson. Nurse is going to lance the abscess and put a dressing on it, and don't forget to take the antibiotics I've prescribed. Make an appointment to see me again in a few days' time before you leave the surgery.' The grime-covered building worker nodded and David went back to deal with the rest of those waiting to consult him.

How could Laurel be so flip? he thought as he waited for his next patient. A rapport had been developing between them, but last night it had disappeared in the strangest of moments and he was amazed at the hurt he felt at the way she'd rejected his offer of comfort.

James was back by lunchtime looking somewhat frazzled, though he was laughing as he told them how Jolyon had altered his lines in the play to his own version and refused to budge until the teachers had agreed he could.

'And the joke of it was that his was better than theirs,' he said. 'I did get a bit hot under the collar at the time, but Jess, who'd gone with me, was in stitches.'

While Laurel and Elaine were having a quick bite before afternoon surgery the practice manager said, 'You haven't told me how you enjoyed last night. Did you have a nice time with David?'

Laurel sighed. 'I did at first, but he asked if I'd ever had a serious relationship. I told him the basic details about Darius and made a fool of myself at the same time by weeping.'

'I think you could be forgiven for that,' Elaine said consolingly.

Having no wish to tell Elaine what had happened afterwards, she said lightly, 'I left David at the gate and went straight to bed.'

'He came for his car this morning while you were upstairs getting ready. Did you see him?'

Laurel shook her head. 'No. I heard your voices but was in the middle of getting dressed. He's been giving me the impersonal treatment all morning, which is fine as I keep telling myself that is how I should be with him.

But it isn't easy. After the Darius episode, and remembering my deficiencies, I know I shouldn't get any closer to him if I don't want to get hurt.'

'We are not talking about your actor friend now,' her aunt protested. 'David Trelawney is in a different class. He has integrity *and* compassion.'

'I didn't say he hadn't, but it isn't pity I'm looking for. I had lots of that when it happened and I'm not complaining. People were lovely, and their sympathy helped to get me through it, but when it comes to the crunch it's up to me now and I'm a mass of uncertainties.'

It was there that the discussion ended. The two doctors had gone on their calls, the surgery would soon be filling up with the second session of the day, and their separate functions awaited them.

As the summer evenings passed Laurel didn't go to the house by the lake any more. She felt that if she did it would contradict the way she was behaving towards David at the surgery.

When it came to health care they admired each other's application to the job, and as she absorbed herself into the routines and demands of the practice Laurel would have been content if there wasn't always a reminder of past happenings to take the edge off everything.

Because of that she was anxious to avoid any more incidents like the one where he'd wanted to offer comfort and she'd pushed him away, and it seemed as if David was only too keen to do likewise.

Yet he hadn't been able to resist mentioning that the sale had gone through, the stone had been delivered, and the builder was already on the job, and he'd been so upbeat about it she'd decided that she was flattering herself by expecting their faltering friendship to be casting any gloom in *his* life.

But what he'd said had made her curious, and one night in July she weakened and went to see for herself what was happening at the house by the lake at a much earlier time than when she'd gone before.

It was still daylight and she gasped with pleasure at the sight before her when she arrived at the building site. The walls were half-up, beautiful new limestone was rising out of the ruins, and she understood how David must have felt when he'd stood in front of what was left of his mother's old home and known that it was going to be his.

She was experiencing a similar sensation herself and so much for that, she thought as she turned away and began to walk slowly back to the village. It wasn't just wishing for the moon. It was wishing for the sun, moon and stars all rolled into one.

When she arrived back at Glenside Lodge David's car was on the drive, and when she went inside he was in the sitting room with Elaine.

'I was passing, Elaine was in the garden, and she invited me in for a coffee,' he said, as if he felt he had to explain his presence.

'So where did you go for your walk?' Elaine asked as she passed her a cup of the steaming brew.

'Oh, here and there,' she said vaguely.

'Not to the lake, then?' David asked casually.

'Yes, I went to the lake,' she said steadily.

'And?'

Knowing how dear the renovating of the house was to his heart she couldn't pretend that she hadn't gone that little bit further to where the building site was, and she told him, 'It's going to look fantastic. The stone that you're using is beautiful, so natural looking and enduring.'

His expression softened and Laurel thought if anyone had told her a month ago that she would be going into raptures over the rebuilding of a derelict property in the middle of a field miles from anywhere she would have laughed in their face. But that was what she was doing and it was all because of the man sitting opposite.

Elaine was about to leave them. 'The last meeting to arrange the party this coming Friday and the Summer Fayre on the Saturday is taking place tonight,' she explained, 'and I need to be there. So I'm going to have to leave you.'

When she'd gone there was silence for a moment and then David asked, 'So are we friends again, Laurel?' and for the life of her she couldn't say no.

'Yes, I suppose so,' she told him awkwardly, without meeting his glance. 'I've felt such a fool after the way I behaved that night.'

He shook his head. 'You mustn't. It was clear that the hurt in you that I'm always aware of comes from your broken engagement. That it must have upset you much more than mine did me and I will respect that, but it doesn't need to come between *us*…does it?'

She was looking down at the carpet as if the pattern on it had her mesmerised. So David thought he had her moods sussed. He wasn't to know it was something much bigger than being dumped by Darius that had blighted her life, even though it had been he who had delivered the final blow. But for the moment the easy way out seemed to be to let him carry on thinking that she wasn't over the break-up.

'No, it doesn't,' she told him, 'and, David, I'd love to be involved in helping you build your house…if you would let me.'

'Of course I will,' he assured her, his expression brightening. 'Didn't I say right at the beginning I would welcome your input? And by the way, are you going to the party in the park on Friday?'

'I wasn't going to but Elaine is insisting that I do so, yes, I'll be there.'

'So once I've done my duty with Mrs Wilkinson perhaps we could get together, us being the two newcomers to the village.'

'Mmm. Why not?' she agreed, and immediately wondered what she had in eveningwear that would cover her shoulders. It wouldn't have to be something skimpy and strappy like she'd always worn before, and thank goodness her hair was growing nicely again.

At that moment she wasn't to know that before Friday an occasion would arise requiring a united front from them, and it would have an appeal all of its own.

On the Thursday night they were the last two out of the practice. Gillian, the other nurse, had rung in sick and James had gone early because it was the twins' birthday and Jess and Helen had organised a special birthday tea.

They would be having a party for their friends on the

Saturday when he was free, but the two women who doted on them wanted to celebrate the actual day with them.

The last patient had left with the receptionists not far behind and Elaine had gone to keep a dental appointment, which left the two of them to clear away and lock up.

It was as they were about to shut the outer door and leave the premises that a man came running out of one of the cottages opposite in a panic. Seeing them, he shouted, 'My wife is pregnant! The baby wasn't due for two weeks but it's coming now. I can see its head!'

Even as he was speaking they were sprinting towards him. Turning, he led the way into a sitting room where a heavily pregnant woman was lying on a couch in a state of advanced labour.

'I can't hang on!' she screamed between contractions. 'I've got to push.'

'OK, Sharon,' David said reassuringly as he examined her. 'But I need to ask you to just hang on for a couple of seconds. I'll tell you when it's the right moment.'

Laurel was holding Sharon's hand and phoning for an ambulance at the same time, while her husband stood by looking as if he was going to collapse.

'Get a clean towel ready,' she told him to keep him occupied, 'and a bowl of warm water.'

The woman cried out again and David said in a low voice, 'She's been coming to the antenatal clinic at the surgery. Her name is Sharon Simpson. It's not her first, so that could be the reason for the speed with which the baby is arriving. She changed her mind about having it at home, and just after I joined the practice she transferred to the maternity clinic at St Gabriel's, so you won't have seen her before.'

He bent to check on progress again and then said urgently, 'Right, Sharon, now you can push.' As she obeyed with an almighty shout, they heard the first cry of the newborn as David gently eased it into the world.

'You have a daughter,' he told them as the man put down the bowl he was carrying and rushed to his wife's side, and as David carefully lifted the child for her to see, Laurel was there with the towel to wrap the baby in before he placed the little one in her mother's arms.

'Lizzie Carmichael was going to deliver my baby,' Sharon said as she looked down at her new daughter. 'She'll be disappointed when she finds out that she's missed the birth because this young miss was in such a hurry.'

'Or relieved that it's just one job less,' the happy father commented whimsically, touching his tiny daughter's face reverently.

'Not Lizzie!' Sharon protested gently, looking up tenderly at her husband. 'She loves what she does.'

'You were fantastic in there,' Laurel told David as they stood on the pavement afterwards and watched the ambulance drive off with mother, father and baby on board.

'Not really,' he protested laughingly. 'I've done quite a bit of gynaecology and obstetrics in my time, but not usually in such cramped surroundings. And what would I have done without *you* there?'

'Managed very well, I would say,' she said dryly, not

wanting him to guess how much it had meant, the two of them being there together at such a time.

He ignored that. 'All the excitement has given me an appetite. What about you? Do you fancy checking to see if the tourist trade has slackened off at Hollyhocks? It *is* climbing up to seven o'clock. Or will Elaine have made a meal?'

She shook her head, the red-gold of her hair catching the evening sunlight. 'Not tonight. She's had quite a lot of dental work done this afternoon and as she'd thought it would be, her mouth is sore. So either I go home and boil an egg, or take you up on your suggestion, and I'll give you two guesses which it's going to be.'

'Come on then,' he said, tucking her arm in his. 'Let's see if they've got anything left at the Tea Rooms.'

It so happened that they had, and as they relaxed in the cosy atmosphere of one of the most popular places in Willowmere, Laurel thought that she was asking for more heart-searching. Yet at that moment she didn't care because this was the first of three days that she and David were going to be around each other away from the surgery.

Tomorrow night was the party in the park, and on Saturday the villagers and the farming community would be combining their efforts at the Fayre, so what more could she ask?

One thing that she certainly wasn't going to dwell on was how she came to be getting so excited about country matters when in the past a movie or a nightclub had always been her scene.

CHAPTER FIVE

THE band was playing in the marquee in the park and as Laurel watched David performing a sedate waltz with Sarah Wilkinson, who was resplendent in dark blue brocade, the moment was taking hold of her.

There were lots of people there from the village and the surrounding countryside and there was an atmosphere of great good humour amongst them. Elaine was at the forefront of things as usual, smartly dressed as always in a long, strappy black dress that enhanced her fair colouring, and Beth and her husband had surfaced from the newly opened delicatessen.

Beth's daughter Jess, James's children's nanny, was there too with her boyfriend, but there was no sign of James himself, which Laurel thought was a shame. Yet she supposed that like most people the senior partner at the practice knew his own affairs best, though it was something she couldn't say for herself.

David had called for her and presented her with a corsage of orchids that went with her colouring perfectly. When she'd opened the door to him she'd seen that his glance had been on her outfit and had known that he was taking in the fact that she was not as well concealed as usual.

Anything strapless or low cut at the back would not have been suitable, but with the anticipation of the night ahead Laurel had chosen to wear a dress of dark green silk with cap sleeves and a short flared skirt, and the high heels were back.

He wasn't to know that the way she was dressed was another step towards the normality that she longed for, the freedom to be herself instead of the stranger that she had become during the long weeks of her recovery.

A sudden longing to tell him what it was all about had come over her as his glance had warmed at the sight of her, but it had been fleeting.

It would take more than a moment of admiration from him to make her lay her soul bare, or her shoulders for that matter. She sometimes dreamt that the scars had gone away, that she was whole again. Awakening to find that it was not so was heartbreaking.

Yet she was coping, mainly because she was learning to live one day at a time and by doing so was slowly getting some of her confidence back, the confidence that Darius had destroyed when he'd made it clear that he didn't want someone less than perfect.

The man who'd come to take her to the ball was playing a major role in the healing process, though he wasn't aware of it, and tonight she was happier than she'd been in a long time as she watched David escort Sarah to her seat when the music stopped.

As he changed direction and began to walk towards her with a smile that was for her alone she let the blissful moment wrap around her. As the band started to play the next number he raised her to her feet, and without betraying by word or glance that hers were not the softest hands he'd ever held David led her onto the dance floor.

It was a slow foxtrot, the most dreamy and romantic of ballroom dances, and this time Laurel thought she wasn't going to shy away from being held close in his arms. She was going to pretend that she had nothing to hide but her pride.

'Your perfume is like you,' David said as they glided around the floor with the short red-gold covering on her head resting beneath his chin. She smiled up at him, green eyes calm and untroubled for once.

'In what way?'

'Elusive. Hard to describe, but mind-blowing.'

She was aware that they were attracting curious glances from some of those there, the new nurse at the practice and the doctor who hadn't been there long himself so engrossed in each other, but she didn't care. Whatever life was like in the cold light of day, tonight was magical, and for the moment she wasn't going to think any further than that.

In the middle of the evening there was the unexpected appearance of Lord Derringham and his wife, who'd stopped by to make sure that all was satisfactory with the marquee that he'd provided, and as Laurel watched them chatting with Elaine and other members of the organising committee she thought that, wealthy though they may be, the Derringhams were very supportive of village life.

David and Laurel danced every dance and during any intervals dawdled outside with the scent of summer flowers all around them and trees festooned with fairy-lights twinkling like jewels beneath the night sky.

At the end of the last waltz Laurel sighed and David asked quizzically, 'Was that an expression of relief or regret?'

'I think you know the answer to that,' she said lightly. She could have said so much more that would have left him in no doubt about how much she'd enjoyed the ball and being with *him*. How the enchantment of it would stay in her heart forever.

But that would be running before she could walk. She had to move slowly in the new life that was opening up before her. She was not the catch of the century in anybody's eyes, far from it, and couldn't face the thought of being hurt again.

As they strolled home amongst the rest of the de-parting guests the centre of the village was full of noise and laughter, but by the time they reached Glenside Lodge there was just the two of them in the quiet night and as they stood at the gate once more David turned to face her and said softly, 'Are you going to run a mile if I kiss you?'

'No! Yes! I don't know!' she faltered, taking a backward step. 'Can't we just stay as we are?'

'What? In a situation where *I'm* never sure what you're going to do or say next, and *you* are happy for it to be that way?'

'Is that really how you see us?'

'How else?'

'It's been a lovely evening. Don't spoil it, David.'

'So are you still pining for the guy that you were engaged to?'

As *if,* she thought miserably and looked away, which brought forth a groan on his part.

'OK,' he said equably. 'Hurts of the heart are not as easily forgotten as some things, so let's change the subject.' Wanting to see her smiling again, he said whimsically, 'So are you any good at bricklaying?'

'Would you expect me to be?' she questioned lightly, relieved to be on safer ground.

'No. I was teasing.'

'My dad was in the building trade before he and my mum got hooked on travelling the world, and he would have liked me to show an interest as he'd always wanted a son, but I didn't want to risk breaking my nails. Why did you ask, though?'

'The builder I'm employing is short of bricklayers, or should I say stone-layers, but as I'm new to the area I couldn't help him on that, I'm afraid.'

'Ask Elaine or James,' she suggested. 'They know everyone around here. What about the fellow with the abscess that we treated? Did he ever come back for a follow-up visit? I wonder what *his* skills were.'

'I could find out, I suppose,' he said absently, 'but I do want the best, and it's late, Laurel. I'd better go.'

'Elaine hasn't come home yet,' she protested, reluctant for the night to end in spite of having behaved like a nervous virgin when he'd wanted to kiss her.

'She's on the committee, so will be helping with the clearing up afterwards, but that doesn't say she won't arrive any moment, so I'll say goodnight.' Their gazes met and he murmured, 'On second thoughts, I'm not leaving without this…'

Taken aback at his sudden change of mind, she didn't resist when he drew her into his arms. He kissed her lightly on the mouth and then putting her away from him said, 'That was merely to say goodnight, a less enthusiastic performance than I first had in mind, but better than nothing.'

With that comment he went, striding off into the darkness, leaving her drained from the mixture of emotions that the night had brought.

When he turned up at the Summer Fayre the next day David found Laurel serving soup and savouries to those strolling amongst the stalls and sideshows and looking anything but comfortable. She was dressed in a long black dress with a white apron and a white mob cap on her head, and when he stopped in front of the table that she was serving from and observed her laughingly she glowered at him.

'It's all right for you!' she muttered. 'Elaine talked me into this because the person who should have been on this stall had a family emergency that has prevented her from taking part.' She groaned. 'I'm supposed to be a serving wench.'

'You look really cute,' he told her, keeping a straight face, and she began to laugh. She'd wept after they'd separated the night before, tears of frustration and regret, but seeing him again in the light of another day was lifting her out of the doldrums.

'Can I offer you a bowl of mulligatawny soup, sir?' she asked, preening at him in the clothes of a bygone age from behind the table. 'It's the very thing to warm the cockles of your heart.'

'Yes, you can, wench,' he told her, his eyes dancing with laughter, 'though I can think of other ways of doing that which would be much more satisfying.'

Laurel gasped theatrically and tried to quell the spark of excitement she'd felt at his words. The queue for soup and savouries was growing and he said, 'Do you have a spare apron, plastic if possible, rather than starched white cotton?'

She pointed to a box in the corner and with ladle in hand said, 'Have a rummage in there.'

He found what he was looking for and within minutes was beside her, serving the soup while Laurel supplied the savouries.

There were smiles from those in the queue and one humorist shouted from the back, 'Can we get the flu jab while we're here?'

When the demand had slackened off they sat on stools beneath the awning that covered the stall and David said, 'When will you be free?'

'Someone is relieving me at two o'clock.'

'I'll circulate for a while, then,' he said, 'and when it's two o'clock I'll be waiting outside the refreshment tent.' She nodded, happy that they were friends again after their flat farewell of the night before.

As David went to explore the Fayre his thoughts were returning to the same moment as he wondered if 'waiting' described what lay ahead for him. Waiting for

Laurel to forget the past and its hurts, whatever they may be, and give *him* the chance to take care of her.

They'd stood side by side when Sarah had won first prize for her Madeira cake and a second rosette for her jam, and then wandered around the event that everyone had turned out for in full force.

It was clear to Laurel that this was a very special weekend for them and no one was going to miss it. Willowmere's tribute to rural living was 'times gone by,' which accounted for Laurel's attire.

As they moved amongst town criers, old-fashioned bobbies with handlebar moustaches and peasants, Laurel was amazed to see Lord Derringham amongst them, dressed appropriately as a country squire, and she said, 'I thought His Lordship wasn't seen in the village very often.'

'Me too,' David agreed absently, 'but it doesn't seem to be the case at the moment.'

He'd been trying to imagine Caroline at an event such as this and couldn't. In fact, he was having difficulty bringing her to mind at all since Laurel had come into his life.

Her thoughts were serious too, but very different. Soon she would have to take stock of what was happening to her, decide if she was really falling for David or was on the rebound, and she wasn't expecting it to be a difficult decision.

He was smiling across at her and she wished she'd met him before the thoughtlessness of others had made a mess of her life. Yet were she to be asked if she would do the same thing again, the answer would have to be yes. She'd chosen a career where the saving of life was the top priority whatever the circumstances.

David hadn't missed the fact that for the last few moments her thoughts had been far away, and if her expression had been anything to go by they hadn't been happy ones.

Yet he was not going to ask any more questions, even though he was curious to know why she dressed as she did. To keep probing was a sure means of putting the blight on their rekindling relationship. If it ever came to anything it would be because Laurel felt she trusted him enough to confide in him.

He'd wondered a few times if her obsession with covering herself up was because of something unsightly, like a regretted tattoo maybe, and had even let his thoughts run along more serious lines, such as domestic violence. Maybe she would open up to him when she was ready. He just hoped that day would eventually come.

When the Fayre was over Laurel and David walked Sarah home. They made her a cup of tea and settled her on the sofa with the prizes she'd won gracing a big oak sideboard, and turned their steps homewards.

He was going to ask her out to dinner when she'd changed out of her costume, and was about to voice the suggestion as his cottage came into sight. But the words hovered on his lips as he watched a taxi pull up outside the surgery, and of all people that he wasn't expecting to see, his father got out of it with a big suitcase and the morning paper tucked under his arm.

'I don't believe it!' he exclaimed. 'That's my dad. He never said he was coming!'

'I'll be on my way, then,' she said immediately. 'Enjoy yourself with your father, David. I'll see you on Monday at the surgery.'

'No, wait!' he protested, but she was moving swiftly in the direction of Glenside Lodge and his father was looking around him with interest as the taxi disappeared.

'You should have let me know you were coming,' he said delightedly as the two men hugged each other.

Jonas laughed. 'Why, so you could have hung the bunting out? It was a spur-of-the-moment thing. I suddenly knew I just had to see what you're doing with the house where your mother lived. How's it coming along?'

'Not as fast as I would like, I'm afraid. There seems to be a shortage of bricklayers. But let's go inside and I have to warn you, Dad, that my accommodation is not large. I have only the one bedroom.'

'Don't worry. I'll stay at the pub. Is it still The Pheasant?'

'Yes, it is, but are you sure? It feels rather inhospitable after you've come all this way.'

'Sure I'm sure,' he declared. 'I've come for the week and if there's anything I can do with regard to the rebuilding you have only to say the word. I'm not a bricklayer, but I'm no mean hand at dry stone walling.'

'You're on,' David told him. 'The walls around the site are in a dreadful state.'

'Lead me to them, then.'

'You won't be able to do much in a week, though,' he reminded him.

'We'll see. I can always come back again. Next time I'll close the cottage and leave one of my friends in charge of the boat so that I can stay longer. I can't believe what you're doing, rebuilding that house up by the lake. I can remember it as if it was yesterday, your grandmother telling me to wipe my feet before I stepped on her carpets. She always looked on me with a jaundiced eye when I went calling on your mother because I wasn't local.'

'There wasn't much of it left when I bought it,' David warned him. 'Just four crumbling walls in an overgrown field.'

'We'll soon have it shipshape,' Jonas promised. 'If nothing else, I'll be able to see to the perimeter walls.'

Instead of taking Laurel for a meal it was his father sitting opposite him in the small dining room of The Pheasant. The landlord had booked Jonas into a firststorey bedroom for a week and now he was absorbing all the sights and sounds of the place that he hadn't been near since he'd lost Rachel, David's mother. But the son so dear to his heart had changed all that, and here he was, back amongst the green fields of Cheshire.

'So are we going up to the house now?' Jonas asked when they'd finished their meal.

'Are you sure you want to after the long journey?' David questioned.

'Oh, yes, I want to.'

'Then, yes, by all means. I'll be keen to know what you think, but bear in mind the builder only started a couple of weeks ago. So far it's been a case of strengthening the foundations and laying the first few courses of the fresh stone before the damp course goes in.'

Laurel had showered and changed, had a sandwich and a mug of tea, and with Elaine still down at the village green supervising the clearing-up process was wondering how she was going to get the evening over with.

She'd been with David for hours at the Fayre and instead of being satisfied with that she was aching to see him again. But if he was going to be entertaining his unexpected guest and showing him around the place that he hadn't visited for thirty years or more, she could at least go and look at the building site and dream a little. There couldn't be any harm in that, and they wouldn't venture so far after his father's twelve-hour journey.

It was quiet and very still as she stood by the gate that led to the field, and on impulse she pulled it open and went on to the site where an assortment of window frames and door frames had already been delivered.

She was imagining where she would arrange everything if she lived there when she heard voices out on the lane and froze. It didn't take two guesses regarding who they belonged to, and she thought that David would think that he couldn't even show his father around the place without having her at his elbow.

'Hi,' he said as she turned slowly to face them, and to the man by his side he said, 'Laurel is a nurse at the surgery, Dad, and also my inspiration when it comes to this place.'

She was smiling as Jonas shook her hand, her composure returning as she said, 'I don't think David needed inspiring. He was captivated from the start, it being his mother's old home, and now I must be off. I do hope that you enjoy your stay, Mr Trelawney.'

'I intend to,' Jonas said with a smile for the man at his side, and when she'd gone with a low-voiced goodbye to his son, he said, 'So what's with Laurel of the lovely green eyes?'

David laughed. 'Nothing, Sherlock, nothing at all. You've just seen her in an upbeat mood, but she isn't always like that. There's a sadness about her sometimes that worries me.'

'So she isn't the one and only that I told you would come along one day?'

'I didn't say that.'

'No, you didn't, did you?' his father said dryly. 'Now, tell me what your plans are for Water Meetings House.'

Elaine was sitting with a glass of wine and her feet up when Laurel returned to Glenside Lodge, and she said, 'I thought maybe you were out with David.'

'No, he's got a visitor.'

'Who would that be?'

'His father, a hale and hearty Cornishman with white hair and blue eyes, has turned up unexpectedly.'

'Really!'

'Yes. I've just met him at the building site.' Before Elaine had any questions about David and herself, she asked, 'Has it been a successful day?'

'Very much so,' she replied. 'Those kind of things are hard work, but well worth it because the community spirit is always there, and I kept getting glimpses of two people who seemed to "commune" very well indeed.'

'You mean David and I?'

'Who else? So when are you going to tell him what it's all about?'

'I'm not. I can't! I do *not* want him feeling sorry for me, or alternatively beating a tactful retreat.'

'You aren't being fair to him, Laurel.'

'Do you think I don't know that?' she cried. 'I'm allowing myself a month and then...'

'What?' Elaine questioned gently.

'I don't know. I wish I did.'

'You've heard about the tangled web we weave when we practise to deceive, I take it?'

'Yes, I have,' she said flatly. 'And have you seen my back and shoulders recently?'

Elaine nodded. There was no answer to that.

On Monday morning at the surgery, the two nurses were busy with the mother-and-baby clinic when Sharon and her newborn daughter appeared.

'She's beautiful,' Laurel said as big eyes looked up at her out of a smooth little face when Sharon placed her on the scales.

'I will never forget how you and Dr Trelawney looked after me at the birth,' she said. 'Is he anywhere around?'

'I'll see if I can find him,' Laurel told her. 'If he's with a patient I can't disturb him. But if he's free I'm sure he'll be delighted to see you both. What have you called her?'

'Elsey. It was my mother's name but we've changed the spelling.'

David had just finished a consultation and was about

to buzz for the next patient when she found him, and when she said, 'A young lady called Elsey is here to see you,' he observed her questioningly. 'You can spare a moment, can't you?'

'Er, yes,' he said, coming from behind the desk. 'Is she a patient?'

'Yes. With big eyes and skin as soft as silk,' she told him. She glanced down at her hands and thought to herself, *Unlike some of us.*

He saw the glance but didn't comment, and followed her down the passage to where the nurses' room was. When he saw Sharon sitting there with the baby in her arms he gave a satisfied nod.

'So this is Elsey!' he exclaimed. 'How have you both been, Sharon?'

'Fine, Doctor,' she told him. 'She's on the breast and is a very contented child considering what a hurry she was in to be born. I've just been telling Laurel how grateful I am for the way you both appeared out of nowhere and took care of me. It was as if you read each other's minds. I don't know what I would have done if you hadn't been there.'

His smile was still in place as he said, 'Yes, there is the odd time when we are in tune, but not always to that extent.' He prepared to go back to his patients and said, 'Take care, Sharon. If you let us know when you're having the baby christened, we'll try and get to the service.'

'That would be lovely,' she said, 'but it will be a couple of months before we can have it as my husband's parents are coming from New Zealand and they can't get away until then.'

'That won't be a problem, will it?' he asked Laurel.

'No, I shouldn't think so,' she replied, and could hear herself telling Elaine that she was going to allow herself another month around David and then it would be decision time.

She could feel the web of deceit that Elaine had talked about clinging around her, and as David left them to get on with the clinic after sending a puzzled look in her direction, the day continued to take its course.

'What was it this morning with Sharon and the baby?' he asked as they were leaving at the end of the day. 'Don't you want to go to the christening, or was it because I spoke for both of us without consulting you first? It didn't occur to me that you might not want to go, and if that's the case I'm sorry.'

Of course she wanted to go. They'd been magical moments when they'd been there for the birth of little Elsey. It had been one more lovely thing to remember him by, but if she kept to her resolve she might not be in Willowmere in two months' time and once she'd gone she wouldn't be able to face coming back, even for something as lovely as a christening.

She managed a smile, unable to bear the thought of David feeling guilty over something that he wasn't aware of. 'No, it wasn't anything like that,' she assured him. 'You just took me by surprise, that's all.' Eager to change the subject, she asked, 'How is your dad getting on with the stone walling round the field?'

'Great. All his life he's vowed he would never leave Cornwall, but I'm starting to feel he might have a rethink once the house is finished. I might add on a grandad flat, just in case the day ever dawns when I have children. But after the Caroline fiasco I'm wary of making another error of judgement. Do you have those kind of feelings about your broken engagement?'

She wasn't going to get involved with any more half-truths, she decided, and told him, 'I keep telling myself that any errors of judgement were on his part.'

'I'm curious. Who was he?'

'An actor called Darius Symonds. He's in one of the soaps.'

'So he's a household name?'

'Not in my house,' she said flippantly, and it was true. David's was the only name she wanted to hear, wherever she might be.

'I'm going straight to the site,' he announced, relieved to hear that she wasn't moping over the Darius fellow as much as he'd thought. 'Dad's meeting me there with a picnic meal from the Hollyhocks. Would you like to join us?

'I told him to bring enough food for three on the off chance you might agree to be our guest. I don't know how you feel, but I'll be glad to get out into the fresh air for a few hours after being at the practice all day.

'I'm anxious to see how the work is progressing, needless to say, then I'm going to have a go at the gardens and I use the term loosely. They are full of wild flowers, weeds and shrubs out of control.'

'I'll help you,' she offered impulsively, and immediately thought she wasn't going to get David out of her mind by working with him on the garden of what was going to be a beautiful stone house by the lake. But she had come to love the place almost as much as he did, and that was a straight course to heartache if ever there was one.

'I'd love to share the picnic,' she told him, 'but will need to go and change out of my uniform first and let Elaine know I'll be eating out.'

'I've got my working clothes in the boot,' he explained, 'and it's great that you're coming, Laurel. It doesn't feel the same if you're not around when I'm at the house, what there is of it!'

The walls that Jonas had been working on were rising out of the piles of fallen stone on the ground, and when she arrived he said with a twinkle in his eye, 'So is it the gardening you've come to do, my dear?'

She laughed and he thought she was an odd-looking young woman but there was something about her that caught the imagination, and without being told he could tell that was how it was with his son, but whether she was going to be *the* one was something yet to be revealed.

'Yes,' she told him. 'Though how much use I'm going to be, I don't know.'

David had been sprawled on the grass, propped up on his elbow with a mug of tea in his hand when she arrived, but now he was standing beside her and saying, 'I thought of getting rid of all the vegetation that has gone haywire and maybe leaving the rest of it half wild with a lawn here and there, a couple of water features and a gazebo overlooking the lake. What do you think, Laurel?'

'I *think* you're making me envious,' she said lightly, 'but, yes, that sounds great. So lead me to the food and then I'll get cracking. As you can see, I'm dressed for the job in a pair of old dungarees belonging to Elaine and a past-its-best sweater, and have borrowed some gardening gloves off her.'

'Yes, by all means take care of your hands,' he said, giving her the chance to explain why they were as they were, but in keeping with the occasion it fell on stony ground and he went on to say, 'There will be lots of brambles out there.'

They worked until the sun was ready to set, with Jonas back on the erecting of the walls and Laurel and David clearing the overgrown garden. It was hot work, the ground was hard from years of neglect, and he went across to where she was pulling out brambles by the roots.

When she looked up he said, 'That's enough for now. It will soon be dark. Why don't the three of us finish the night off at the pub? I don't know about you but I could do with a long, cold drink.' Taking off his gardening gloves, he reached out towards her and rubbed a grimy mark off her cheek with gentle fingers.

'Not like this, I don't think,' she said softly as their glances locked. 'I'll have to go home, have a shower and change into some decent clothes.'

It was a timeless sort of moment, the two of them in the garden of his mother's home, both of them hot and grimy, yet so aware of each other it could have gone on and on.

But they were not alone. There was a third member of the working party and he was calling from the bottom of the field, 'So what now? Is that it for today?' Smiling wryly, David signalled for Jonas to down tools.

'We'll drop you off at Elaine's house, then Dad and

I will go and get cleaned up at my place and we'll pick you up in an hour, say?' he said as normality returned.

'Yes, all right,' she agreed, knowing that she should call it a day when they arrived at Glenside Lodge, instead of spending any more time with David. Why couldn't she be satisfied with being near him all day at the surgery and working side by side with him in what would one day be a beautiful garden?

CHAPTER SIX

WHEN David was dropping Laurel off at Glenside Lodge some minutes later he said, 'Why not see if Elaine wants to join us at The Pheasant if she's available?'

'Yes, of course,' she agreed, and as soon as she was inside put the question to her aunt who had just come in from weeding her own garden.

'I'd love to,' she said. 'For one thing I'd like to meet David's father. My dad used to have a boat when I was small and we used to go sailing on the Norfolk Broads with him at every opportunity, so we will have something to talk about. But like you I need to freshen up and change my clothes. So who's first for the shower?'

'Huh?' Laurel said absently. She was back at the site in her mind, helping to make David's dream come true, and feeling that, after those spellbound moments in the garden, if he should appear at that moment she would be able to face up to telling him what it was that lay so heavy on her heart.

If the opportunity came later in the evening she would grasp it and clear the air between them. For once she felt strong enough to unburden herself to him.

She knew that Elaine was of the opinion she should have done so long ago and that perhaps she was making too big a thing of what had happened to her on a quiet night in the men's ward.

But only she knew how ugly she felt when she saw the bright red eruptions on her back and shoulders and the tight, unsightly skin of her hands. She was no different from any other woman in wanting to be beautiful for the man she was falling in love with, but the pleasure was being denied her.

They were seated at a table for four in the beer garden at the back of The Pheasant and as Elaine and Jonas chatted nonstop about boats, Cornwall and the Norfolk Broads, David said in a low voice, 'Those two are getting on famously, aren't they?' He smiled at his silent companion. 'You are very quiet, though. Are you all right, Laurel?'

'Yes. I'm fine,' she told him, and wondered what he would say if she told him she was trying to decide how to tell him what had happened to her before she'd come to Willowmere.

The best idea was to suggest they go for a stroll and leave the others to their conversation, and she was about to suggest it when David said, 'I noticed Sarah Wilkinson in one of the rooms back there. I'm just going to say hello. I won't be long.'

When he'd gone, Laurel went into the bar to buy another round of drinks. As she was about to step out into the garden, balancing a tray of full glasses, she paused as she overheard Jonas say, 'I suppose you know that David was engaged to be married to an American woman before he came to work in Cheshire and he broke it off.'

'Er, yes, I do,' Elaine told him uncomfortably.

He sighed. 'I don't know the full story but break-ups are never easy, are they? She was very attractive and they made a striking couple. I can't help but worry about him. Do you really think he's happy with his life here?'

'Yes, I think David seems very happy here,' Elaine butted in quickly as Laurel arrived at the table, knowing she'd heard and that Jonas's casual comments would be like a slap in the face to her niece. It seemed that she was not wrong in that assumption.

'I'm sorry, but I've got to go. Say goodbye to David for me, will you?' Laurel said as she put the tray down. Elaine watched in dismay as she left the beer garden by a side gate and began to walk along the main street at a brisk pace.

Laurel brushed away stinging tears. If she'd had any doubts about what she'd intended to do, David's father in all innocence had just made it very clear that it would be a mistake, and her newfound confidence was disappearing like water down a drain.

When David came back to the table he said immediately, 'Where's Laurel?'

'Oh…she left,' Elaine said awkwardly.

'Why?'

'I'm not sure.. She looked tired so maybe she's decided to have an early night.'

'Without saying goodbye?'

'She asked us to say it for her.'

'Right, I see,' he said levelly, and thought nothing had changed. Laurel was still as unpredictable as when they'd first met and he was crazy to think he was beginning to understand her.

On a sudden impulse he said, 'Which way did she go?'

'Down the main street,' Elaine informed him.

'I need to make sure she's all right...don't I?' he questioned.

'Yes, you do,' she told him gravely.

When he'd gone striding off Jonas said wryly, 'And then there were two.' In a more serious manner he went on, 'Oh, dear. I didn't mean Laurel to hear me talking about Caroline. You must think I'm completely tactless. I did sense an affinity between my son and your niece.'

'Yes, you need have no doubts about that,' she told him flatly. 'But don't expect anything to come of it as far as Laurel is concerned.'

'Why not? She seems a sparky young lass.'

'Yes, she is, she has to be, and that is all I'm going to say.'

'So shall I redeem myself for spoiling the evening by walking you home before I turn in?'

'No,' she told him, managing a smile. 'It's still daylight and I've been doing my own thing for years. It's been great to meet you and hear all about life on the Cornish coast.'

Jonas flashed her a craggy smile as she departed in the opposite direction to the one that Laurel and David had taken, and commented to no one in particular, 'And then there was one.'

* * *

There was no sign of Laurel on the way to Glenside Lodge, which was not surprising as she'd had a few minutes' start on him, David thought as he drove to the old stone lodge at the end of the interminable drive that sloped up to the moors.

When he'd rung the doorbell several times and there was no answer he had to accept that either she didn't want to talk to him, had gone straight to bed and was already asleep, or she wasn't there, but if that was the case, where was she?

It was clear that in those few moments when he'd been chatting to Sarah something had upset Laurel and he hoped it wasn't something his father had said as Elaine would never do anything to cause her to leave so suddenly. With his hand on the gate latch, a thought struck him. Supposing she'd gone to the house? Yet surely it was the last place she would want to go to if it was his dad who had somehow put his foot in it.

One thing he knew, he had to make sure, and he drove off in the direction of the lake, relieved that he'd gone to pick up his car that he'd parked outside the cottage after giving Laurel and Elaine a lift to The Pheasant.

It was dark, lightless, with no moon shining in silver shafts between the willows tonight, and no slender figure standing where he'd found her on other occasions looking out over the building site. He turned the car round despondently and drove back to the village.

Laurel *had* gone home and when she'd let herself into the quiet house she'd gone straight up to her room and stood by the window looking down blankly onto the lane below.

She'd seen David drive up and come striding quickly along the path that led to the front door and had moved back out of sight, and each time he'd rung the doorbell she'd covered her ears with her hands.

She knew she should go down and apologise for the way she'd rushed off while he'd been talking to Sarah. It had been a selfish thing to do, making him suffer for her inadequacies, but she couldn't do it. Her legs wouldn't support her down the stairs.

Hidden in the bedroom she'd watched him leave and seen his momentary hesitation before he'd got back into the car and driven off in the direction of the lake, and the shame of causing him so much anxiety brought the use back to her legs.

She dashed down the stairs to flag him down, but was too late. All that could be seen were the taillights of the car driving off into the night.

In the absence of a war memorial in Willowmere a peace garden had been created by the locals and it formed an attractive centrepiece in the village. It was a circular arrangement made out of local stone and, whatever the season, was always a mass of flowers.

There was seating around it for anyone who wanted to stop and rest, and it was very popular with ramblers and others who visited the village or were stopping off en route to other parts of the Cheshire countryside.

It was only a short distance from where David lived and was always illuminated in the evenings once daylight had gone. It was as he drove the last few yards to the cottage that he saw her and relief washed over him.

Laurel was hunched on one of the benches that encircled the peace garden and when he stopped the car she got slowly to her feet.

He wound the window down and when she drew alongside asked levelly, 'So what's going on? You left the beer garden with not so much as a word. I was only chatting to Sarah for a matter of minutes. Surely you didn't object to that!'

'No, of course I didn't,' she said quickly, wondering what excuse she could come up with to avoid telling him that his father had made her even more aware of her shortcomings in those moments while he'd been gone.

'It was just that Elaine and your father were engrossed in their common interests, you had gone elsewhere, and I felt that I might as well leave you all to it and have an early night,' she explained in a low voice.

'And so why didn't you? If that was the case, what are you doing here? I've been chasing around looking for you like someone demented. You were happy enough before I went to speak to Sarah, so what went wrong in that short time, Laurel?'

'Nothing!' she cried. 'Will you please stop badgering me?'

'If the day ever dawns when I understand the workings of your mind there will be a flag flying over Willowmere,' he told her, still in the driver's seat, 'and now if you will get in the car I'll take you home.'

She obeyed without speaking and he drove to Glenside Lodge once more, this time with an easier mind because he'd found her, or more correctly she'd found him, but there was no joy in him.

Maybe he should ease off. Perhaps she felt suffocated by him. Yet she was the one who'd wanted to help with the garden, the one who was as interested as he was in the rebuilding of Water Meetings House.

But somewhere along the line she'd been hurt. He could sense it all the time and he didn't think it was just her broken engagement. She'd been in some kind of trauma that it seemed she didn't want to talk about and he had the choice of giving up on her or waiting until she was ready to open her heart to him.

She knew it was the moment to tell him where her hurts and fears lay, Laurel was thinking as he pulled up in front of the lodge, but she couldn't face it after the way his father had described his ex-fiancée. A striking couple he'd said they were, and a tear ran down her cheek at the thought.

As he switched off the engine David turned to observe her, saw it and, dismayed, fished a clean handkerchief out of his pocket. 'I can't bear to see you cry,' he said gently, wiping it away, 'especially when I'm responsible for your tears. Can you forgive me for being so unfeeling, Laurel?'

'I can forgive you anything and everything,' she told him on a sob, 'and in any case there's nothing to forgive.' She leaned over and kissed him fleetingly on the cheek. 'Good night, David.'

When he would have reached across for her she opened the car door, slid out of the passenger seat and said, 'I'll see you at the surgery in the morning.'

As she went quickly inside and closed the door after her, he thought wryly that her words of farewell were the only sure thing he could hold on to. He *would* see her tomorrow, and the day after, and the day after that, and would be thankful because he knew deep down that there was no way he could give up on Laurel.

Hard to understand or not, she had him enchanted and captivated, and he would just have to wait until she was ready to tell him what it was all about.

Elaine had returned and she said, 'I felt for you back there in the beer garden of The Pheasant. Jonas was upset after you'd gone. He didn't know you were there and realised he'd been rather tactless in bringing up the subject. It seems that he's picked up on the bond between David and yourself and I'm sure he would never have said what he did if he'd known what happened to you.'

'It doesn't matter anyway,' Laurel said flatly. 'I shouldn't have eavesdropped. But I was weakening—really he's done me a good turn.'

It wasn't true, of course. Jonas had inadvertently diminished her returning confidence.

After a brief greeting by Reception the next morning there was no time to talk even if Laurel and David had wanted to. The pollen count was high and quite a few asthma sufferers had arrived seeking relief. Added to that there was an incident in the waiting room when a toddler wandering around on wobbly legs toppled over and was knocked senseless as he hit his head on the side of a radiator.

The mother's horrified cries brought David forth from the middle of a consultation and Laurel flying out of the nurses' room to find patients crowding around mother and child and general chaos ensuing.

'Quiet, everyone,' he commanded as he bent over the stricken child, who was opening his eyes slowly and letting out a frightened wail.

'Don't try to move him,' he told his mother as she bent over him, 'not yet.'

The side of the toddler's head was beginning to come up in a soft, spongy swelling and both doctor and nurse were thinking the same thing—haematoma.

'So what's the situation?' the first of two paramedics asked when the ambulance pulled up outside the surgery where Laurel had gone to greet them.

'We have a small child who has fallen against the hard edge of a radiator and knocked himself unconscious for a few moments,' she said as she hurried them inside. 'There is swelling of the skull that needs checking out in case it's a haematoma.'

'What's that?' the anxious mother asked.

'Bleeding inside the head,' Laurel told her gently. 'It's just as a precaution, that's all.'

'Come on then, young fella,' the other paramedic said as they lifted the child carefully onto a stretcher, adding to his mother, 'They'll soon sort him out at St Gabriel's.'

'I do hope so,' she sobbed. 'I shouldn't have let go of him back there in the surgery. Oliver has only just started to walk and wants to do it all on his own. He doesn't like having to hold my hand.'

* * *

James hadn't been present during all the commotion. He'd driven up to the moors above the village in answer to an urgent request for a visit from one of the isolated farms up there and had arrived back at the surgery just as the ambulance was driving off at some speed, which meant that by the time he'd been put in the picture and helped David deal with the backlog that had arisen in the waiting room, it was lunchtime.

The delicatessen had opened officially that morning and when Laurel went across to buy a snack of some kind she found that David had done the same thing. When they'd been served and duly admired the new venture they walked back together in silence until he broke into it by saying, 'We're getting to be quite a good double act in a crisis, aren't we? First there was Sharon and the baby, then today little Oliver. I wonder what will be next.'

It was the last thing she was expecting him to say and she said the first thought that came into her head. 'Someone else's crisis maybe, but I'm not so good when it comes to my own.'

She'd coped with the emergency on the ward that night with speed and coolness, but the aftermath of it had become a personal crisis that went on and on. It wasn't going to go away, ever.

'Are you referring to a broken engagement?' he couldn't help asking.

'No, though that wasn't pleasant. You've been there yourself, haven't you? But at least you were the one who finished it. You weren't cast aside.'

'Not on the face of it maybe,' he replied. 'As for what

happened to you, sometimes there is no accounting for the stupidity of others. After my relationship with Caroline folded I decided to steer free of any other issues. That was until I met you, but having promised myself that nothing can be worse than making you cry, I'm staying on the sidelines, Laurel. Let me know if anything changes, will you?'

'So we are just going to be friends?' she said stiffly.

That made him smile. 'Yes, we are, Miss Prim. And would I be stepping out of line if I told you that your hair is looking very fetching?'

'No, not at all, I'll allow you that,' she replied, 'as long as you're not just saying it to make me feel better.'

He hadn't been wrong, he thought. It hadn't been a hairdresser who'd got carried away, and he'd seen her hands. Those two things were nothing to do with tattoos, but until she'd thrown off the protective clothing that she wore like a second skin he wasn't going to get any answers, and in the current state of their relationship that wasn't going to happen, not in his presence anyway.

When he'd eaten the salad he'd bought at the delicatessen David called in at The Pheasant to have a word with his father before he started his home visits, and discovered from the landlord that Jonas had gone to the building site once again. So it was a matter of having his anxieties of the night before brought back as he drove past the lake, though he didn't need any reminding.

'I don't usually see you at this time of day,' Jonas said when he pulled up on the overgrown drive of the house. 'Aren't there any sick people in Willowmere?'

'I'm only here for a moment,' he explained. 'I've

come to ask what you said to Laurel last night that made her get up and go.'

'You mean Elaine hasn't told you?'

'So you *did* say something, and what has Elaine got to do with it?'

'I didn't know Laurel was there—she'd gone to get more drinks. But I just mentioned that Caroline was attractive and how you'd made a striking couple. I also meant to say that she wasn't the right one for you, but Laurel was up and off. So I wasn't wrong when I thought there was something between the two of you.'

'Yes, well, for the record Laurel and I are just friends and that isn't going to change in the near future.'

'But you wish it would?'

'Yes, but she is a woman with a secret and until she's ready to tell me what it is, Dad, I'll settle for friendship.' He turned to set off. 'I'll see you about half six if you haven't already had enough.'

'I'll be here,' Jonas informed him stoutly, 'and I'm sorry for poking my nose into your affairs, lad. You know that your happiness means a lot to me.'

'Yes, but do please remember that I'm capable of sorting out my own life,' he said with a smile for the man who had been both mother and father to him for many years.

'Aye, I know,' Jonas replied, and ruffled his son's dark thatch with a soil-stained hand before turning back to his dry stone walling.

So had Laurel felt she was being found wanting in what his father had said? David wondered as he did the calls he'd set out to do. He hoped not, but the odds were that she had, and somehow, without actually putting it into words, he had to find a way to reassure her. It wasn't going to be easy as every time he tried to get closer to her she was on the defensive.

When he arrived back at the surgery she was chatting to Jess Jackson, the slender brown-haired girl who was nanny to James's children, and when she'd taken Pollyanna and Jolyon through to see their father Laurel said casually, 'Jess was asking me if I miss living in London.'

'And do you?'

'I did at first, but not now.'

Willowmere was casting its spell over her and so was he, but she wasn't going to tell him that. Instead she said, 'I'm going there for the day in a couple of weeks so it will be interesting to see if I have any yearnings.'

'Are you going for anything special?' he asked casually, breaking his promise to himself not to ask questions.

'I have an appointment to keep. Fortunately it's on a Saturday so I won't be missing from the practice at all. It will give me the chance to collect any mail that has been delivered to my apartment while I'm there. I've kept it on as it is always somewhere to go if I need a bolt-hole.'

'That is an odd thing to say. Why would you need somewhere to hide?' he asked quizzically. 'You haven't committed a crime, have you?'

'Not yet, and regarding it being an odd thing to say, I am an odd person, David. You've found that out already, haven't you?'

'Not odd, different maybe, but I like a challenge,' he

told her as the thought of her running back to London took his spirits down to zero.

When they'd both gone back to their respective functions in the practice Laurel wondered what he would have said if she'd told David it was a hospital appointment that she had to keep with the doctors who had done their best to repair her damaged skin.

They would decide if further grafts were necessary and if they were there might be no way of keeping her painful secret from David, but she would meet that problem when it came. If she had to be absent from the practice for a while maybe she could think of another reason for it, and then there was always the dismal alternative that she'd mentioned to Elaine, leaving Willowmere and moving back to London.

That evening she told Elaine that David knew she was going to London for the day and was curious why.

'And I don't suppose you satisfied his curiosity?' she said.

'Er...no...I didn't,' Laurel replied flatly. 'I said I had an appointment but didn't say where. After his father's description of the ex-fiancée I know I can't compete and have accepted it.'

Elaine shook her head despairingly. 'That doesn't sound like the gutsy girl who is the light of my life,' she protested. 'If you wanted David enough you would tell him what happened to you.'

'Don't you see it's because I'm so in love with him that I can't tell him?' she protested. 'When it happened I never thought that anyone would find me so unpleasant to look at as Darius did and that thought is going to stay with me always. In a weird kind of way I'm fortunate that all the scarring is where I can't see it. When I look in the mirror there is no sign of it. But that wouldn't apply to anyone I slept with, would it?'

There was only one answer to that, Elaine thought, and if Laurel would only give him the chance David Trelawney might provide it. *He* wasn't Darius.

Like others before it, the conversation wasn't getting them anywhere and on a lighter note she suggested, 'Why don't you go and give some help with the garden again on Saturday and when they've finished for the day invite David and his father back here for a barbecue? I'm sure the men would enjoy some freshly cooked food after their labours.'

'I suppose I could,' she replied with a dubious frown, 'but you know I'm no cook.'

'You'll be fine. It's just a matter of putting sausages, bacon and chicken drumsticks onto a hot grid and turning them over every so often. David will get the equipment working for you.'

'All right, I'll do it,' she said decisively. 'It's a nice idea just as long as it doesn't rain and Jonas is there to chaperon us so that I don't send out any wrong signals.'

He won't be there if I can help it, Elaine thought. She had plans for Jonas that would make him absent from the building site for most of the day on Saturday, leaving David and Laurel alone for a few hours.

There was a maritime exhibition on in the nearest town and she was going to ask him if he would like to visit it with her. It might seem a bit pushy as she'd only just met the man, but they had a few things in common, boats and the sea for starters, as well as the happiness of those they loved...

A big brown duck was waddling along the pavement in front of the practice when Laurel arrived the next morning. There had been a heavy shower shortly before, and each time it came to a puddle it stopped to drink.

As she watched it, fascinated, David came out of his cottage and on seeing what it was that had her attention he exclaimed laughingly, 'I don't believe it! There are lots of them on the river and this one must have come up the bank to investigate what lies on either side. It must be "quackers", drinking from puddles when it has all the river at its beak.'

As she joined in his laughter and left the duck to pursue its way, Laurel thought that only a few weeks ago the idea of being so enchanted at the sight of a duck waddling down the street would have seemed ludicrous, but she had to admit it, the countryside had taken her into its embrace. She was captive to its peaceful perfection, and even more so to the charismatic man beside her.

In the last few moments before the surgery doors opened she put Elaine's suggestion to David and he said, 'Are you sure? You've already discovered that it's hard work getting that garden to come out from under years of weeds and undergrowth without feeding us too.'

'Yes. I'm sure,' she said breezily, 'and if you are willing to risk the results of my cooking, the barbecue is on, as long as you'll sort out the technicalities of it for me.'

'Of course I will,' he assured her, with the thought of the approaching weekend becoming more appealing with every moment.

Clare from the picture gallery near the vicarage was one of the patients sent to the nurses' room for blood tests during the morning. She was still in remission from ovarian cancer and much happier for it, but James wasn't taking any chances, and as part of a routine check-up he'd asked for the tests to be done.

She was a pleasant woman in her fifties, unmarried, and ready to chat as she explained that she'd been Georgina Adams's patient until the dark-haired doctor that Laurel had glimpsed that first day with her baby had remarried her husband and given him another child.

'I'm little Arran's godmother,' Clare informed the two nurses with a wealth of affection in her voice. 'The Fates have lately been most kind to me. My cancer has disappeared, I was asked to be part of Arran's life, and my mother, who lives with me and can be difficult, has been a changed character since I was ill.'

When she'd gone Gillian, the other nurse, said, 'There goes a very happy woman and a brave one too. I've never once heard her complain about the cancer.'

Maybe there is a message for me somewhere in that, Laurel thought as she greeted the next person to be summoned from the chairs in the corridor, but it isn't ever going to stop the awful ache I feel inside when I think about David.

When she arrived at the house by the lake on the Saturday morning she gasped at the progress that was being made.

All the walls were up and the builder and his crew were on site, getting ready to put the slates on a new roof.

It was taking shape, she thought wistfully, and wished she could be a permanent part of it. As he went to greet her David was observing her expression. Would Laurel ever let him get near enough to tell her that Water Meetings House could turn out to be an empty dream without her there beside him?

There was one thing he was sure of. He knew that he wasn't going to be able to wait forever to discover what it was that always reared its head every time she was weakening in her resolve to keep him on the edge of her life. He told himself frequently that he could and would, and when they were apart the resolve was still there, but the moment he saw her again the longing to hold her close and tell her how much he cared was so strong he could almost taste it.

She was looking around her. 'I don't see your father. Isn't he here?'

'I thought you would know,' he said in surprise. 'Dad has gone to a maritime exhibition with Elaine.'

'No, I didn't know,' she said slowly, 'but it explains why she was out early and vague about how she was going to spend the day…and who with.'

'So it's just you and me,' he said. 'Do you think you can cope with that?'

'I'll have to, won't I?' she replied, and he gave her a long, level look and went back to his digging.

CHAPTER SEVEN

IT WAS late afternoon. The workmen had gone home to relax for the rest of the weekend, and Laurel and David, hot and grimy, were about to do the same when he asked, 'What kind of a barbecue is it?'

'Gas,' she replied. 'One of those cylinder things has to be attached to it.'

He was laughing. 'Spoken like a true handywoman.'

She pulled a face at him. 'I'm a city girl, don't forget, an expert in fashion, take-aways and theatre tickets.'

'So you haven't fallen in love with Willowmere?'

She was admitting to herself frequently that she had. She'd fallen in love with everything about the place and him in particular, but it was a moment for evasions rather than honesty and she said casually, 'It's a nice place.'

His heart sank. He hadn't forgotten that she was going back to her roots in two weeks. Would she want to stay there when she'd renewed her acquaintance with the capital city?

They were back at Glenside Lodge, scrubbed and clean after their efforts at the building site, and it was time for the barbecue. David had used the main bathroom to shower and Laurel the one in the en suite in her room, and there'd been an awkward moment when he'd heard her lock the door as he'd been crossing the landing.

'You're quite safe, you know,' he'd said coolly from the other side. 'I'm not going to suggest that we shower together, or anything else that would be as remote from your thinking as the heavens above.' And when she hadn't replied, he'd gone on his way.

She'd closed her eyes in anguish. Yet there'd been no signs of distress when she'd reappeared in one of the inevitable high-necked tops and a long cotton skirt, and David's moment of rebuke seemed to have been just that because he was smiling as he said, 'The barbecue is up and running on the patio. I've connected it to the propane and the gas is lit. All we need now is the food. Are you sure you're up to this, though? You've had a strenuous day so far. I'll do the cooking if you like.'

'No. I'm going to do it,' she informed him. 'I know you think I'm pretty useless so it's time I showed you that I'm not.' She gave him a gentle push towards the garden chairs out on the lawn. 'Go and relax and I'll call you when it's ready.'

'All right,' he agreed, 'but be sure to adjust the flame if you think the food is cooking too quickly.'

It was all going to plan. The sausages and the chicken legs that Elaine had suggested were all sizzling nicely on the grid. Laurel turned away to prepare the bacon for cooking, not realising in those first few seconds that smoke was rising from fat that had dripped through. She turned around to see flames leaping up from the barbecue.

She was back on the ward, but this time fear didn't lend wings to her feet. She was transfixed, and David came leaping onto the patio and dampened the flames with water from the bucket they'd put nearby. The fire went out with a loud hissing sound, and at the same moment that he turned to reassure her that it was all right, just a minor hiccup, Laurel was swaying on her feet.

He caught her before she crumpled and carried her into the sitting room, thinking as he did so how limp and helpless she felt in his arms. For a few seconds no words issued from the mouth that had refused his kisses, no bright eyes looked up at him. There had been fear in them when the flames had appeared and now they were closed in a still, white face.

As he laid her down on the sofa, as he'd done on the day she'd arrived in the village, David was thinking that it *had* been a bit worrying, but it had soon been sorted. It wasn't as if the house had been on fire. It was such a shame that Laurel's intention to cook for him had been thwarted, but more important was for her to realise that now there was nothing to be afraid of.

She opened her eyes and the panic was still there. 'It's all right,' he said gently. 'Everything is sorted. You saw me put out the fire and I've turned the gas off. It was my fault. I should have stayed beside you while you were cooking the food.'

She turned her head into the pillow and said in a muffled voice, 'You must think I'm stupid. I just panicked.'

He shook his head. 'You're not stupid, Laurel. You

are bright and funny, clever and kind, but why were you so distressed?'

'It was probably because everything I touch is a disaster,' she said evasively. 'My engagement was a catastrophe, and now I can't even cook you a meal without almost setting the place on fire.'

He stroked her cheek gently. 'That's twice you've fainted on me. I hope you're not going to make a habit of it.'

'I'll try not to,' she promised weakly, and raised herself up on the cushions. 'I'm all right now, David. It was just the shock of seeing the flames leaping up, that's all.'

He nodded understandingly yet wasn't convinced, but if Laurel wanted him to think that he would go along with it for the present.

The sound of voices on the front path indicated that Elaine and Jonas were back and he sighed. So much for time alone with Laurel. 'Stay where you are,' he said. 'I'll go and explain what's happened to Elaine.'

'No,' she protested, getting off the sofa. 'I don't want to worry her. I'm fine now.'

'All right,' he agreed doubtfully, 'but...'

'I'm OK, David, I promise,' she insisted, and said with a pale smile, 'Thanks for being there for me once again. I'm sure you never expected to be lumbered with me in your life ever since you lifted my cases off the train that day at the station. I'm a nuisance, aren't I?'

He was smiling for the first time since she'd fainted. 'If being a top-notch nurse at the surgery, working beside me in that jungle I call a garden, and brightening my days with your presence constitutes being a nuisance then, yes, you are. And now, if you're sure you are up to it, I think we should present ourselves to Dad and Elaine, who are bound to have smelt the smoke and will be wondering where we are.'

He took her hand and as they went out into the hall together she wished that his firm, reassuring clasp could be there for her always in darkness and in light.

Elaine and Jonas had gone straight to the garden via the kitchen and were lounging with long, cold drinks in front of them when they appeared. Without any reference to lingering odours, her aunt said, 'Have you had a nice day?'

'The barbecue seemed to be cooking too fast and some of the food got overdone, so I'm taking David somewhere for a decent meal to make up for it,' Laurel announced, and met Jonas's shrewd blue gaze with, 'We'll see you two later.'

'Well done!' David said as they drove to the village. 'I couldn't have done better myself.'

'Oh, I'll bet you could,' she teased, happy that she had him to herself after all. 'Let's hope that they have a free table somewhere.'

'If they haven't, we can go to my place and I'll rustle up something to eat,' he suggested.

He was waiting to see her reaction to that idea and wasn't surprised when she said hurriedly, 'That wouldn't be fair. I'm supposed to be entertaining you. If they can't fit us in at the pub, Hollyhocks might still be open.'

'Sure,' he said easily. 'We'll just play it as it comes,' and wondered why Laurel had been keen for them to spend the evening alone before and now she was chickening out at the thought of him taking her to the cottage.

There wasn't a free table at The Pheasant, and Hollyhocks Tea Rooms *had* closed, so because of Laurel's reluctance to take up his offer of eating at his place David said, 'I think something is telling us to call it a day, don't you?'

'I suppose you're right,' she agreed, and on a crazy impulse that she knew she might regret said, 'But I *would* like to see where you live if you haven't changed your mind.'

'It will be my pleasure,' he said, 'but when I've made you a sandwich and you've sampled a glass of Helen's home-made elderberry wine, I *am* going to take you home. You did pass out earlier after your scare *and* you were helping me with the garden for a long time before that, so it's an early night for you, Nurse Maddox.'

'Who is Helen who makes the wine?' she asked, turning a deaf ear to his solicitations on her behalf.

'She is James's elderly housekeeper, who often sends round something nice when she has baked too much.'

As they walked up the path to the cottage David said, 'It's very small, compact in every detail but small. James offered me the annexe to the surgery when I moved to Willowmere. It's where his sister Anna used to live, but I saw this place and liked it and here I am, though hopefully not for long.

'I saw Lizzie Carmichael, one of the midwives at St Gabriel's, the other day. She'd heard about my building project and asked if I would let her know when I'm moving out of here as she's interested in coming to live in Willowmere and would like to rent the cottage if possible when it comes empty.

'She's a great girl but a bit of a mystery. Doesn't seem to be in a relationship of any kind, which is surprising, but I think that Lizzie is in love with the job. She's a born mother, so it must be a strange feeling to be delivering other people's babies all the time and never one of your own.'

He was turning the key in the lock and when the door swung back he stepped inside and waited for her to pass him in a hallway that was so narrow she couldn't help but brush against him as he pointed towards a sitting room that was attractively furnished but also quite small.

The brief moment of contact had made her blood warm, but Laurel controlled the urge to throw herself into his arms and looked around her. She could understand why David was rather cramped in this place and wanted his own space. It also explained why his father was staying at The Pheasant.

'Take a seat while I prepare something to eat and pour the wine,' he said, 'and if Helen's wine isn't to your liking, I'll make tea or coffee.'

When he brought in the food and drink he said, 'I'll be going from one extreme to the other when I move into Water Meetings House, leaving a tiny cottage for a large detached one. It can't come too soon, although I was happy enough here until I saw my mother's old home.' *And met you*, he wanted to tell her, but the thing she didn't want him to know lay between them as heavy as lead.

'Will you have a housewarming?' she wanted to know, and he shrugged the suggestion off as if it was of no account.

'It all depends on circumstances.'

'Such as?'

'Whether I want one.'

'Why wouldn't you?'

'I would have expected you to know the answer to that,' he said, stung by her casual questioning. He'd made his feelings for her clear enough. Did he have to express them in neon lights for her to take notice?

Laurel knew she'd upset him, and fighting an insane urge to take off her top and show him the reason why she was always holding back she got up to go.

'I can see myself home,' she told him. 'It's still daylight and you were right about me needing an early night, David. It *has* been a long day and I want to give the barbecue a quick clean before I go to bed after my catastrophic performance on it.'

'You're making too much of what happened,' he said gently, his good humour returning. 'It wasn't the end of the world.'

She gave a vestige of a smile. 'True, but one's world can end in a matter of seconds in some circumstances.'

'Are we talking about your broken engagement again by any chance?'

'Again...no.'

She was moving towards the narrow hallway. 'Thank you for a lovely day, David,' she said gravely. 'I'm sorry I'm so difficult to deal with.' And before he could reply she was gone, walking slowly in the direction of Glenside Lodge. Remembering how she'd made it clear that she didn't want him to walk her home, he didn't go after her.

* * *

Elaine was waiting up for her when she got there and her first words were, 'What happened with the barbecue, Laurel?'

'The food caught fire.'

'Oh, no, I should never have suggested it! That has never happened before. What did you do?'

'Froze to the spot, and while David was extinguishing the flames I fainted.'

'How awful that you of all people should have had such a fright.'

'Mmm, and I missed its only compensation. When I came out of the faint I was lying on the sofa, so David must have carried me there from the patio. He must rue the day he ever set eyes on me,' she said with droll regret.

Elaine had to smile in spite of her consternation. 'At least he must feel that life is never boring when he's around you, and so I take it that the food was spoilt?'

'Yes, it was burnt, then soaked. Before I go to bed I'm going to give the barbecue a good clean.'

'Too late, it's done and put away,' she was told.

'Thanks for that,' she breathed, and sinking down onto the nearest chair asked, 'And so how was your day with the ship's captain?'

'You are the cheeky one,' Elaine said laughingly. 'Jonas is a nice guy who loves his son the way I love you. He says he'll take me out in his boat if ever I'm in Cornwall.'

'And are you going to take him up on the offer?' Laurel asked curiously.

'Yes, if ever I'm in Cornwall, which is hardly likely.'

With a feeling that Elaine didn't want to pursue that topic Laurel headed off to bed. She paused on the bottom step of the stairs and said, 'It's been a strange day, full of peaks and valleys. It will be a relief to go to London to chill out when the time comes. I might even be looking forward to it if my reason for going wasn't my check-up.'

'I'm sorry I can't go with you for moral support,' Elaine said, 'but as you know it's the quarterly audit at the practice then and James and I will be bogged down with it all day Saturday.'

'I'll be fine on my own,' Laurel told her. 'If I have to have more skin grafts it won't be so soon.' With that she climbed the rest of the stairs and went to bed.

Sleep came fast. She was too tired to dwell on the day's events, but on awakening the next morning they came crowding back, and as she lay reliving them the worst thought that came to mind was knowing that it was going to be a long time before she ceased to see incidents like yesterday's as moments of terror…

She'd been involved in a nightmare happening not so long ago due to the duplicity and carelessness of others, and it was going to be etched in her mind *and* on her body for ever more. Now she was nervous at the drop of a hat.

The *best* part of the day had been coming out of the faint to find David looking down at her with his eyes full of concern. She didn't deserve him, she thought dejectedly. She was continually disrupting his life, blowing hot and cold and attracting catastrophes like a magnet.

Yet when the phone beside her bed rang and it was

him, every other thought was wiped out in the pleasure of hearing his voice.

'Just checking that you are all right after yesterday's trauma,' he said.

'Yes, I'm fine,' she told him. 'Are you all right?'

'Of course. I'm all right when you're all right.' She could tell from his voice that he was smiling. 'But promise me that you'll have a complete rest today. As your doctor I recommend no exertion. Dad and I won't be around. We're going to spend the day at the site as he's going home tomorrow and wants to get another day in on the walls. He's coming back soon, but for now he wants to make sure that his boat, *The Sea Nymph*, is all right. She's the woman in his life.' *And a lot easier to handle than the one in mine*, he thought.

Laurel's mind was moving in a different direction. Jonas's boat might be the love of his life, but it would be no good for holding close in the night. What if Elaine did decide to go to Cornwall?

When Laurel arrived at the surgery on Monday morning Georgina's husband, Ben Allardyce, and the father of baby Arran was in Reception, reading a poster that someone had put up over the weekend advertising a charity walk that was to take place the coming Saturday.

When she halted beside him he said, 'Georgina and I would love to take Arran on this walk, but the terrain gets a bit rugged out there.'

'So couldn't one of you go, and the other stay behind with Arran?' she questioned.

Ben's expression was sombre. 'I think not. We spent

years apart for reasons I won't go into, and now every moment together is so precious that we do everything as a family. What about you, Laurel? Are you into walking?'

'It would give you the chance to see more of the Cheshire countryside, should you want to,' a voice said from behind, and when she turned David was there. She watched as he added his name to the list of volunteers and then, raising a questioning eyebrow, passed her the pen.

It went without saying that she was going to write her name under his, she thought. Just the mere sight of him always sent common sense flying out of the window.

The patients were arriving and that was the end of the discussion, but when surgery was over she caught him as he was about to set off on his calls and asked, 'So where does the charity walk take us? Do I need to wear walking boots and suchlike?'

'I would say so,' he informed her, and then he remembered the day when she'd tottered off the train in high heels. 'Whatever you do, don't come in your stilettos. Part of it is over rough terrain and if there has been much rain beforehand it can be boggy.'

'So you haven't forgotten the day I arrived in Willowmere?' she teased as he opened his car door and slid into the driver's seat.

'Of course I haven't,' he said in wry amusement. 'How could I? You were like a package that came without instructions or warnings.'

On that he prepared to drive off into the summer morning. Resisting the temptation to get in beside him,

Laurel went back to blood tests, injections and the rest of the duties of a practice nurse.

It was late afternoon and the second surgery was in full spate when David came into the nurses' room and said, 'I have the vicar's wife outside. Could I have an ECG, please?'

Gillian had some time owing and was due to finish early, so when Catherine Beesley presented herself it was Laurel who greeted her and explained the procedure.

'I came because I thought I had a hernia,' she explained as Laurel was positioning the rubber discs on her chest, stomach and feet, 'but when I mentioned to Dr Trelawney that for the first time ever I'm aware of my heartbeat all the time and it is quite fast, he said that must be dealt with first. I was amazed when he said the test could be done here in the surgery. I was expecting to have to go to St Gabriel's.'

'Just a short time ago that would have been the case,' Laurel told her, 'but not now. We're all high tech and will have the result of the ECG in a matter of minutes, printed out for Dr Trelawney to see.

'We will be in direct communication with the cardiology department at the hospital while you're wired up, and they will decide whether you have a problem or not.'

The vicar's wife was a sensible, homely sort of woman and as the equipment registered six level beats and then a hop, skip and jump, it didn't take a genius to work out that something was not quite right.

'The test has shown that you have two heart problems,' David explained when she went back into his room for the results. 'The first is that the electric impulses of it are not working correctly, and the other, which we do come across now and then, is that at some time in the past you've had a minor heart attack.'

'If that's the case, I don't know when!' Catherine exclaimed in disbelief. 'Are these two things anything to worry about?' she questioned. 'The vicar relies on me so much with his work in the parish, I haven't time to be ill.'

'I don't think either are anything too serious,' he told her, 'but I'm going to arrange for you to see a cardiologist, and now if you'll go back to the nurses' room I'll examine the area where you feel you might have pulled something out of place. The nurse will tell you what to take off and will be there all the time for reassurance.'

After the examination, he smiled reassuringly at Catherine. 'Nothing out of the ordinary there,' he said. 'Just a bit of muscle strain, but be sure to come back to see me if it persists.'

When she'd gone, looking somewhat dazed, Laurel said, 'Who would be a vicar's wife? In spite of being told unexpectedly that she has a heart problem, Catherine Beesley remembered to ask if any of us have put our names down for the charity walk.'

'And did you tell her that the best ramblers have signed up for it?' he quipped as he went back to the rest of his patients.

'I don't want to wear boots. They'll hurt my feet,' she said to his disappearing back.

He swivelled round. 'Strong shoes, then, and don't forget a hat in case there's a downpour.'

It all sounded wildly exciting, she thought as she went back into the nurses' room to tidy up.

Laurel awoke on Saturday morning to the sound of heavy rain and when she padded across to the window, sure enough, there was a downpour pelting out of dismal skies.

There was no pleasure to be had from the lake sparkling in the distance today, she decided, and was turning away when she caught her breath. Rising above the willow trees, some of them huge with age, were the sturdy grey slates of the roof of David's house.

It was a sight that she would have expected to be excited by, but instead she felt lost and lonely. She had dreamed that David had married the midwife, Lizzie, who was readily available, with a house full of babies that she'd delivered herself. In the dream, Elaine had laughed as she sailed into salt spray with Jonas out on the open sea, while she, Laurel, had fallen into the role of the perennial godmother-cum-maiden aunt with drawers full of high-necked jumpers.

As she caught a glimpse of herself in the dressing-table mirror she thought wistfully that at least she wouldn't end up wearing a wig. Her red-gold hair had grown longer and she rejoiced every time she saw it.

While she was in London she intended visiting her regular hairdresser and having it styled. Hopefully, when she came back, David might be impressed.

When she went down to breakfast, Elaine observed her expression and said, 'I know, the weather is dreadful, but it's early yet. By the time you are ready to leave, it might have cleared up.'

'I wish you were coming instead of going shopping,' Laurel told her.

'You won't need me around while David is there,' she replied. 'I'm not going on the walk because I don't want to cramp your style.'

'And what style would that be?' she enquired flatly, nibbling on a piece of toast.

Elaine's mind had switched to basics. 'Don't forget to make a packed lunch and take a bottle of water with you. Ramblers often stop to eat miles away from anywhere.'

Laurel was observing her in sudden consternation. 'A rucksack!' she exclaimed.

'I've got one you can use.'

'No, I don't mean that. I can't stand anything rubbing against my back.'

'I never thought of that,' Elaine said slowly. 'You'll have to carry it in your hand, so be sure to just take the basics.'

The weather had reduced the numbers of those who'd signed up for the charity walk and there were only a dozen or so stalwarts waiting outside the village hall when Elaine dropped Laurel off at the starting point.

The rain had eased off for the moment and a watery sun was filtering through the clouds as David came striding out of the cottage suitably clad in sensible clothes.

She saw that he was casting a dubious glance over her and when he reached her side he said in a low voice, 'The rucksack is made to be strapped on to your back for convenience.'

'Yes, I do know that,' she told him coolly, 'but I find it easier to carry it in my hand.'

He shrugged. 'OK. Just don't trip over it, that's all.'

'I won't,' she said sweetly, and he laughed.

'All right, I get the message, but at the risk of being told that you're quite capable of taking care of yourself, and knowing that not to be so, I suggest that you stay by me all the time. There are some dangerous places up there among the peaks, especially if a mist comes down, which it often does after rain.'

'Yes, all right,' she agreed meekly, having no intention of being anywhere else other than close by his side. After all, that was why she was there. It was to be with him that she was going to spend the day tramping around the countryside.

The vicar and his long-suffering wife were in charge and they explained that the route they were going to take was past Willow Lake, through the next village, up the hill road, and onto the moors for a short distance, eventually descending at the other side of Willowmere, having done ten miles in all.

'And in case any of you are apprehensive regarding minor injuries that you might sustain during the walk, Dr Trelawney has a comprehensively kitted out first-aid box in his rucksack,' the vicar announced jovially.

'So that's what we're here for,' Laurel whispered, 'to render first aid.'

'Not necessarily,' he replied. 'I'm here because I want to spend the day with you, and I hope that you feel the same.'

There was a mischievous twinkle in her eye. 'What? That I want to spend the day with me?'

'You know what I mean. Are *you* here because of *me*?'

'I might be.'

He rolled his eyes heavenwards and took her hand in his as the walkers set off on what was going to be the easiest few miles.

After a long dry spell the rain had brought freshness to the air. The green fields looked greener, raindrops sparkled on leaves and flowers, and as a grey squirrel climbed quickly up a nearby tree at their approach and disappeared amongst its branches, Laurel wondered how she could have been reluctant to come to live amongst all this.

As they passed the lake she and David exchanged secret smiles at the surprised comments of the rest of the party when they saw that Water Meetings House was rising out of the disrepair of years, and as the next village came into sight with the hill road just beyond, there was a happy camaraderie amongst those heading for the moors that lay beneath the shadow of the rugged peaks.

CHAPTER EIGHT

As THE walking party strode up towards the moors in no particular kind of order, the promise of the day was faltering again. The sky was darkening with rainclouds and all too soon it was pelting down on them.

They were on the edge of the moors now, with the peaks towering above them and steep gullies on either side of the path. Laurel and David were at the back of the single file of walkers. It was a time for care and caution, and even the two high-spirited youths who'd come along for a lark and were just in front of them were treading with caution when a moorland sheep, disturbed by the sound of heavy boots on the rocky path and the voices of those passing its grazing place, came careering out onto the path in a fright and ran straight towards one of the youngsters.

Startled, the lad stepped back to avoid the impact, teetering on the edge of the steep drop behind him for a second, then lost his balance completely and fell with a frantic cry into the gully below, where he landed beside loose debris that had fallen from the rock face over the years.

'Go and get the vicar!' David bellowed to the lad's friend, who was standing dumbstruck beside them as the sheep changed direction and went careering down the path they'd just come up.

Turning to Laurel, he thrust his mobile phone into her hand. 'Phone for an ambulance, but get our exact position from the vicar before you do. Better still, ask for a helicopter.' He looked down at the still figure at the bottom of the gully. 'They'll never bring him up on a stretcher. It's too steep and treacherous with bogs and dangerous overhangs of rock all over the place. I'm going down there while you direct operations up here, Laurel.'

'I'm coming with you!' she cried as the rest of the party came back after being told what had happened. 'Someone else can do that. I'm a nurse, for heaven's sake, and I'll be needed. Have you got the first-aid kit?'

'Yes, it's in my rucksack, and it would seem that I've got you too,' he said dryly. 'Do you ever do what you're told?'

'It depends on the circumstances,' she said, already taking note of what lay ahead on the way down to the unfortunate youth.

'Is an ambulance coming?' the vicar asked as he joined them at that moment.

'Helicopter,' David said tersely, as Laurel handed the phone to the panting clergyman and began to ease herself carefully down the steep hillside that in parts was made up of jagged rocks.

He was behind her in a flash and when she held out her hand to him David took it in his firm grip and together they began what was to be a perilously slow descent.

There was no way they dared rush it, no matter how badly injured the lad was, he thought as they picked their way amongst nettles in the undergrowth and stepped over fallen tree branches littering the place. There were rock falls everywhere and the overhangs above had a menacing atmosphere about them.

But there was no point in dwelling on things that might or might not happen. They had a life to save and if the frightened sheep had done the youth no favours in sending him careering over the edge, the Fates weren't being too unkind to him. They were sending him a doctor and a nurse—if he was still alive.

He was breathing but unconscious when they got to him and as David wrenched the rucksack off his back and bent to examine him, Laurel brought out the first-aid kit and prepared to follow orders.

'Breathing seems OK, pulse rather weak,' he said as the rain continued to fall in torrents, 'and from the odd angle that he's lying at I'd say that both his legs are fractured.'

Laurel was crouching over him to protect him from the rain, while trying to stem blood gushing from a head wound with one hand and unbuttoning the lad's shirt at the neck with the other to help his breathing, and David began strapping the boy's legs together.

He was pale and shivering, his skin cold and clammy from shock and the unwelcome downpour. David was taking off his waterproof jacket and then removing the thick sweater underneath it that was warm from his body heat and placing it over him, but they weren't enough to cover his injured legs.

Laurel knew that she had to do the same, whatever the

consequences, and followed suit, taking off her coat and removing the sweater underneath to provide more warmth.

David was bending over him, checking pulse and heartbeat again, and when he glanced up momentarily she'd replaced her jacket, but not before he'd caught a brief glimpse of scarring.

He made no comment, but as he bent to his task again she'd seen his expression and wondered what was going through his mind. Whatever it was he was halfway to knowing she'd received serious burns to the top half of her back and she wondered what he would have to say when or if he saw the full extent of them.

She could hear the sound of a helicopter approaching and in the relief of the moment everything else was forgotten as they waited to see if the pilot would be able to find enough space to land.

While he was hovering they continued to monitor the young victim and David gave a satisfied nod as his body heat began to rise and the shivering lessened.

She'd worked with a lot of doctors since she'd taken up nursing, Laurel thought, but there had never before been a situation as rewarding as this, working with David as they tried to save a life.

Maybe it was because she hadn't been in love with those other guys. Whatever it was, she wouldn't forget today. They were united in their professions, perfectly in tune. If only she was as sure of herself and him in the rest of their lives.

The pilot was flying as low as he could and bellowing above the noise of the engine, 'There's nowhere to land. We're going to have to winch him up. A paramedic is coming down to you now and one of the crew is going to follow him to supervise the winching.'

Almost as he spoke the door opened and the paramedic they'd been promised came swinging down on the end of a winch line, followed seconds later by a member of the crew.

When they landed beside them David explained briefly that there were suspected leg fractures, a head wound, cuts and grazes from the fall, and possible shock that they'd prevented for the moment with their own clothing.

'We've immobilised his legs to avoid further injury to the fractured bones,' he said as they prepared to winch the lad up to the helicopter, and the paramedic nodded.

'OK, Doc. We'll get him to A and E as fast as we can. He's had a bad fall but it was the kid's lucky day that you people were on the spot. I've seen you somewhere before, haven't I?' he said as they fastened the patient onto a lightweight stretcher and prepared to lift him upwards. 'Didn't you used to be at St Gabriel's?'

'Yes, that's right,' he said absently as the winch line began to work.

'And now you're a country GP,' Laurel said, as they began the slow climb back up to the road above.

'Yes, I am without any doubt,' he agreed. 'And what about you? Are you going to feel the pull of the city when you go back there next weekend?'

'I won't know until I get there, will I?' she said, grateful that any comments he was going to make about what he'd seen were being put on hold. 'But Elaine won't let me go back there yet. She says I have to stay here until I have roses in my cheeks.'

The top still seemed a long way off and when they stopped to rest David said, 'You are an amazing woman, Laurel. Do you know that?'

'Why?' she asked, acutely aware that her top coat was chafing her shoulders under the scarf. She was longing to throw it off but what would she wear then? Her jumper was stuffed inside the rucksack.

'Surely you don't need to ask! You faint at the slightest thing, yet in a situation as dangerous as this has been you don't bat an eyelid.'

'I only perform well when I'm centre stage,' she said with another shiver. 'Although I think you outclassed me on this occasion so I'll step back when they're handing out the medals.'

He sighed. 'I give up. Why are you always on the defensive when I say nice things to you?'

'It must be because I'm not used to it.'

The rest of the walkers were peering over the edge of the drop, watching them climb up, and before David could question that oblique remark someone shouted, 'Watch out, we're throwing you a rope. Tie it around your waists and we'll haul you up.'

When it came down she eyed it hesitantly, imagining the discomfort it was going to cause, but it was the lesser of two evils, she supposed, and let David tie it around her and then attach it to himself.

'I suggest that we carry on with the walk,' someone said when they had all reassembled beside the winding road. 'The lad's been taken to hospital faster than he could have ever dreamed. There's nothing else we can do.'

The vicar was about to comment, but as he was clearing his throat another member of the group said, 'You know who he is, don't you?' Turning to the injured lad's companion, he said, 'Tell them who your mate is, laddie.'

'Alistair's father is Lord Derringham. I'm staying up at the house with him while his parents are abroad on holiday. I'll have to let them know he's been hurt, I suppose,' he said gloomily. 'We only came on the walk for a laugh.'

'His Lordship's son? Oh, dear!' exclaimed the vicar. 'We must indeed let him know what has happened, but not out here. The reception is not good for imparting a message of such urgency. My wife and I will go back to Kestrel Court with you so that we are there for support when you make the call, or maybe we should put it into the hands of the estate manager?'

'That's Gillian's husband,' David told Laurel. 'He'll be the best person to break the bad news, and they can tell His Lordship to speak to us if he wants on-the-spot information, though the best plan would be for his parents to ring St Gabriel's for news of their son's condition.

'And now you need to go home for a hot drink, a bath and some clean clothes,' he said, still with no reference to what he'd seen. For the information of the rest of the party he added, 'We're off to get cleaned up and dried out.'

She nodded thankfully as her coat was making her back sore.

'Is Elaine going to be in when we get to the lodge?' he asked as they retraced their steps beneath a warm sun that would have been most welcome when they'd been at the bottom of the gully. At least it was helping them to dry out now.

'She said she was going shopping,' Laurel replied, hoping Elaine would be there so that the inevitable questions would be postponed, but her aunt was nowhere to be seen.

'I'll make hot drinks while you shower and change your clothes,' David said. 'Then we need to talk, Laurel, don't we?'

She nodded mutely and went to do as he suggested.

When he was alone, David's mind went back to what he'd caught a glimpse of on her shoulder when she'd been removing her jumper to cover the lad.

He was no fool, knew the scars left by burns when he saw them, and he wondered, as he'd done a few times, if she'd been the victim of domestic abuse. Was that why she was afraid of getting close to him? It was a likely theory. There was the fractured knee, the redness of her hands, the short hair she so clearly hated... Had it been caused by her ex?

The thought of anyone hurting her was too horrendous to contemplate, but he was a doctor and knew that kind of thing happened all the time, sometimes in the least expected relationships.

When she came down scrubbed, clean and dressed in dry clothes, he handed her a hot toddy and waited while she drank it before saying gravely, 'I got sight of the kind of scarring that serious burns leave when you were taking your sweater off down in the gully. How did that come about?'

'I was caught up in a situation that I couldn't get out

of,' she said in a low voice. 'The result being that I feel ugly all the time.'

So he hadn't been wrong. 'Domestic abuse?' he questioned gently, and watched her mouth go slack with surprise.

'No. Nothing like *that*!' she exclaimed, and as he waited for what was to come next he heard Elaine's key in the door and groaned silently. The moment that was going to bring clarity to their relationship had been there. Now it was gone and the way she greeted her aunt was proof enough that Laurel was relieved.

'What is this I hear about Alistair Derringham having a serious accident?' Elaine said as she came bustling into the sitting room. 'They were talking about it when I stopped off at the post office for some stamps, and I was told that the two of you risked your own necks to treat the poor lad at the bottom of some gully on the moors.'

'I'll let Laurel tell you all about it, Elaine,' he said, getting to his feet. He was accepting that he was going to have to wait a little longer to find out what had happened to Laurel in the past. At least he knew that the Darius fellow hadn't hurt her—well, physically at least.

She went to the door with him to say goodbye and as if the conversation that Elaine had interrupted had been about the day's events in general said, 'Shall I ring St Gabriel's to enquire after Alistair, or will you?'

'I'll do it,' he offered, taking note of how pale and exhausted she looked. It was making him think he should have waited until another time to ask about the scarring on her shoulder. He was aching to offer comfort, but he'd done that once before and Laurel hadn't wanted to know.

But after all they'd been through on the ill-fated walk he couldn't just stride off without letting her see that he cared, cared a lot, and would continue to do so whether she wanted him to or not.

Taking her limp hand in his, he bent and planted a kiss on the rough palm, then curled her fingers around it protectively and told her softly, 'Don't worry if you lose it. There are lots more kisses just waiting for their moment.'

Before she could reply he'd gone, tall and straight in the summer afternoon, and she had to hold on to the doorpost to stop herself from running after him.

She gazed at the hand he had kissed, aware that David had only seen a small part of the damaged skin of her back and shoulders. He'd known what had caused it, of course, but hadn't been aware of the extent of it. That was something he had yet to discover if ever she could bring herself to show him after Darius's unconcealed revulsion, but for now that was how it stood. Maybe when she'd been to London on Saturday to see the consultant, she might see the way ahead clearer.

When he phoned St Gabriel's, David was told that Alistair was conscious and had just come back from Radiography, where his leg fractures had been X-rayed. He would shortly be operated on. When he asked about the head wound he was told that no internal bleeding had been shown inside the skull, but the patient was still being monitored for shock.

'The lad's father is on the board of governors here,' the doctor in A and E told him, 'and has already been on the phone from some faraway place. He was ringing from the airport where he and his family were about to board the first available flight.

'I can't see roast lamb being on the menu for some time to come for that household,' he said. 'Or on the other hand that might be where they will prefer to see it, on a plate.

'He's got a lot of heavy bruising and cuts and scratches as well as the more serious injuries,' he went on to say, 'but it's amazing that a doctor and nurse were on the spot. At least it's one thing in his favour. There's no telling what would have been the outcome if the two of you hadn't been there.

'Alistair says that he's always being told off by his father for things that he is to blame for, but this time His Lordship can't complain as he did nothing wrong, *and* in any case it was one of his sheep. He owns that part of the moors.'

It was Wednesday morning and James had called David and Laurel into his consulting room for a quick chat.

He was smiling when they went in and Laurel thought with a sinking feeling that he was about to tell them that his sister and her husband were on their way home, which would be joy for him and the children but could mean an abrupt ending to her short stay as practice nurse if Anna wanted to take up her old job at the surgery. She accepted that she was employed on a temporary arrangement but had been hoping that it wouldn't be this brief.

She was wrong in her surmising and her eyes widened when James said, 'I've called you both in to give you some good news.' As she and David exchanged puzzled glances he said, 'Lord and Lady Derringham are calling in later this morning to thank you for what you did for their son, and while he's here he wants to discuss making some kind of gesture in a practical way connected with village health care. What do you think of that?'

'Amazing!' David exclaimed. 'We were only doing what we've been trained to do.'

'Maybe, but in very difficult and dangerous circumstances and His Lordship is aware of that.'

'The main thing is, how is Alistair?' Laurel said.

'He has both legs in plaster and the head wound will take some time to heal, but his parents are aware that it could have been much worse if it hadn't been for you two.'

'How about a complete makeover of the surgery?' she suggested.

'I'm not sure that His Lordship has something like that in mind,' James said. 'He might be thinking of just a plaque on the wall or something similar.'

'I hope not!' David exclaimed. 'Save that kind of thing for someone who deserves it, but we need to hang on until he's been and I think Elaine should be in on it.'

The Derringhams were in James's office for an hour, and afterwards they came out and thanked Laurel and David profusely for what they'd done for their son. To Laurel's surprise they'd had a toddler with them and Her Ladyship explained, 'Alistair is our eldest and Oliver, who is a year old, is our youngest. In the middle we have twin girls.'

'I wanted to do something for health care in the village to express our gratitude,' her husband said, 'and

I intend to be generous. So we've talked with James about funding a much-needed community midwife position based in the surgery.'

James nodded and smiled. 'This is a great chance to develop our antenatal care and is something we've wanted to do for ages. Rather than mothers from here and the surrounding villages having to travel to St Gabriel's, they can visit a midwife here and have the best of care on their doorsteps, so to speak. When Lord Derringham suggested the maternity clinic idea to the hospital trust they were all for it, especially if someone on their board of governors is prepared to fund it.

'They've already recommended a midwife for the position. What do you think about the idea?'

'Fantastic,' David said.

'Incredibly generous.' Elaine and Laurel echoed his sentiments.

'The midwife referred to would be Lizzie Carmichael, I think,' David told him. 'I've seen her at work and she would be an excellent choice.'

'So we are agreed, then?' His Lordship said, and observing their delighted expressions went on to say, 'I am also funding the refurbishment of a room for the clinic, and the equipment you will need. We have a young family of our own and both my wife and I are keen to see that mothers-to-be receive the best possible care.'

'That will be just what we need!' James exclaimed when the Derringhams had left to go and visit their son. 'We hope our brand-new maternity clinic will be up and running as soon as possible.'

* * *

When morning surgery was over James called all the staff into the big office below stairs and said, 'I'm inviting you all to Bracken House tonight to drink a toast to Laurel and David, who by being the kind of people they are have brought about this amazing offer from His Lordship.

'A community midwife in the village will be like a dream come true. He is a very generous man. So eight-thirty tonight if you can make it,' he concluded amid delighted applause.

Laurel's glance met David's deep blue gaze as they all went back to their duties and she knew that this was where she wanted to be, here in Willowmere with David and Elaine and the friends she'd made at the surgery, but with him most of all, in the house by the lake that was rising out of the rubble.

'What's wrong?' Elaine asked as they dressed to go to James's house that evening. 'You've hardly said a word since we came home. Is it the hospital visit on Saturday that is on your mind?'

Laurel managed a smile. 'No, whatever they say it won't make that much difference, will it? More skin grafts can only bring a slight improvement.'

'But you'll agree if they suggest it?'

'Yes, of course,' she replied flatly.

'It's the David situation that is really getting to you, isn't it? You are crazy, Laurel. That man is a king among men. If he loves you it won't matter to him that you have severe scarring. He will want you for what you are.'

'It sounds so simple when you put it like that,' she

protested, 'but suppose that he wants me for what *he* wants me to be and I don't live up to it. I know he isn't like Darius, but you remember what Jonas said, don't you? That the American woman was very beautiful and they made a striking couple. No one is ever going to say that when he's with me. An odd couple maybe, but never striking.'

CHAPTER NINE

IT WAS a merry gathering assembled there when they arrived at Bracken House, but as Laurel's glance went round the room she realised that there was no David. As if she read her thoughts, Gillian said, 'David has gone to collect his father from the station. He's back for another visit.'

'Oh, I see,' she said, and wondered if Jonas's return was connected with dry stone walling or Elaine, who was chatting to Ben and Georgina who had brought baby Arran along. Could it be that he'd returned to cement his friendship with the aunt who was also her loving friend?

More likely it was a bit of both, she thought whimsically, and was trying to work out what relation she would be to David if Elaine married his father when he came striding into the room. Now it was his turn to glance around those present until he found her standing by the window with a glass in her hand.

He came across immediately and said, 'Hi. Did they tell you where I was?'

'Yes,' she replied, smiling up at him. 'Your father has

come back, which makes me wonder what has brought him to Willowmere once more—whether it's the house or Elaine. If she is the reason, what would *our* relationship be if they tied the knot?'

He was observing her with raised brows. 'You are racing on a bit, aren't you? Elaine is a lovely woman, but Dad has never shown any interest in anyone else since he lost my mother and that's a long, long time ago. But going back to what you were thinking—' and he was laughing now '—if that ever happened, Elaine would be my stepmother, my dad your step-uncle, and we would be, er…I'm not sure, step-cousins maybe?'

He had ideas of a much deeper relationship than that for them, but the snag was did Laurel have the same yearnings?

But at least she was with him now, looking happy enough. He hoped she was beginning to trust him. That she was beginning to feel that whatever it was that she hadn't been able to discuss with him would be easier to bear if he was there to share it.

He loved her, wanted her as he'd never wanted anyone before, and if it took the rest of his life to convince her of that, it was how it was going to be.

He hadn't forgotten what his father had said when his engagement to Caroline had fallen apart. 'You will know when the right one comes along,' he'd told him, and it was true. It was as if he'd been hit by a bolt from the blue.

Even on that first day when she'd come wobbling off the train in her high heels he'd had a feeling that his life had changed, though at the time he'd thought it was for the worse as the strange female who was Elaine's niece had been everywhere he turned in the days that followed.

He often smiled when he thought back to when they'd first met. Laurel had turned out to be the most interesting and appealing woman he'd ever known.

She was observing Georgina's baby, he noticed, gurgling in his father's arms, and he thought he saw regret in her glance, yet why? Was it because she had no partner to make a baby with, or for some other reason that he knew nothing of, connected with the secret that was weighing her down?

'Let's go outside for a breath of air,' he suggested, and taking her hand in his led her into the garden at the back of the house and to a secluded gazebo at the far end.

'Why have you brought me out here?' she asked.

'It's not to seduce you, if that's what you're thinking,' he said lightly. 'I wanted to get you on your own for a few moments to find out what your arrangements for Saturday are, such as what train you're travelling to London on.'

'Why? Are you coming to see me off?' she teased.

'Do you want me to?'

'Er…yes, if you feel like getting up at the crack of dawn. I'm going on the quarter past seven train from Manchester.'

'No problem. I don't suppose it's any use my asking why you're going to London.'

'I told you. I have an appointment, a long-term one. I'll be back in the evening.' Steering the conversation away from her comings and goings, she asked, 'How is the house coming along? It's a few days since I was up there but I'll be back on the job on Sunday if you want me to continue helping with the garden.'

'Of course I do, but I think I should find you something less strenuous, such as choosing wall coverings, carpets and furniture. The builder has given me a completion date for the end of August.'

'So soon!' she exclaimed.

'Yes, the windows and doors are in, the plasterers have finished, and joiners and plumbers have taken over now. I have a decorator on hold so the end is in sight.

'The builder has quite a few contracts in the pipeline and hasn't let the grass grow under his feet, though that would seem to refer to the garden more than the house. And when it's all finished, *are* you still going to help me choose furnishings and fabrics?'

'I'd love to,' she said with a lump in her throat.

When he'd first suggested it weeks ago she'd been mildly surprised but had thought nothing of it, but now everything had changed and it would be a bittersweet experience if she never had the chance to live there with him.

As he watched the expressions cross her face David thought it would be so easy to tell her that the house would be empty and silent without her there. But first Laurel had to find the confidence to confide in him without any persuasion on his part, and, as he kept telling himself, he could wait a little longer.

And while that was happening he was going to buy a ring with emeralds to match her eyes and diamonds to sparkle as she sparkled when she was happy. As there was nothing wrong with *his* confidence he intended to see it on her finger sooner or later.

When he looked up Elaine was beckoning to them from the patio doors and they left the gazebo reluctantly and went back to join the others.

'James is going to propose a toast to Lord Derringham and the hero and heroine of the peaks and gullies,' she said, 'so be prepared.'

As they went inside the practice staff circled them and raised their glasses as James said, 'Will you all please drink a toast to the generosity of Lord Derringham?' And when they'd done that he went on to say, 'And to Laurel and David, who acted as true medical professionals.'

'I'm going your way,' David said as the gathering began to break up. 'I want to call at The Pheasant to make sure that Dad has settled in all right. We had no time to talk when I picked him up at the station with only minutes to spare before I was due here.'

When they were about to separate outside the pub he said, 'It's been a great day, hasn't it? A locally based midwife promised for the village, and the practice staff all together on a rare social occasion at James's house. I don't know about you, but I felt as if I really belonged as I haven't been here much longer than you.'

'The village has a timeless magic of its own,' she said. 'I never imagined I would ever hear myself say it, but if I had to choose it would be here that I would want to live.' Though only with you, her heart said. And before she proclaimed it out loud she left him to go and find Jonas and walked slowly back to Glenside Lodge.

Elaine was there before her and as they chatted over a bedtime drink she said, 'Georgina told me tonight that when Ben first came to join us at the surgery she took him with her on home visits to help him to get to know the area. When they were driving along that same road up on the moors, a sheep ran in front of the car and she had to brake sharply to avoid an accident.'

'I don't suppose much can be done about that sort of thing if they graze free up there,' Laurel commented, 'but that won't be much comfort to Alistair when he's hobbling about with two legs in casts. The only solution would be to have fencing along both sides of the road, or for walkers to take less hazardous routes.'

Once they'd exhausted the subject of the lost sheep, she said flatly, 'David has asked me why I'm going to London.'

'And did you tell him?'

'No, I want to put what the consultant has to say in perspective before I do anything else. David knows I've got scarring, but not to what extent, and when I come back I'm going to show him. I'm going to put my dithering days behind me, even though we only can boast half of a striking pair.'

'Put that comment behind you,' Elaine insisted. 'Jonas didn't mean anything by it. David will have seen worse scars than yours, bad as they are.'

'Maybe, but not on someone he might want to make love to.' And with that dismal thought the last thing in her mind she went up to bed.

On the Friday night before she was due to go to London there was to be a barn supper at Meadowlands, a farm on the edge of the village, and when Laurel asked what it would be like she was told that there would be lots of wholesome food in the form of crusty bread, various cheeses, home-made pickles and sauces, savouries, apple pies and lots of fresh fruit from various orchards, along with country and western dancing to work up an appetite.

'So are you going to go?' Gillian asked when the vicar's wife came in, selling tickets. Catherine Beesley had had the cardiogram that David had arranged and was waiting to see the cardiologist for the result. In the meantime it would seem that she was still busy with parish work and would continue to be so.

'I suppose so,' Laurel said half-heartedly. She knew that Elaine would be there and maybe Jonas as the light was beginning to fade earlier in the evenings with midsummer's day having been and gone some weeks ago, and he wouldn't be able to see to carry on with the task that he'd set himself up at the house.

Every time she thought about what *her* input was going to be in the resurrection of it she couldn't help but feel pleasure at the prospect of being asked to make suggestions about the interior, but there was always the feeling behind it that she was going to be on the outside of things.

Yet it didn't stop her from pretending that she wouldn't be, and she would conjure up visions of children with their mother's odd colouring or their father's dark handsomeness playing in the garden, or sleeping in one the spacious bedrooms, but always the memory of a certain night on the wards, its aftermath, and the undeniable evidence of it came to spoil it.

On the morning after they'd all gathered at James's

house David said, 'Have you ever been to a barn supper, Laurel?'

She laughed. 'No. Until I came to Willowmere I didn't know what a barn was. There is going to be one on Friday in someone's actual barn, I believe.'

'Yes, and from what my patients tell me it is not to be missed, so are we going?'

'I don't know,' she replied, as if the question hadn't made her heart beat faster. 'I have an early start on Saturday morning.'

'I am hardly likely to forget that, but we don't have to stay late, do we?'

'No, I suppose not, and it will be an experience.' She couldn't pass by the chance of spending extra time with him before the day of revelation approached.

The reaction of Darius when he'd seen her back was imprinted in her mind and she knew that whatever David felt he would conceal it. He would never be so unkind, yet she wasn't expecting him to be the same afterwards.

There would be lots of people at the barn supper so there would be no opportunities for heart-to-heart talking on *that* occasion, and in any case she was going to wait until she'd been to London to see if there was any chance of improvement of the damaged skin in the future.

Once again Elaine was helping with the arrangements for the occasion that everyone seemed to be looking forward to and had gone on ahead when David called for Laurel on the Friday night and found her waiting at the gate dressed in jeans, a checked shirt and high boots.

He smiled when he saw that her outfit was almost a

replica of his own and offered her one of the two Stetson-type hats he was carrying.

'I found these in a cupboard at the cottage,' he said, 'and thought we may as well go the whole way for the country and western.'

'Why not?' she said, sparkling up at him. He was such a joy to be with and he cared for her, she thought mistily, though she sometimes felt that his feelings were more protective than passionate.

They had a wonderful time in the huge barn, which was clean and fragrant. The atmosphere was relaxed and friendly, the food plentiful and good to eat, and the music foot-tapping and rhythmic.

Jonas wasn't there and when she questioned David about his absence he said, 'I tried to get Dad to come, but I think he was a bit shy. He's more at ease with boats than a lot of people. I'll take you to Cornwall some time if you like. It's a small fishing village where I was brought up and it has its own particular charm, like the rest of the county.'

When there was no reply forthcoming he said wryly, 'You're not exactly bubbling over with enthusiasm at the suggestion.'

'That's because I'm not sure what the future holds,' she told him awkwardly, 'but it's nice of you to offer.'

In one of his rare moments of irritation he replied, 'I'm not trying to be "nice", Laurel. I can't think of a more inane word to describe me. I have much stronger motives in suggesting it. For one thing I'd like to show you where my mother is buried, as you are taking such an interest in her old home. It's on a headland looking out to sea, not far from Dad's cottage.

'It would seem that between us we have a triangle of locations that mean a lot to us. Willowmere, Cornwall and London, and I have to say that it is this village that comes top of the list.'

She couldn't agree more, Laurel thought, but she wouldn't want to live there without him in her life. She could tell from the way he was talking that David had his own ideas about that. He was wanting to be with her more and more and it was so hard to say no when it was what she wanted too…

But she had nightmares about saying yes if he asked her to marry him and then him finding out on their wedding night that she was less than desirable.

It was why she had to tell him soon, before it went any further between them, and not having changed her mind on that score she made the most of the night in the barn. She danced every dance with the hat on her head and the boots on her feet, until David protested he needed a drink and went to get them glasses of cider on tap from a wooden cask.

They left before it was over with the early start in mind, and as he walked her home David thought wryly of the number of times they had separated at the gates of the old stone lodge.

The day couldn't come soon enough when they lived in Water Meetings House, together for always. He didn't care how much Laurel shied away when he asked her to marry him. He would woo her until she had no refusals or doubts left.

He held her close for a brief moment as they parted, releasing her before she had the chance to wriggle out of his arms, and said, 'So I'll see you at the station at what time in the morning?'

'I need to get the six-thirty local train to get me to Manchester in time for the inter-city connection,' she told him, 'but you don't have to come, David. Why not have a lie-in?'

He shook his head. When was Laurel going to get the message that he wanted to be with her every minute of the day...and in the night too?

Reaching up, she brushed her lips against his cheek but he kept his arms by his sides, and as he strode off down the lane she watched him without moving until he was out of sight.

He was waiting for her in early sunlight when she arrived at the small station that Walter looked after so painstakingly, and as she walked towards him he said, 'So you didn't oversleep?'

'Does it look like it?' she parried. 'Though I don't mind telling you it was an effort to get up after all the dancing and the cider.'

'I'm coming with you as far as Manchester,' he told her. 'I want to do some shopping.'

'Fine,' she said, and went to book her ticket in the small office at the entrance to the platform.

'Aren't you the young lady who helped the doctor take care of His Lordship's son?' Walter asked from behind the glass that separated him from the travelling public.

'Er…yes,' she replied, and thought if she'd been in London she could have been the Queen of Sheba for all he would have known.

'The village folks have really taken you to their hearts after that,' he informed her, and as she prepared to join David, who was standing just a few feet away, he said, 'Have a nice day, my dear.'

'That is what it's all about, isn't it?' she said as she and David walked along the platform. 'People around here take the time to get to know each other.'

'Mmm, that is so,' he agreed as the train came chugging into the station. When they were settled in an almost empty carriage he said, 'Are you glad that you took the time to get to know *me*?'

'Yes and no,' she told him. 'Life was less complicated when I didn't, but I wouldn't have missed it for the world.'

'There is an element of the past tense in what you've just said,' he remarked, observing her keenly, 'but I'll try to keep an open mind.'

They arrived in Manchester after a short time and when she would have left him at the barrier he ignored it and walked to the door of the carriage with her. As she turned to say goodbye with one foot on the step he said gravely, 'Take care, Laurel. Come back to me.'

She nodded and without speaking boarded the train. When she'd found a seat by the window she flashed him a half-smile and thought if David was under the impression that she was looking forward to the day ahead he was mistaken. The only impetus that was taking her away from him was the hope that there might be some way she could be made to look less un-attractive than she did now.

'Are you creaming the affected area regularly and keeping the skin out of direct sunlight?' the consultant asked when he'd examined her back.

'Yes, of course,' she declared. 'My back rarely sees the light of day. It isn't something I would ever want to flaunt. It still looks dreadful.'

'I know,' he said sympathetically, 'but you have to remember they were third-degree burns that you received. We did everything possible at the time to repair the damage, but it won't ever completely disappear. It will become less noticeable as time goes by, but the scars will always be there. We could try plastic surgery. We've gone the limit with skin grafts. Would you consider that?'

'Yes, anything,' she said flatly.

'We're pretty booked up at the moment. It could be a while before we get round to it, yet I will certainly put you on the list if you're sure, but again there is no certainty that it will be other than a small improvement. That is all I can guarantee.'

His words stayed with her all the time during her homeward journey and she asked herself dismally what she had expected. A promise of perfection, hardly, but she'd hoped for some joy to come out of the visit to the burns unit.

When she got off the local train at Willowmere her eyes widened. David was waiting for her on the platform.

'How did you know which train I would be on?' she questioned, and he smiled.

'I didn't. I've just been meeting each one as it came in and finally hit the jackpot. What sort of a day have you had?'

'Average,' she told him wearily. 'It's good to be back.'

'Let me take you for a meal,' he suggested, 'or if you want I'll cook for us at my place. Would you like that?'

'Yes, I think I would.'

She was going to keep to her vow of telling him about the full extent of the damage to her skin and the sooner the better, she was thinking. If they went to Glenside Lodge Elaine might be there, and Jonas maybe, and she would lose her nerve.

David was watching her as they ate the food he'd prepared and the thought of the ring he'd bought was uppermost in his mind. If she was in agreement when the meal was over, why didn't he take Laurel to see the progress that had been made with the house and then surprise her by asking her to marry him in the place that meant so much to them both?

He'd vowed to wait until she showed that she trusted him, but did it matter? She would do in time, he would make sure of that.

She was tired, but when David suggested they go to the house Laurel couldn't resist, even though it was putting off the moment of truth. There would always be another time, she told herself.

'The electricity supply was connected today,' he said as he turned the key in the door, 'otherwise I wouldn't have suggested we come.' And when it swung back he flicked on a light switch and the hall was flooded with light.

As she looked around her at oak panelling and a domed ceiling Laurel didn't have to say anything. The expression of delight on her face was answer enough if he'd had any doubts about her reaction, and as they went from room to room he watched her pleasure increase until they were back in a sitting room that was waiting to be enhanced by some furniture.

'The house is beautiful, David,' she breathed.

'And so are you,' he said softly. 'Will you marry me, Laurel, and live with me here?'

He saw her expression change. 'I'm not beautiful!' she cried. 'And I can't marry you. It wouldn't be fair.'

'Why not?' he exclaimed, unaware that his proposal had taken away her one chance of showing him that she trusted him. If she told him how scarred she was now he was going to think that she'd saved it until she was sure of him, and it wasn't like that at all. Over recent months she hadn't been sure of anything, least of all the reactions of others.

'I'm waiting,' he reminded her in a flat tone. 'If nothing else, you owe me an explanation, Laurel.'

Suddenly it was all too much. She was wearing an outdoor jacket and clutching her handbag in a clammy hand, and almost in one movement she flung the bag to one side and wrenched off the jacket. Then as he watched in stunned disbelief she took off one of the high-necked sweaters that he'd seen her in so often, and turned slowly to present her back to him.

She heard his sharp intake of breath like a death knell

about to toll. 'So this is what you couldn't bring yourself to tell me. Who or what did that to you?'

'Does it matter?' she said dismissively. 'It's there and isn't going to go away. I've been to London for a check-up at the burns unit where I was treated, hoping there might be a chance of some sort of cosmetic improvement, but didn't get much joy out of the visit.'

'And you couldn't tell me any of this,' he said in a low voice. 'You thought so little of me that you couldn't share your heartache. What kind of a person do you think I am, Laurel?'

She didn't answer the question. Instead she had one of her own. 'Would you want to wake up to this patchwork quilt every morning?' she asked flatly, still with her back to him. 'Take me home please, David,' she begged as she replaced the clothes she'd taken off, and after switching off the lights and locking the door he did as she'd asked in the silence that had fallen upon them.

CHAPTER TEN

WHEN they arrived at Glenside Lodge she opened the car door and was out of it before he'd had the chance to break the silence, and he thought dismally there would be no lingering under the streetlamp tonight.

The lights were on so he waited until she was safely inside and then drove home to the cottage and sat staring into space. Every time he visualised what Laurel had gone through he felt sick inside. He still didn't know what had happened, but he was a doctor and knew that it must have been something terrible to have done that to her skin. No wonder his father's comment about Caroline had sent Laurel running for cover.

If he'd been there he would have made sure that she'd also got the message that there hadn't been much else to commend his ex-fiancée, but he hadn't been and she'd fled to hide her hurt.

When he'd found her she could have told him then, but she hadn't. He hadn't been entirely convinced by her reaction with the barbecue and had thought there was more to it than just a scare. Now he knew that it had been with just cause on her part and his heart ached when he thought of the pain she must have suffered. He wished he could turn the clock back and wipe out the times he'd told her she was unpredictable and difficult to deal with.

She'd asked him to take her home, and his dismay at what she'd revealed to him had been so acute he'd done as she asked instead of telling her that he loved her as she was and wanted her in his arms, in his bed, in his life for always.

The midnight hour was long past. Dawn would soon be breaking over the sleeping village, and he thought determinedly that he had to make things right between them before another day took its course.

When Laurel let herself into the house there was no sign of Elaine, and a note on the hall table said, *Have gone to mind Arran for Georgina and Ben. They're dining out with a Swedish colleague of his and have suggested I stay the night as they might be late back. Hope all went well with the check-up. See you soon, love Elaine.*

She breathed a sigh of relief. She had the place to herself, thank goodness. If Elaine saw the state she was in she would to know what was wrong, and she felt as if she would choke on it if she had to explain.

Sleep wasn't swift in coming, which was not surprising as her thoughts were going round and round in a miserable circle, and eventually she slipped on the fleecy robe that she'd been wearing on the night David had found her asleep on the sofa and went to sit out in the garden.

It was hot and airless with only a sliver of moon up above, and as she sat alone in the silence Laurel thought she'd behaved like a crazy woman, throwing the words she'd longed to hear back in his face. So much for dignity. She'd intended telling him calmly and without drama so that he could walk away without embarrassment if he felt the need. She hadn't expected him to be as cruel as Darius had been, but neither had she expected him to be so hurt and condemning when she'd finally shown him the scars. He hadn't said a word after that. It was as if a shutter had come down between them and she doubted it would ever be raised again.

When the car swished to a halt at the gate in the light of the streetlamp and David came up the path to where she was huddled on a wooden bench Laurel remained motionless.

He stopped in front of her and beckoned for her to rise. 'Come with me and don't ask questions,' he said in a low voice, and she obeyed.

When he'd tucked her into the car she found her voice. 'Where are we going?'

'You'll soon see,' he said, and she lapsed into silence again.

When the lake with the house behind it came into sight she shrank down in the seat and pulled the robe more closely around her, and he smiled across at her.

'I don't think anyone is going to be around to note your strange attire at this hour and there isn't any need to cover yourself up any more, is there?'

He'd stopped the car in front of the house, but instead of taking her in that direction he took her hand and walked her down to where the waters of the lake lapped against a small stone landing stage.

'It was here that you cast your spell over me,' he said, embracing the lake and the field where the house stood with a sweeping gesture, 'and it is here that I want us to be for ever and always, loving and living in the house back there once I've convinced you that I love everything about you, including the scars.

'I love you for your spirit that must have been almost quenched by what happened to you, for the forthright person that you are in everything except the thing that you mistakenly thought set you apart from other women.

'It is what I should have told you when you showed me your back, but I was so taken aback I said the first thing that came into my head. Can you forgive me, Laurel?'

'I've told you before, David. I can forgive you anything,' she said softly as dawn began to lighten the sky, 'and I do so want to live with you in Water Meetings House.'

'And you shall,' he promised, 'because I'm going to ask you again. Will you marry me, Laurel?'

'Yes, I will,' she told him with sweet gravity, and this time she went into his arms knowing it was where she belonged.

Later, as daylight began to slant across the water, he said gently, 'So are you going to tell me what happened?'

She nodded, with the dread having left her. 'Yes. It is long overdue.' She held his hand tightly. 'I was on night duty on Men's Surgical along with another nurse who had gone for a break when it happened.

'I was settling in a patient who had been brought up from the high-dependency unit when I smelt smoke and saw that the door of a small side ward was shut, which was against regulations.

'When I flung it open I was horrified to discover that the bed was on fire with the patient still in it. The curtains nearby were also on fire. Smoke was filling the room and I knew I had to get him out of there fast.

'The fire alarm had gone off and help would soon be arriving, but there wasn't time to wait so I ran across and half lifted, half dragged him off the bed and began to carry him towards the door in the choking smoke.

'It had swung to behind me and as I opened the door the draught turned the blaze into a flash fire and caught my back as I staggered out into the corridor with him. I collapsed with one leg crushed beneath me and the patient on top of me.

'I could hear raised voices and pounding feet but they seemed a long way off and I remembered nothing else until I surfaced two days later with a doctor looking down at me sympathetically as he was about to explain that I'd got third-degree burns on my back, that my hands were all blistered, and my hair was burnt.

'The only good thing to come out of it was that the fire had been contained to the one room. No other patients had been hurt, just myself and the old guy who hadn't been able to resist lighting a cigarette. He too had severe scarring but amazingly made some degree of recovery.

'They told me when I surfaced for those first few moments in the burns unit that I had some painful times ahead of me and that skin grafts might be required once the extent of the damage to my skin had been calculated, but I was so heavily sedated not much of what I was being told registered. Though it registered fast enough when at last I was conscious enough to see for myself what the fire had done to me.

'There were no-smoking notices all over the hospital, but the old guy had pleaded with his visitors to leave cigarettes and matches, and aware that they were breaking hospital rules they'd closed the door after them when they'd left.

'He'd confessed afterwards that he'd lit up as soon as they'd left and after the first few puffs, weak and ill, he'd dozed off and let the lighted cigarette fall on the sheets, then panicked and threw it away, setting light to the curtains. It changed my life for ever.'

Overwhelmed with tenderness, David had listened without interrupting as she'd told him what he'd wanted to know ever since they'd met. And now, as she turned towards him, he said, 'You are so brave and so beautiful it takes my breath away. Don't ever be afraid of the reactions of others, Laurel.'

Her smile was rueful. 'They wanted to give me an award but I didn't want one. I just wanted my skin back, and it was Darius who made me lose confidence about the scarring. I showed him my back on one of his infrequent visits to the hospital and he couldn't take it, said it was nauseating. I finished with him soon after.'

When he would have expressed his disgust she told him gently, 'Shush, David. It's forgotten. If he hadn't been like that I would never have met you.'

She couldn't believe it was happening. The black despair of the last few hours had disappeared. He really wanted her, she thought joyfully. David wanted her as much as she wanted him and he wasn't fazed by what he'd seen on her back, even though it did look like a map of the Pennines.

He was taking a small jeweller's box out of his pocket, and when he opened it and she saw the emerald surrounded with diamonds glowing on its velvet bed she turned to him with eyes wide with amazement.

'When did you get that?' she breathed.

He laughed. 'Do you remember me saying that I was going shopping in Manchester?'

There were tears on her lashes as she told him, 'After Darius I didn't think any man would ever want me. Then I met you when I was looking a sight and hating the thought of living in the countryside.

'When I discovered that you were a local *and* a doctor in the village practice it all became so much more bearable, though it didn't make me any more confident regarding my appearance or eager to expose my disfigurement.'

'I'm not "any man",' he said steadily. 'I'm the one who will love you no matter what, through thick and thin, in sickness and in health. I want you to wear this ring on your finger to show that you belong to me and soon I hope, very soon, I'm going to place a gold wedding band next to it. How soon do you think we can arrange a wedding? A week? A fortnight?'

'And you're sure that this is what you want?' she asked, with the feeling that it was all a dream.

'I'm sure all right,' he said softly, 'and will be happy to demonstrate how much whenever the opportunity occurs.'

The emerald was on her finger, and the first of the demonstrations that David had promised was so satisfactory they repeated it several times.

As Willowmere basked in glorious September sunshine, Edwina Crabtree and her fellow bellringers were out in full force. The vicar had raised his eyebrows at holding a wedding at such short notice, but for David and Laurel he was happy to make an exception.

Their families and friends were gathered in the church to share in their special day. Everyone from the surgery was there to wish them well, along with Pollyanna and Jolyon in the charge of Jess and Helen, while their father was occupied with his duties of best man.

Sarah Wilkinson had brought out the blue brocade again, and Clare, proudly holding baby Arran, was there too.

The Derringhams had also put in an appearance and there was much sympathy for Alistair on his crutches.

A newcomer to local health care was also one of the guests—David's acquaintance from St Gabriel's, Lizzie Carmichael. She'd been appointed as the new community midwife and had introduced herself to James. Lord Derringham's plans for the maternity clinic were taking shape and everyone was very excited.

At that moment the organist began to play the wedding march and as everyone got to their feet she was there, his bride, breathtaking in a white satin gown, wide-eyed and beautiful with Elaine beside her.

Unknown to Laurel, Elaine had discovered the whereabouts of her parents and that morning they'd turned up at Glenside Lodge to watch their daughter marry the man who held her heart.

They would be off again the next day if they ran true to form, but she'd long learned to live with that and it was good to see them, though they would never hold a place in her affections like Elaine did.

So it was Elaine who walked Laurel down the aisle, proud and happy to be giving the niece she loved so much to the man of her dreams. David waited at the altar, tall and handsome in his morning suit. James stood next to him, equally tall and handsome, as best man.

Jonas, as happy as Elaine because his cherished son had found the love of his life, smiled at them from the front pew, and passed Elaine his handkerchief to dab her eyes.

The reception was to be held at the completed Water Meetings House, and when David carried Laurel over the threshold it would be the moment that their hopes and dreams became the reality that he had promised. Maybe, somewhere in the ether, his mother would be smiling down on them as they began their life in what had once been her childhood home.

The day was finally over and the newlyweds were alone. They walked hand in hand to where Willow Lake, beautiful and timeless, would always be there to enchant them, and then wandered blissfully back to Water Meetings House. At last, Laurel lay in David's arms, and as he kissed the scars that she'd tried to hide from him she knew beyond doubt how much he loved her.

MILLS & BOON®
By Request

RELIVE THE ROMANCE WITH THE BEST OF THE BEST

A sneak peek at next month's titles...

In stores from 10th August 2017:

- **The Delicious De Campos –** Jennifer Hayward

- **Expecting His Child –** Paula Roe, Tessa Radley & Cat Schield

In stores from 24th August 2017:

- **Big Little Secrets –** Sophie Pembroke, Rebecca Winters & Soraya Lane

- **Forbidden Desires –** Dani Collins, Lindsay Armstrong, Marion Lennox

Just can't wait?
Buy our books online before they hit the shops!
www.millsandboon.co.uk

Also available as eBooks.

MILLS & BOON ®

Why shop at millsandboon.co.uk?

Each year, thousands of romance readers find their perfect read at millsandboon.co.uk. That's because we're passionate about bringing you the very best romantic fiction. Here are some of the advantages of shopping at www.millsandboon.co.uk:

* **Get new books first**—you'll be able to buy your favourite books one month before they hit the shops

* **Get exclusive discounts**—you'll also be able to buy our specially created monthly collections, with up to 50% off the RRP

* **Find your favourite authors**—latest news, interviews and new releases for all your favourite authors and series on our website, plus ideas for what to try next

* **Join in**—once you've bought your favourite books, don't forget to register with us to rate, review and join in the discussions

Visit **www.millsandboon.co.uk** for all this and more today!